MAGNOLIA HOUSE

KATHRYN TRATTNER

eBook ISBN: 979-8-9872112-2-9

Paperback ISBN: 979-8-9872112-3-6

Editor: Jackie Hritz - Bloom Editing

Cover Designer: Maria Spada

www.kathryntrattner.com

for my friends who read it first

CONTENTS

MAGNOLIA HOUSE

WEDNESDAY

My past is
An armor
I cannot
Take off,
No matter
How many times
You tell me
The war
Is over.

- Jessica Katoff

CHAPTER ONE
WEDNESDAY

I leaned forward, taking in the texture of the woman's skin, the layer of makeup, and false eyelashes. I hadn't realized until I was closer that they were fake. Something about that seemed so right. It was absolutely Vivian, right down to vanity in death.

"You're dead," I whispered.

The funeral home was cold. I'd known it would be, I'd brought a sweater, but the chill crept in under the fabric. The scent of embalming fluid and jasmine perfume filled the air, the two mixing unpleasantly, clinging to me, crawling into my nose.

"And you stink."

I studied her face. Even in death, there was something compelling about her. The mortician had made her up beautifully, and she'd been young still. I'd never realized how young Vivian had been when I was born. Looking down at her pale face, wrinkles mostly smoothed away, and thick, dark hair threaded with silver, I could see it. She'd only turned fifty in January.

She could have been sleeping.

I reached out but hesitated, my fingers dropping to the edge of the metal table she rested on. I didn't want to touch her. Even this was too close. I pulled back and brought my hand to my mouth, blowing on it like a child with a burn, hoping my breath would drive away the chill.

Mr. Laurent had murmured apologetically about giving me a moment in this awkward space. The viewing rooms were occupied, and he didn't want me in the preparation area. So he'd abandoned us here, the door closing behind him with a final ominous click. I wished he hadn't. I felt like I had to linger, like they were expecting me to mourn her here, in this barren space. If I left too early, they'd talk—that special variety of bless-her-heart poison, sweet Southern gossip disguised as compassion.

Well, they'd be talking anyway.

Crossing my arms, I looked around, taking it all in but her. It was a private room at the back of the building, neither one area nor another, an in-between place. It wasn't public, not really, there was no carpet—only flecked linoleum tiles—and the walls were a bare industrial beige. It had two wide doors, the one I'd come through and one opposite, but no windows, and a low paneled ceiling.

This room felt like an afterthought, a space meant to exist for these five minutes and no more. Would it pop out of existence when I walked through the door? Maybe. A little like limbo, which seemed fitting for this moment between mother and daughter. She'd known I'd never come back while she was alive. If anyone had asked, I would have said I wouldn't have come back even if she'd died. But she must have known I would.

After all, here I was.

Even lying on the metal table, she was tall. They'd dressed her in the outfit she'd specified; a floor-length, long-sleeved red velvet dress with a high neck, polished black heels, and a hairpin with a gold magnolia on it. Nothing else, which surprised me. I'd expected her to be weighted down in her prized jewelry—diamond earrings, bracelets, and rings for each finger—taking it all to the grave because she could never stand the idea of me touching any of it.

Instead, she was elegant in a minimal way. The dress was snug but not too tight, and I could see that she'd gotten soft here and there. Maybe she'd finally started eating instead of living off air and too much bourbon. Maybe after I'd left she'd given in to herself a little, shown herself the grace she could never show me.

Cancer was on the death certificate. But Mr. Laurent had lowered his voice to inform me that ultimately it had been a drug overdose. It made sense. The cancer diagnosis had come several months ago, already too far gone. It hit close to home for her, attacking her appearance—the only thing she ever valued. She'd opted out of treatment. She barely tolerated doctors, so there had been pain management but nothing else.

It made sense. I couldn't picture her waiting in hospitals or being patient with nurses. She'd always pushed to the front of the line, rolling over people's toes in her wheelchair, while I followed meekly behind.

It had been a strange way to grow up, watching her push herself into whatever conversation she felt she should be a part of. Into church meetings and potlucks, grocery shopping and snooping on the ladies gossiping at the drug store, gliding into private offices, a sweet smile on her lips and cold determination in her blue-violet eyes. But without me to push her around, to take the blame for crushing toes and bruised shins, it must have been harder.

A sharp stab of guilt hit me, and I almost winced. If I'd been here to take her, would she still be alive? Was it my fault? But another part of my brain was screaming already. *You got out! Don't let her pull you back in! This is a game! Pay attention!*

I looked at the woman in front of me, white and cold, and very, very dead.

Vivian Taylor.

She'd been my mother a long time ago, in another life. Though I don't think *mother* was the right word. She'd given birth to me, so a part of her must have cared for me a little at some point.

But whatever part of her had loved me had died long before now. Maybe about the time I'd pulled air into my lungs and cried for the first time—a pale baby streaked with blood, a separate soul from her own. Her kind of love was a short-lived flame, quickly extinguished, nothing but a smoking hint of what had been.

Anger caressed me, tender, familiar. All these years, everything that had happened in my childhood, all the time I'd spent with a therapist working to build a life that was completely my own, no one else's, had been snatched away. She'd reached out and given my life one last turn, flipping it all on end.

She would have laughed in my face.

"You can't hurt me anymore," I said aloud, voice steady —rusted, brittle iron in my backbone, but iron all the same. I needed to hear it again, to know it was true. I licked my lips, pulling in a breath, filling the very bottom of my lungs. "You're dead."

My ears rang, my voice harsh and coming back to me, bouncing up from the floor, down from the paneled ceiling. I don't know what I expected: to have her sit up and begin yelling, for an unseen observer to ask what I thought I was doing talking to my mother like that. I expected something, *anything*, but nothing happened. She remained motionless, air conditioning humming through the vents, people talking several rooms away, and blood thumping in my ears.

I straightened, feeling foolish, and took a breath.

I was alone. There was no one here to contradict me, to claim the past had been anything other than what I remembered. Crossing my arms over my chest, I turned away, heading for the door that led back into the public part of the building.

Behind me, something moved, rustling, fabric shifting. A faint breathy sigh filled my ears. I froze. The air conditioning continued humming, but this had been a different kind of sound, an exhalation, a chuckle. The hair on the back of my neck rose, goose flesh covering every inch of skin as cold washed over me.

Something crouched behind me, the pressure in the room changing.

I'd been alone before; there hadn't been anyone living in the room aside from me. She'd been so obviously dead. So gloriously and finally gone. I'd been so sure.

Now I wasn't.

If I turned back, what would I see? Open milky eyes? Red mouth curved into that wicked three-corner smile she'd perfected?

Don't look back.

I wanted to run, my legs trembling with the desire to move. I needed to know. I needed to be able to turn and face this, face her, conquer the moment. But my stomach churned; I was ten again and terrified of meeting her gaze and having to explain some situation I'd gotten myself into.

She'd want to know why it had taken me so long to get here. She'd want to know why I hadn't made her a priority. She'd let me know right up front that I hadn't done much with my life and she wasn't surprised.

Your father would have been so disappointed in you. You're such a waste.

The air conditioner cycled off, leaving the room silent. The space begged to be filled, and in it, I could hear her breathing. In and out, out and in, steady and rhythmic, and if breathing could have a hard edge, a little bit of hatred, this one did.

Turn around and face me.

"No," I said, pushing through the door without a backward glance.

"She wanted to be entombed with your father in the family mausoleum. In your mother's words, they belonged together. There's a place for you as well. I don't know if you've considered that at all?" Mr. Laurent spoke smoothly, shuffling paperwork on his desk and looking everywhere but directly at me.

"No. I haven't." I wanted to laugh. Buried next to Vivian for all eternity? I shook my head. "And I have the final say in the burial?"

"Well, yes. Though it would be the right thing to honor what she'd laid out so plainly. Your mother wanted a viewing as soon as possible and then cremation right after. She'll be taken over to Mr. Fontenot in Fairview. I realize you've only just arrived and have yet to get settled, but would tomorrow be convenient?"

I looked down at my hands folded carefully in my lap:

long elegant fingers, buffed nails. I had to concentrate on not clenching them together, stop myself from picking at my cuticles, stop myself from twisting them into claws.

"Can I take some time to decide?" I hurried on when a flicker of impatience crossed his plump face. "The viewing tomorrow is fine. I meant about afterward."

"Why don't we have the viewing Saturday evening then? That would give you some time to get settled. It's a lot to handle when you've been away for so long."

Not long enough.

"Thank you."

The rest of what I might have said stuck in my throat, a lump of false friendliness and forced politeness. I couldn't bring myself to expel it. He paused, giving me a moment to continue, and when I didn't, he cleared his own throat.

"Let me know as soon as you've made a choice, and we'll take care of everything from there."

"I appreciate it. You've been so kind."

"I'm more than happy to help. Please don't hesitate to get in touch if you need anything at all. Your mother will be very much missed around here."

"I'll miss her too."

It was a bald-faced lie, and he could tell.

CHAPTER TWO

WEDNESDAY

I sat in the rental car, an older compact, the last sad car on the lot, for several minutes, gripping the steering wheel, staring at the side of the building—dark-red brick, white trim, a sign in black flowing script, *Joseph Laurent and Sons Funeral Home*. The man inside, tall and well-groomed, judgment and curiosity plain on his face. His questions, the decisions I needed to make about Vivian, weighed on me.

There was so much I needed to handle, that no one else could take care of, and I didn't want to do any of it. I wanted to drive back toward the highway and speed toward the airport. I wanted to go home, Oregon home, and leave her here to rot on that table.

But I was going to Magnolia House.

The funeral home served the whole area, situated between several towns of various sizes, with the largest cemetery nearby. Not the kind with flat placards in the ground or the blocky granite stones with engraved names and dates. This cemetery held neat rows of mausoleums and tombs, all above ground, white and watchful, peacefully waiting for the living to visit. My dad was there.

Hey, kiddo. How ya been?

My father's voice. He'd only ever been the one to call me kiddo. Vivian never would have been so informal. I shook it off, the familiar voice so easily pulled from memory, dredged up from childhood. I'd see the house first, get the bad over with before I could deal with the good. As good as visiting my father's grave could be. It was sad that in this place that was the only thing to look forward to.

When the car started, I was relieved. It had died twice between here and New Orleans. I just needed it for a week, maybe less, and then it could be put to rest.

You just gotta make it a week.

Was I telling myself or dad?

Pulling out of the funeral home parking lot, I glanced back, catching movement out of the corner of my eye. The funeral director was standing toward the rear of the building, a little back from the parking lot, smoking a cigarette and watching me. He held up a hand, a goodbye, and I returned the gesture. But his gaze wasn't friendly.

———

It was a thirty-minute drive to my old stomping grounds, down narrow roads and past isolated houses. Most were abandoned, shells standing in tall weeds or shadowed under close-growing trees: broken windows and missing doors, siding falling off, and holes in the roofs. The places that were still occupied were sometimes in a similar state, with dead cars sitting in foot-high weeds and porches crowded with old sofas. But here and there a house sat at the center of a mown lawn, neat gravel drives connecting to the road, with bright red or blue mailboxes. Not everyone had given up yet.

I passed a faded billboard with heavy black lettering —*Hell Is Real*—and another down the way a bit, *Repent*.

What did I have to ask forgiveness for? Abandoning Vivian? The half truths? The whole lies? The moments I'd hurt someone, the phone calls I promised I would make and didn't? The cat I'd run over on my way to work one morning? I'd cried all the way there, heartbroken for days and desperate to heal the wound. I would repent for that. I would go back and right that wrong. The moments I'd been needlessly cruel or unintentionally so.

Repent the rest? The things that came along with living and trying to keep it all from imploding day to day? It wouldn't be honest of me, to say I would and not feel it with my whole heart. And wasn't lying a sin too?

I eased to a stop at a four-way intersection, the red reflective signs riddled with buckshot. Straight ahead was the place I'd grown up. Back of Beyond, Louisiana—not only name of this small out of the way place but a true description. Magnolia House. If I went right, the road would eventually lead me to another small town, and if I went left, I would find the highway. A moment of hesitation so small it almost wasn't there, and then I was passing through the intersection.

The road leading to town was cracked, potholes here and there, breaking down over time and never repaired. What would it take to get the parish road crew to finally get out here and fix it? Divine intervention maybe. It looked the same as it had on the day I'd left. It would probably be the same in another five years or until the next flood raged through here.

Trees grew right up to the shoulder, underbrush

reaching out, gangly sunflowers and tall grass, knee-high poison oak, with nameless vines tangling it all together. High over the road branches met, dappled light shifting beneath them, a tunnel of living woods, nature ready and willing to reclaim the space.

The bridge was coming up. I didn't need to see it to know it was there, to feel the point of no return coming. It spanned a creek, slow dark water, connecting to a deeper channel—more decaying concrete, furry with moss and other green things. The only way in and out of town. I saw it then and gunned the engine, lifting my feet off the floorboards of the car as it rattled and rolled over the creek. A piece of superstition, a gift from my dad.

Always lift your feet going over water.

Then I was on the other side and within town limits. The sign stood where it had always been, *Back of Beyond – Population 2238.* I was betting it was a lot less by now. Who knew when the last time was that the census people had been out to count the residents. The bridge, the sign, was the official boundary, and from here on out, I was officially home.

It wasn't a triumphant return. I wasn't coming back a huge success, rich and famous, handsome husband and beautiful children in tow. As if the car understood my hesitancy, it lurched, the engine groaning, before catching and carrying me forward.

I was coming from a small life, quiet and built around books and the routines of a university—grading papers and student questions, office politics that I purposely avoided. Teaching wasn't glamorous. Especially when it was a college lit course that rarely reached the student limit. I taught other things when I had to, picking up classes randomly and filling in. I went to work and came home, came home and went to work. Between those times I occasionally had a night out with friends, a relationship here and there—nothing too intimate, no one too close. But it wasn't any different, any better or greater or bigger, than anyone else's life.

And right now, there was no one waiting for me to come home.

The road improved as I reached the center of town, and soon I was passing a few outlying buildings. Some tidy houses were set back from the road, and a woman in a robe watering a front yard full of lilies turned to watch me go by. There were another few houses on either side of the road and then an old feed store, empty and dusty, weeds growing up around the foundation. On the side of the building, someone had spray-painted something, and I slowed, reading it.

There will be no miracles here.

My stomach twisted, a fleeting moment of unease surfaced before I shoved it down. In and out, there and back. Home in Oregon before a week passed. How long would it take to bury Vivian and get the house in order? Less than a week. I'd be gone in no time.

The whole place was about the same. What wasn't empty was worn out, fresh paint or trimmed grass unable to draw the eye away from the decay. A few cars passed, and I saw more people. Life here was slower and looked like it had gotten harder after I'd gone. The place had been dying then. Maybe this was after death, maybe this was the resurrected body of a town that needed to give up and become a ghost.

The town center was built around the two-story post office, built in 1850 and surrounded by huge live oak trees draped in Spanish moss. A few cars sat out front in the shade, windows cracked to keep the heat from building up. There was a tiny police station with a plate glass window, a barbershop, a diner, even an old one-screen theatre, and lots of buildings with orange *for rent* or *for sale* signs in the windows. I passed slowly through, looking at everything, feeling like a stranger in the place I'd grown up.

On the other side of the town square was a church: white and fresh, unreal and glowing in the sunshine. The grass around it was lush and perfectly manicured with flowering trees surrounding gathered around like worshipers. A white sign stood out front, the different services and times listed. *First Southern Baptist Church.* It seemed so out of place, bright and hard to look at after everything else. The big front door was open, but beyond there was just darkness. Nothingness.

I turned away, heart rate picking up. Magnolia House was close now. It had always seemed like a short ride on Sundays to church.

Just past the church, the car began to slow, the engine ticking loudly, before lurching to a halt. I groaned. I knew nothing about cars. I couldn't even pretend to know what was wrong with this one. With a swear, I twisted the key in the ignition, turning it off, trying to start it again. Nothing happened.

Leaning forward, I rested my forehead against the steering wheel. I felt like crying. I wanted to scream. I wanted to just get this over with. Fumbling through my purse, I dug my cell phone out. Reception had been spotty since I'd landed, but maybe I'd have enough bars to make a call. But the phone was dead too. *Great.*

Great.

I got out of the car, slammed the door behind me, and looked up and down the street. Wet heat and the smell of summer pressed against my skin, sticking to me, my clothes too heavy for the afternoon. As soon as possible I'd change into shorts and a tank top. It had been pointless to wear this silky blouse and jeans, the sweater to keep me warm in the funeral home. Not exactly the fanciest of dead-mother-viewing attire, but I'd made an effort. For myself or the town though? I wasn't sure. But it hadn't been for Vivian.

The church or the gas station? If I kept going, the gas station would appear, around the bend in the road. I couldn't see it, but I knew it would still be there. Or the hot white perfection of the church and that dark entrance. I'd rather walk a little bit farther than spend any more time in that church than I had to.

I grabbed my purse and locked the car. My bags were in the trunk, and I didn't think anyone would steal them. But it was habit to lock the car, one picked up out there in the real world. Even if rules like that didn't apply to a place like this, I wasn't going to give them up. If I ever made it back to civilization, I was going to need them.

Sweat had soaked through my bra by the time I made it to the gas station. The two pumps outside were old with numbers that rolled over instead of the familiar digital display with a card reader. The building was covered in advertisements for energy drinks, cigarettes, and scratch-off lottery tickets. Underneath all of that must have been windows, but I couldn't see them.

Air conditioning washed over me as soon as I pushed the door open, bell chiming, the relief instant. It was ferocious, the air on high, and I felt sorry for whoever paid the electric bill, because being in this much air conditioning felt expensive.

The interior was as crowded as the exterior. Rows of snacks and candy were packed in, the aisles narrow, barely wide enough for an adult to shuffle down. There was a rack with sunglasses next to one full of ball caps, liters of coke were stacked and tilting here and there, several on the verge of falling over. Along the far wall, refrigerated cases hummed, cooling beer and other beverages.

"Hey there," the man behind the counter said. "Help you with anything?"

"Hi," I said, pushing my sunglasses on top of my head. "My car broke down a little way down the road. Do you know a good mechanic nearby that could come look at it? Or a towing service?"

"Yeah, I sure do." The man, really a big kid, didn't look any older than eighteen, picked up a cordless phone, and dialed a number from memory. He smiled at me while it rang.

"Thanks," I said.

He nodded, waving a hand at me. "No problem. Oh! Hey, Josh! This is Izaak down at the gas station. I've got a lady here that needs some help. Her car broke down not too far from the church on main, and it needs towed to your place. Can you help her out?"

I waited, trying to catch the other end of the conversation as the kid nodded, listening.

"Thanks, man, I'll let her know." He hung up, his smile broadening. "Josh is the nearest mechanic, and he'll have to call a tow truck to pick up your car. But it'll be a few hours. He couldn't say for sure because it depends on their schedule. But they'll pick it up and bring it to him."

"Great." It was late afternoon already, and waiting a few hours would mean waiting in the dark. It was that or walk to Magnolia House. Neither one sounded like a good option in this heat. I gave the kid a tight smile. "Thanks for calling."

"Don't worry about the waiting." He gestured with his hands, trying to erase all the worry and stress in the world, a soothing, wax on, wax off motion. "He's sending one of his part-time mechanics, I think he said Jake, over to pick you up and take you where you need to go."

"Oh wow." I hesitated, already knowing I was asking the impossible. "That's really great, and I appreciate it, but can't I call a cab or something? Does anyone drive over from Covington?"

He laughed. "No one would make that drive. But Josh is great, and his people are good too. I could call the sheriff's office if you'd like, and they could run out here. Or do you have someone else you wanna call?"

I shook my head, a little horrified at the thought of calling the sheriff for a ride. "No, you don't need to call the sheriff."

"You sure? I don't mind!" He reached for the phone again, but I waved him off. "You can borrow the phone too, if you've got someone you need to call."

"Oh, no, I don't. Thanks though."

"Sure, sure." He eyed me, his curiosity a solid force in the room. "So, you just passing through? We're not really on the way to anywhere, is all. It's funny getting strangers in here."

I raised an eyebrow.

"I mean," he stumbled over his words. "I mean, yeah, we get people passing through. It's not like we're out in the middle of nowhere. It's just rare. You know, on this end of town. It's practically a dead end here. Nothing at all except the big house down the way a bit and the bayou."

He was starting to turn red, stammering a little. I nodded, unsure of what to say. Did I tell him I knew this place like the back of my hand? That nothing had changed and that it would probably always be this way? Or did I tell him all about the big house on down the way and the woman that had lived there? And once upon a time her daughter too.

"I'm going to grab some water," I said, turning to the row of cold cases. I grabbed two bottles of water, so cold they burned my fingers, and then considered the beer. I ended up with a bottle of cheap white wine. I wasn't driving, and seeing Vivian, being in this place again, was wearing on me. I set the bottles on the counter, daring the kid to say something.

"Yeah, it's awful hot out there. Got your ID? We got rain coming. Did you see the news? There's a tropical storm moving our way across the gulf. Craziest thing. Usually don't get them this early in the year, but here we are. The weather guy said it'll probably be a hurricane by the time it hits us."

"They have a name for it yet?" I asked.

Hurricane season ran from June to November and June first had barely passed us by. I hadn't even considered checking the weather before I left Oregon. But it seemed fitting to come home and be greeted in such a fashion. If I was lucky, I'd be out before it even decided Back of Beyond seemed like an easy target.

They're calling it Angela." He made a face. "But that's my mom's name so we're calling it Angie. Between you, me, and the fridge over there she's got a temper so Angela fits."

I smiled in a noncommittal way—maybe the hurricane should have been called Vivian if we were going to compare mothers. He scanned the bottles of water and then the wine, waiting while I dug around in my wallet for my driver's license. I handed it over, and he glanced at the birth date. I held my breath, hoping he'd miss the last name. But his expression changed. I saw the moment he realized who I was, looking up to meet my eyes.

"Emma Taylor? Mrs. Taylor's daughter?"

I nodded. If he'd been curious before, it was nothing compared to now. I could practically feel the questions whirling around his brain. I hadn't recognized him, but that didn't mean he didn't know who Vivian was. Everyone had known her. She made sure of it. And even if he'd never met her personally, I'd bet there were plenty of stories out there still making the rounds.

"Oh." He grabbed a plastic sack and stuck my bottles inside, the plastic sticking to the cold surfaces as he slid it toward me. "So you're on your way home then."

I stared at him. It shouldn't feel this way, like a punch to the gut, to hear Magnolia House referred to as home. Home was Oregon. Home was a tiny apartment filled with plants and sunshine. But here, to this stranger who only meant to be kind, Magnolia House was home.

"Yes," I said, pushing my sunglasses back over my eyes and grabbing the sack. "Thanks for calling the mechanic. I'm going to wait with the car."

"Yeah, of course." He leaned across the counter, face somber. "I'm really sorry about your mom."

Only because you didn't really know her. But I didn't say it, couldn't make the words leave my mouth. Instead, I smiled tightly and nodded. "Thank you. I appreciate all the help."

He waved as I shouldered the door open, bell chiming overhead, fleeing the glorious air conditioning and his suffocating pity.

The walk back to the car seemed longer, even under the shade of pine trees, and with a bottle of cold water pressed to my temple. I took a gulp, holding it in my mouth, wondering what the kid might say to other people. Not that there was anything to say. *Emma Taylor's car broke down, and she bought a bottle of wine at the gas station.* I couldn't imagine anyone being interested in that bit of news. They all had to know I'd be coming back; she'd died, of course, I had to come back and handle it.

Reaching the car, I unlocked it and sat in the front passenger seat with the door open. I rolled the bottle of water across my forehead, listening to the whine of insects and wishing the temperature would drop ten degrees. Or twenty, anything to ease the sticky heat. Moving the bottle over the back of my neck, I looked down and froze, a knot forming in my stomach. The noises around me faded, drawing back, pausing with my held breath.

A dead bird lay between the curb and the back tire. It was crushed, a mass of black feathers with one twisted foot. A grackle or some other dark species. I couldn't tell how long it had been there. It seemed to be fresh, a recent tragedy I'd stumbled across, a new sorrow. Had I run it over? Was that why my car had stopped? A mechanical protest to my human inattention? Or had it been waiting for me? Waiting to be seen and properly mourned?

Something my dad had told me once surfaced in my mind, his voice clear.

Dead birds are bad luck, kiddo. You just move right along.

"I'm sorry," I whispered, squeezing my eyes shut and pulling back.

I slid over to the driver's side, shoving the key in the ignition and praying the car would start. It clicked but didn't roll over. I'd been half hoping the air would come on, blow cool on my face, give me a little bit of relief. But that failed to happen as well. I was stuck, trapped between my dead car and a dead bird, my dead mother behind me, Magnolia House before me.

The neighborhood was quiet, houses small and tidy, older cars sitting in driveways. A low buzzing hum filled the air, the quiet filling my ears the way an ocean would, the pounding incessant, determined to conquer beaches, to wreck minds. I wasn't sure how much longer I could sit here, waiting, listening to the fullness of the world. I could always go back to the gas station or go on down to the church to soak up some of their cool air, explore other silences.

Cicadas hummed, thrumming, the air heavy. A slight breeze drifted by, shifting through Spanish moss and oak, pine trees swaying as it passed. But it wasn't enough to chase the heat away. It somehow made it worse.

I'd forgotten how Back of Beyond got under my skin; muggy air coming in close and getting everywhere I didn't want it to be. It had been one of the things I'd forgotten first, along with the humidity and the taste of bug spray. All things I would have thought impossible to forget.

This whole place was right under my skin again. The way the funeral director had talked to me, the way Vivian had lain there, motionless, lifeless on the table, and the kid at the gas station looking at me like I was some kind of ghost.

The ghost of Vivian Taylor.

I took a mouth full of water and swished it around. Wednesday morning, yesterday felt like a lifetime ago, I'd woken up in my apartment and gotten ready for my day. All without thinking of her. I'd had lunch and worked and graded papers and read, all without thinking of her. I'd gone almost the whole day without her creeping in. I hadn't at all until the attorney called. And then I'd discovered she'd been thinking about me all along.

I reached for the bottle of wine, inspecting it, wondering if I'd need a corkscrew. I turned it over, watching the liquid inside, thinking about the dead woman I'd seen on the table. The scent of the funeral home filled my nose, plastic floral air refresher and bleach, and the faint, almost not there scent of synthetic jasmine. The cold space and the sound of people talking in another room voices low, but knowing they were talking about Vivian. And about me.

Lucky for me, the bottle was a screw top and came off with a twist, seal cracking, metal threads pulling apart beneath my fingers. I sniffed it. Cheap white wine and probably terrible. I didn't recognize the label at all, and I was a fan of the cheap stuff. Give me a box with a pour spout any night of the week.

Vivian alive, violet eyes sharp, the hushing whisper of the wheelchair crossing the old wood floors, flashed through me. The last time I'd seen her alive. I didn't care about cheap and probably terrible wine. The first sip was pretty bad, but it improved on the second. By the third, it wasn't that bad at all. I lifted it, toasted the memory, welcoming the distance between the girl I'd been and the woman I was now.

Overhead the trees moved lazily, shadows shifting, patterns of light and shade moving over me. I watched them, the movement, and pushed everything else away. Today had been enough. I'd do more tomorrow. Right now, I'd drink wine straight from the bottle and wait for the mechanic to show up. I wasn't going to see any of these people again. I didn't care what they thought. I didn't care how Vivian might have presented the situation after I'd gone.

She would have turned it all to her advantage, weaving a story of loss and motherly love, her desire to do the best she could for me, her quiet stubborn daughter. She wanted to provide for me, guide me, be the strong influence in my life that I so desperately needed in the wake of my dad's death. She was a single mother, making ends meet, sheltering me from the world. And after I was gone, she probably told them how ungrateful I had always been. Damaged. Traumatized.

Had any of them, just one, ever wondered what Magnolia House was like at night?

A shudder passed through me, leaving me cold in the heat, and I took another sip of wine. How long had I been here? Stewing in the past, turning over memory after memory, even after I'd pushed them all away. But they'd come back. They always would. I held out the bottle, inspecting it. I'd been waiting exactly half a bottle's worth of time.

———

A car was coming down the street, rumbling along, and I leaned out far enough to get a good look. It was a big black truck with dark-tinted windows and a slight dent in the front bumper. The closer it got, the more imperfections I could see, a few obvious scrapes and hail dents, plus a thin layer of dirt over it all.

A working truck. Or more likely, a fishing truck. I'd seen them a million times, but this one pulled up right behind my car. I blew out a sigh, putting the cap back on the wine, not wanting to stand up yet. I wondered who was in the truck. I didn't know what I'd been expecting, but this wasn't it. Would I want this person to give me a ride home?

The door opened, and a man stepped out. He wore jeans and a white T-shirt with a few dark greasy streaks across it, a scuffed-up pair of boots, and black sunglasses. He looked like he'd skipped a few haircuts, hair dark and shaggy, but the grown-out look suited him. The same went for the stubble along his jawline. He had fine features, but his nose was slightly crooked, just enough to give him a bit of character, one imperfect thing amongst perfection so you'd know he was the real deal. He walked past me without a glance, tapping a knuckle on the hood of the car, and reaching down to feel for the latch.

"Pop it open, and let's see what's going on."

I scrambled to find the latch. The wine had gotten to me. I thought I'd been fine; I'd been drinking water as well. But the alcohol had snuck in like the heat, getting under my skin and turning me clumsy. I found the latch and pulled it, watching as he lifted the hood and looked inside.

I watched him as he pushed his sunglasses up and squinted at the engine. Blue eyes, the color of storms, like hurricanes in the off-season and water along the Oregon coast. He pulled at a few things, leaned in, and looked down into the engine. Maybe he'd be able to fix it here and now. I'd be able to drive myself home, and I wouldn't have to rely on a stranger. Not drive, I amended. Call someone. Ask the kid at the gas station for a ride home. Die here on the side of the road and become mummified like the poor bird.

"Are you Jake?" I asked finally, leaning out of the driver's seat trying to get a better look. He was so focused on the engine. I had no idea machinery could be that fascinating.

"Yep." His tone was uninterested, a little of the Southern accent slinking in.

The hood slammed shut, and he wiped his hands on the hem of his already dirty shirt, exposing his flat stomach. That explained the grease stains at least. He came to stand in front of me, and I looked up, a question about the car on my tongue.

But his look stopped me.

"You're the Taylor woman. The daughter."

The daughter.

"How can you tell?"

"You look like your mom."

Maybe he meant it as a compliment. But to me, it wasn't one. I jerked my chin at the engine. "Is it fixable?"

"Not here," he said with a shrug. "Josh has a tow truck coming in a few hours, and he'll take a look at it as soon as it gets back to the shop. He'll get you taken care of in no time. Until then, I can give you a ride to the house. Need help with your bags?"

"How do you know where I'm going?" I narrowed my eyes.

"Because you're a Taylor, and there's only one Magnolia House."

I found the release for the trunk and pulled, the latch popping free with a thump. *Abandon ship!* I grabbed the rental keys and shouldered my purse, sliding out of the car and shutting the door behind me with a hip. I held out the keys to Jake. He accepted them and slid them into his front pocket.

"You taking that with you?" he asked, his voice deep and smooth, an undercurrent of humor running through it.

"What?"

He raised an eyebrow and nodded at my hand. I was

still holding the half-empty bottle of wine. I had a moment where I considered downing the rest of it in one go but decided against it. I held it out to him instead.

"Drink?"

He shook his head.

"That's fine. I've had a tough day and really didn't feel like sharing. Anyway," I said, digging in my purse for the lid and magically discovering it. "It has a lid. I won't drink while you drive."

"Appreciate that," he said.

I gave him a smile, one of the good ones, and moved around him to the trunk of the car. There wasn't much. A black rolling suitcase and backpack stuffed to bursting with two feather pillows. I'd grabbed two pillows at the last minute because I didn't want to sleep on any of Vivian's. And I hadn't packed much else.

"I'll take those." Jake reached past me and grabbed the suitcase with one hand, taking the bottle of wine from me with the other. "Grab your backpack."

The interior of the truck was cool, and I leaned back against the seat, grateful for the reprieve from the heat. I stuffed the pillows around my legs, feeling foolish now for dragging them all this way. Jake transferred my luggage and then made sure the rental car was locked before sliding into the driver's seat beside me.

"Any place you need to go before I drop you off?"

"I can't think of any place, but thanks for asking."

"You got a cell phone with reception?"

I glanced at him. "No. Is that an issue around here for everyone else as well?"

"Most of the time." He shrugged. "The house has a landline, right?"

It had when I was little, it had right before I'd left, and I couldn't imagine Vivian getting rid of it. But I honestly had no idea about the condition of the house I was returning to. It could turn out to be anything, everything, or nothing at all like what I remembered.

Maybe I'd get lucky, and it wouldn't be at all like some of the things I'd tried to forget.

"Maybe," I said.

He glanced at me, pulling away from the curb and leaving the rental car behind. The neighborhood looked different from this high up, an altered perspective, a fresh view. The town didn't seem so forlorn, so worn down and dirty. It was a strange shift, the world moving just enough, becoming another place entirely with this stranger beside me.

I leaned back against the seat, head back, watching the little bit of town that was left roll on by. A metallic scent lingered in the cab of the truck, some mechanical shop scent, but over that was the harsh smell of lemon cleaner, sharp and intense. I glanced behind me, into the bed of the truck, and spotted a beat-up tackle box.

The man beside me focused on the road, hands loose on the wheel, confident in his knowledge of what the road had to offer. How well did he know his way to Magnolia House? Had he ever been out there? I searched his face in quick glances, searching for the familiar, the hint that I might have known him in my other life. But I couldn't be sure.

As we approached the edge of town, I shifted back to the window, catching the words of a billboard just before the trees began. Big letters, bold and black, hand-painted and dripping over a stark white background.

Hell Is Real.

"Is it?" I asked, hearing the pastor from my childhood, thumping the pulpit, red in the face as his voice rose and he damned us all. The white church. Vivian's head bent in prayer. And all that anger spreading through me like fire.

"What?" Jake asked.

"What?" I turned to him, not realizing I'd spoken aloud until he'd responded.

"What did you just ask?"

I waved vaguely at the window, the sign now behind us. "That's the second one of those billboards I've seen today. 'Hell is real.' It's just a sign. I didn't realize I'd said it out loud."

He gave me a blank look.

"I've had a long day," I added.

He nodded without saying anything. There had been something in his face when he'd realized who I was, a flash of recognition. Or surprise? Now, though, he couldn't be less interested. He gave off an air of *don't talk to me*, and all I really wanted to do was talk to someone.

I wanted to drown out the memories that were rising like a tide. I was a little drunk and full of emotion that I didn't want to examine too closely. There might have been some sadness in there somewhere, but it was getting drowned out by a lot of anger. And more fear than I wanted to admit to.

"So, do you believe it's real?" I asked.

"What?"

"Hell."

He glanced at me—from the road to me and back—eyebrows pulled together. "What?"

It was too much. I burst out laughing. "*What* is the only word you know, isn't it? And I've just been hallucinating everything else you've said."

He looked at me like I was crazy. I felt crazy. I held my hands up. "Sorry. I'm not making a ton of sense, and I apologize. I'm overtired. Thank you for coming to check out the car and chauffeuring me to the house. You didn't have to, and I appreciate you taking the time."

"Not a problem."

I nodded, embarrassment joining the swamp of other emotions roiling in my gut. When I was a child to the drive from Magnolia House had seemed long. I'd counted in my head as a kid, finding my own personal landmarks along the way. But now it seemed longer. Maybe my distance from the past made it longer, drawing it out into this never-ending drive.

Jake remained silent beside me. I'd thrown a few glances his way, the alcohol in my system blurring the edges of everything a little. I wanted him to talk to me. I wanted to know how he'd ended up staying in this place when everyone should have gotten out like I had. Because that had been smart, right? To leave? And yet, here I was. So maybe not as smart as I'd thought.

No matter how many times I turned my eyes back to the road, they slid back to Jake. He was compelling, the set of his jaw, and the line of his brow. His big hands gripping the steering wheel were rough and tan and so steady. He looked like he spent too much time out in the sun. I wondered if there was someone to remind him to put sunscreen on.

I shook myself. None of that mattered. I wasn't inter-ested. I was only looking for distractions, anything to keep me from thinking about Vivian. For a split second, I'd almost thought of her as Mom; it had crept in, a surprise attack, those cruel eyes turning up at the corners as a sneer touched beautiful lips.

Vivian was gone. Dead. Soon to be buried. I had Magnolia House and her debts. I had bills to figure out and a possible visit with the bank if the attorney hadn't sorted it all out already. I would settle her worldly affairs, and she'd go on to find out if hell were real or not.

She'd made it real for me.

Out of the corner of my eye, I caught Jake glancing at me, face smooth and expressionless, but he looked away as I met his gaze. I wondered what he was seeing. Hopefully not the complete mess I felt like. But he'd picked me up, and I'd already been through half a bottle of wine in a broken-down car.

I was pretty sure he knew exactly what kind of mess I was.

———

Live oaks lined the long, winding drive up to Magnolia House. Spanish moss reached out, long tendrils stretching, almost touching the roof of the truck as we passed beneath low branches. The lawn, once a smooth expanse of short grass, was now waist-high brush and weeds. The trees had always masked the house, making it almost impossible to see until you were right in front of it. But even now, having grown up in this place, I wasn't sure when the trees would part.

Magnolia House would appear in its own time, a sly, deceptive magic trick.

The drive, the trees, the Spanish moss, it was all alien to me now. I held my breath as the drive turned and a memory overtook me. Vivian waiting on the porch for me after school in the eighth grade, sitting at the top of the ramp with a tight smile on her face. Would she be there now? Was the woman in the funeral home an impostor? My stomach dropped, toes curling as we followed the final curve and the house came into view.

A classic white plantation house, a staple of Southern magazines and movies, the imposing pillars, black shutters, touches of wrought iron, and carriage lamps. Now it was decaying, overgrown, with an air of loneliness.

It was almost completely covered in star jasmine and honeysuckle vines. When I'd been little, my dad had kept them in check, trained them to follow the thoughtfully placed lattice, and later there had been gardeners to trim them back when necessary. Now they'd taken over, obscuring windows and lining the wide verandah and balcony on the front of the house. Vines crawled up the roof and twisted around the chimneys, moving beyond the brick and mortar, curling into the sky, stretching and reaching for the clouds.

The main part of the house was built up on brick pylons, lifting it a few feet above the ground and out of the reach of floodwaters. Or whatever else might come along. The space between the house and the earth was covered in a latticework of brick covered in vines. The white paint on the wooden stairs was peeling, gray wood peeking through. Without seeing it, I knew the roof of the verandah would be haint blue, the color meant to trick and confuse a spirit, to keep it from entering a house.

Did it work? Or would I go in and find Vivian still there?

The garden around the house was overgrown and had gone past wild; it was now something else, something prehistoric. The magnolia tree that had been some distance from the house was now a thicket of dark shiny leaves, branches brushing against the siding. A mass of rose bushes grew close to the house, half covered in jasmine, thorns and star-shaped flowers vying for space.

Vivian had made sure each detail of the house had been right—usually with that overly sweet Southern drawl and an iron fist. When I was growing up, it had looked like the kind of house you'd see in a magazine. When the ramp for her wheelchair had been added, it had gone on the back of the house by the kitchen door, out of sight and without ruining the classic architecture. Even the places that had seemed slightly overgrown in my youth had been done for effect. Vivian had perfected the windblown, lovely look for herself, and transferred it to the house.

This place had always been an extension of herself.

Magnolia House.

Vivian's house.

I'd grown up here. This was the house my dad had never returned to. Vivian had rolled through the halls screaming and crying until the dust settled and we found a tense routine. None of it had gotten easier with time. I'd left a few days after my seventeenth birthday, swearing on everything that was holy I would never come back.

And yet, here I was.

The truck came to a stop, and I hesitated, not knowing what I'd find inside, not sure I wanted to face it after coming all this way.

"You staying here?"

"What?"

"Are you spending the night in the house?"

I tore my gaze away from the building and met his eyes, searching his face. There was something in his voice I didn't understand, an edge, emotion lurking beneath the words I couldn't name. "I don't know. Does it matter?"

He shrugged, leaning forward against the steering wheel, and studying the facade. "Is it livable? Does it have electricity? Running water?"

I laughed. Those things hadn't always been guaranteed when I was growing up. The house was old, over a hundred and fifty years at this point, and repair issues had been constant and dramatic. Only the first floor had running water, courtesy of a great-grandmother in the late thirties. The kitchen had been renovated and a bathroom installed. But it was the only one in the house.

As far as electricity, that was only downstairs as well. There had never been enough money or desire to refit the rest of the house. And after the accident, Vivian never bothered with the upstairs. Partly because her wheelchair kept her on the ground floor and partly out of spite. If she couldn't enjoy it, neither could I. But that had come later. I didn't move upstairs until after my dad died.

In a high wind or in the middle of a storm, the electricity went out. Hot water was a luxury I rarely enjoyed unless I put the big black kettle on the gas stove to boil. There had been a tiny water heater, small and high on the wall, but it didn't hold much. And that hot water wasn't for me. Vivian made sure I understood that early on.

Home sweet home.

"It never really had those things to begin with."

I started to open the door, and he reached out, putting a warm hand on my arm. The touch was gentle, soft, and gone before I had a chance to look down. He pulled back, gesturing at the house, dark eyes searching mine.

"You can't stay in there like this. The weather lady is talking about a hurricane rolling through in the next few days. You'll end up stuck out here."

"It'll be fine."

I eased out of the truck, tugging my purse higher on my shoulder and taking a few steps toward the house. My clothes felt tight and hot, and all I wanted to do was stand in a cold shower for an hour and drink the rest of the wine. But maybe he was right. It would be silly to strand myself out here with no way of getting in touch with anyone. Already evening light filled the sky, the world on the verge of going soft and golden. Soon it would be dark. Soon the night would be here.

Jake got out of the truck, and I heard him get my suitcase out of the back.

"If you're staying, you're staying. Fine. But you still need to get back to your rental car. Thought about that at all?"

I hadn't. Panic pounced, heart picking up, and I turned to him. "Could you come back in the morning? And take me to the mechanic? Please?"

He didn't say anything.

"I honestly hadn't thought about that part. I'm sorry. It would be a huge help if you could come back in the morning." I stammered, tripping over my words. "I could pay you! Or maybe you could call a cab for me when you get home?" My voice trailed off, and I groaned. "But there aren't any cabs out here."

"Or," he said, "I could take you back to town, and you can find a hotel room for the night out by the interstate. Call yourself a cab from there to the shop."

For a moment I saw how that would all work. The only place that would be open or have a phone that I could use would be the gas station. I'd call one of the hotel chains along the interstate and get a room for the night. Maybe for however long it took to settle things. I'd figure out another rental car. It would be all cold sheets and boring mass-produced artwork, cable television, and security bolts on steel doors.

But that was all at least an hour away, and it would take more money than I had. I wasn't prepared to pay for a week of hotel rooms on top of gas and the rental. Even though I dreaded going inside the house, it was the only place I could go.

I shook my head, reaching for my suitcase in his hand.

He set it at my feet and turned away. "You're an idiot."

"Excuse me?"

He kept walking, back to his truck and swinging inside. The door slammed, ringing in my ears. He rolled down the passenger side window and said loudly, "Tomorrow morning at eight."

And that was it.

CHAPTER THREE

WEDNESDAY

I walked slowly up the stairs to the verandah, heart picking up, blood ringing in my ears. I could feel it, feel it in the way you feel a toothache coming on, a pulled muscle in your back getting worse instead of better. The scent of overgrown vegetation and old wood surrounded me, beneath that rich soil and recent rain, the edges of the bayou less than a mile away—black water and cypress trees.

I paused on the top step, poised to step forward but motionless, flash-frozen in fear. The setting sun lowering in the sky, a pair of birds racing the sunset to find a roost. Their song passed over me, a warning or blessing, receding quickly. Sweet jasmine filled the air here, as if the house were wearing perfume, the intense scent so different from the artificial jasmine at the funeral home.

The front door was open, not standing wide, but cracked as if the latch hadn't caught when the last person had passed over the threshold. Had it been Vivian? Had someone come to take her to the hospital or discovered her dead?

Come inside, come inside, and find out for yourself.
Or are you afraid?

The last step creaked, boards shifting beneath me as I crossed to the door, beneath the blue ceiling of the verandah, and into the breathing space of Magnolia House. I stopped there, setting my bag down, pushing the door open —crackled white paint beneath my fingertips, heavy leaded glass windows to either side. As it swung back, hinges silent, the large foyer came into view, polished wood floors, the white staircase leading up. Elegant arched openings to the left and right led to formal sitting areas, the dining room, and places to entertain guests—areas that had been reserved for Vivian alone.

She was there in the shadows, looking down on me— pale face with that beautiful smile, perfectly styled hair, large diamond earrings, with a ruby ring on her left hand, in the other she held a large magnolia blossom. A young woman in an elegant white dress—not a wedding dress, no, but something for an event, silk and bare shoulders. A young Vivian, as I had never known her, a woman with secrets behind her violet-blue eyes.

I gasped, stepping back, half turned to go back the way I'd come. But I paused, realizing it was the portrait. She'd commissioned it right after they'd been married, a wedding gift to herself. I'd forgotten about it. When I'd lived here, the back of the house had been my domain—the kitchen door and garden, the winding paths out of sight. I'd moved down narrow passages meant for servants, steep stairs, and small rooms behind these open, airy spaces.

"Hello?" I cleared my throat, tense and uneasy, and raised my voice. "Anyone here?"

Nothing in the house moved. The interior was so quiet and still that it sucked in the noise from outside, muting it, smothering it. The world pressed against my back—my life in Oregon, the peace I'd built outside of this place, beyond the pull of Vivian and Magnolia House. The empty rooms gave me nothing, offered me nothing.

Would it remember the sound of my feet on wooden floors, the feel of my fingertips as I flipped on light switches and closed doors?

That's stupid. Stop being stupid. The place is empty. Someone forgot to lock the door on the way out. Just go inside and get it over with.

Crossing the threshold and stepping into the house was like arriving in another country. A place untouchable from the outside, set apart and distant. This place had always been that way, but it was even more so now, eight years later and seemingly empty.

"Hello?"

The house swallowed the word. Consumed it, ate it, caressing me as the sound disappeared from my throat. Memories, some bleak and hard, the others, the ones with my dad, bright enough to chase the darkest shadows away for an instant. I lifted my chin and straightened my shoulders. I wanted to tell the house this situation was temporary, that I didn't like it any more than it did. We just had to make it through the week together.

Don't be an idiot. It's just a house.

The crystal chandelier buzzed into life with one flick of the switch, warm light filling the room, small rainbows trembling against the white plaster ceiling, catching in the crown molding—delicate, swirling fleur-de-lis. I sighed, some of the tension inside uncoiling. I hadn't been sure the power would be on. Or that it would work. It had always been an issue growing up, and I'd gotten used to using candles. I would still need them for the second floor and attics. There had never been any electricity there.

With the lights on, the colors of the room were bright—fresh cream and various shades of green, pops of sunny yellow, and that beautiful blue carried in from the verandah ceiling. Paintings of birds and detailed botanical prints were framed in antique gold, pretty painted porcelain dishes hung from ribbons, and objects simply meant to be beautiful and appealing filled in the gaps. The antique oval mirrors were draped with sheer black fabric—dark ghosts suspended on each wall.

If you opened a book on architecture and home decorating, this room would be in it—one of those big glossy coffee-table books simply meant to be beautiful. The whole downstairs could have filled pages. A timeless and classic old house with polished parquet and marble tables, fresh flowers, and the deep chime of a grandfather clock.

I noticed it then, the absence of the ticking. The grandfather clock was silent. It had always been the heartbeat of the house—a constant rhythm, counting down the hours, a minute-by-minute account of my childhood. My lonely existence here.

It was stopped at three in the morning, the little moon on the face of the clock suspended over a field of painted stars. The estimated time of death. Vivian must have stopped it herself, knowing exactly how and when she would go. No one else would have been here at that time to follow the tradition of stopping the clocks for the dead.

Without thinking about it too much, refusing to examine the impulse, I opened the polished case and restarted it. I didn't bother to fix the time, simply set the pendulum in motion. It began to tick, a strange comfort in this strange place, picking up where it had been stopped and beginning to count this new chapter of my life.

As I turned away, satisfied that in a small way I'd already left some kind of mark on this place, I caught a flash of movement. The hair on the back of my neck rose, my stomach a solid lump. Slowly, holding my breath and afraid to move, I twisted my head to see what was in the room with me.

The foyer was empty. The grandfather clock ticking. Vivian, the perfect painted woman on the canvas, stared down at me with malicious satisfaction. Had her smile been that pointed before? Lips so red? I stared back, limbs going cold, skin crawling.

It's just a painting. Nothing else.

Before it got dark, I needed to check the rest of the house, make sure nothing had crept through the open door and was now lying in wait. Move. Inspect. Uncover. I went over these things, knowing I would need candles or a lantern, and it needed to happen soon. Now. But I was pinned to the parquet, unable to move, as the portrait watched me.

I sidestepped to the door, eyes never leaving the painting, and I realized it hadn't been looking at me. A trick of the light, a shiver of crystal across the eyes. That was all. Paint and canvas and a gaudy gilded frame. There was nothing else it could be.

Evening was approaching, the world slowing down, the night poised to take over. It would be easier to check the upper floors now, while I could open the curtains and find something more than the night sky on the other side.

There would be candles in the kitchen; stashed in a lower cabinet with enough matches to set a thousand fires. I rolled my suitcase inside and shut the door, pausing before I locked it, wondering if I was locking myself in with someone—or something. The bolt slid into place, the click running up my arm, into my shoulder. The house was dim. Vivian had covered all the windows with blackout curtains because sunlight would damage the expensive fabrics throughout the house. The result was a space full of shadows, even on the brightest afternoon.

I didn't look into either of the sitting rooms off the entryway, or up the stairs; instead, I moved purposefully toward the back of the house. I could go left or right. In one direction the kitchen, bathroom, and my dad's study—his refuge—waited for inspection.

In the other was Vivian's room.

I glanced toward the door, dreading the moment it would turn in my hand and swing open. I had to make sure it was empty. But the thought made me shiver. Reaching the hall, I flipped the switch, memory coursing through me, my body knowing right where it would be. The fixtures along the length of the hall snapped on in unison—four tinkling, shivering crystal wall sconces that matched the chandelier in the foyer. The fixture by the kitchen door popped, snapping off, and leaving a white spot in my vision.

Cold enveloped me, the buzzing of the fixture nearest me growing, a hum that filled the air. A gust of air brushed my hand, a swirl of nothing moving past me. Blinking, heart pounding, my vision cleared, and the hall came into focus. The old house shifted, as all old houses do, occupied after an absence. There was nothing unusual in a light bulb burning out or a ripple of fresh air flitting through the space.

A thin film of dust lay on the baseboards and down the center of the hall I could see the clear track the wheelchair had made as she'd gone back and forth. The marks of her life were so apparent, the condition I'd left her in so clear. A disabled woman alone in this huge old house, miles from town, the nearest emergency services forty-five minutes away. I'd left her all alone out here.

I sucked in a breath. *Breathe*, I reminded myself. It was done. I'd done what was necessary, vital, to keep my life, to keep whatever shreds of myself remained—the pieces she hadn't managed to smother.

Walking down the hall, steps brisk and shoulders straight, I opened the doors and turned on all the lights. I wanted the house to fill up the night, to keep whatever darkness there might be waiting to enter at bay. Maybe it would even be enough to keep the darkness from coming down the stairs.

My room was up there. I'd lived a strange life in a modern world without electricity and running water, set apart from the world, while downstairs had every luxury—always so close but held just out of reach. I'd crept down-stairs for snacks and showers and restroom necessities. Vivian's voice cutting through the creak of stairs, her hearing as sharp as any hunting hound. Time and again her strident tone had sent my heart stuttering, mind racing for a reply, for justification.

What do you think you're doing downstairs?

Before that, a long time before that, I'd had a room across the hall from my parents. It had been full of light with lacy curtains on the windows and a quilt covered in patterned birds on the bed. There had been a light switch. But after my dad died, I'd moved upstairs. Not right away, nothing to make anyone talk if anyone had known. It had been a gradual shift. Vivian had needed the room for this or that, and of course, she couldn't go upstairs. I was the one with a pair of working legs.

Evening light filled the kitchen, coming in through the window over the sink and glass half of the back door. I fumbled for the switch on the wall. The plain overhead light came on, showing the wear on the black and white linoleum floor, the age of the appliances. A potted violet sat on the window ledge—velvet leaves and intense purple blooms.

Vivian had loved violets; loved it when strangers said her eyes were violet blue.

Cold touched me, another breeze or draft, brushing past me, disappearing further into the house. The back door was open, wide open, pushed back all the way to the wall. The screen door was closed but didn't have a lock. There was no way to keep it open anyway. Not unless you put a rock down to keep it in place. It didn't have any springs to recoil, just the hinges, and I could still hear the crash it made when I'd pushed through it and gone running off into the woods as a kid.

I crossed to the door, heart pounding, and pushed it closed. The snap of it shutting echoed in the house, rushing out of the kitchen, rippling out. The top half of the door was glass, and it rattled slightly as I locked it.

Through the window I studied the overgrown kitchen garden—half herbs and half flowers. Now it was mostly weeds. Even when I was a child, the garden behind the house had been messy and haphazard. All of Vivian's time and attention had been concentrated on the front of the house, the facade, the only side the casual visitor saw. The gardener and his crew had only ever been paid for the front.

At the edge of the half-civilized garden were tall trees, tangled woods, and beyond that and unseen, the bayou.

The waterway snaked close to the house, lazy and slow, but if you had a boat, it led to other places, to deeper water. My dad had taken me fishing a few times, borrowed a flat-bottomed boat and pushed away from the half-rotted jetty attached to the property. He'd shown me how our small place connected to a wider world.

A world I might someday escape to.

I turned back to the kitchen, looking around, wondering if the candles and matches had been moved—wondering what else might be in here. The space was clean, cleaner and less worn than the hall appeared. She must have had someone coming in to do some basic housekeeping. Lord knew that woman had never cleaned a day in her life.

The floor was cheap linoleum, from my grandmother's era, placed over the original wooden floorboards. Eventually it would have been white marble, that's what Vivian had kept promising. But the money always flowed into the main rooms of the house or the gardens. White floor-to-ceiling cabinets covered the kitchen, a few inset with glass, exposing the fine dishes and crystal glasses within. The counters were white marble, immaculate, and cool to the touch.

Overhead the ceiling was blue, that haint blue of the front porch, a ward against any spirit that might have somehow made it through the back door. A chandelier hung from the medallion in the center of the room. It wasn't fancy, nothing like the one in the foyer, but it was still much grander than most kitchens might have. That had been a Vivian addition. She ignored the out-of-date floors in favor of something with some sparkle.

A cobalt-blue kettle sat on the stove with a box of matches beside it. The stove was older, the kind of gas range you had to light yourself. There had always been a box of matches there. Something else that hadn't changed in eight years. Candles would be in the lower cabinet or the butler's pantry.

It wasn't all the same. Things had shifted and migrated —the candles no longer in the place I'd expected, stacks of dishrags there instead, and a drawer full of mundane plastic silverware. I found the candles though, across the room from the stove with a few other household odds and ends. Brass candlesticks, an oil lamp, silver polish, and a shoebox full of old keys—a mix of sizes and shapes, shiny silver and dull brass.

I poked through them, wondering what they were all for. They were new to me, and I didn't remember the house having that many locks. I pick one out, a small silver key that might have belonged to a lockbox, and examined it briefly. Maybe I would find what it went to as I sorted through the contents of the house.

Dropping it back into the box, I grabbed a plain brass candleholder and one of the white tapers. A snort of laughter escaped. How very gothic romance it all was. The old house and candlelight, the night coming on fast, and a woman all alone.

I wasn't afraid, of course I wasn't, but if this had been any kind of fiction—book or movie—the character would've been terrified. I would have been terrified. I reminded myself that nothing was going to get me. There was nothing in this house that could hurt me. Not anymore.

The matchstick sparkled into life as soon as I struck it, wick catching, and the flame blossoming. My hand didn't shake at all.

I'd used my right hand, something Vivian had always insisted I do, along with a hoard of other superstitions. I'd done it without thinking about it. The muscle memory had been there. Magnolia House had resurrected it from what-ever shallow grave I'd buried it in. Other things would come back too, I had no doubt about that. I'd just do my best to shed them all again when my time here was over.

I moved back to the hall, pausing, the fear I'd refused to acknowledge touching me. The lights in the hall had gone out. The kitchen around me remained bright, making the shadows seem darker, the space deeper. At the very end, where Vivian's room waited, the shadows condensed and thickened.

That was where she'd been the last time. The final time. Backlit by the window, turned toward me, face blurred and left in shadow. A figure in a wheelchair at the end of a dark hall. If I squinted or let my eyes drift out of focus, would a figure appear? Would I still be able to see her there?

I shivered.

You're dead.

Nothing changed, the space around me the same, all of it as it had been before. Straightening my shoulders, I moved to the front of the house, shielding the small flame as I crossed the foyer and started up the stairs.

Pausing at the top, holding the candle high, I looked to the left and then the right. Light caught peeling wallpaper and the bare wooden floors. The white doors to the rooms were closed, and at the end of the hall in either direction were two large windows covered with heavy drapes.

I went to the right, toward my old bedroom, moving too quickly, the candle flame streaming—a thin line of wax melted down the length. I slowed—my breathing, my heart, my feet.

Don't hurry. Don't rush. You have nothing to be afraid of.

I reached the window and jerked back the curtains. They pulled away from the wall with a snap, and I stumbled back as heavy fabric and curtain rod came down with a thud. Dust filled the air, and I covered my nose and mouth with an arm, coughing, blinking back tears, stepping back and waiting for it to settle.

The window was grimy, the inside as dirty as the outside. Dead flies, blue and black and desiccated, littered the windowsill. Taking a corner of my T-shirt, I tried to wipe some of the grime away. It smeared, streaking, but through it, I could see the overgrown expanse of the side yard, stretching away in the dusk.

I turned to my room, wondering what she had done with it after I'd gone. Left it as it was, locked the door, and never gone in again? Emptied it? Burned the contents and abandoned it all to rot?

There was only one way to find out.

The knob turned easily enough, a little stiff, as if it hadn't moved in a hundred years, a stale smell drifting out to greet me. Pale light from the windows facing the front yard filled the room, showing the emptiness, and high-lighting the lack of furnishing. Nothing on the walls, nothing on the floor. Once upon a time, there had been a brass bed and a large wardrobe, a bedside table with an oil lamp, a pine dresser with stacks of books on the top. Even the curtains had been taken down.

Crossing to the large windows, I took in the view I'd known so well as a child—live oaks and magnolia, the winding drive, jasmine vines rustling in a passing breeze, the glass smooth and cool beneath my fingertips. I remembered it all as clearly as if I'd stood here yesterday. I would be able to recall it with perfect clarity until the day I died.

I stood there only a moment, long enough to take in the changes, and turned to explore the rest of the house.

After that, the rooms went more quickly. I didn't check the entire attic, I stood at the top of the stairs for a moment, holding the candle high—candle flame shivering with an unseen draft as I listened with my whole body. I locked the door behind me when I came down.

A few of the second-floor bedrooms were filled with old furniture, stacked boxes, and wooden packing crates. Some things were covered in canvas tarps, and there was one full room of paintings, all facing the wall.

I glanced through them, recognizing my maternal grandparents, a distant great-uncle, an aunt, a handful of cousins down the years. All of them belonged to my mother, all of them strangers to me. I knew them because my dad had taken the time to tell me their names, show me their faces.

None of them were from his side of the family.

But mostly the rooms were empty. There was less than I'd expected. I thought the house would be cluttered and overflowing—furniture, knickknacks, clothes, books, everything that was collected around someone as they lived out their lives. I was worried it would take me weeks to organize and sort through. The fact that there was less worried me a little. What had she done with it all?

The hallway light had returned when I got back downstairs—faulty wiring and not the pop of an old bulb dying after all. I opened every door on the ground floor as well. A few of the rooms were empty, a few with labeled boxes, a room stacked high with books. No shelves, no tables, only the floor, bare walls, and knee-high to waist-high stacks of paperbacks. I picked one off the nearest pile. A historical romance. The one below it was a thriller. There were nonfiction histories and all kinds of fiction—the variety of a voracious reader.

My dad's study was next. There were more books here, but these were on the floor-to-ceiling oak shelves. The room was lined with them, all four walls, even built around the window. His desk sat before the window, sunlight falling across the paperwork. Other times he'd sat with the window to his back, and when I'd come in with a question, he'd been a figure, a shadow, outlined in light.

Both of my parents were figures in dim light and surrounded by shadows in my memory.

Now though, the window was dark. I turned the desk lamp on, green glass and brass, something that had always seemed so elegant when I was little. Across from the desk was an old sofa, rolled arms and tufted, a chesterfield in warm brown leather, with his favorite spot worn from heavy use.

I was surprised that it was as I remembered. When he'd died, Vivian had closed the door and never gone in again— it had hurt too much for me. But now it wasn't even dusty. This study, this space, which had been so clearly his, was warm and safe after the rest of the house.

I missed him all the more for that, for the comfort he provided even now. His death seemed so far away now, and not enough memories were left. I longed for more. I wanted years. Decades. But I'd had five years and was left wanting but grateful.

I missed him. Even if I hadn't known him. The hole in my life was there, very real, and even now it pulled at me, lingered in the corners of life. If he'd been here, I wouldn't be doing this alone. If he'd been here, maybe Vivian would have been kinder.

After his death, she'd refused to talk about him. There

had been nothing. She refused to let me attend the funeral. Too young. Too little. I'd make a scene. I'd gone to preschool one morning with a dad, and by the end of the day, he was gone. There had been no goodbye for me.

With a sigh, I sat on the sofa, easing back, looking up at the blank ceiling. I'd sleep here. It was comfortable enough. There were no beds in the rest of the house anyway. There was more than enough room for me; the sofa was wide and long, with enough space to stretch out. Plus, I didn't want to go upstairs again, and this was nearer the bathroom and kitchen anyway.

I'd gone over the whole house. All of it. Except for Vivian's room. Pushing to my feet, I stretched. She'd made it very clear I was never to enter her room. I'd only been brave enough a few times when I was small, creeping in to look at the sparkling things on her dressing table—unable to resist the urge, a magpie child with nothing shiny of her own.

The window at the end of the hall was a dark rectangle now, rippled glass throwing back the light, my reflection. Floorboards creaked as I walked down the hall, moving quickly, swinging my arms as if I could bustle my way out of this feeling, and refusing to think about it.

It was just a room. Empty space. She wasn't here to stop me. But my stomach clenched as I neared the door, the air cooling around me. The hair on the back of my neck rose, goose flesh popping up, covering me.

Someone stood behind me. Eyes on me. The presence was physical. But I refused to look. There was no one there. The house was empty. I'd just walked down the empty hall. I'd looked in each room to make sure no one else was here. I knew I was alone.

Her door was like all the others. The knob had once

been polished brass, but now it was faded, worn down like old gold, the same creamy white paint and woodwork. Just like all the others. There was nothing special here.

You're the one that isn't special.

Her voice or mine? The echo of it in my mind faded, and I couldn't be sure. Maybe it was both, our voices twining together, twisting in my brain. All of the doubt she'd planted and fed and watered. I'd carried it forward, nurturing it even after she'd been unable to touch me in person. I'd carried her in my mind and on into the future.

I'd carried her all the way to Oregon.

"Screw you," I said.

But my voice was flat and weak—lacking force and conviction. I'd felt it there, at the back of my throat, the bottom of my stomach, and it had been angry starting out. But saying it aloud, to her, right here and now, was as scary as saying it to her as if she'd been alive.

Nothing had changed. Not in me. Not after all these years.

I reached out, hesitating, breathing heavily. My ears buzzed, a swarm of invisible flies circling me, vision narrowing down to the knob—dull and mundane, nothing more than hardware. I gripped it. Ice cold. So cold it burned. I jerked back, hand to mouth, muffling the cry that slipped out. I curled my other hand against my chest, staring at the doorknob.

Brass like all the others, worn from being held and twisted, turned and shut. It was everything I expected, everything I knew it would be. A doorknob was a doorknob. But it was cold as winter. I stepped back, easing away. The floorboards shifted beneath me, creaking, and something beyond the door creaked too.

I froze. The silence of the house deepened. I listened to

it, listened to it listening to me, and I could feel the pressure of watchfulness at my back. I took another step back, then another, turning to hurry toward the study. I rushed inside, slamming the door shut, taking in the room at a glance. The books were the same, the room was as I'd left it, and here the feeling of being watched disappeared. Leaning against the door, I fumbled with the lock, only breathing a sigh of relief when I heard it slot into place.

CHAPTER FOUR
WEDNESDAY

I'm not sure how long I sat there. Minutes. Hours. My cell phone was dead, and I'd left my bags in the foyer. The door remained locked, a barrier between me and the rest of the house. I'd been straining to catch the faintest sound—a whisper, a creak—and holding my breath. But there had been nothing.

The cold was my imagination. Nothing else. I'd seen Vivian dead today. Vivian. Dead on a table and pale as death because she *was* dead. And then I'd gotten almost drunk in my broken-down car in the middle of town because I was a woman who made great life choices. And whatever that had been with Jake. What had that been? I wasn't sure. And now I'd scared myself so badly that I'd locked myself in the study.

I needed to use the restroom. I was hungry. I wanted to find my phone charger and figure out what time it was. There wasn't anything trying to get me. It was just an old house. I stood, stretching sore muscles. Writing off the last hour as a result of too much wine on an empty stomach.

From the front of the house came a muffled knocking. I

stopped, heart racing, and listened. *Don't be an idiot.* It wasn't coming from Vivian's room. It was the front door.

Unlocking the study, I headed in that direction, avoiding looking down the length of the hall, grateful all the lights were still on. The knocking stopped and then started again, more insistent this time.

"Just a second!" I called, hurrying to grab the door and throwing it open without checking to see who it might be. The light of the chandelier fell across Jake, one hand raised to knock again. A June bug raced through the open door, fleeing the night and curious about Magnolia House.

"Jake," I said, brows coming together. I hadn't expected to see him until morning. My ears were burning, a flush creeping up my cheeks. I'd been thinking about him, and now here he was. "What are you doing back?"

He held up two plastic bags. "I wouldn't be a very good Southerner if I didn't offer a little hospitality. So I brought you dinner."

I took the sacks he extended toward me, peeking in at the junk food. "This is dinner?"

"Well, if you don't want it—" He moved to take them back.

"No!" I said, stepping out of reach. "I want them. I didn't mean to be rude. This is great, thank you. I really appreciate it. There's not anything to eat in the house."

"I kind of figured that. Vivian didn't seem to eat much."

I opened my mouth and shut it. Had he known her? But that was stupid, of course he had. Everyone had. This place was too small not to know the faces around you every day. I searched his face, on the verge of asking, when he took a step back, something like a smile flashing across his features.

"I'll see you in the morning."

"Yeah. Thanks," I said.

The sacks were full. It was almost an apology for being rude earlier. A small flash of kindness. But what else? *Vivian didn't seem to eat much.*

I remained at the door, watching as he crossed the verandah and got in his truck, taillights glowing red in the night. A mosquito bit me, others circling, and I ducked back inside before going through the sacks more thoroughly. They contained a variety of chips and snack cakes, beef jerky, a bottle of water, and a coke. Everything had probably been purchased at the small gas station in town, the kid behind the counter talking about Vivian Taylor's daughter.

It didn't matter. The kid could talk, and the food was perfect.

Grabbing the rolling suitcase as I went by, juggling the bags and my pillows, I headed for the kitchen. There hadn't even been a box of crackers or a forgotten can of green beans in the cabinets. I was grateful Jake had taken pity on me and come back with supplies.

Setting the food on the counter, I dug around in my bag until I located a charger and plugged my cell phone in. I crossed my fingers as I did. *Please work. Please don't start a fire.* A charging battery appeared on the screen, and I smiled.

Unwrapping a chocolate cupcake, I took a bite, the filling sweet with an artificial aftertaste, then I moved to stand at the back door. I couldn't see much beyond the glass. It was a mirror, my face blurred and washed out, a pale figure in another place.

Today I'd come back to a place I'd sworn never to return to. I'd seen Vivian. I'd drunk wine in a hot car and dealt with a man who didn't want to be dealing with me. But he'd been kind enough to bring me dinner.

I shoved the remainder of the cupcake in my mouth and went to wash my hand—blue dish soap and cold water, the pipes groaning as the water flowed. Glancing up, out through the window over the sink, I froze. A light moved in the woods. A flashlight maybe? A distant car? But there weren't any roads behind the house. It was all protected wildlife land and bayou.

There shouldn't be any lights out there.

I went to the back door and put my hand on the knob, intention coiled in me like a snake, a rattle of fear, a warning. There was no light now. Nothing moving in the trees. Nothing but the night.

The house had scared me earlier. No, not the house. *I* had scared me. But there was nothing to be afraid of. It was an old house, and old houses did weird things. It was just that I'd forgotten. Growing up, none of this had bothered me. It was silly to let it get to me now.

Letting go of the knob, I stepped back, crossing my arms over my chest, listening to the house—the nothingness and everything, quiet expectation pressed up against me, breathing across my skin.

I let it stay there, kept it close. I would take the silence over anything else right now.

THURSDAY

I think hell is something you carry around with you.
Not somewhere you go.

- Neil Gaiman

CHAPTER FIVE
THURSDAY

A quick succession of knocks echoed through the house—a rattle of small boulders, a prelude to a full-on pounding landslide. I looked up, pulled out of the crinkling newspapers in my hands, fingertips blackened with ink, dust clinging to the inside of my nose-old paper and heat, a faint trace of rot, something hidden and long dead high in the rafters of the attic. My back ached from sitting cross-legged on the rough floorboards—toes tingling and on the verge of going numb.

I'd been up since before sunrise, watching light creep in through the window, listening to something small rustling in the overgrown rose bushes outside. I hadn't been able to go back to sleep, so I'd finished the snack cakes for breakfast, taken a quick tepid shower, and started going through things at the top of the house.

The attic around me was dusty, already hot, and I'd started with a small cardboard box nearest the stairs. I hadn't gotten any farther. I looked over the newspaper clippings again, the paper crackling with age, the edges smooth and sharp—precisely cut. I wasn't sure I wanted to answer the door now. If I stayed here, would he go away? How would I get my car back? I shuffled through the headlines.

Suspect Arrested in the Murder of Local Woman
White Held Without Bail — Victim's Father Speaks
Justice for Alice Kent
Jake White Acquitted
The Search for Alice Kent's Killer

Both names were familiar. I doubled checked the dates. They would have been a year ahead of me in high school, years ahead of me in life experiences. But I couldn't picture the man I'd met yesterday as a teenager. Had I ever talked to him? I doubted it. I'd rarely spoken to anyone, and no one had ever made the effort to get to know me.

I flipped through the articles again. There were so many. A whole box full. Papers from all over the state, and few national ones had even picked the story up. Vivian had saved them, cutting them out and taping pieces together when necessary. They weren't in any kind of order, the dates all over the place as I sifted through them. But most were dated to almost eight years ago. Just after I'd left town, putting Back of Beyond, Louisiana firmly in my past.

Jake had been acquitted. Several articles talked about the lack of physical evidence, no DNA, no witnesses. She'd been his girlfriend, he'd been the last one to see her, and her family, who had loved him, believed he'd done it. He'd been poor, in a single-parent household, but with decent grades, and working a part-time job. She'd been smart and talented and going places. But it had all fallen apart. And he'd been eighteen, so he faced the court system as an adult.

The jury hadn't convicted him, the press seemed split between innocence and guilt. Despite the not-guilty verdict, there were people who assumed, felt they knew, he was the murderer. There were opinion pieces with writers comparing this story to others about women killed by loving partners or about women who'd tried to escape a bad situation.

Why had Vivian kept all these?

And Jake was here, knocking on the door now, insistent, demanding.

I lay the clippings carefully back in the box, hands shaking a little. He hadn't been convicted. I didn't know the whole story; it wasn't fair to assume things. I thought about the way he'd looked getting out of his truck, big and intimidating, his face set and voice rough. He'd helped me but didn't want to. He'd been an ass about it. But he'd also come back with dinner.

It didn't matter. I'd get my car back today, and I wouldn't need to spend any more time with him. I'd settle the house and go home. This would end up being part of the strange story of Vivian's death, a small, odd detail I shared with friends.

I tried to clear my mind as I hurried downstairs, wondering if he would appear any different to me now. I didn't know what to think. I didn't how I felt about it. Uneasy mostly, unsure maybe. The justice system made mistakes all the time; the wrong people had been convicted before. Too many things could go wrong or couldn't be accounted for.

At the door I paused, taking a breath and trying to steady my heart and put a polite smile on. It'd be nice. I'd say *please* and *thank you* and not let him know I'd discovered his past in the attic of Vivian's house.

What if he was guilty? What if he'd gotten away with it?

I opened the door, smile trembling.

"Hello, Emma! My how you've grown! I can't believe how beautiful you are! Just like your momma!"

The older woman, short and plump with artificially curled dark hair, spoke several volumes above normal, each sentence exclaimed with enthusiasm. I could practically see the exclamation points. The woman beside her was tall and thin, with a severe face and mass of white hair curled and piled on her head, making her appear even taller. She held a covered casserole dish in skinny hands, nails painted a deep red.

"Hi," I said, looking from one to the other, one face open and friendly, the other sour. "Can I help you?"

"Oh, dear! No, not at all! We're here to help you! We've known Vivian, your momma, for years! We were on the lunch committee at First Baptist together. I'm sure you remember us."

She paused for a response, carrying on with a wave of her hand when I didn't speak up right away.

"I remember you when you were little! So skinny. And pale, oh my gosh so pale, like you never even went outside. Then of course you left so suddenly! None of us knew what to think! But here you are! Back home! Your momma would be so pleased. She was so proud of you, off doing literary things out there in the big world! Of course, you could have come back for a visit more often, but that's neither here nor there."

Off doing literary things.

How had she known? I would never find out now. A chill slid through me at the thought, and I smiled tightly. I didn't remember these two specifically, though they looked familiar. Vivian had always had guests coming and going, a constant rotation, like a spider at the center of a web. But I was expected to stay out of the way. In her view, children were meant to be seen and not heard, except when someone specifically addressed you, and then the appropriate response would always be *yes, no, thank you, sir* or *ma'am.*

Not for a second did I believe she'd ever been proud of me. She might have told these ladies she was, she might have told the whole town and put up billboards and stood in the pulpit on Sundays, but when we were alone, she'd always made her feelings about me very clear.

"I'm sorry," I said. "I don't remember you."

The women exchanged a glance.

"Well," the short one said, voice indignant. "You've been away a long time. I suppose your life is very busy. I'm Sadie McDonnell, and this is Irene Oster."

Sadie, Sadie married lady popped into my head immediately and I had to stop myself from saying it out loud. I held out a hand, trying to warm myself up, already wishing they'd leave, and shook their hands. "Pleased to meet you."

"It's a pleasure to meet you again, dear," Sadie said.

"Have you seen your mother yet?" asked Irene.

"Yes," I said. "I stopped by the funeral home on the way here yesterday. The viewing will be tomorrow night."

The pair exchanged another glance.

"No, dear," said Sadie. "She meant, have you seen her *here.*" She pointed at the ceiling—haint blue, cautionary blue—and raised both eyebrows.

I shook my head, refusing to think about the light in the woods or the cold spots in the house last night. I listened now; I could feel it like someone looking over my shoulder. "I don't think the house is haunted."

"Honey, it's the South," Sadie smirked. "Of course, it's haunted."

They both laughed.

"Of course, you've been living out there on the West Coast doing California things. You've probably forgotten what it's like to live here."

With decent folks and real culture and people who actually care about each other.

It was all implied, the unsaid words hanging in the air between us. She gave me a bright smile, something vicious flashing behind her eyes. But as soon as it appeared, when she realized I'd seen it, she put it away, bringing out something more genuine.

"It's Oregon, " I said. "I live in Oregon."

"Your mother said California," Irene said as if I was the one with the wrong information. "Told us all about it when you got your GED and graduated from that fancy college of yours."

"How did she know?" My tone was too sharp and surprise touched their faces.

Irene opened her mouth but nothing came out.

"We brought you a casserole!" Sadie jumped in, gesturing to the dish Irene held, a brittle edge to her voice. "Chicken and green rice. We thought you might not have time to cook since it's all up to you to deal with this great big place and the funeral arrangements. We're just so sorry we can't do more. Your momma was a treasure. We all miss her so much. She was very private, you know, at the end. I wish I could have been with her at the end. I know you do too."

"Thank you." I hesitated, looking at the glass dish, not wanting it at all. They were waiting for me to invite them in, Southern hospitality and all that. But I wanted them to leave. "I appreciate your kindness so much. I'll take this to the kitchen—"

"Oh, don't worry yourself about that at all," Sadie said,

brushing past me. Irene followed, the corners of her mouth going up as she passed, mimicking a smile. "We know the way! We'll pop this in the fridge for you! And if you need help organizing a few things, we can help!"

They walked briskly through the foyer and turned toward the kitchen. I watched them go, shocked that they'd let themselves inside, and worried I'd never get them to leave now. Shutting the door quickly, I followed, catching their conversation about the kitchen.

"You know, I thought for sure she was going to update this terrible linoleum. I'm just so disappointed. This old place deserves something grand. This place ought to be on the historical register list. How do we do that? Can we submit it? We should take care of that for her."

I caught up with the pair as Irene slid the dish into the empty refrigerator. Sadie was putting the empty snack cake wrappers I'd left on the counter in a trash bin under the sink, making sure the bottle of coke was closed before tucking that in beside the casserole. I stood helplessly in the doorway, watching them tidy, opening and closing cabinets to inspect the contents. Then Sadie went to the back door and pulled it open, sticking her head out and getting a good look at the mess the kitchen garden was in.

"You know, your momma never did think much of gardening. Even before the accident. But I seem to remember your daddy having a bit of a green thumb."

I swallowed a lump in my throat at the mention of my dad. "I don't remember."

"Well, I guess not. You really weren't very old when he passed and I'm sure the sorrow of losing him overshadows everything else. But I do remember how pretty the garden was while he was alive, there was a party every year, around the Fourth of July. The whole town would come out.

Not on the Fourth, but the weekend before or after. Your momma went all out for those parties."

The tall woman nodded.

"I don't remember any of that," I said. She was describing someone else's life.

"Oh, well, a lot of things changed after you were born, and of course, there was the accident. Your momma mostly had the ladies' group from church visit after that, and a few college friends, I think."

I nodded. I remembered the small gatherings, women sitting on the stiff antique sofas and sipping tea out of floral-patterned porcelain—small tea cakes and triangle sandwiches with the crusts removed. Some things she prepared herself, but most had come from the bakery in the next town over, orders delivered in pink boxes, flowers arriving in bunches so she could arrange them herself. Groceries were always delivered, brought around to the back door, and she'd be ready with a small tip and a smile.

"It's a shame Vivian hasn't kept up the place. But that's to be expected, I suppose."

"Yeah," I said weakly, wondering how I could get them out of the kitchen, and usher them through the front door.

I wanted them gone. I wanted to go back upstairs and read more of the newspapers. I wanted to know exactly when Jake was going to show up. And what would I say to him when he did?

"After your daddy passed, there weren't any more big parties. It must have been so hard for your momma." Sadie shook her head, pity in her eyes, a false sense of understanding. "It was so hard for her after the accident. She was just one of those people, you know? Just one of a kind."

I nodded, wondering what these two would say if I told them about the horror she'd been capable of inflicting even when her body didn't cooperate. It hadn't stopped her. I glanced around the room, anywhere but at Sadie, because she was trying hard to catch my eye. In a moment I knew she'd reach out, try to take my hand, touch me. I didn't think I'd be able to stand it.

"Thank you so much for the casserole," I said, taking a step toward the door, hoping to lead them back down the hall. "I appreciate it so much. You know, there wasn't any food in the house when I got here, and it didn't occur to me to go grocery shopping first."

"Oh! I had no idea. Well, we'll just have to bring you a few more things. We can't have you starving while you're here!" Sadie smiled, and Irene nodded. "I just assumed there'd be something left, but maybe Andrew cleared it all out."

"Andrew?" I hadn't heard the name before.

Sadie shot me a look. "You didn't know?"

"Know what?"

"Vivian had someone coming in a few times a week to help her with the house. Meals and such, light cleaning. A kind of caretaker or home nurse or something. I forgot the word she used. He's the nicest boy though, but he's not local. He was coming over from Fairview, and that's an hour drive each way. Henry Owens didn't tell you?"

"I still need to go over a lot of details with him."

We were moving down the hall now. They were so close to being gone. I needed a moment to process these new pieces of information about Vivian—a woman I had no desire to know, not even now. But it seemed I'd be getting to know her after all.

"He's very nice, you'll like him," Irene said.

"Oh yes, he's very handsome!" Sadie added. "I'm sure you two would hit it off."

The polite smile I'd been wearing froze on my face. The last thing I wanted was to have this stranger decide to play matchmaker. I had no interest in whatever stories he might have to share about Vivian, and I didn't want to explain to anyone why I didn't want to hear them.

We turned the corner from the back hall into the foyer, their steps behind me lingering, hopeful that I'd invite them to see the rest of the house. The entryway was full of morning sunshine, and dust motes shifted in the light streaming through the window above the door. I hurried forward and pulled it open, letting in the muggy heat and blackbird song. I held it open, waiting for them to pass through it, a smile stretching my cheeks.

"Thank you again for coming to check on me. And the food. I'll make sure to get the dish back to you."

"Oh, don't worry about that at all!" Sadie looked around the foyer, obviously wanting to stay and searching for an excuse. "I can come by in a few days to pick it up. Plus, I want to bring you a few provisions. The weather people keep saying that a tropical storm is going to hit us. But they've been wrong plenty of times before. It's still better to be prepared."

"Better safe than sorry," Irene said.

"Your momma would never forgive us if we didn't take care of you now that you're home. That's what we do after all. We take care of each other."

"You don't have to, it's really okay. I'm planning to make a run to the store later today after I pick up my car." I shook my head, biting the inside of my cheek. The edge in her tone said it all.

"We know that, dear. I know you regret not being here for her. I know it just must be eating at your heart. We can't let you carry the weight of it all on your own."

Sadie and Irene smiled. They'd be back no matter what I might say. I needed to remain polite. I didn't want to make my time here any more difficult than it was already going to be. The idea of them poking through the house and asking a thousand questions about why I'd left made my skin crawl. I opened my mouth, on the verge of saying something I'd regret, when the sound of gravel crunching filled the air.

A familiar truck was easing up the drive. Jake was here.

They looked at me and then back to the truck, their sly condescending expressions turning to shock and distaste.

"My dear sweet child," Sadie said, reaching out, bubble-gum-pink nails digging into my skin. "Do you know that man?"

I fought the urge to jerk away and nodded. "Yes, I met him yesterday. My rental broke down, and he gave me a ride. The mechanic working on the car sent him."

And in the attic was a box full of newspaper clippings saying he'd killed his high school sweetheart. For a moment I'd forgotten about the headlines, the heat of accusation they carried radiating through the house, stretching to touch me, to remind me. He'd killed a woman.

"I know you haven't been in town long, and I don't know how well you and your momma kept up, but Jake White is not a man you should ever be alone with."

"He's dangerous. No matter what Vivian thought." Irene's voice was cold, her hard gaze focused on the truck now.

"Vivian knew him?" My voice came out sharp. I was trapped between them, Sadie's hand heavy, as if she would stop me from stepping forward or shush me if I spoke his name. I looked from one to the other, wondering what wild gossip was making the rounds. "I don't know anything about him. He was really nice yesterday, a lot of help."

The women exchanged a look.

"They say he killed that poor Kent girl because she was going to leave him. You remember Alice? Such a sweet young thing. It was all over the papers. There was a trial and everything." Sadie whispered hurriedly, watching the truck. "I shouldn't repeat gossip, but really, it's not gossip if it's a safety warning. Emma dear, this is serious. He killed that girl."

"And got away with it," Irene said.

My heart thumped, hearing it from them after reading it in the clippings made it feel more solid. I put as much doubt and dismissiveness in my tone as possible. "But he didn't go to jail? I'm sure he'd be in jail if he had."

They shook their heads, and I sighed. The fact that they thought Vivian had been their friend and was a kind, caring person scared me more than the man sitting in his truck. I'd take that man over these two any day.

"Well, it doesn't matter. He's here to take me to my car."

"Oh no! You can't!"

They spoke at the same time, words overlapping, voices raised. I laughed, they sounded so absurd. I patted Sadie's hand and her eyes narrowed. Their dislike of Jake was perfect. He would keep them way better than I ever could. "It's really okay. I'll see you at the viewing. Thank you again for the casserole."

I waved at the truck, beckoning. Jake eased out with his black sunglasses on. He was bigger than I remembered, taller and broader. In the newspaper clippings, he'd still been a kid, a boy really, thin and lean, not filled out yet. The man coming toward us was years away from that kid. An improbable knight in shining armor arrived in the nick of time to save me from a pair of meddling witches.

It seemed too early for him. He hadn't shaved, his hair

damp and all over the place, with an outfit similar to yesterday's. It looked good on him, all of it. *He* looked good. Not like someone who might have murdered a woman. But what would I know about how a murderer looked? I watched him closely as he came up the stairs, moving slowly, maybe in an effort to seem less intimidating, the wood creaking beneath him. Halfway up, he paused.

"Morning, ladies," he said with a nod. When they didn't respond, he turned to me. "You ready?"

"I'll grab my purse and lock up."

Sadie squeezed my shoulder, but I slipped away, back into the house. I'd left my purse in the study and wanted to hurry, wondering what might happen if I left the three of them alone for too long. Nothing. He wasn't a killer. And they were just old women with nothing better to do than gossip and remember the dead fondly. If they'd been so convinced of Vivian's goodness, they obviously had no clue about the people around them.

My purse was on the desk, and I picked it up, glancing out the window. I caught something, a flash, and paused, heart skipping. There was nothing there, trees and overgrown grass, everything that had been there before and nothing that hadn't. I looked at the old glass, the wave of it distorting the world, curving the reflected room around me. I froze.

Someone was in the room.

The hairs on the back of my neck rose. Floorboards creaked in the hall, not with the pressure from footsteps, but a rolling creak, the weight distributed differently. I was a child, standing in a room, listening as anger and pain came toward me. I couldn't stop it. Nothing would keep her away, nothing would delay whatever I had coming—words sharp as knives, relentlessly attacking.

You're not real.

Tension pulled at me, shoulders aching, back taut. Fear kept me motionless, but I wanted to turn, I wanted to see, because I knew there would be nothing there. Old houses creaked. Magnolia House was decaying; it would fall into the swamp with the next big storm, and I'd be far away when it happened.

You're not real.

Oregon. My tiny desk covered in sticky notes. The half-dead plant in my bathroom. The sound of my favorite pair of running shoes hitting the pavement. My favorite song coming out of the living room speakers. The feel of the leather purse strap in my hand. All of these were real things, solid and true beyond reasoning. Nothing you could change or talk yourself out of. Or into.

You're dead.

I turned, half convinced she'd be there, framed in the doorway, watching me with cold violet eyes. More beautiful than any woman I'd ever met, with a perfect face, cold as white marble and glacial ice.

But no. The door was empty, the hall bare.

The only people here, besides me, were the three on the verandah. Two women who had had the nerve to ask me if I'd seen Vivian yet. And the man who would take me away. I hurried to the front door, almost jogging, wanting more than anything to feel the click of the door handle locking tight. I was coming to love locks, desperate for the sounds they made, the protection they offered.

"Thanks for picking me up," I said to Jake, sweeping out of the house, all hurry and bustle, slamming the front door shut. I looked up at the pale blue ceiling and crossed my fingers. If it kept things from coming in would it also keep things from going out? Superstitious. I hadn't thought of these things in years. I'd shed them all—moved on. I'd been a child living under intense pressure, full of fear and desperate to find anything to keep the bad things at bay.

But the moment I'd crossed the creek, they'd come back.

Sadie stepped between Jake and I, voice low and hurried. "Emma, dear. I don't think we should leave you alone with him. He's dangerous."

"You don't think I could get away with it again, do you?" Jake said loudly, voice vicious and biting.

There was real fear on Sadie's face, naked desperation in her eyes. *Come with us.* I could almost hear the plea. But I couldn't listen to anything more about Vivian. I would end up being ferried around, hand clutched tight like some kind of child, and paraded in front of everyone else. They'd beat the rest of the town to Magnolia House's front door; they would tell all their friends they'd been inside, that they'd met the long-lost daughter. They would try to own as much of this ordeal as possible.

"Thank you for bringing the casserole. Sadie, Irene, you've both been so generous with your time. I can't thank you enough."

Their mouths were pressed into identical thin lines. I'd been firm, leaving no doubt about who I was getting into a car with. Disgust and fear, the light of *I told you so* already in their eyes.

"If you need anything else, just let us know," Irene said. "There's a piece of paper with Sadie's phone number tucked between the aluminum foil on the casserole."

"Yes, absolutely please call," Sadie said with a nod.

"And you know," Irene continued, stepping closer and taking my hand, "I think your momma was waiting on you to come home. You'll run into her eventually. It'll be the peace you need. The peace you both need."

I bit the inside of my cheek to keep in a sharp response. The only peace I needed would be the kind that came from these two leaving. "Thank you."

They walked away together, voices low, throwing glances over their shoulders. I waited until they reached the gold Lincoln Town Car before I turned to Jake, my eyebrows raised. He shrugged and went down the steps, headed for his truck without looking back. *Take it or leave it* his actions said. I followed him.

Sadie and Irene sat in their car waiting. Irene behind the wheel, Sadie in the passenger seat, the two of them watching us like a pair of buzzards. Jake walked past them without a glance, getting in the truck and starting the engine. I tried to ignore them too, but I could feel them watching as I went around to the passenger side of the truck, irritated when the door didn't open right way. I wanted to get out of their line of vision.

"You wanna open this?"

He hit the unlock button, and I slid inside, thankful for the dark tint. I leaned back with a sigh, closing my eyes. Sweat prickled my skin; already I was sweating from the heat and humidity, even this early in the morning it felt like ninety degrees.

I refused to consider that it might have been a reaction to the cold inside the house, the way it had crept up on me —touched me.

Jake eased the truck back, maneuvering until it pointed down the drive, directed toward town. I checked the side mirror. The Town Car followed, the two women talking, both using their hands, mouths open wide.

"They're yelling at each other." I glanced at him,

looking for a reaction, but he didn't respond, didn't even look at me. "You shouldn't have said that back there."

"Maybe not," he said tersely.

I laughed a little, making an effort to ease the tension, to show him I wasn't interested in Back of Beyond gossip. I wasn't going to be forming any knee-jerk opinions about a man I'd just met. A man who had been accused of murder but acquitted. Would it bother some people? Shouldn't it bother me? His younger face filled my mind—black and white photo, caught in a harsh camera flash. He must know this town was too small to keep any secrets for long.

But I hadn't just met him, had I? I glanced at him, taking in his profile—a face I should recognize. The school had been small, but several counties were bussed to a central location and there had been enough kids to get lost in. I'd been young for a senior, the other kids a year older than me, and I'd slipped under the radar as much as possible.

Jake shot me a look and I blushed, gaze darting away— caught red handed. I turned my attention to the interior of the truck. Tidy and impersonal except for two unopened energy drinks in the cup holders between us. He must have had a long night after dropping me off, gone on to do what- ever else needed doing. For a split second I wondered what that meant. Another job? Someone waiting at home? But that wasn't my business.

The drive into town took a long time in the silence, Irene and Millie on our tail the entire time. We were a procession of two cars rolling down main street, and I wondered if anyone noticed. Maybe they all kept a lookout for Jake's big black truck, the whole town on high alert all the time.

"Is everyone in town still like that? Minding everyone

else's business all the time?" I gestured to the car behind us. For a moment I wasn't sure he'd answer, holding onto his silence with both hands and a shut mouth.

"No," he said finally, glancing at me before continuing. "Not anymore at least."

"Just the little old ladies?"

"Yeah, mostly just them." He smiled, shooting me another look. "They getting on your nerves too?"

For a moment I wanted to tell him all about Vivian Taylor and the oppressive house I'd grown up in. I wanted to tell him about the chill in the halls and the sound of a nonexistent wheelchair filling the house. I had no one else to talk to here, and their version of Vivian was so far removed from mine. They were so convinced I needed comforting. They saw me as some terrible daughter, abandoning her invalid mother, only coming home to collect whatever valuables were left. They had no clue.

'Maybe." I shrugged, biting my tongue to keep it all in.

His eyebrows went up, a silent question, wanting more than a one-word answer. "Sounds like a lot more than maybe."

"Everyone has this version of Vivian, who they thought she was. This beautiful, kind woman with a tragic history. Someone to be admired and pitied. Her life was so hard; my dad died, and she was paralyzed and left to raise a child on her own in a drafty house in the middle of nowhere. Poor her. Poor Vivian." My tone turned bitter, more frustration showing than I'd intended. All of that more than I'd intended. He probably thought of her like the rest of this place did, seeing a long-suffering woman with a heart of gold.

Monster.

"Not everyone thinks that," he said.

I turned to him, studying his face, the clenched jaw. "No?"

He shrugged, a roll of his shoulders, one hand still on the wheel. "I think she was good at fooling people, making them see what she wanted them to. I can see why you got out when you did. I would have wanted out too."

"How well did you know her?"

I wished he'd take his sunglasses off so I could see his eyes, guess at whatever expression might be there. Did he know about the attic full of newspaper clippings?

"Knew her well enough to say hello to, I guess."

"She could be very charming," I said.

He nodded but didn't say anything. I let the quiet between us grow, not wanting to fill it and not minding that he didn't want to either. We kept a strange kind of companion, a third passenger.

The mechanic was on the other side of town, almost halfway between us and the next little wide spot in the road. The big four-car garage had all the doors open, cars up on lifts inside, a couple of guys in blue jumpsuits working on them. As we pulled up, one of the men came toward us, shading his eyes from the morning sun.

"Looks like they finally gave up," I said, unbuckling my seatbelt as the truck stopped. Sadie and Irene drove past the shop, faces turned to us, taking it all in as they went. "Thanks for the ride."

"Sure." A slight smile curved his mouth. "Anytime."

The smile caught me off guard. I liked it. I liked the way he looked at me with a smile on his face, the way the air changed between us. I smiled back, a flutter of pleasure going through me. Sun hit my face as I opened the truck door, warming me, blinding after the dim interior.

Jake waited until I was a few steps away before leaving.

I waved, feeling silly, and dropped my hand quickly. But he raised a finger from the steering wheel in acknowledgment.

"Emma Taylor?"

I turned to the man that had come out of the garage. "Yes?"

"I'm Josh. Izaak down at that gas station gave me a call yesterday about your car. I'm sorry I didn't get a chance to talk to you in person."

"It's okay. It's nice to meet you, Josh." I extended a hand. He showed me how dirty his hands were, even though he'd been wiping them on a clean rag when I'd seen him coming out of the garage. I smiled and shrugged. "I don't mind."

"It's nice to meet you too," he said, taking my hand gingerly, barely making contact. He stepped back, gesturing to where the rental was parked. "I took a good look at the car but I have to tell you if it needs any real work you're going to need to get in touch in the rental company."

I followed him across the lot, wondering how much it was going to cost and what to do about contacting the rental company. I should have already called them. But it felt easier to start here. I didn't want to deal with getting a new rental, all the time it would take, too much time when all I wanted to do was get things done and get the hell out.

"I think you got stuck with a lemon."

Josh stood with hands on hips, shaking his head. The car was shiny and new, a model I wouldn't have minded driving every day. I even liked the color. But he was looking at it as if it were responsible for all the carbon emissions on the planet.

"A what?"

"You know, a lemon? Just a flat-out bad car," he

shrugged. " I checked it over. Looked over every inch. Can't figure out why it died on you yesterday. It looks fine."

"So, it's okay?"

"It looks fine. Can't promise it won't die on you again though."

I nodded, studying the car, wondering what would happen if I got stranded again a lot farther from the gas station next time. The thought of the car dying at Magnolia House, of having no easy way to leave after last night, made me uneasy.

"If you want, I can loan you a beater. I've got a hatchback I save for customers when I've got to work on their car for more than a few days."

I shook my head. "No, it's okay. Thank you, though. I can always take this one back to the rental place."

"Sure, sure."

"Thanks for taking a look at it. How much?"

He waved a hand. "Free of charge. Nothing to fix, nothing to pay."

"Really?"

"Really."

"Listen," I said, digging in my purse and pulling out my wallet. "I wasted your time with this. I can't not compensate you."

"Tell you what," he said, meeting my eyes. "Next time you're in town and not dealing with a death, you can cover the inspection charges."

I sucked in a breath, on the verge of saying something I shouldn't. Her death didn't mean anything to me. Vivian didn't mean anything to me. But everyone thought I was grieving. And he was being kind; he thought he was easing my burden in a small way.

I smiled and said weakly, "Thanks."

"My pleasure. Anything you need at all, just let me know. We'll get you fixed up."

"Thank you. I appreciate that so much. I do have a quick question though. Can you tell me how to get to Mr. Owen's office? He's an attorney here in town."

Josh gave me the directions, easy enough to remember, and turned to go back to his office. I was already thinking ahead, to the conversation that came next, the decision I would need to make. The car beeped and the lights flashed when I hit the button, my chariot waiting to take me to a difficult destination.

"Oh, Emma, I almost forgot. This fell out when I opened the driver's side door."

He held out a silver disc the size of a half dollar. It shone in his hand, bright and fresh, so shiny and new. There was a woman on it, head bowed, hands clasped. It looked vaguely religious and unfamiliar.

"It's the Saint Rita of Cascia. You don't recognize it?"

"No. It's not mine." I shook my head. "What is she the saint of?"

"Well, I gotta admit that I'm more of a lapsed Catholic these days. So I had to look her up. But from what I read, she's the patron saint of lost and impossible causes and abuse victims."

"Someone must be missing it," I said, heat flushing my cheeks, fanning out across my skin. "Probably the last person who had the car."

Glancing up, I caught curiosity in his face and a trace of understanding.

"Maybe they didn't need it anymore. Sometimes things come along for us at the right time. You hold on to it just in case."

I took it, warm from being in his pocket, closing my

fingers around it and feeling the raised figure of the woman —this saint of impossible mothers. I dropped it in the cupholder as I got into the car, willing to take whatever good luck and kind, watchful eyes I could get on this journey.

CHAPTER SIX
THURSDAY

"No, of course I didn't say anything. What am I supposed to say?" There was a pause. "She looks just like her. You wouldn't believe it. You know that photo Momma has of the two of them together? Same face. Only Emma has shorter hair."

I sat in the waiting room of the law offices, an old brick house that had been converted sometime in the last twenty years, two attorneys sharing the space with one secretary. I wasn't trying to eavesdrop, but it was impossible not to. Even in another room, Becky's voice was clear, though I could tell she was trying to keep it down.

Connie, her younger sister, had been a classmate, and they were only a few years apart. I remembered vividly Becky picking her up in a worn-out white sedan, windows down, country music blaring—honkey-tonk and blue jeans. I'd envied them. Not only for the transportation and ability to come and go as they pleased but the relationship too. They clearly loved each other. I would have given anything to have that.

"I think maybe Vivian was prettier though, just something about her personality. I remember thinking how much I wanted to be like her when I grew up. She was so vibrant." Becky typed as she talked, hitting the back button repeatedly to fix something before continuing. "Do you remember when she left? It was wild."

There was a pause, the typing coming to a halt. "Are you serious? With Jake White? Who told you that!"

The typing picked back up, the conversation continuing. My stomach churned, my ears hot, and I bit the inside of my cheek to keep from responding. Nothing I said would change anyone's mind. It was better to let them think whatever they wanted.

I flipped the pages of a home decorating magazine that was a few months old, but I wasn't really reading it. I needed something to keep my hands busy—glossy pages rustling back and forth, azaleas and hydrangeas and pink dogwood trees. If I stepped outside right now, I'd find all three crowded in around the building—tucked tight and mulched, well cared for, the manicured lawn vibrant green.

No pale blooms on the dogwoods though, it was too late in the season. Summer was here, the weather across the South oppressive and heavy, all of it made worse by a tropical storm rolling our way.

Right now, I was thankful for the air conditioning blasting through the vents—a fresh scent coming with it, clean and crisp. The high constant hum covered almost all noise, apart from Becky's conversation. It was hard to tell if the attorneys were present. All the doors along the hall were closed. I flipped another page, wondering how much time it would take and how soon I could get the funeral arrangements settled. Then I'd leave all this Southern comfort behind.

Vivian had liked azaleas and dogwood trees. She'd

loved all things quintessentially Southern. She'd built a life around sweet tea and visiting church ladies. The big old house full of history, the lemony scents of magnolia blooms brought indoors, the sly *bless your heart.*

It was all lovely in its own way, and I'd loved it all when I was younger. But now, I would take the pounding of the waves and the peaceful redwood groves any day. They fit my soul. A sharp stab of homesickness hit me, tears pricking my eyes. I wanted to go home, and I didn't want to take any of this place with me.

I'll follow you home.

I froze, staring straight ahead, every muscle in my body tense. The voice, Vivian's voice, had been so clear—a whisper in my ear, the tickle of indrawn breath, words a malicious caress.

A door opened down the hall, a man's voice spilling out, a woman's soft response.

"Not to worry, Mrs. Watson. I'll get it all under control."

A dark-haired woman came into view—puffy red face and eyes, more tears threatening. Her clothes, a rumpled pair of black slacks and an oversized blue blouse swallowed her, several sizes too large. The man was older, possibly in his fifties, and balding, with a button-down dress shirt rolled up to his elbows, dark-gray slacks. Tall, maybe six feet, and thin, he reminded me of a great blue heron, all legs and sharp nose.

He spoke kindly, warmth in his tone, in the way he met her worried gaze, steering her down the hall and through the waiting room. He glanced at me as they passed, sharing a gentle smile.

Seeing him now, after the steadiness on the phone, the calm that had radiated through the line made sense. He'd hesitated after giving me the news, giving me a moment for grief, but the tears never came. If he'd been surprised, he hadn't let on.

"Well then, Ms. Taylor," he said, coming back in alone and holding out a hand. "I'm Henry Owens. It's a pleasure to speak to you in person. I'm sorry I had to give you such bad news over the phone."

I smiled, shaking his hand. He'd picked the thought right out of my head. Maybe it had been on my face already. "Hello, Mr. Owens. I'm glad you were able to find my information and let me know."

"Henry, please. No reason to stand on ceremony here." He gave me a warm smile. "And your momma left the contact information with me some time ago."

Momma.

"I didn't realize she had it."

I'd never shared it with her, and even now, even with her gone, it made me uneasy. All this time, through distance and years, she'd known where I was. He studied my face. I couldn't tell how much he saw, what I gave away. But I tried to smooth my expression, call back the poker face I'd once been a master of.

"Why don't you come on back? I'll lay it all out for you, and then you can make some decisions."

"Thank you."

We passed paintings in the hall, more landscapes full of azaleas and dogwood trees—bright pastel washes of pinks and greens, blue skies, white clouds. They surrounded me even here, indoors and out, a riot of color and texture. But these were a little soft focus, impressions of flowers, the idea of them, instead of hard facts. Flowers of the past and future, no present here.

The office was everything I'd ever imagined an attorney's office should be. The back wall was lined with bookshelves, not pressboard or plywood, but dark polished hardwood. Law books, wide and skinny, maroon and deep blue, a few very dark green with gold lettering, sat in neat rows. The oversized desk was the same wood, and I wondered how they'd managed to get it in the room. Maybe the whole house had been built around it. Papers covered the surface, tan file folders, a few large brown envelopes. A closed laptop perched on the edge, on the verge of falling off. I glanced at the photographs on the walls—old buildings, courthouses, and local public spaces.

"Have a seat," he said, gesturing to one of the hard chairs before his desk. "I'll read the will, explain any sections you might have questions about, and give you copies of all the paperwork. There are also a few things here your momma left with me. They're sealed in an envelope, so I can't tell you what they might be. But she left explicit instructions that you get them as soon as possible."

I sat, dwarfed by the huge desk, feeling like a kid in front of the principal—purse balanced on my knees, hands folded neatly. Behind the desk he seemed less kind, more businesslike, as he began to read the will.

Nothing personal in it, details of inheriting the house, less than a thousand dollars in a bank account that I now had access to. Vivian had lived extravagantly, but every-thing coming in, the large payout remaining from my dad's death and investments in the stock market, had all been spent in some fashion leading up to her death.

She'd even sold her beloved classic Mercedes before her passing—after the accident the car had sat for years until I'd learned to drive. I assumed it had gone back to sitting abandoned in the carriage house after I'd gone. Her final wish was to be entombed with my dad in the family crypt.

The instructions were detailed; all the arrangements were made and paid for.

"But I get to make the final choice? About her burial?"

The thought of her being with my dad, a man she'd barely tolerated, made me livid. She hadn't wanted to stand next to him in life, why would she choose to in death?

Mr. Owens eyed me, hesitating. "Yes, you do. While these things have been paid for, everything set with the funeral home and the church, she's made it very clear that as executor and heir, you have final say."

"I don't understand," I said. "Why would she leave this up to me?"

He shook his head, eyes shifting back to the will. "I can't tell you that. I only know what's in these pages. She gave you the final say."

Why? Why would she do this? To have it eat at me? To make a choice that would once again prove to this whole town how awful I'd always been to her? My stomach churned. The choice was mine.

"I don't want her with my dad." My tone was harder than I'd intended, the edge startling. I was angrier than I should be, more than I wanted him to see.

"Would you like me to make alternate arrangements?" His tone was neutral, eyes on the papers in his hand as he shuffled through them.

"I've talked to the funeral director a little already. I can call him when we're done here."

"Of course. Yes. Well, if you decide you need some assistance, I am more than happy to help."

"Thank you, I appreciate that. Is there anything I need to sign? Or do?"

"I have the deed for you to sign, and I've made copies of all the tax information you will need. I suggest you review it all and get an attorney in Oregon to go over it with you when you get home. This is a large piece of property, even though your parents had begun to sell off pieces of the land, there are still fifty acres and the house. Of course, what's left is mostly swamp, and Magnolia House could use some work."

I nodded, signing the documents he slid toward me, my sloppy signature harsh against the white page. Without thinking about it, unable to process the reality of fifty acres and an aging Greek-revival relic that began its life well before the Civil War.

"I'll have Becky make you copies, and we'll send them out to the house." He shifted the stacks of folders on his desk, reading the labels until he found the one he was looking for. "Here is your copy of the will. And," he leaned back, pulling open a desk drawer and lifting out a thick tan mailing envelope. "This is the package she left for you."

I took it, feeling the weight, wondering what she'd leave me that she didn't want the attorney to see. I broke the seal and looked inside. He watched, as curious as I was, as I lifted out a red leather diary.

Her name was on the inside, larger than life, with a flourish at the end. I remembered the signature from childhood, signed grudgingly across report cards and permission slips. I could see the face as she signed, concentration as she added the final looping embellishment. I closed it and slipped it back inside the envelope. Besides the diary was a crisp white envelope, blank on the front, no name or date, and an old brass house key with a rough star cut into the grip. The edges of the shape were raw, sharp against my fingertips, like someone had cut it out themselves.

"Can I ask you something?" I hesitated, wondering if

he'd think it was impolite, not sure I wanted to know the answer.

"Of course," he said, smiling.

"Can you give me any more details about her death? I know you shared the basics when you called but—"

I held out my hands in silent invitation. What he'd only hinted at, Mr. Laurent had filled in the rest at the funeral home. I don't know why I needed more details—to know the horror of her decline. But I needed assurance she was really gone, finally dead.

He coughed, glancing down, away from my eyes, and I knew. He didn't need to say it. I could see it in the way his face went carefully blank, his shoulders stiff. "You said you've spoken to the funeral director?"

"Yes, but very briefly. I told him I wanted to change the arrangements, and he suggested I speak with you first." I let it hang there between us, waiting for him to fill the silence.

"Well, as I said before she had stage four breast cancer. She found out rather late."

"Yes," I prompted. "Mr. Laurent mentioned cause of death might have been something other than cancer."

He glanced down, moving a folder on his desk a few inches, sliding it back again. I waited. I could see how uncomfortable he was. The silence grew, I embraced it, listening to the sound of the air conditioner humming through the room and Becky's ongoing phone conversation down the hall.

"She came to me last week and wanted to get her will in order. She laid it all out, made sure there was enough money to pay for everything. She was refusing treatment. I'm not even sure she'd been back to the doctor once the initial diagnosis was made." He sighed. "She didn't tell me what she was planning, but it was pretty clear. I've helped other people facing the end of things, older mostly, knowing what's coming and wanting to make sure their affairs are in order."

"And she killed herself." It was a statement of fact, my voice firm.

Mr. Owens nodded. "An overdose. Mr. Laurent shared the details with me, and it fit with everything she'd laid out. You have my deepest sympathies. I know how hard this must be. Coming home to all this extra grief on top of losing your momma. I didn't want to tell you over the phone, but I didn't want it coming to you through the grapevine either."

"Thank you," I said, keeping my voice quiet. It wasn't extra grief for me. It was all the same, and most of what filled me, sustained me, was an incredible relief.

He was nodding again, shifting things on his desk, hands busy and eyes off my face. Maybe he was waiting for me to cry, giving me room for sorrow. Everyone seemed to think I needed it. But I didn't have that in myself to give him. After a minute, he cleared his throat.

"Thank you again for coming in, Ms. Taylor. I am so sorry for your loss. Are you sure you wouldn't like me to call Mr. Laurent for you? Or Pastor Roberts? You said you wanted some changes?"

Pastor Roberts. The name made me queasy.

"No, thank you. I'll speak with them myself."

"If there's anything else you might need, please give me a call."

"I will, thank you."

"One more thing, I almost forgot. I don't know if you're aware, but your momma had a person coming in twice a week to help with the house. I can give you his information if you're interested in speaking with him? His name is Andrew Barns. I think they might have gotten quite close."

I shook my head. "No, I don't need to speak with him."

Curiosity flashed across his face, the expression there and gone as he carefully smoothed his features. I stood, and he did too, coming around the edge of the desk. I clutched the envelope to my chest, aware of the hard edge of the diary inside, the key. I would have to open the blank envelope eventually. But not yet.

I'll be waiting.

Magnolia House flashed across my mind, the empty rooms and dust, boxes and mess that I didn't want to keep.

"I do have one thing, Mr. Owens, that I could use your advice on."

"Absolutely, how may I help?" He seemed pleased to be asked, thankful to finally be helpful.

"Can you recommend someone to deal with the estate? Vivian didn't say what would happen with the contents of the house."

"Oh. Well." He looked at me carefully, finally starting to see that my relationship with the woman might not have been what he'd thought. "I believe she intended for you to keep Magnolia House and the contents. It's been in your family for generations."

"I don't have any plans to sell the house right now. I honestly don't know what I'm going to do with it all. But I'd like to know what my options are."

He was nodding, studying my face, and I wondered if he could see the lie. I knew what I was going to do with the house. I knew what I planned to do with the contents. I just didn't know how to make it all happen.

"Give me a moment, I have a card for a trustworthy estate company." He ducked back into his office and returned with a cream-colored card with black scrollwork and a looping font. "Give these people a call and let them know I sent you. They're good people."

I smiled, taking the card. "Thank you."

"Absolutely, Ms. Taylor. You call me any time."

Going from the cool office to the wet heat of the afternoon was like getting smacked in the face with a damp towel—sweat prickling under my arms as I made my way to the rental car. After starting the engine, I leaned back, closing my eyes, breathing out hot and breathing in cold.

She'd killed herself. I wasn't sure what to think about that. It didn't surprise me. She'd liked control and had never let any situation get the best of her. No matter what, she would always win. Vivian wasn't a loser.

I tipped the envelope upside down and the contents slid out onto my lap. The key caught the light, holding my attention for a moment before I tucked it in my pocket—whatever lock it might open would come later, a mystery for another time. Flipping through the diary, I scanned the contents without reading the words—page after page of beautiful cursive. Vivian in written form. It felt like peeking in someone's window in the middle of the night—a life exposed to harsh light, only half the story told.

But it couldn't be trespassing if she'd left it for me. It felt like an invitation. It felt like a threat. If she'd left it for me, made sure it would be placed in my hands, it was because she wanted something from me.

CHAPTER SEVEN

THURSDAY

The doors to the church were open—a maw, a creature waiting to swallow me whole.

Come in.

I hesitated under the hot sun, wanting nothing more than shade and a moment to breathe. But there would be no reprieve, no solace offered beyond those doors. How many times had I pushed her inside, only to stand patiently behind her while she talked about me as if I weren't there? She would reach for me, take my hand, not because she loved me, but because she liked the image it presented.

Poor Vivian. Poor, beautiful Vivian and her daughter.

The memory of that day swallowed me, filling my vision, all-consuming.

You should be grateful I even let you stand beside me.

I stand in the aisle of the church, my vision blurs, and my chest heaves with frustration and blinding red anger. I thought seeing red was a myth. It's not. The world is tinged crimson, the voices of the parishioners far away, muffled by the roar of blood in my ears.

Madness grips me, a snapping pair of iron teeth, a steel trap springing closed, digging in. I am a wild animal, making the decision hard and fast, right there in front of God and everybody.

I am going to chew my own foot off and escape this place.

I grip the black padded handles of the chair, heart racing, legs shaking with adrenaline. She is light, so light, weighing almost nothing. Even the chair is light, a custom-built slim creation of polished silver. I stare at the back of her head, the elegant twist, dark hair coiled at the base of her neck, a golden magnolia-blossom clip to hold it in place. She is wearing one of her favorite Sunday dresses—white cotton and tiny pink blossoms. Magnolia blossoms.

I hate her with everything that I am, everything I will ever be.

I hate her so much there is nothing left.

I make no sound, give no warning, simply lift and tilt, one foot on the brake as I move the chair. Vivian shifts, half turning to meet my eyes, cheeks reddening with rage, eyes narrowed. For a moment she is poised, a fledging bird not quite ready to leave the nest but taking the plunge against her wishes. Then she is sprawling across the waxed hardwood floor, legs at an awkward angle, holding herself up with both arms.

Light from the stained-glass windows falls across her— lemon yellow, cherry red, lime green. She is bathed in color. A fallen angel, a displaced queen.

Shock and horror fill me, stomach dropping, trembling as the anger leaves me cold.

I have done this.

Harsh breaths fill my ears, my lungs struggle—I can't get enough oxygen, the tight grip on my chest is crushing. I can't hear anything else. I don't see the pastor approaching us, don't see him raise his hand. The slap connects with such force that I bite my tongue, tasting blood, cheek stinging.

Then the memory faded, leaving me with a sinking

dread. Shivering now, with so much time between that moment and this, I touched my cheek, hot with remembered shame. Vivian's expression in the aftermath had been one of pleasure and delight, crumpled on the floor in an elegant heap. The pastor standing over me, clenching and unclenching his fist.

Everything in me screamed to run. I didn't want to talk to this man, try to justify or explain my actions from years before, and I hated that standing here now, shame and disgust gathered around me. But she'd pushed me all that day, the night before, and the years before. She kept pushing, wondering what it would take to break me.

I could walk away, make a phone call, and let the attorney handle it all.

Baby, sometimes we just have to do the hard things.

My dad's voice, soft and sad. I closed my eyes, holding on to it.

"Emma. Welcome. I was wondering when you would be by."

His voice came out of the darkness of the church, a figure materializing, walking toward me out of memory. He was older now but still tall, straight-backed, and thin, with dark hair going gray. When I had been younger, he'd seemed so much taller than I was; even when I was seventeen, he'd towered over me. Nothing had changed. All those years in Oregon—living my life, conquering fears and insecurities, and doing the hard work of fighting everything that had made me feel small and worthless—vanished.

With the sound of his voice, I was seventeen again, and Vivian was alive.

No. You're dead. I whispered inside my head, repeating it, needing it to be true. Because it was true.

"Hello, Pastor Roberts," I said, struggling to keep my

tone emotionless. The pressure to be kind and respectful pressed on me, touching a long-forgotten bruise. I needed to put on the show, a song and dance, so this man wouldn't see how he affected me.

"I'm so glad that you came. I've been looking forward to speaking with you. I was with Vivian the last few days. We talked about a lot of things, and I know you might have some questions."

I shook my head. "No, I don't have any questions. Mr. Laurent said Vivian arranged for a viewing and services before she passed. I've come to go over some changes."

A dark eyebrow rose, his pale eyes sharpening. "You mean your mother?"

"Vivian."

I let the name land between us. Not a description, but identification. Not mother, but a woman who hadn't loved me. His mouth twitched, a frown beginning to pull his face down, an edge of anger exposed at my rudeness, my ungratefulness after all these years.

Maybe he'd been willing to give me another chance to prove myself a better person than the one he remembered. Yet I'd shown myself to be exactly who he thought I was. He wouldn't be making an effort to be polite now. I was fine with that. He'd never shown me any kindness or decency when I was a kid.

I didn't want it from him now.

"Yes, well," he said icily. He gestured toward the open doors. "You should come on inside. We can speak in my office."

He led the way, walking out of the Louisiana sun and into the shady silence of nave—empty wooden benches covered in thin hunter-green cushions, the backs with built-in pockets for bibles and hymn books waiting to be opened. Fans spun lazily overhead, moving warm air around the room without cooling the space.

Stained-glass windows threw colored patches of light —blue and green, bright yellow, a deep red. Colors that had fallen across Vivian, highlighting her hair, pooling in the folds of her dress, falling across my hands as they gripped the wheelchair.

I glanced at the panes of leaded glass—geometric patterns and simple crosses, everything exactly as it had been. Directly ahead of us was a dais with a plain wooden lectern where the pastor stood on Sunday mornings. At the very back, a large cross hung on the wall, simple and polished smooth, fake flowers gathered beneath it, lit from above in stark white light.

We'd always sat at the front, Vivian and I, in full view of the congregation. I knew how hard the pew would be if I sat, the padding little more than a piece of fabric folded twice and stapled down. Sitting wasn't encouraged. You were expected to stand, to sing, to hold hands with the person beside you as you bowed your head to pray. Everyone stood, even the small children. Only Vivian stayed where she was, songbook open on her lap, perfectly aware of the eyes that touched her and moved away, the unspoken relief that it was her and not themselves bound to a wheelchair.

"My office is through here," Pastor Roberts said, indicating a door to the right of the dais.

I nodded, thanked him for holding the door for me as I passed, and took in the small space. A window unit blew frosty air in the room, the temperature between here and the rest of the church significant. There was a small desk with a comfortable chair behind it, two chairs before it, and a painting of Jesus preaching on a hill before hundreds of people.

Another office, another man watching me thoughtfully behind a desk, struggling to understand my relationship with Vivian. But this man wasn't wondering. He thought he already knew.

"Have a seat," Pastor Roberts said, indicating a chair.

The wooden chairs in front of the desk were hard, the seats worn smooth from a countless number of people coming and going Sunday after Sunday. I perched on the edge, ready to leave, prepared to say *thank you for your time* and be done. Pastor Roberts sat on the corner of his desk, hands clasped around one knee, poised above me like a Mississippi kite ready to strike.

"Now," he said, studying my face. "What questions do you have? How can I help?"

"The services," I began, hesitating under the direct harshness of his gaze.

He cut in with a dismissive gesture. "Yes, everything is in place. I'm sure you've spoken to Mr. Owens? Vivian left all the details with him. Mr. Laurent will bring her here for services, we talked many times about how important it was to her to have them here at the church, and then she'll be taken to be interned beside your father."

I shook my head, steeling myself for his reaction, knowing already what it would be. "No. She won't be entombed beside my father."

He laughed, a small condescending sound that bounced off the walls, catching in my ears, tinkling into my brain. "Emma, it's been decided. Perfectly clear instructions have been given."

"No," I said again. "I have final say."

"What do you think that means exactly?"

"I make the decision, she doesn't."

"You would go against your mother's wishes?" His face hardened, eyes burning as he stared at me. His hand twitched. "Even now, you would deny her the ability to rest peacefully beside her husband?"

Swallowing hard, desperate to breathe, pressure building in my chest, I watched his hands. It took everything I had to keep from cringing away, to keep from leaning out of reach, to keep the tears from my eyes, to keep from apologizing. But I wasn't sorry this time. I wasn't going to put that woman with my father. And I wasn't a child anymore. He couldn't slap me like he had back then. He wouldn't dare.

I met his gaze, the hardness in it, and said softly, "I have final say. I've spoken with the attorney."

He opened his mouth, face red, but I held up a hand to stop him.

"The viewing will be Saturday evening with services Sunday afternoon, as she requested. But after the service, Mr. Laurent will collect her, and she will be cremated. There will be no graveside ceremony."

At first, he didn't respond, and I waited, watching as his face went from red to white, mouth pressed into a thin line. I squeezed my hands together, the cold room warming with his anger.

"I thought," he began, voice hard and tight, hissing between stiff lips, "that after all these years you would have grown into a more compassionate and understanding young woman. I am deeply saddened by your choosing to ignore your mother's final wishes and refusing to place her beside her husband, a man she loved dearly. That is cruel, Emma. Cruel. I am disgusted that you've made this decision."

I stood, trembling, fighting to control it. I didn't want him to see it, to know that after all this time, I was still afraid. But it didn't matter. He knew. I spoke stiffly, gripping my purse strap, heart pounding in my ears. "If you'll excuse me, I need to go see Mr. Laurent to let him know the final details."

He shook his head, watching me, face pinched tight around his rage. I turned to go, desperate to leave, to feel the hot sun on my face, pull in the scent of dry summer grass and baking pavement into my lungs. I would never complain about the heat again. I would never rush for air conditioning and sigh with relief as long as I got away from this man. I found my keys in my purse as I passed through the empty church, the pastor following. I could feel him at my back, stalking behind me, seething.

Remaining calm was important, to appear unshakable and in control, but I hurried. I couldn't help it.

Birds sang beyond the open doors, making promises to the blue sky, swearing allegiance to the green earth. I crossed the threshold of the church, grateful to give up the chill, welcoming humidity and punishing heat. I hurried down the steps, hitting the unlock button on the keys, and the car waiting at the curb beeped.

"There's still time to do the right thing, Emma," Pastor Roberts called.

I didn't turn around. The urge to cry was taking over, out of anger or fear, I wasn't sure. Both. All of it. I wanted to get away from this man. I wanted to get away from this town.

You're so close, kiddo.

Dad again—calm and supportive.

Reaching the car and opening the door, I finally looked back. Pastor Roberts was standing in the doorway of the church, hands in pockets, glaring at me. I looked away, regretting the contact, wishing I'd kept my eyes averted. But he'd seen how close I was to breaking. He called out to me, pleased with himself for getting under my skin.

"I'll see you at the viewing, Ms. Taylor."

CHAPTER EIGHT

THURSDAY

For once my cell phone worked—enough charge and one whole bar of service. I called before both vanished. Mr. Laurent didn't question my decision: yes, Vivian would have a viewing at the funeral home on Saturday; yes, Vivian would have services at the church Sunday afternoon; yes, Vivian would be cremated that evening over in Fairview by special request.

She'd arranged it all, secured time and dates because she was after all, Vivian and she always got her way. It was settled, the hardest part done, and I could concentrate on getting the house taken care of. I could take the time to see my dad.

I parked and wondered what he would have to say about me being gone all this time. Maybe nothing. Maybe he'd understand and forgive me for trying to forget. He'd spent plenty of years shielding me, steering me away from whatever explosion might be coming next. But he'd never been brave enough to stand up, to put his foot down and say no. When emotional strength was being passed out, he must have been standing at the back of the line.

The cemetery was walled, the brick crumbling, ferns growing from between the bricks. Live oaks hung with Spanish moss swaying, moving in the breeze. I turned into it, closing my eyes as it caressed my face. I wiped tears away. I hadn't realized I'd been crying. I would make my peace, try to explain and go back.

This was just another thing to put behind me so I could run away.

Again.

It's funny how some memories never fade, how the moment you come to a half-remembered place, suddenly your brain can tell you to turn left or right. I passed beneath the wrought iron arch at the entrance, moving swiftly down the path to the family mausoleum. Left at the statue of the angel weeping, right at the memorial for the LeBlanc family, a mix of gravel and oyster shells crunching beneath my feet.

You're almost there.

Vivian had never come to see him. Not after he'd been sealed into the mausoleum, the casket simple pine covered in black velvet—a detail shared with me much later. Velvet had been the only small luxury she'd bestowed on him. Even with the life insurance money in the bank. Vivian had smiled and said he'd wanted it this way, he'd wanted her to keep everything for herself.

Vivian never even mentioned my name.

I had never mattered.

All around me headstones and mausoleums sat above the ground. There was too much water here, beneath the surface, waiting to swamp the caskets, waiting to push the dead back to the surface. So everything sat above ground— various colors of weatherworn cement and granite, white marble with moss growing in the cracks, all sunburned and aged to a uniform whitish gray.

Some of the names I recognized; others I didn't. But I wasn't here for any of them. It wouldn't matter to them if I had been. No one here knew me; no one in town wanted me.

Only him.

Dad.

I caught sight of the familiar mausoleum, the family name at the top, generations of Taylors sealed inside. The names went back to the 1800s, the time the big house was built, the time the merchant patriarch had settled at the edge of town. Even now, where he'd gotten his money was in question. Not by any legal means, not without slitting throats and squeezing blood from stone. A conman. A smuggler. A thief.

I traced my dad's name, Brian Ethan Taylor, before easing down on the steps before it, pulling grass from between the walkway stones, thinking about the last time I'd seen him. So long ago, on the way out the door—a hurried kiss, a too brief hug.

I'll see you in the morning, baby. Just driving your momma over to the charity event. I'll be here when you wake up.

But of course, he hadn't been. Their car had gone off the road and slammed into a tree. He'd died instantly, or so they said. And Vivian had been thrown from the car, breaking her back, paralyzed from the waist down.

He hadn't been there in the morning.

It hurt still. It hurt so bad I wanted to wail, the pain of it here, in this place too much. Everything he could have been, gone. The comfort and support it would have taken to survive those last few years snatched away. I'd held on, clinging with nails bitten to the quick, fighting to make it out of this place. But if he'd survived, things would have been different. Maybe it would have been the two of us against the world. We might have been beaten down by Vivian, but at least we would have had each other.

Jasmine—fresh and living green—filled my senses, as if my thoughts had conjured her, and something wet and cold touched my cheek. I brought a hand up, covering the spot, looking up to see if it was the rain finally arriving, the hurricane here early. Not a cloud in the sky. It was blue as blue could be.

Crying to your daddy, Emma?

Footsteps rang out, the swift sure steps I remembered from my childhood—high heels on hardwood, click-clacking down a long hall, striding confidently through the rooms of Magnolia House. My breath caught in my chest. I held it, focused on the soft sound of someone walking toward me. I couldn't turn, stunned and frozen by a will other than my own. I could only remain, waiting for punishment to arrive. I knew that feeling all too well.

I knew the thing that was slowly approaching.

The mausoleum, my dad right here, a place I expected to be safe. How could she come here? Here of all places, a place she'd only ever come to once while she lived. She hadn't cared for him, hadn't loved him, not the way I had, not in a way that kept him close to a beating heart, his kind smile living on, the soft words of encouragement keeping me going.

I let out my held breath, needing to breathe, unable to hold it any longer. The steps sped up, the person, the thing coming faster, my heart picking up with it, pounding with each step. I closed my eyes, squeezing them tight, welcoming the darkness behind the lids, knowing what was coming but unable to stop it.

A hand clamped down on my shoulder, biting into my skin, hard and vicious, anger coming with it. I bit my lip, fighting the urge to move, to jump up and run. Running had only ever made it worse. The only hope I'd ever had was to hide. But it was too late. She'd found me. Jasmine enveloped me, the prick of manicured nails digging in, the hiss of her voice raising the hair on the back of my neck.

What have I told you about running to your father and telling lies?

I shook my head, memory flooding me—her tight grip and red nails leaving little half-moons on my arms or cheeks, the way she'd seized my face, tilting my chin up until I could see her staring down at me. Beneath the perfect face, moisturized and made up, the threat of something so much darker—resentment boiling and spilling over. The pressure of her hand on my face was real, the demand to turn, look up, and meet her gaze.

"No," I whispered. "You haven't been able to walk in years. You're dead."

I leaned back, trying to pull away, but she held on. The pressure increased. The grip tightened.

"Emma?"

The grip vanished, the scent of jasmine gone with it.

I knew the voice, already knew him, and that made my heart hurt just a little. I turned to Jake, tears on my cheeks, cold and scared and desperate to leave. I wasn't going to question why he was here, wouldn't think past it for this moment, embracing the relief he brought, the end to the cold, gripping horror.

"What're you doing here?" I asked.

He waved back toward the parking area, "I was passing by and saw your car. I wondered if maybe it had died on you again since it was in an odd spot, so I stopped."

I nodded, grateful, unable to put into words how relieved I was that he'd shown up. He held out a hand, offering to pull me up, and I took it. He was warm and real, hands gentle as he steadied me, and held on longer than necessary. His eyes were so blue, and I wanted to lean into him, pull him to me, to have his arms wrap around me. His gaze shifted beyond me, reading the name, understanding without my having to explain.

"You want me to leave you alone?"

I couldn't tell if he'd prefer it that way or not. If he was ready to be on his way, duty complete; Southern hospitality was a thing even he was able to muster in the rare moment.

"No," I said, voice soft, suppressing a shiver. "I'm not staying any longer."

He nodded, uncertain, and stepped back. I wanted to tell him *no, no stay, stay and help me keep the monster at bay. Stay and hold me, keep me safe.* But I had no right to ask that of him, to cling to him when he barely knew me.

"I have to go," he said, taking another step away, not offering more.

I sucked in a breath, a voice inside me scolding. What did I think would happen? I smiled, cheeks stiff, wondering if I would get home and see small half-moon indentions fading on my skin.

"Thanks for stopping."

A flash of color to the right caught my attention—a ripple of movement. I wasn't sure. But there was something. *See me,* it seemed to say. I scanned the cemetery. There were no birds, no breezes drifting through the trees, no insects singing their incessant songs. Overhead the sky was clear—a false face. Soon a hurricane would hit, the water coming before it, driven unstoppably forward, rain and tidal surges. I should be gone when it hit. No matter what the blue sky implied, I was running out of time.

"Sure," he said, glancing in the direction I was watching. "Have a good day."

I nodded without looking at him, concentrating on what I thought I'd seen.

Crossing to the next row of tombs I caught the shape—a shadow moving quickly, someone keeping out of sight. I moved faster, following, needing to know who it was. I don't know why it mattered, it shouldn't, maybe it was someone like myself, who'd come out to share a peaceful moment with the memory of a loved one.

But I needed to see. I needed to know. Tension kept my shoulders tight, jaw clenched, the moment of confrontation hurtling toward me. It mattered. I didn't have to understand this feeling to know that it was true.

I jogged between rows, crossing from the newer sections to the old part of the cemetery—past extravagant tombs with weeping women, columns, and peaked roofs. No one spent money like this anymore, not in the Back of Beyond. The living kept the money here, putting it to better use than opulent mausoleums, feeding families and making car payments. The people with the kind of money to put toward stone angels had moved on long ago.

Pausing where several paths converged, I looked around, spinning slowly, searching. I'd lost them. I was deep into the cemetery now, the arched sign out of sight, the road invisible. If cars passed, I couldn't hear them; if anything moved in the world beyond this place, I was unaware of it. Jake seemed to be gone as well, on his way to visit his own ghosts maybe.

Shaking my head, *you're such an idiot sometimes*, I dug my keys out of my purse and began walking toward my car.

There was still so much to do. I'd get in touch with the estate company and arrange for the contents of the house to be sold. And after that? What would happen to the house? I hadn't really considered that, even now I wasn't sure what I wanted to do.

I would never come back to this place, never set foot in that house again if I could help it, but selling it was daunting. I could keep it, let it sit, and leave it to decay while I paid property taxes from a distance. I could rent it out. I could turn it into a bed and breakfast. I could do a hundred things with it. Anything I wanted.

Magnolia House is mine.

Reaching the car, I slid in behind the wheel, staring forward without seeing. I touched my cheek, searching for the little half-moon indentions on my skin, wondering if a mirror would reflect them back at me—cold and hard and true. I didn't want to know. It was better not to. Putting the car into gear, I pulled away from the curb, passing the entrance to the cemetery. A flash of red to my right caught my eye, movement, a sway of fabric, a hand raised. I paused, glancing at the cemetery.

Vivian.

She stood beneath an oak tree near the back, a distant figure in the shade, watching me.

I slammed on the brakes, jerking forward against the seatbelt, heart hammering. I slammed the car into park, turning my full attention to the tree at the end of the long row of mausoleums and vaults. Nothing. No one. I fumbled in the cup holder, searching for the medallion without taking my eyes off the tree, relief touching me when I found the cool metal disc.

She's not real.

It was imagination, frayed nerves, stress, and anxiety, and beneath that possibly a small core of grief. I was seeing things. Nothing more than that.

CHAPTER NINE
THURSDAY

The shop was crowded, with surfaces a mishmash of dishes and figurines, small white stickers with prices, chunky ashtrays, and green glass. I caught my reflection in a frameless antique beveled mirror, the silver backing cracked, edges worn away.

Vivian's face stared back at me.

I stopped, caught, and feeling instant shame. For what, I had no idea. Discovered and found unacceptable, selling the contents of her house, tossing the last few remnants of her away. The face in the mirror showed the emotion, guilt visible on my features. They all said I looked like her, and I'd never seen it. But it was my face in the mirror, me and only me.

"Hey there! Can I help you find something?"

Turning, gathering calm around me, I faced the speaker. A woman smiled at me, wide and welcoming, with dyed red hair and gray roots peeking through. She was warm, her smile and eyes, the way she spoke. I felt as if I'd met her before, known her somehow, and I couldn't help the smile that touched my mouth. She was infectious.

"Hi," I said. "I'm looking for Laura Kennedy. Mr. Owens recommended her."

"Oh! You must be Emma Taylor. Henry said you might be getting in touch. Why don't you come on back? We can talk about what you might need done out at the house."

She led the way, and I followed, weaving between large pieces of furniture, lamps, and artwork, a rack of vintage linen dotted with embroidered magnolias. At the very back, between a monster of a carved wardrobe and the wall, was a desk. This one was clean, completely bare, with two chairs in front of it, and an old swivel chair behind it. It was like the others in a way—the attorney, the pastor, the funeral home director. I would forever be perching on the edge of chairs before serious desks, meeting eyes full of curiosity or anger.

"Go ahead and have a seat," she said, waving at the chairs.

I took one, and to my surprise, she sat beside me instead of sitting behind the desk.

"I hope you don't mind that Henry called. He didn't share anything personal. Just that he had a client that would be needing some help with an estate. With Magnolia House actually. And here you are, so I guess he was right."

"He was. Is. I need to settle what's left of the estate, and I don't want the contents of the house. I was hoping to sell it all before I leave."

"Nothing off-limits for the sale, huh? Well, that makes it easy. We can evaluate and price everything, then run the sale for you. And whatever doesn't sell we can take on as consignment. What won't work for our place we can drop off at the Goodwill in Fairview."

"Would you be willing to take it all if I sold it at a

discount? No consignment. I'm really hoping to get it all settled and not have to think about it again."

The woman studied me, searching for something they all did. I couldn't guess at what it might be. "We could maybe do that. I'll need to talk with my husband. He handles all the money things. I'm just in for the shiny stuff." She laughed, and I smiled, grateful for her easy kindness.

"I'd really appreciate it. I know it might seem strange, but I don't want to get a check in the mail six months from now and dredge up all these memories."

Why had I shared that? It was too personal, too much for this strictly business conversation.

"I think it might be more common than you think. I can let you know if we can do that after we inventory the house. What's a good time to come by and appraise the contents?"

"As soon as possible, any time really."

"Monday? After the services?"

"Sure, that's perfect. What do I owe you? Can I give you my card now?"

"Oh no, nothing for appraisal. That's free. We usually take a small fee for setup and then a portion of the sale. I can give you more solid numbers after we've taken a look at it all."

"Sounds good," I said, standing and shouldering my purse. "I'll see you tomorrow at noon."

She stood with me, gesturing to the door and walking me out. "It was nice to meet you, Emma."

"You too, Laura," I said, reaching the door and pushing it open. Sunlight hit me, cloud shadows racing across the parking lot; rain threatened away on the horizon. "Looks like rain."

"I'm sorry about your mom," the woman said, sincere as hell.

A shadow bathed me, cooling the heat in my skin. I didn't know if I could handle hearing that anymore. It would break soon, yell and refuse all condolences, tell these strangers to save them for someone who wanted them. I didn't. But I said thanks and let the door shut behind me, forgetting the face in the mirror, avoiding my reflection in the huge plate-glass windows.

CHAPTER TEN

THURSDAY

Standing at the study window I thought about everything I'd accomplished so far, cradling a mug of tea to my chest—grateful for the warmth. The sun was sinking, settling into a cooling sky, the world going dark around the edges.

I'd come home and bustled around like a fly with a blue bottom—restless and busy without accomplishing much. The key from the envelope the attorney had given me hadn't fit a single lock in the house. I'd given up and added it to the box beneath the cabinet—a question for another day or another person. Then I'd spent some time in the room with all the books, looking through titles and sorting stacks half-heartedly, trying to forget what had happened earlier.

The experience at the cemetery had gotten under my skin.

Vivian had gotten under my skin.

I kept telling myself that I'd built the right barriers, I'd learned the right things. My therapist had helped me to face trauma, years of it laid bare in a sparse office overlooking a parking lot. I'd shifted through it all and moved past it. Or thought I had.

But here I was, terrified of her all over again. The fear had convinced my brain things were happening, that she was still here, that she'd been waiting for me. But it was just my brain. None of it was real.

Vivian was dead, and there was no afterlife, no such thing as ghosts.

You sure about that kiddo?

The Mercury dime warmed in my shoe. I set my mug on the desk, slipped the shoe off and shook out the coin. It landed on my palm, worn smooth with so many years, so many other people rubbing the relief of Lady Liberty with her winged cap. Silver for luck. If I truly believed that there were no ghosts, that superstitions were stories people shared, I would leave the dime on the desk and not think twice about it.

It clicked against the hardwood, snapping into place, all my weight on it, pressing it into the surface. When I'd been little, my dad had slipped the first silver dime in my shoe. *For prosperity and good luck, baby.* Somehow, after all these years, I still carried one in my purse, a token of him, a reminder. But when I'd reached town I'd put it in my shoe, as he had all those years ago. In this place, it mattered.

In Magnolia House, it worked.

After replacing the dime, I slipped my shoe back on. My hands were cold, the sun retreated, and I wanted another cup of tea. I should have worked on the house again today, gone up into the attic to rustle around old paper, touch tarnished frames of the family paintings.

But those were daylight things, chores to be accomplished with the sun high in the sky, warm on my shoulders. There was nothing left to be in the darkness except drink tea and read.

I wasn't going to give in to fear again.

I was the sole resident of this house now.

———

Beyond the glass, distorted and wavering, lights moved between the trees.

I dropped the coffee mug, and it shattered in the sink—a tinkle of shards, a prickle of cold sliding through me. Blood rushed in my ears, mind going blank as I watched them move. I blinked, and the light vanished, flickering and gone, already a dream or figment of my imagination.

The whole place was getting to me—the town, the house, the people. I was getting tired of it all, scared but getting close to the point of pushing back. Nothing had happened at the cemetery, and there was nothing happening here.

I'd prove it.

I grabbed a cheap plastic flashlight out of a kitchen drawer. Jake had included it in the bag of supplies he'd dropped off the other night. I was grateful for it, flicking it on and off to make sure the batteries hadn't died.

Everything that came into the house seemed to die or go bad—batteries, fruit, my cell phone charger. Even the candles I burned seemed to go out more quickly than any I'd ever used at home. This house picked away at the edges of my mind. I shook off the thought, pulling open the back door and breathing in the humid night as I stepped out on to the back steps.

The world was a blue-black space under a moving overcast sky. Clouds raced across the moon and stars, driven and chased by an invisible wind. But beneath them, here where I stood, it was windless, the humidity rushing into my clothes, laying close to my skin. My underarms prickled, the hair on the back of my neck rising ever so slightly. A cricket sang from beneath the steps, and another answered it from the overgrown garden, more frog and insect chirps coming from the trees. They sang to each other, the music amplified and echoed, a greeting to the night.

The steps creaked with my weight on the way down, louder than I'd expected, the voices going quiet. I hesitated, wondering if whoever was out there in the woods had heard me too. Not that it mattered. They'd see me coming with the flashlight anyway.

Panning the light across the garden, moving beyond to the trees, I wondered what I was doing. Wasn't it safer in the house? I wasn't so sure, so I pushed the thought away, concentrating on the woods, on the moment before me. The darkness between the trees was deeper than the night, gathered between trunks, thick beneath leaves, and caught in branches. It seemed touchable, moveable as if I could reach out and part it like a curtain, move beyond it, and into a wood bathed in sunlight.

A mosquito buzzed my ear, and I waved around my head, already regretting the lack of bug spray. But if I went back inside, I might not come back out again. On the other side of the door I was brave, confident in myself and my ability to face whatever might come next. Out here, under the open sky and with the woods ahead of me, I was less sure of myself.

Out or in.

Forward or back.

In the woods, for a brief instant, a light appeared and then vanished.

A flashlight? Lantern? Candle? I couldn't tell.

Go on.

It wasn't her voice, not even my own. It came from some other part, from some other moment. But I accepted it and stepped forward. The paving stones soon gave way to overgrown grass and then knee-high weeds, the low brush below the trees took over, and then I was under the canopy.

The flashlight lit a narrow swath straight ahead, greenery washed out, spider webs glistening, insects crossed the beam—black, then harshly illuminated, before going dark again as they moved away. Old leaves and sticks rustled and snapped beneath my feet, the earth soft and spongy.

There wasn't a path or even an animal track, but I pushed forward in the direction I'd last seen the light. Around me the sounds of the night continued, thrumming, ignoring my intrusion as I swatted away bugs and tried not to shriek when I passed through a trailing filament of spider silk.

I glanced behind me, wondering how far I'd come, and was surprised to see how close the house sat. The entire downstairs was lit up, the warm yellow windows watching me. Beyond the panes of glass, I could see the study and the kitchen, the world contained inside seeming miniature and foreign—an abandoned dollhouse.

It was tall in the night, solid against the sky, the upper stories stretching to meet the low clouds. I hesitated with the woods at my back, the house before me. I was watched by both, observed by things that had no eyes to see, no mouths to speak.

A sharp crack split the air, loud as gunfire, and so close I could almost feel the pressure change in the air. Spinning, flashlight bouncing, I searched the trees, terrified of what I might see. Shadows jumped, and the trunks appeared to shiver, as jittery as I was. The night noises vanished, the pounding of my heart as audible as each shaky breath I pulled in.

Nothing. There was nothing. Whatever the woods contained, beyond myself here trembling in a dim halo of light, they didn't reveal themselves to me. The night beyond my circle felt darker, deeper, more watchful than before, and now silent.

I held a ragged breath, straining to hear anything—crunching leaves, branches being pushed back and broken. A breeze touched my face, moving a strand of hair, but it didn't do much to relieve the heat sitting so close to my skin. It pressed on me like everything else, *don't forget I'm here.*

I didn't care about the light. I didn't need to know. It didn't matter. It had been stupid to come out here, picking my way in the dark and determined to face some unnamable thing. Stupid.

I turned toward the house, toward the golden-lighted windows and the promise of a cold drink from the tap. I was suddenly thirsty, desperate for even the mossy-tasting water that came out of the pipes here.

A crash off to my right stopped me, anchoring my feet to the earth, as something big ran through the trees. It was approaching quickly, racing toward me. It was close, too close, and I darted for the house. Branches scratched at my face, pulling my hair, yanking some free as I stumbled and went down on one knee. The thundering approached, coming right up behind me as I shoved myself up and forward again.

In a blur, the thing was beside me, large and invisible, and so close in the dark. The air changed, the space around me suddenly full as I panted and tried to scream. But there was no breath, nothing but overwhelming panic as I stumbled back into a tree, landing on my backside with an *oomph*.

In the beam of the flashlight, shaking so badly I was barely able to hold it up, I caught a deer. A doe. Long delicate legs, gray-brown fur, a reflective pair of eyes alert and aware, large ears turned toward me. She passed in an instant, faster than blinking, faster than my attempt to scream. She was gone, leaving behind nothing visible, only the sounds of her passage, her continued rush forward.

I sat, the dampness from the earth soaking into my jeans, the rough tree bark at my back, my head throbbing where I'd hit it against the tree. I touched the spot gingerly. The skin wasn't broken, and there was no blood on my fingers when I shined the flashlight on them. I waited for my heart to even out, for my breathing to steady, before pushing to my feet. My knees only shook a little as I picked my way more carefully than before toward the house.

The pressure at my back was more intense than before, my brain convinced someone was in the woods watching, that they had seen me fall and maybe even chased the deer toward me in the dark. But as soon as the thought crossed my mind, I dismissed it. It was too much, even for me, even after the last few days here.

Passing through the last of the trees, I stepped back into the kitchen garden, back into reality. I hurried toward the backdoor, flashlight jittering as I started to jog, light bouncing over the facade, glass catching it, throwing it back to me.

Movement caught my attention. I swung the flashlight in that direction and caught the deer, frozen in the light, and watching me as intently as I watched her. She was just a few feet away, frame tight, muscles poised to leap. I hesitated, waiting, not wanting to scare her any more than I already had, even though I was pretty sure she'd scared me more.

"Hello," I whispered, clamping down on the urge to laugh with relief.

At the sound of my voice, she sprang away, up and to the side, melting back into the darkness with her white tail held high. I watched her go, standing alone in the dark, the house empty and waiting for me.

Suddenly I couldn't stand the thought of going back inside. I'd wanted it only moments before; I'd wanted doors and locks and to forget about the strange light in the woods. But now? I wanted people. I wanted noise and laughter.

I didn't want to feel alone.

CHAPTER ELEVEN

THURSDAY

The Fishing Hole was a bar forty minutes away—practically next door. And the perfect place to be surrounded by people without needing to speak to any of them. I wanted noise, not conversation—a stiff drink and to pretend that Magnolia House hadn't gotten under my skin.

It was a square building, covered in aged wood siding, without any windows. The gravel parking lot was almost full, but I found a spot in the back beneath the overhanging trees. I hurried from the car, double-checking that my keys were in my purse, and I hadn't accidentally locked myself out. As I reached the door, a neon sign fizzled softly in the night as I passed beneath, bathing me in a green and yellow glow.

Noise flowed out as I pulled the door open and stepped inside. Smoke, beer, and the heavy, greasy scent of fried foods greeted me. The bar was half booths and half high-top tables with bar stools grouped around them. The place was packed—men and women playing pool with longnecks in their hands, couples at tables, men sharing pitchers of pale beer.

I scanned the space, looking for a free spot. There were a few places at the bar, but I didn't want to sit there, exposed and out in the open. I'd grab a drink and then find a booth. I went up and waved the bartender down.

"Could I get gin and tonic?"

"The good stuff or the cheap stuff?" she asked. The woman smiled at me, friendly and welcoming, feeling more like a friend than any stranger had a right to be.

"The stuff that will help me forget."

She chuckled. "Might as well go expensive. Not that our high end is very high."

"Sounds good to me."

"Want to start a tab?" she asked, exchanging the drink for the card and taking it to the register.

"Yeah, let's go ahead and do that."

She swiped my card, double-checking the name. "All right, Emma. You're all set." She handed it back to me, noticing I was still looking around. "Booth or table?"

I smiled gratefully. "Booth. A quiet corner would be perfect."

"If you go all the way back by the pool tables, there are usually a few empty booths this early in the evening. Maddie is floating around here somewhere, and she'll bring you whatever you want."

"Thanks," I said, taking my drink and heading off in that direction.

I got a few looks on my way—curious but mostly unfamiliar. This was the nearest bar to Back of Beyond and the closest to Magnolia House. I was thankful for the strange faces—the people who didn't know I was a Taylor. But a few faces I recognized the deeper I got; no one by name, but maybe they'd known Vivian. I almost set my drink down and walked away. I didn't want to deal with any of those people tonight, didn't want to be crucified by their judgment.

But the thought of getting back in the car and going somewhere else, or even going back to the house, was unbearable. I just wanted to sit in a place where I wasn't alone. And there was only so much driving around I could do on a half-empty tank. And walking around a store with a shopping cart just to get out of the house didn't sound like a lot of fun either. So, the nearest bar, a stiff drink, a paperback thriller from the collection in the room down the hall, and Vivian's diary in my purse would be enough for tonight.

There were four pool tables in the back, the room widening out and the whole space seeming larger than it had from the outside. Booths lined two walls, and on the others were a juke box blasting country music and a wall of pool cues separated by neon beer signs. Low lights hung over the tables, the corners of the room dim, and overall, it was much quieter than the area around the bar. There were fewer people, and they were clustered around the pool tables. One booth held a couple having a tense whispered conversation, and I chose a table farthest from them.

Setting my drink down, I slid into the booth, sitting with my back to the wall and stretching my legs along the bench. Hopefully taking up the space on the bench and keeping the book out would be enough to discourage anyone in the mood to make conversation.

It was easy to tune out the noise and fall into the book. Much easier than I'd expected. I'd gotten several chapters in and something extra gruesome was about to happen when someone spoke, drawing my attention.

"Want a refill on that?"

The woman standing at the end of the table had a small tray in one hand and an empty pitcher in the other. She was short and curvy, and everything about her generous—figure, smile, eyes. And I liked her right away.

"Sure," I said, pushing my glass toward her. I'd been so focused on the book that I'd finished the drink without realizing it, ice and all. "Gin and tonic please."

"Sounds good. Name on the tab?"

"Emma."

"Be back in a sec. Try not to dry out."

I laughed as she walked away. The room had filled while I'd read. The volume inching upward but only noticeable now that I'd set the book down. The couple I'd seen hissing at each other was gone, and a group of women with several pitchers between them was crowded around that booth. The others had filled up too, couples and group; no one seemed on their own tonight except me.

The same group of young guys was playing pool at the table nearest me. The other three tables had games going as well. There was so much talk and laughter and chatter and noise. I was surprised I'd been able to tune it all out.

I set my book in my lap, pages down to mark my spot. People watching had always been a favorite pastime. It's easier to watch than take part. I'd learned early on with Vivian that it tended to be the safest option as well. Maddie was making her way back to me, and behind her there was another figure I recognized. Jake. I fumbled with my book, dropping it and picking it up again, flipping through the pages for where I'd left off.

"Here you go," Maddie said, reaching my table and setting down the gin along with a glass of water. "I'll be by to keep you topped up. Need anything else? I can grab you a menu if you want. It's all fried stuff, you know? Fried okra. Fried pickles. Fried cheese. Fried tomatoes. Fried alligator. French fries, fried of course. That's the best option if you want my opinion. Fries, I mean. The tomatoes are nice, but you'll need a fork. Fries are just easy. But you might not want to get your book all greasy. I'll just bring you a ton of napkins."

"Thanks," I said, focusing on her face and a little overwhelmed by the flow of information. Food was a good idea. I couldn't remember the last time I'd eaten. "Fries would be great. And lots of ketchup too please."

"Sure thing! I'll get that order in right away. I'll bring you some ranch too."

I thanked her again and pulled the water glass closer. It tasted a little odd, like deep well water without all the city additives, but I didn't mind. Maybe someone was out back pulling up buckets and fishing the newts and frogs out before pouring it into the glass. It was cold and did a little bit to lower my temperature. My cheeks were hot, and I could feel myself turning pink.

Glancing up, I met Jake's gaze across the room. He was standing at the pool table farthest from me, one hand in the pocket of his jeans, the other holding a beer. He looked casual and relaxed, and somehow different from the man who had driven me around town. Here, he was a stranger.

Every time I turned around in this Back of Beyond place, there he was. I looked away before he could, working on indifference and hoping I was pulling it off. It surprised me that he was here; he seemed like such a loner, and no one liked him in town. But maybe this place was far enough away, maybe here he could escape the stigma of a woman's death that hadn't been his fault. Here, he might be a stranger.

I wished I could have read his expression. He'd seemed surprised to see me, but that wasn't saying much. I had no clue what he was thinking.

It was harder to get back to my book. The main character was getting chased through an abandoned building, running for her life, but I couldn't have cared less. Jake was across the room. If I looked up, would I find his eyes on me? I hated my curiosity, the desire that lay beneath it. I was here for Vivian. I was here to bury the past and then run away with my tail tucked between my legs. I wasn't here for a handsome stranger. I wasn't here for a man with a history of trouble and some pitch-black secrets in his past.

I looked up anyway. He was playing pool with another man. Not a big group of rowdy guys like the table closest to me. Jake and his friend were having a quiet game, holding beers in one hand while they talked, gesturing, telling jokes. He laughed, and my heart skipped, a quick one two before catching up again. He turned, moving to pick up pool cue, his eyes catching mine. I stopped breathing, couldn't help it.

"Here we are," Maddie said, putting a basket of fries on the table. She pulled a bottle of ketchup from her apron with a flourish. "You want anything else? Another drink?"

"No thanks, I'm stopping with this one."

"You wanna tab out now?"

My stomach rumbled and my mouth watered as the scent of crisp salty fries reached me. "Would it be weird if I said no, just in case I want more fries?"

"Hell no!" She laughed. "Not at all! Give me a wave when you're ready."

"Thanks."

Settling back on the bench, I opened the book, eating fries with one hand, turning pages carefully with the other.

Adding carbs to the alcohol was good. Good idea. Much better than drinking on an empty stomach and getting trashed alone in public. I'd already done that once this week. Halfway through the basket of fries, and right as the main character was cornered in an impossible situation, someone sat down across from me with a lot of noise.

"Noticed you sitting here all by yourself and thought I'd come say hello."

It was one of the men from the group at the pool table nearest me. He was midtwenties, with brown hair and eyes, cute in a baby-fat kind of way, with a boyish smile. He flashed it at me now, glancing over to his friends to make sure they were watching.

A flush began to work its way across my cheeks, irritation pinching my mouth shut. He wasn't going to be happy with just a hello. He was planning to take up much more of my time than I was willing to give. I resented him already, and a few drinks made it easier to let him know.

"I'm not interested in making friends. Have a good night," I said, going back to my book.

A chorus of oohs broke from his audience.

Damnit. He'd been embarrassed, and now he'd feel the need to make up for it. I could have just smiled and been polite, but the day had been so long, and I'd been dealing with too much to fake it for an asshole in a bar.

"I'm Ryan. You're Emma Taylor, right? I haven't seen you in here before," he said, trying to get my attention. "It's been a while since you were in town. I could show you around if you're interested."

Something sharp lurked beneath the words, his tone implying much more. If I looked up and around, would someone see? Would they read the plea for help on my face?

Gotta help yourself, kiddo.

"No, thank you." I kept my tone flat and eyes on the book, staring at the pages but unable to read a single line.

He coughed, the table creaking as he leaned forward, his voice lowered. "You don't have a whole lot of friends in town, do you? It gets lonely at night 'round here, not a whole lot to do, you know? And you seem like a nice person despite all the gossip. And I'm a nice guy. Nicest guy in town."

Nice guy. I bit back my reply, fighting to keep my face expressionless. No more. I wasn't going to say anything else. He'd get bored with the one-sided conversation eventually and leave. But his friends were watching, murmured encouragement and derisive laughter reaching us.

"Hey," he said, reaching out and pushing the book out of my hands. "I'm trying to make conversation here, and you're being rude."

I met his eyes, hands beginning to tremble, adrenaline and an edge of fear building—fight or flight kicking in. "I'm sorry but I don't want to have a conversation."

"Then why come to a bar?"

"It wasn't to pick up strangers. I didn't approach you. Please leave."

His face reddened, eyes narrowing. "Bitch."

My stomach knotted, skin prickling. The tables nearest us had gone silent, people watching with passive curiosity. His friends returned to their game, laughing too loudly, ignoring us now. I swept the room, and Jake caught my eye; maybe he'd seen the whole thing, or at least caught the last word.

"Hey! You want that second order of fries?" Maddie arrived, armed with a pitcher of ice water. She filled my glass, making a point to keep her body turned toward me, freezing out the man in the other half of my booth. "Or could I get you something else? Steve just put on a new pot of coffee, and I could get you some vanilla creamer. I've got a private stash back in the kitchen."

I loved this woman. "Coffee sounds really great actually."

"You wanna come on up to the bar and grab it? My hands are really full right now, and you'd be doing me a huge favor. Jessica, the woman working the bar, has an empty stool right by the pot, so you could just help yourself."

I eased out of the booth, a little stiff from sitting for so long, and grabbed my purse. Maddie turned from me to the man, moving slightly to keep him from following. I focused on the floor as I passed his friends who'd been encouraging him, aware of their scornful eyes. Everyone watched, studying me, wondering. Ryan's last word hung in the air.

Then I was passing Jake, so close I could have touched him, reached out with a single finger to run it along his arm, slide in close. I was more aware of him than my own feet or beating heart. I held my breath, trying to stop myself from wanting him to talk to me, to stop me in front of all these people, to do more than watch me across a crowded room. I looked up, bracing myself for the shock of blue eyes, for the way my face would betray me. He gave the slightest of nods and turned away, recognition and dismissal all in one.

I made it to the bar, smoothing out the anxiousness twisting inside of me, and sat by the coffee pot. It didn't matter that Jake hadn't said anything. It didn't matter what Ryan had said. None of these people mattered.

Jessica brought me a white mug and filled it up without a bunch of small talk, which I really appreciated. Then she went back to working the bar and being a good listener for everyone else sitting there—a few regulars, one man with a crumpled newspaper.

I patted my purse, meaning to pull out the novel, but it wasn't there. I groaned. I'd left it on the table, and there was no way I'd go back. It wasn't worth it. Instead, I pulled out Vivian's diary—cover smooth against my fingers, cream-colored pages. A trace of jasmine reached me, her perfume finding me even here. Ruffling the pages, I noticed the scent grew stronger. She must have sprayed them sometime in her last few days.

The contents were basic. She listed what she ate for the day, a little masochistic since it wasn't much, and right below that she'd list her weight. Tall and thin, classically beautiful, like the starlets in black and white movies. She maintained it all on one hardboiled egg, no more than five celery sticks, black coffee, and enough whiskey to keep a horse afloat.

It sounded awful. Maybe she'd been so terrible all those years because she'd been starving herself to death. I didn't have one memory of her eating, not even when my dad was alive. Those Sunday afternoon teas with delicate porcelain plates full of small crustless sandwiches and tarts, glistening and full of butter and heavy cream. All full but never touched. Aside from that, the weather got recorded, the phases of the moon, her menstrual cycle, and a daily tarot card.

"Hey," Maddie leaned against the bar beside me. "I'm really sorry about that back there. Ryan can get mean when he's drunk. You okay?"

"Yeah, thanks for saving me."

"I'm sorry I didn't see you sooner though. If you stick around for a bit, Steve can walk you out later."

"Steve?"

"Oh! The cook! And sometimes bouncer. He's nice, you'll like him. He's so tall!" She held her arm over her head and stood on tiptoe. "And he really can't stand Ryan."

"I like him already," I said. "I was going to have some more coffee and hang out. I'm not ready to drive home just yet."

She patted my arm. "Good idea. Fries?"

I nodded. "I absolutely need fries."

"Done."

I looked over another couple pages of the diary, but it was more of the same. Diet and weather and weight and daily card. She never made any remark about the card, just that she'd pulled a card. That part did surprise me. I'd never seen her with a deck, but she'd been deeply superstitious woman. Maybe there was a deck tucked away in a drawer in her room, waiting to be found—the past, present, and future of Vivian Taylor.

If I pulled a card from her deck, would it be the one for death?

I flipped through more pages until I reached the end of the diary—each page was filled out, nothing empty or left for some future date. A small newspaper clipping fell out, barely three paragraphs, no photo, only text. I picked it up, the twist of anxiety returning, a dread creeping up on me as something headed my way—something that would hit me like a coal train.

An obituary.

I scanned it quickly, going back to read it a second time to make sure I'd gotten the name right. It was for the woman, the girl, Alice. Jake's high school sweetheart. It was brief, skimming over her short life, birth to death with not much in between—happy baby, beautiful soul, taken too soon. My heart ached for her, sorry that her life had been cut short with such a brutal end.

The clipping reminded me of the others in the attic. Stacks worth of words, sentences, and paragraphs asserting guilt or suspicious innocence. I would need to deal with those. And the remaining contents of the house. But that was a tomorrow worry. Flipping to the back of the diary I found the pages it had been tucked between.

There was more written here than anywhere else. Just three words.

They found her.

My skin crawled. The words were so simple and direct. *Found. Her.* It didn't mean they held anything harmful; it could have been a simple observation. But I knew Vivian. I didn't know how she was connected to this girl, but she must have been. Boxes full of newspaper clippings and now this simple sentence. There was something here that scared me. It worried me even more that she'd left the diary for me, purposefully, intentionally, with this inside.

I closed the diary, tucked it back in my purse, and then pulled my phone out. It was almost midnight, and I still didn't have any service. The battery wasn't staying charged either. It was less than a year old, brand-new, and shouldn't have all these issues. But this place seemed to take pleasure in keeping things from the outside from working.

The phone was useless. I had no service at the house or anywhere else in town. I'd been able to make one phone call to Mr. Laurent, then the signal bars had vanished, never to return. Stranded, stuck here, and disconnected from it all. It was like being a kid again. There was no way to really escape, no hope to distract myself or go someplace better.

I was here, and here I'd stay.

Who would be on the other end of the phone anyway?

Ann? She was always swamped in the English department, buried under her own workload and now covering my classes as well. Rachel? Or Cody? With a frown I realized they were all coworkers. There wasn't anyone outside of the university to call, no one with connections to my personal life.

I didn't have a personal life.

Aside from that, they all knew I was dealing with a death in the family and I'd be out of touch for a week. I hadn't told anyone it had been Vivian. No one knew it was my mother. After all these years, I'd never gotten close to any of them. I'd kept everyone at arm's length. And now none of them would expect me to reach out.

The crowd in the bar began to thin. There were fewer patrons at the tables and sitting along the bar. Even in the back, where it seemed almost everyone had ended up, it wasn't as loud as it had been earlier. I'd had several cups of coffee and had tabbed out, sipping water and thinking about the diary, the box of newspaper clippings in the attic, and the way Vivian had watched the world when there was no one watching her.

No one but me.

The bartender wandered over. "We're getting ready to announce last call. You want me call someone for you? Have Steve walk you out?"

I shook my head. "No thanks. I'll be okay."

"Sure? Wouldn't be a problem at all."

"Yeah, I'm okay. Thank you again for everything. I really needed to get out of the house tonight and be around people, you know?"

She nodded, leaning against the bar. "Absolutely. I get like that too sometimes. Come back again, and we'll save you a seat. I'm sorry you had that issue with Ryan. He's such an asshole."

"It's okay," I said, pulling my keys out and standing up. "It happens."

"Hey! You leaving?"

I turned to Maddie coming over, her expression worried.

"Yeah, I'm heading out. Thank you for everything tonight."

You want Steve to walk you out?"

I laughed. "No, it's okay. Thank you though."

"Well, okay then. Be safe getting home."

I shouldered my purse and turned toward the door with a wave. "Thanks, have a good night!"

CHAPTER TWELVE
THURSDAY

Gravel crunched beneath my sneakers as I crossed the lot, humming to myself to keep an uneasy feeling at bay. Worry over going back to Magnolia House, worry over the night so close around me, the sky overcast with racing clouds, patches of blue-black sky peeking through, a handful of stars, and a thin silver moon watching me. I carried a low-level insistent worry.

I hit the unlock button on the rental car, and the lights flashed at the back of the lot. It had been full when I'd arrived, and the last few spots had been under the trees that overhung the back corner. Now it was almost empty.

Jake's truck stood out to me. My stomach flopped, wondering whether he was in it, wondering whether he'd waited for me, wondering whether I'd hear the door open behind me and he'd say my name. But he could have talked to me at any point in the bar; he could have said something when that man had harassed me. He hadn't. And that told me everything I needed to know.

I pushed that all away.

Magnolia House.

It waited, enduring at the edge of the bayou, confident of my return. The sooner I dealt with the past the better. Figuring out what to do with everything was another step toward home. The antique dealer would help with most of that, but there might be things I'd want to take back with me. The thought of bits and pieces of Vivian in my tiny apartment made me shiver. But there would be things that belonged to my dad—books, photos, his gold watch. Those things I would keep.

The rest of it? I'd be happy to leave it all behind.

But what about the newspaper clippings? The diary? Who could I ask? I wasn't sure. The attorney? But maybe it would be better to throw those things away too, no point in dredging up the past and reminding everyone of bad blood.

Why had she kept it all then?

The crunch of gravel made me turn. I hadn't realized someone had come out behind me, and I squashed a flash of excitement. Even if Jake was heading out to his truck, I wasn't going to get anything more than a passing nod.

But the person behind me was shorter and smiling. My stomach dropped. The guy from the bar. Ryan. He was walking toward me, hands out in a calming gesture.

"Hey there, didn't realize you were heading out too. Maybe I should walk you to your car."

Go faster. Leave now.

Turning away, I refused to respond, walking more quickly as my heart raced. Dumb. I should have waited and had Steve walk me to my car. I focused on the car, wanting nothing more than metal and glass between us. He grabbed my arm, jerking me back, spinning me around. A small noise of pain escaped as he dug his fingers into my arm, so far into the muscle it felt like he was touching bone.

"What the hell is wrong with you? Maybe your mom

was right when she said you were a stuck-up bitch who abandoned her," he hissed. "Are you too good for me to walk you out?"

Pain and panic and fear swamped me, mind spinning—soothe him, calm him down, and get to the car. I'd get in and drive and never, never, never come back to this bar. If I was really lucky, I'd never even see him again, not even passing through town. I tried to pull free, but his grip tightened.

"That your car?" He nodded to the rental, snatching the keys out of my hand and pressing the lock button.

It gave a cheerful little beep, and the lights flashed, red warmth washing over us, highlighting his face, casting deep shadows. I'd never heard a car noise that was that happy. I wouldn't complain ever again about the issues it had had since I'd picked it up as long as I could keep hearing that stupid chirpy beep.

He tossed the keys up in the air and caught them with one hand, the smile widening on his face as he pulled back and threw them into the woods. They crashed and rattled, hitting foliage, dropping through the bushes, to land with a jangle in the dirt somewhere.

I couldn't stop the noise that came out of me. A small animal noise—fear and defeat. I looked back to the bar, but the lights seemed so far away, like a distant star. If I pulled free, would I get that far? If I screamed would someone hear me? I sucked in a breath.

A slap landed hard across my cheek, slamming my teeth together, stopping any sound I might have made. He hit me again, and I tasted blood, my lip cracking, stinging. I don't know why I'd stayed quiet before, why I'd let him bully me. The pain brought me back to myself.

"Let me go," I yelled, kicking at his knees, and pulling away. "Help! Help me! Fire!"

"Shut up!" he screamed.

I pushed him with my free arm, scratching, biting the hand that was trying to cover my mouth. He was strong, bigger than me, and he pushed me down into the gravel, right there in the parking lot. There were so many people, they were so close. I could see the lights of the bar, the stars overhead. He was breathing heavily, wheezing, smothering me with his weight.

"Shut up, shut up, shut up."

Sharp stones cut into me, through my jeans and T-shirt, small points of pain from my head to my feet. Everywhere my skin met the gravel, it hurt. I tried to knee him in the balls, arching my back in an effort to move him, to give myself a little bit of space. But he was so heavy, and it was hard to breathe. I gasped through the hand covering my mouth, tasting salt and dirt, the corners of my vision blurring—little bits of speckled darkness closing in.

Then he was off me, his weight gone, his words gone. He'd vanished. I sucked in air, rolling onto my side to study the gravel. It was just gravel. Gray stone crushed and jagged, the kind of gravel you'd find anywhere. I waited, concentrating on my lungs as my breathing slowed, came back to me. I was hearing something. I didn't know what it was. Not the sounds of the night, not insects or night birds, but something heavy and pounding.

Sitting up, I looked around, steady meaty thuds coming from very close to me.

Jake had the man pinned to the ground. He was pale in the darkness, taller and bigger, more like a monster than a man at this angle. His knuckles were black in the night, wet with blood, and each time his fist connected, there was a noise of pain, a bubbling sound, a grunt. I watched, stunned, my jaw aching, the scrapes on my shoulders stinging.

I pushed to my feet, shaking, feeling every joint as I stumbled to my purse and picked it up out of the dirt. Nothing had fallen out, and it was just a little dirty. You couldn't even tell what had happened minutes before. It was unchanged, without a mark.

"Stop," I said, too softly to be heard. I moved until I could see Jake's face, the careful mask of nothing he had in place. I cleared my throat and said louder, "Jake. Stop."

He paused, eyes flicking up to mine, fists stalled in midair. The man in the gravel was motionless. In the dark I couldn't see much, but I could see the blood, and he didn't look conscious. Was he dead? Did I care? I shuddered. I held out a hand for Jake, beckoning, asking him silently to come to me.

"You okay?" he asked, leaving the guy in the gravel, that gray and sharp crushed stone I'd studied so carefully a moment before. Maybe he was looking at it too. Jake came to stand close, leaning down to look at my face, and he reached out to touch my lip but stopped. Fierce eyes stared into mine. "What do you need me to do?"

I'd never seen anyone so angry.

"Leave him," I said, turning to stumble toward my car. "I just want to go home."

"You should go to the ER and get your face looked at. He hit you pretty hard, you could have a concussion." He walked beside me, a hand outstretched and ready to steady me.

I shook my head, unable to stop the wince that sped across my face. "No."

"You need to get checked out."

"No," I said again, louder this time, the back of my throat scratchy and sore. "I'm not going to the ER. I'm going home. That's it."

"You can't drive," he said.

"I just want to go home." My voice sounded pitiful even to my own ears.

I saw him throw your keys into the trees right as I was walking out. I have no idea where they are, but we won't be able to find them in the dark. I can come back in the morning and look for them."

"What?" I checked my pockets, my purse. I could still feel the weight of them, the comfort they'd provided until they'd been snatched away. But he'd thrown them, cutting me off, isolating me.

"Let me take you home."

Jake pointed across the lot to his truck—familiar and strangely comforting. I glanced at the rental car. It looked lonely at the back of the lot. Ryan lay in the gravel between us, sprawled out, beginning to groan.

"I'll take you home," Jake said.

I didn't move, staring at the man, numb all over except for the hot pain of my split lip. I touched it, running a finger along my bottom row of teeth, tasting blood. Jake moved to stand behind me, solid and real. His anger, the rage, was there too, a physical thing in the air beside us. But it wasn't for me. He was protecting me, and that changed everything.

"Come on, sweetheart," he said softly. "I'm going to drive you home and make sure you get in safe. Okay?"

I didn't say anything, but I leaned back into his chest, and he supported me, arms coming around, encircling me. I didn't move. I couldn't. The man on the ground groaned, a hand scrabbling in the gravel. The things I wanted in this moment, watching him, unable to look away, were dark, a swirling mix of anger and fear.

"I'm taking you home," Jake said against my hair.

"Yes," I whispered finally, nodding.

He moved, putting one arm under my knees, and lifted me up, cradling me to his chest. I leaned into him, resting my head on his shoulder, listening to his steady breathing. He carried me to his truck, covering the distance quickly. At the passenger door, he set me on my feet and pulled the keys from his front pocket to unlock it. He opened it and the dome light came on, harsh and yellow, lighting us both up. I brushed dirt from my jeans, hands shaking.

"Leave it," he said. "A little more dirt isn't going to hurt anything."

I nodded, letting him help me in, sitting perfectly still as he reached across to buckle my seatbelt, his face coming close to mine as he leaned across me. He glanced at me, pausing when he found me watching. I was surprised at all the gentleness, the softness beneath his hard features.

He studied me, inches away, his blue eyes dark, the pupils large. My breath caught, heat flooding me as tension coiled between us. I reached out, touching his cheek with the fingertips of one hand, lifting the other to reach for him. But he stopped me. He took my hands and put them gently on my lap, looking away as he did, double-checking the seatbelt and shutting the door. Then he was in the driver's seat and throwing the truck into reverse, headlights picking out the parking lot.

Ryan lay where Jake had left him. Where I had left him. *Run him over.* I almost said it aloud, speaking desire into motion, willing reality to fill in the gaps. I wanted to crush that man into the gravel and make sure he'd never get up again. I wanted it with a brutality that scared me. Rejecting the image, shuddering at the discovery of violence in my soul, I turned away, focusing on Jake's hands on the steering wheel.

I'd never ridden in a car for such a stretch when it seemed to fly by quickly and drag at the same time. I sorted through the last few hours, examining each piece, tucking them away for later—to be turned over and understood, when the emotional wherewithal returned.

The thing in the parking lot. Incident. It was a thing that had happened. That had been done to me. The worst part was that this moment joined a myriad of other instances of quiet or outright brutality: men who had taken advantage, times I'd felt unsafe, preyed upon.

Every woman had their share of stories. It didn't make it right; it didn't make it easier to deal with. But nothing, no matter how bad it was, could touch Vivian's cruelty. That was the measure of all things for me. Was it worse than that? No. Then I could handle it.

Jake didn't talk as he drove. He'd turned the radio on as soon as we'd left the parking lot behind, but it was turned down so low that I couldn't make out what was playing— whispering hushed voice, low mournful chords. I didn't mind another quiet car ride with him. Leaning back in the seat, I watched Jake. His knuckles were bloody, hands wrapped tight around the steering wheel, gripping it so tight I thought he might rip it from the dashboard.

The truck eventually swung onto the drive leading up to Magnolia House, and I could see the downstairs lights on. I'd turned everything on before I'd left, knowing I would come back in the night and not wanting the house to be dark as well. I was glad I'd done that now, especially now. The place had never been inviting, but for the first time in longer than I could remember. I was happy to see the house, decay and all. I let out a sigh as Jake parked the truck, grateful to be home, the end of the night only a few feet and locked door away.

Before he could say anything, I fumbled my seatbelt off and opened the passenger door. The moment in the truck when his face had been so close to mine, I'd touched his cheek, felt the heat of his skin, and had wanted nothing more than to kiss him, to have him kiss me back. I wanted to forget the gravel parking lot, the empty house, this whole place. I wanted something clean to wash the horror away, to take the taste out of my mouth.

"Thanks for the ride," I said, grabbing my purse and sliding out of the truck.

He was out and around it, beside me almost before I knew it, and shutting the door for me. I couldn't see him clearly; he was an imposing shadowed figure beside me, waiting silently.

We went up the stairs together, my arm brushing his, a cricket singing nearby going quiet as the steps creaked. The scent of jasmine wrapped around us, stronger somehow when I closed my eyes, sweet with unknowable promises. What would I ask of it? What could it give me? I smiled, pain sparking in my lip, mind spinning and making no sense.

I paused at the top, light from the windows around the door catching the edges of Jake's face—a savage and unexpected protector, a brutal avenger.

"Do you have an extra key?" he asked.

"What?"

He gestured at the door. "You got an extra key to get in?"

"Oh, yeah. I think so."

You didn't have to have two brain cells to rub together to discover the hiding place. It wasn't even really a hiding place. Though I hadn't checked it since I'd been home, I was certain there'd still be an extra key in a small hollow in the underside of the railing along the verandah, tucked tight and held fast by rotting wood.

I moved to the spot, feeling for it, an instant of worry that it might be gone, but then relief when I felt it move. Dull brass and older than I was, the key felt heavier than the one the attorney had given me, weighted with memory —my father's key.

"You need to fix that first thing," Jake said.

"What?" I fit the key in the lock, metal against metal, sliding the bolt back.

"Don't put it back. Find a better place to keep a spare key. Has it always been there?"

"Well, yeah." I glanced at him, forehead wrinkling. "It's always been there. Not like anyone ever came out here anyway. At least not when I was a kid. And I guess, since she was in a wheelchair it was easier to leave it for someone instead of answering the door herself."

I pushed the door open, light falling full on our faces, pushing the night out and away, sending it rushing from us. He was watching me, looking at the key in my hand. His brows drew together, worry or irritation, something he worked to smooth away before meeting questioning gaze. The voices of insects and frogs filled my ears, the humid night coming back to get a good look at us, a slow-moving breeze rustling by.

Stepping forward, heart pounding, unable to stop myself, I touched his arm. I held my breath, poised for motion, unsure of what might happen next. I kept coming back to this, an attraction that couldn't be one-sided. There had been something there, in the car, in the parking lot. He'd touched me as if I was something he could ruin, as if I might be something he wanted to keep from breaking.

"Thank you," I said, keeping my eyes lowered. I waited, for his hand to cover mine, for him to speak, for anything at all to happen. "Thank you for everything."

I felt like an idiot for saying it, for not having someone walk me to my car. The feeling intensified when he didn't respond. I stepped back, dropping my hand, smiling tightly, and wincing at the pain in my lip. I jumped when he grasped my chin, lifting my face to the light, turning me slightly so he could see my mouth clearly. He focused on my lip, the line between his brows back, his own mouth pressed into a flat line.

"If I said you should go to the ER, would you?"

I shook my head slightly, and whispered, "No."

His hand moved, the pressure of his fingers gentling as he cupped my face, taking a step toward me. The space between us vanished, gone, each breath hitching as I watched him come closer.

"Emma," he breathed out, the sound more exasperation than anything else. "Next time, let someone walk you to your car."

I nodded, and he let go, turning to go down the steps, back to his truck. For a moment, I thought he'd kiss me. I'd felt it there between us, expectation, a delicate strange bird hatched from a shared moment of bloodletting.

"Jake!" I called as he reached the bottom step, everything on the verge of coming out, desire and confusion and the desperation to keep too many things at bay. Too much, too fast.

"Goodnight, Emma," he said without turning.

He got in the truck, the engine rumbling into life, headlights slashing a path across the yard—magnolia, live oak hung with Spanish moss, the tall grass almost waist-high in places. I watched as red taillights disappeared down the drive, the sound of tires on gravel fading away, leaving the world to the night creatures. Farther away came the sound of slow-moving water, not really there but the kind of thing you'd notice if it were gone. I stood on the verandah, putting off the moment when I'd have to go inside, skin pricking with the heat, every muscle sore, and thought about home.

Home.

Oregon home. Where I'd walk out of my apartment at night and stand under a big sky, gazing up at the stars, the breeze laden with scents of the ocean and spruce. The taste of first snow, smooth coffee, and wildness.

Would it still feel like home when I got back? Or had I already been here too long, wallowing in the strangeness of my childhood? Would every other place in the world feel alien from now on? This Southern place, a mix of the divine and flawed, imperfect while being perfectly what it was. Back of Beyond, Louisiana, my birthplace and spiritual graveyard.

In the yard, beyond the circle of light thrown by the open door, something moved. I froze, heart thumping so hard it hurt, immobilized, waiting. The grass rustled and an armadillo scurried across the small open patch where the truck had been parked. I laughed, the sound false and hollow, forced, with no one else even to hear it.

But I felt better for it anyway. The tension in my shoulders eased, and I went inside, locking the door firmly behind me.

FRIDAY

Time:
The healer
And the
Killer.

- d.j.

CHAPTER THIRTEEN

FRIDAY

Knocking jolted me awake. Midmorning light filled the study, sliding in, coming curiously through the lace curtain to browse the bookshelves and lay languidly on the Persian rug. I listened, wondering if I'd dreamed it, still half asleep. Then it came again, echoing through the house.

I groaned as I sat up, head aching, back sore. I fumbled with the jeans I'd left on the floor the night before, pulling them up, wincing at the sore places they touched, and glanced around for a shirt. The one from the night before smelled gross—full of sweat and dirt and cigarette smoke, and the one I had on was old with a few holes and a stretched-out neck. There was a sloth on it. I grabbed my plain nude bra and snatched the first clean shirt I saw in my suitcase. Nothing special, a light gray crew neck T-shirt. At least it didn't have a sloth on it. Tugging it over my head, I walked quickly to the front door, wondering if it was another nosey old church lady.

"Emma Taylor? You home?"

A male voice, strong and loud, trying to penetrate the

house. Not one I recognized. I turned the lock on the door, wondering if I should have checked the window first to see who it might be, but opened the door anyway. It was becoming a bad habit, opening without looking, and if last night had taught me anything, it was that I couldn't underestimate this place.

A man in a blue police officer uniform stood on the verandah, buzzed light-brown hair and dark eyes, the utility belt he wore had a gun in a black holster and a few other items snapped on. He was in good shape, taller than me, and his eyes swept over my body, up and down and back again. I could tell it wasn't because he thought I was attractive. He was doing an inventory, and already he'd catalogued any visible injuries.

"Good morning, ma'am." He held out a hand and gave me a firm handshake. "I'm Officer Hatcomb."

"Nice to meet you." The night before came rushing back —the man Jake had left in the parking lot, the bite of gravel, the way the attacker's weight had been lifted, suddenly, miraculously. I touched my lip. "What can I do for you?"

"Ryan do that?"

I covered my mouth, not responding.

"Mind if I come in? I've got a few questions about last night. You're not in any kind of trouble," he held up a hand, his face serious but voice kind. "Just want to talk to you for a few minutes."

"Sure," I said, stepping back and letting him through the door. I pushed it closed, leaning against it for a second before turning and gesturing to the sitting room to the right. "Living room is this way, that okay?"

"Perfect," he said, following me, head swiveling this way and that as he took in the house.

"Can I get you anything? Water or tea? Or I could make some coffee?"

"Don't plan to be there that long, but I appreciate the offer, Ms. Taylor."

I nodded, sinking onto the stiff cushions of the formal sofa—blue and cream damask, magnolia blossoms, and jasmine. I hadn't turned the lights on when we'd come through because there was enough sunshine coming through the windows. It caught in the cut glass of the curio cabinet on the far wall, lingered in the reflections of the brass knickknacks on the delicate writing desk beside the arched entrance. The sofa and matching chairs were antiques, with feet like lions, sharp clawed and dangerous.

Mirrors on the walls showed Officer Hatcomb and a young Vivian—prim and proper, hands folded in her lap—seated together. I looked down at my hands and realized I was the look-alike, an inferior imitation. The longer I lingered, wading through this business of death, the more like her I became.

Somewhere deep in the house, something creaked, timbers settling, floors or walls taking on weight. I looked to the arch, expecting Vivian to be there—beautiful face calm, eyes bright with fury. She'd forbidden me to come into this room, and it had been off-limits for as long as I'd lived in this house.

But that space was empty, and if Officer Hatcomb heard the noise, he gave no sign as he eased down into a chair opposite me, wood creaking, and he glanced down, obviously hoping it would hold his weight. Then he looked me right in the eye—gaze direct, a no-nonsense manner emanating from him.

"You want to tell me what happened last night?"

"Have you..." My voice trailed off, and I brought my

hands together, palm to palm, before returning the to my lap, fighting to keep myself from wringing them together.

"I've spoken with several people. Now I would like to hear what you have to say."

"I went to the Fishing Hole to get of the house for a bit. It's been quiet here, and being around people sounded nice. Um. I sat and read and talked to the bartender and waitress some. Then, uh, I left, and a guy stopped me in the parking lot." I was rambling, not sure how to explain what happened next, not sure what to even say. "He'd talked to me in the bar before that, but I told him I wasn't interested. He didn't take that well. I ended up moving seats and sitting at the bar for a bit. He left me alone after that."

"And the parking lot?"

"He followed me out to my car. He tossed my keys into some bushes just outside the parking area. He said some things." I stopped, breath hitching, heart pounding. It was hard to pull in air, to push it out. I didn't want to think about it. I didn't want to talk about it. The officer waited, watching silently, letting it grow between us, leaving it all for me to fill. I started again, slowly. "And Jake stopped him."

He nodded, pulling a small spiral notebook from his breast pocket and made a note in it with a black pen. I watched his hand move, unable to read it, wondering what it might be. "Are you willing to come down to the station and fill out a report?"

I shook my head, not even having to think about it. He stared at me, face impassive.

"Listen, you haven't lived here in years, and I don't know how much you still talked to your momma, but Jake isn't one of the good guys. Maybe he was acquitted all those years ago, but he killed that girl. And whatever else happened in that parking lot last night, he wasn't the hero."

I nodded, staring at my hands as he spoke. I heard what he was saying, the emotion behind the words, the things he wasn't saying but wanted to.

Stay away from Jake.

"You want to press charges?"

"What?"

"Charges." He indicated my lip. "A blind man could see you've been assaulted. I'm not saying what Jake did was right or wrong, and he's not one of the good guys, but I can understand it. Whatever happened in that parking lot last night isn't okay. But the police should have been the first call. We can fill out a report right here, I got the paperwork in the car, and get the process started."

My head ached, the split lip a sharp stab each time I spoke. I wanted to forget about it, all of it, and leave. "No, I don't want to press charges. I just want to handle everything with the house and go home. I'm hoping to be gone in a few days."

He tapped the pen against the open notebook, eyes narrowed. Finally, he nodded and slipped the pen and notebook back in his pocket. "Okay, well. I'll take care of it. Legally. And if you don't want to press charges, that's your choice, and I can't force you to. But it's the right thing to do, and I'm not going to sugarcoat that."

I nodded, not wanting to say anything else.

"I'm having your car towed here. We'll figure out a set of keys. Or hell, maybe I'll even get lucky and find the set the asshole threw in the bushes. You said it was close?"

"Yeah. I heard them land, but beyond that, I couldn't say where."

"That's fine, no worries if we don't find them. I'll call

the rental company or the dealership up on the interstate about cutting a new set."

"You really don't have to do all that. I mean, I'm grateful, I really am. But I can figure this out."

He held up a hand. "Ma'am, I'm sorry, but you're just going to have to allow me to help you. I'm more than a little irritated you're not pressing charges, and since I can't control that situation, I'm going to do the best I can by you this way. Not to say that we won't make the choice to charge him ourselves. That's always an option."

I nodded, wondering what would happen. I shouldn't feel guilty, none of it was my fault, but I did. "I just want to get back home."

"I can respect that."

"Thank you."

"You're welcome," he said, standing up and glancing down at the creaky chair. "I don't agree with it though. If you change your mind, doesn't matter where or when, I'll get the paperwork started."

"Thank you, Officer Hatcomb."

"Anytime, Ms. Taylor."

I walked with him to the door and out onto the verandah. The morning was calm, and the sky was so blue overhead it reminded me of watercolors and robins' eggs, with not a cloud in sight, birdsong filling the air.

"Hurricane is coming this way, but you'd never know it looking at this pretty day," he said.

"Think it's going to be as bad as they're saying?"

He looked around, the big old house and live oaks draped in Spanish moss, the magnolia tree sprawled out across the lawn, rose and jasmine overgrown everywhere. Then he nodded thoughtfully. "I think it will be for some people. You got a plan for this place?"

"No."

"Well, you might want to come up with one. You're near a lot of water here." He pointed toward the rotting jetty and bayou. "A good-sized waterway too. If we get the amount of rain they're talking, I think you'll have a problem. Not to mention the winds. Those will be something fierce."

Magnolia House had been here for almost two hundred years, and I expected it to stand for another hundred more. But maybe this storm would prove me wrong. And if it did? I looked up at the house, the tangled wreck of it all, everything it represented. It wouldn't bother me one bit if it fell down.

"Ms. Taylor," Officer Hatcomb cleared his throat, face serious. "I'm going to give you a card with all my info, personal cell number too. If you change your mind or you need some help, you let me know. I cannot stress enough that you should keep your distance from certain people. I can see where you might not understand that, but if maybe you get into an uncomfortable position later on, if you understand me, and you need some help, you call. Okay?"

I hesitated, accepting the card he held out, studying it. An official seal on cream heavy cardstock, very formal, and exactly what you'd expect a police officer's card to look like. I rubbed a thumb over the black and gold embossing, considering it.

"I know you don't think he's a good guy." I spoke softly, feeling his irritation between us, because he knew what was coming. "But he did the right thing last night."

"Ma'am. He put that boy in the hospital. You should not have been attacked, I'm sick to my stomach knowing you were. I don't want that going on in my town. But it wasn't handled the way it should have been. The police should have been called, that kid should be sitting in jail right now, waiting to get in front of a judge.

"Instead, you're standing here refusing to press charges with a split lip, and that kid is going to get out of the hospital and do it again somewhere down the line. And that's something you could have an impact on. I want you to think about that.

"Right now, he doesn't have a record, though it's pretty well known he's not real good about taking no for an answer. But I can't charge him if I don't see it and no one officially tells me. Oh, I hear rumors. But nothing that seems to stick to him."

He turned away, after one last hard look, and headed toward his cruiser. I stared down at the card, turning it over in my hand, feeling the edge of it, fine-grained heavy paper. I heard the door to the car open and looked up.

"That tow truck will be here sometime this afternoon with your car, and I'll make sure there are keys."

"Thank you," I called. "I really appreciate it."

"Not a problem. You have a good day, Ms. Taylor." He waved, ducking into his car, pausing before he shut the door. "Put some ice on that lip."

———

The rental car arrived on a flatbed tow truck less than an hour later—the driver honking the horn as he reached the house. I came down the steps, arms crossed, watching as the large sunburned man unloaded it. He wore overalls with a dark-blue shirt and a faded red ball cap with a sports team logo. A red bandanna was half in one pocket, and his work boots were well-worn.

He told me his name was Bill, and he talked constantly.

When the car was sitting on the gravel drive, he had me sign for it and passed me a set of keys.

"Officer Hatcomb found these, which is awful lucky for you. It would've been a pain to get a new set. And this being a rental, they'd probably charge you an arm and a leg. Where did you rent the car from? It's got Texas plates, but I thought maybe if it was local, we'd get you sorted if the keys didn't show up. But here they are! Not to worry then. Though lord only knows why they had it towed. Maybe not enough manpower or time for a pick up or drop off. Lucky for you though either way."

"Yeah, it was," I agreed, studying the keys.

They were the same as before, unchanged by the events of the night.

"And I have to say, Ms. Taylor, how very sorry I am to hear about your mom. Cancer is a tough way to go. Paw Jim had lung cancer, and the chemo just about killed him. But that man was tougher than pig iron. It was the heart attack that got him. So sorry for your loss, ma'am. Heartbreaking stuff."

"Thank you," I said, working to keep my expression placid.

"Sure, sure." He looked over the paperwork I'd signed, double-checking my signature was in the right spot. "We're all set. No offense meant, but I hope we don't run into each other again. Not that you don't seem nice, but with her being freshly departed, as it were, I'd like to avoid the ghost."

"Ghost?" My voice was shaky, and I glanced over my shoulder to the house. The front door was open—the interior shadowed beyond, an observer, a consciousness lurking beneath the facade. Jasmine vines swayed, and a robin began to sing, the building seeming to shiver as a breeze touched it.

"One hundred and ten percent, ma'am. You would never believe how long Paw Jim stuck around for. Moving Sweet Gran's teeth in the night, blowing out the pilot light on the gas. He was trouble with a capital T."

I nodded, not sure how to respond to the flood of information. I thanked him again for dropping the car off, and he touched the bill of his ball cap and gave me a jaunty bow. He kept up the chatter after he'd told me to have a nice day and headed back to his truck.

Gripping the keys in one hand, I waved goodbye with the other. The car eased the tension in my shoulders, the ache at the back of my head gone. But a heaviness remained. The house, the contents of the rooms, waited for me. I couldn't face it. I kept running away, avoiding those empty rooms, and I knew I should stay.

All of it would be here when I got back.

You always were a coward.

Vivian's voice this time, sharp as poison darts.

"There's nothing wrong with a strategic retreat," I said loud, self-soothing.

But I wasn't being honest with myself. I wanted to find Jake.

Running inside, I grabbed my purse, making sure everything was there—wallet, useless phone with no reception, and sunglasses. I told myself I was going into town. I'd pick up a few groceries for the half-empty refrigerator—something fresh, apples and sweet strawberries, vanilla creamer for my coffee, sugar for the iced tea. Then I could drive aimlessly, windows down and music loud; I would enjoy the freedom the car offered.

Excitement flowed through me, gathering in my stomach, butterflies unfolding delicate wings.

But I didn't stop when I passed the grocery store. I kept driving, letting my hands take me where I wanted to go. Refusing to examine the desire that had filled me as soon as my foot touched the gas pedal.

The mechanic shop had its bay doors open and a blinking sign lit up in the window of the little office. I pulled into the lot, classic rock greeting me as soon as I opened my car door. Bad idea or good, I had committed.

Josh came out from one of the open doors, meeting me halfway. He nodded to the car and asked, "Everything okay with it?"

"Yeah, yeah it's good. I was hoping Jake would be working today."

"Nah, he's off Friday, Saturday, and Sundays. He might be moving furniture for those antique people though. Or home." He studied me thoughtfully, taking in my split lip and dark circles beneath my eyes. "I heard about last night. You need to get a hold of him?"

I nodded. "I was hoping to. Do you have his address?"

"An address?" An eyebrow went up, surprise all over his face.

"For Jake?"

"Yeah, I got his address. Hold on a second. I've got it written down in the office. You wanna come in and get out of the heat? You want a coke?"

"No thanks, I'm good."

"Well, to be honest, you don't look it. I'll grab you that coke."

"Thanks," I said, smiling a little and touching my bottom lip to ease the sting.

He waved a hand, urging me to follow, and I went with

him to the small office. Another office, another desk and set of chairs. Unlike the others I'd seen over the last few days, this one was a mess—stacks of paperwork and car manuals covered every surface, oily car parts perched on top. There was a collection of mugs grouped around an old coffee machine and a few empty coke cans scattered throughout.

A door was open between the office and the shop, the sound of heavy power tools and music filling the room. An AC unit in the window was doing its best to cool the space, but it only managed to ruffle the paperwork and spread the scent of oil and gasoline.

"Have a seat," he said, plopping into the cracked leather chair behind the desk.

I took the single plastic chair shoved in the corner for visitors, moving a stack of car manuals to the floor. As I got settled, Josh reached under his desk and dug around.

"Here we are." He held out a cold can, and I took it. "Perks of being the boss around here. My own private mini fridge under the desk."

"Must come in handy," I said.

"Well, you'd think it would, but Bobby out there keeps drinking my cokes and leaving me quarters everywhere." He nodded toward the mason jar full of silver on the bookshelf behind him as he rolled the mouse around to wake the computer up. "I'd rather he just replace the coke and save me a trip to the store."

"That's fair," I agreed, popping the top, enjoying the fizz of bubbles. I sipped it slowly, the cold can soothing against my lip.

"I've got it Jake's info here somewhere," he said, clicking through things until he found what he was looking for. Grabbing a pen from the mess on the desk he scribbled the address on a yellow sticky note. "Before I hand this over, I need to clear some things up."

"Okay," I said warily, gripping the can so tight it caved in a bit.

"Jake isn't the man all those busybodies in town say he is." He gave me a stern look. "And I don't think you're the woman your mom said you were. But people talk, you get that right? And at the end of this, you're leaving, and he isn't."

I swallowed, nodding.

"I know I sound like a mother hen, but I can't help it. Jake is like a little brother to me, and after everything that's happened, someone needs to look out for him. Hatcomb has been asking questions about last night. And now everyone is talking again, not like they ever stopped though. I'm just asking that you not add fuel to the fire if you can help it. Don't let anyone think Jake did that to your lip."

"But Officer Hatcomb knows it wasn't—" I began, rushing to defend myself, to defend Jake.

"I know it," he sighed. "People in this town have a hard time letting go of the past. A lot of them are just plain stupid and wouldn't know the truth if it hit them with a two-by-four. It's easy to paint him as the villain. I think you might know a little bit about how that feels."

I nodded.

"Now," he said, leaning back in his chair and watching me with curiosity. "It's a bit hard to find. You wanna go down the road slow or you'll miss the turn. It's just a single lane in some trees, there's an old green mailbox with faded numbers and that's it. Just head on down to the stop sign out here and turn left. You'll go aways before you see it."

"Thanks," I said, standing and heading for the door. "I appreciate it."

"Not a problem." He stood and came around the desk, holding the door open for me. "Come on back if you have any car issues, and we'll get you fixed up."

"I will. Thank you."

If he had questions, he kept them to himself. But I was asking my own. Was thanking Jake the only reason I wanted to see him? What did I think would happen if I went out there? What would it accomplish? He'd been nice, sort of, but hadn't seemed interested. Not in the way I'd found myself being interested in him.

I was drawn to him. It was the wrong time, the wrong place. But I didn't care. It was complicated and messy, and last night had been a nightmare, but when he'd stood on the verandah with me, everything else had faded from my mind.

My skin prickled as I got back behind the wheel, cranking the air conditioning up as high as it would go. Everything was hot here, the moments between car and building, building and car, as brief as they were, were enough to make me sweat. I'd forgotten all of this after living on the West Coast for so long. Everything got so close here, invading your private space, inspecting you with hot velvet fingers—the heat, the vegetation, the insects, and memories.

Hello, Emma, good to see you again. Let me get a good look at you. You've been away for so long. Do you remember me now?

I followed Josh's directions, turning at the stop sign and taking the least traveled path. The two-lane road was narrow and full of potholes and bad patches. Some of the repairs went down the middle, and the yellow dividing line had worn away. The radio cut in and out, the low classic rock eventually turning to white noise and the occasional high-pitched hiss. I shut it off, the hum of tires on asphalt and the blast of the air conditioning filling my ears.

Trees and underbrush crowded the road, threatening to leave the verges, to spread roots into gray asphalt and break it up piece by piece. Tall bald cypress, feathery fronds reaching out, interlocked and tangled above me. The world was made up of sunshine and shadow, changeable and mysterious, and I traveled through it, suspended in the moment—like a butterfly in sweet molasses or tupelo honey. The scents of decayed vegetation rushed in through the windows, fresh grass, and slow-moving water.

I kept an eye out for the mailbox, worried I'd miss it, slowing well below the forty-five speed limit. Even going thirty, I missed the turn, the narrow gap between the trees flashing past—a tunnel of vegetation hinted at then gone. I hit the brakes, checked my rearview mirror, and then carefully reversed, hoping no one else would come speeding up behind me.

The mailbox listed to the right, caught in the middle of a slow-motion fall. It was barely visible from the road, and I wondered if the mail carrier even bothered to stop. It would be a chore to get out of the car and pray this wasn't the day the whole thing slid down the embankment to be greeted by alligators and curious mud hens.

It was swampland here—rich and dark, vibrant green with pale purple water hyacinth. Civilization, whatever that was, ended with the mailbox. A raised narrow road, barely wide enough for a car, wove into the trees, twisting, the end unseen and unknowable. Water lay on either side, bald cypress rising from it, small plants floating on the surface.

I eased the car forward, bumping along, clenching the

steering wheel and hoping I wouldn't mess up a tire. The swamp was so close here, eating away at the embankment. Did it ever flood here? Was Jake worried about the impending hurricane? Maybe that would be a good conversation opener. My stomach flip-flopped, and I had no idea what I was going to say when I saw him.

Hey, thanks for taking me home last night. I'm here uninvited, and maybe I should have called first. But here I am!

The narrow drive snaked through the swamp, and with each bend I expected to see a house. But it kept going, deeper into the trees, farther and farther away from the little bit of familiarity the beat-up road behind me offered.

As I went along, the trees thinned, water rising, cypress sending up knobby knees, the water covered here and there with green growing things. Patches of sunlight made it through, columns of light that fell on calm water.

Then a weatherworn cabin came into view, small beneath the trees, with a wide porch that wrapped all the way around. To the right, a short walkway leading to a dock, a clear channel leading off into deeper water. His truck sat in the small turnaround space in front, pointed toward the road and taking up all the space. He obviously wasn't expecting anyone else to come out here.

I parked in the middle of the little road, blocking the truck in, but not sure what else to do. Taking a deep breath, wondering what I would say. I wouldn't know until he stood in front of me. There was only one way to find out. I eased out of the car and shut the door, the sharp sound breaking through the stillness. I watched the cabin, sure he must have seen or heard me coming and was waiting for the front door to open.

But no one appeared, and I couldn't take the pounding in my chest any longer.

What're you waiting for?

I crossed quickly to the cabin, up the creaking wooden steps, and knocked on the screen door. There was no way I was going back now. The old door behind the screen was closed, but the top half was clear glass, and I could see down a short narrow hall. To the right was the living room and to the left the kitchen, and out of sight must be the bedroom and bathroom. The cabin wasn't big enough to hold more.

The interior was sparse. The wooden floor looked new, maybe a project he'd completed recently, with a glossy shine that hinted at cleanliness and polish. The walls were pale blue, recalling afternoon skies and clear tropical waters, and I could just see the corner of a painting that hung above the overstuffed leather sofa.

I knocked again, glass rattling, touching my tongue to the sore place on my lip as I waited for him to appear from the back of the house. Nothing moved. Silence reigned, absolute, but not the kind where someone lurked, waiting for the visitor to leave. The house felt empty. No one was home.

Glancing at the truck, I knocked again. Third time's a charm. Three wishes. Good and bad things come in threes. My dad believed in the power of three. I guess I did too. The empty house continued to be empty.

His truck was here, where else would he be? I'd worked myself up, gotten his address, and come all this way only to find him gone. I'd risked my life coming down this crumbling dirt track pretending to be a road to stand here and knock on his door. The least he could have done was be home. It was the only polite option. Where was his Southern hospitality?

I didn't want to leave yet, surprised at the amount of

disappointment filling me—more than I had any right to feel. He hadn't gone out of his way to be friendly beyond the rescue last night. Maybe he was back there hiding and waiting for me to vacate his porch.

I surveyed the property. There was a window on either side of the door, and a pair of rubber boots tucked beneath a short bench. I wandered around the corner of the cabin to get a look at the dock. A Deepfreeze hummed, and there were white five-gallon buckets stacked neatly in pairs, fishing poles, several crawdad traps, and worn floats. There was one window on this side of the cabin, on the far corner, maybe a bedroom. A set of steps led down, a wooden walkway connecting the house and dock.

There was a light pole with a single industrial light that shone warmly, even in the daylight. The dock had metal moorings, and there were several carefully wound ropes. The area looked taken of and tidy. He must have a fishing boat.

I returned to the car, hoping there was something I could use to leave a note. I lucked out, finding a pen in the cup holder with the medallion of Saint Rita of Cascia. I paused, considering it. Right time, right place. Josh had said something like that, right?

Quickly, I scribbled a note. I'd tuck it between the glass and screen door.

A rumble came across the water, the uniform reverberation of a small engine reaching me. I stared at the words I'd written, just seven, my heart skipping, picking up.

Thank you for being there last night.

I could leave it. I didn't have to stay, even after coming all this way. I'd wanted to see him, but I'd been a little relieved when he wasn't home. Last night seemed so far away now, in the daylight, at his house.

The house of a man who had murdered a girl.

He'd saved me, rescued me, last night. It sounded dramatic, but that was what he'd done. I'd lain in the gravel listening to the sound his fist hitting that man's face, thudding and wet and bone crunching. Part of me, a deep, secret, dark part of my soul, had wanted it to go on and on. Something inside of me clenched, pulled tight, an unsettling combination of fear and triumph flowing through me.

A moment of hesitation, and then the boat came into sight, Jake sitting at the back with a hand on the tiller of a small engine. The boat was green with a flat bottom, the kind I'd seen people fishing from in the bayous before. He had a dark-blue ball cap on, shading his face so I couldn't make out his expression from this distance.

It was too late to leave now. He'd seen me standing on his porch, all the way out there in the middle of nowhere. It wasn't like I could even pretend I'd been passing by. I'd come here for him. And he knew it. I shrugged, feeling a little bit like a kid getting caught doing something wrong, and sat down on the top step of the cabin to wait. I folded the envelope in half, hiding the words, hands shaking a little with the rush of anticipation.

Jake steered the boat closer, focused on the dock and engine, going through it all and ignoring me. He was purposefully not looking at me, I could see the tautness in his shoulders, the way he made sure he didn't even glance in the direction of the cabin. He stood, boat shifting beneath him, as he secured it to the dock.

I watched as he worked, wondering what he thought about me being here. If the stiffness of his movements was anything to go by, he wasn't exactly pleased. But expectation roiled inside of me, picking up momentum. I wanted more than anything to hear his voice, have his gaze fall on me.

He looked like he'd been fishing for several hot hours already, even though it was barely noon. The khaki cargo shorts he wore appeared worn even from here, the T-shirt faded, and the pair of sneakers muddy. He lifted a fishing rod and white five-gallon bucket from the boat and finally turned to the cabin—turned to me.

"I see you got your car back. You lost?" he asked, walking toward me along the dock with his gear. He continued past me, bringing the smell of hot summer, leaving me with a hint of mud and fish.

I stayed seated, turning to lean against the beam supporting the porch, watching as he put the fishing rod in its place, setting the bucket on top of the Deepfreeze. Whatever had been there the night before, the tenderness was gone. But I'd half expected it. Last night was a memory. Today he was back to being a bit of an asshole. None of that altered the tension between us, a taut line humming with expectation.

"Not lost," I said, watching his back, willing him to turn to me, to face me.

I wanted to tell him what Officer Hatcomb had said. Jake had killed that girl. I didn't believe it. But I wanted Jake to say it—tell me it wasn't true. I wanted it more than I had any right to. He owed me nothing. And after last night, I owed him everything. And I wanted him. It was impossible to ignore it. Not now, not when was within reach.

"I came out to say thank you," I said.

"It's not necessary." He turned to me, arms crossed, and focused out across the water.

"It is. I don't know what would have happened to me if

you hadn't saved me." I shrugged and tried to shake it off. "Well, I do know. But you were there."

He made a noise, dismissing the word *saved*.

"Jake," I stood, brushing dirt off my backside and sighing. "Thank you. You don't have to accept it, but I'm offering it anyway."

His blue eyes swept over my face, a flash of emotion there and gone. "I wouldn't thank me just yet. I'm sure someone will want to ask you some questions about last night. I've already gotten a phone call."

Had Officer Hatcomb spoken to him first then? His warning rolled through me. *He's a killer.*

"I've talked to someone already," I said. "An officer came to the house."

Jake gave a stiff nod and turned away, back to the bucket. He pulled out several fish, already gutted, flashing pink-white insides as he laid them inside the Deepfreeze. There was a tub of wet wipes tucked between the crawfish traps, and he grabbed a few, carefully cleaning his hands.

"You pressing charges?" he asked.

"No." I shook my head and shrugged. "I just want to get out of here."

"Probably a good thing," he said. "Getting out of town, I mean."

"Yeah. But what about you? What was your phone call about?"

"The guy ended up in the hospital with a concussion and a busted nose."

"Is he pressing charges against you?"

"No," Jake hesitated, adding, "and Officer Hatcomb isn't going to file any. I guess Ryan admitted to harassing you, and the waitress and bartender witnessed it in the bar. Maybe it's not right, but I guess it'll pass for justice for right now. Especially if you're not taking him to court."

"No, I just—"

"Want to get out," he said, finishing my sentence. "I know the feeling. How soon are you leaving?"

A laugh escaped me—small and bittersweet. "In a hurry to see me gone?"

"I wouldn't be here if I didn't have to be." He shrugged.

"Why do you have to be?"

"And why are you here, Emma?" Jack met my eyes, a line between his brows. My heart thudded, frozen with the intensity in his voice, the expression on his face.

"I came to tell you—"

"Not my house." He pointed at the dirt beneath our feet. "Here, in Back of Beyond?"

"For—"

"A dead woman?"

I nodded.

"Maybe that's why I've stayed."

We stared at each other, the sharp edges of his words shivering in the silence.

"When are the services?" he asked abruptly.

"What?" My brow wrinkled; I'd been caught off guard by the change of subject.

"The services for Vivian. Viewing and burial?"

"Oh, right." I hesitated. "Um. Viewing is tomorrow, and services are Sunday."

"Saturday and Sunday night, huh? Your mom pick out the days?"

A sharp laugh escaped me, bitterness on my tongue. "Yeah, actually she did."

"Sounds just about right."

"You knew her pretty well then?" My stomach dropped,

a shiver traveling across my skin as I watched him, waiting. How had he known Vivian? The woman the whole town had loved and the man they all hated.

"Not really." He looked down at the wad of cleaning wipes in his hand, flexing his fingers. "But it was obvious she enjoyed being the center of attention. Can't get much more attention in this place than booking the church on a Sunday."

Rooms of curious and distrustful people, each one observing every move, watching for tears. They would be furious in their happiness; it would be a great victory to see Vivian's daughter turn out to be exactly who they thought she was. Cold. Uncaring. Selfish.

It would give them something else to talk about for the next twenty years. These people thought they knew her. Some had considered themselves friends. Pastor Roberts would watch me with that cold expression, disgust in every line of his body, as he talked about how Vivian Taylor had been a gift from God.

"Are you going?" I asked, suddenly desperate not to be there alone. "Would you come?"

Jake met my gaze, eyes deep blue and unreadable. Anything he thought or felt, he kept to himself. There was nothing but his blank expression. Not even a question. I closed the space between us, only a few steps, and reached out tentatively, fingertips to his forearm. He looked down at my hand and then up at my face.

"If you'd like me to."

"I would like you to be there." I pulled away, trying to smooth over the raw gratefulness that suddenly filled me. "I don't want to be alone."

"You won't be alone," he said. "There will be—"

"No," I shook my head. He didn't get it. He hadn't really

known her after all. Maybe he'd never experienced that special kind of excruciating loneliness that could come from someone who was supposed to love you but didn't. How they could make you feel small and isolated, convince you that no one would ever listen, no one would believe anything you had to say.

"I'll be there, Emma."

The way he said my name melted through me, sinking into my muscle and bone. I wanted to lean into him and feel his arms go around me. But right now, I'd have to settle for him agreeing to come to the services.

"Thank you," I said, turning toward the car, and fumbling for my keys. "I'll see you there."

He made a noise of agreement as I walked away, and I could feel him watching me. I wondered what it was he thought about. Not me, not wanting me, but about Vivian and myself maybe, wondering why a stranger would ask another stranger to be there for a mother's funeral. Not a mother though. Vivian.

When I got to the car, he was out of sight, around the back of the cabin or inside, or just vanished into thin air. I held my breath as I turned the key, letting it out when the engine started. I eased down the gravel track, checking the review only once, hoping he might be there—to have it mean something.

Instead, I drove on without a witness, heading back toward the harsh reality of Back of Beyond and the bubbling mess Vivian had left for me.

SATURDAY

Be patient and tough:
someday this pain will be useful to you.

- Ovid

CHAPTER FOURTEEN

SATURDAY

The parking lot at the funeral home was full: dusty pickups and recently washed Lincolns, one or two beaters, dented with worn paint. I didn't know who they all belonged to. But I didn't need to know. I might recognize some of the people, but none were friends. There weren't going to be any friendly hellos or welcoming glances when I got in there.

I parked and sat in the car, the engine humming as the air conditioner blasted icy air in my face. My stomach rumbled, a dull ache settling in, and I fumbled in my purse for an antacid. I hadn't eaten much that day, but I hadn't been hungry either. The idea of food made me nauseous. Maybe I would have felt better walking in there with a full stomach, but it was too late now. I chewed a few chalky tabs, gulping down half a bottle of water that was warm from having sat in the car for too long.

Now or never.

It had to be now. I got out of the rental and shouldered my purse, tugged my top into place, and set off across the lot toward the front door. The white building threw back the sun, the glaringly white siding shimmering with evening heat. Sweat prickled between my shoulder blades and beneath my arms, the places where my bra touched skin warming. I moved faster, wanting to get into the air conditioning, and hoping no one would get close enough to realize I'd forgotten deodorant.

Pausing at the door, I sucked in a breath and settled my face into a pleasant blankness. neither happy or sad, not angry or unforgiving. I practiced the careful lack of emotion I'd cultivated as a child. It had helped me then. It was going to help me now.

I pulled the door open and stepped into a room full of whispered conversations. There were so many people, too many to count at first glance, and I hesitated on the threshold. Several faces turned to me, suspicion in their gazes, mouths puckered around sour thoughts. Men wearing Sunday clothes and women with high heels and cardigans with mother-of-pearl buttons.

"Ms. Taylor," Mr. Laurent said, moving forward to take my hand. "Please accept my deepest condolences. Let me take you to your momma."

I nodded, murmuring a *thank you,* and avoided meeting anyone else's eyes. I could feel them on me, searching for a weak spot, wondering what it might take to teach me a lesson. They were those kinds of people, determined to right an injustice, set on letting the ungrateful child know her place in all of this.

But Vivian had never altered her will or estate. She could have removed me at any point, disowned me, banished me from her life. Maybe they didn't know that. Maybe they thought I was here for whatever money she had left, whatever might be valuable in Magnolia House. But of course, it was the house. They'd all think I was here for that old place. None of them would believe me if I said I didn't want it. And Vivian had known. She'd known I'd come home, summoned by a sense of duty, blood being thicker than water, and with just enough time passed between the going and the returning to dull the edges of memory, let me forget how truly terrible it had been.

Being back here reminded me of it all. Things I'd buried had risen to the surface of my mind, my heart in my throat, tears trembling on lashes. That's why she'd never disowned me. She'd wanted me to come back and relive all of this again. She'd forced open old wounds and left them for the people of this town to inspect.

I walked through clouds of powdery perfume, the scent of aftershave, and green flowers. Cold air hissed through the vents, the air conditioner working overtime to fill the space with icy air. Several conversations were happening at once, little groups of people huddled together, watching as the director led me to a set of closed doors.

"I thought you should have a moment alone with her before I opened the doors to everyone else. She's been waiting for you."

He smiled at me, trying to be kind, but his words sunk through me like lead.

"You didn't have to wait for me," I stammered, feeling the room at my back, full of judgment and vicious eyes. "All of these people…"

"Of course we did." He pulled one of the doors back, a pocket door that slid into the wall, revealing a dim room beyond. "I'll give you a moment before I open the room up for everyone else."

"Thank you," I said, stretching my cheeks to mimic a smile.

My eyes shifted to the room, the casket lit by overhead

lights while the rest of the room was dark. I stepped inside, the conversation and cool air were cut off as he pulled the door shut behind me, leaving me in an empty room. An almost empty room. I sucked in a breath and set my shoulders back, the sweat still not dry, and walked down the aisle to Vivian.

The lid of the casket was open, silk lining a deep rich red, the color fresh blood and day-old poppies, the color on the verge of going dark and congealing. She lay nestled in it, her red dress a few shades lighter, dark hair perfectly curled around her face. A beautiful woman even in death. She'd cultivated a certain look, an old-school Hollywood charm, and she'd mastered it. I envied her for the ease with which she moved through the world, this beautiful untouchable woman. Like a snake moving through grass.

I didn't want to approach the casket, didn't need to see how thickly the makeup was caked on, how the false eyelashes might be barely attached, or if those perfect hands should have had a manicure first. I sat heavily in the front row, into a seat right on the aisle, my body half turned to run and escape.

Flowers ringed the casket, giant sprays of roses in various shades of red and pink, the purple blue of irises with yellow throats, and spots of collected baby's breath. There were house plants in woven baskets with red bows, white cards stuck on plastic sticks protruding like sharp-edged blossoms, and vases full of mixed bouquets. Off to the side was a large wreath of magnolia flowers, creamy white with deep glossy leaves, the lemony scent seeping into the room.

Hushed voices carried from the room behind me, coming from under the door and between the cracks. I pressed my hands flat to my knees, putting pressure on them to stop the tremble.

"Don't you want to say goodbye?"

I jumped, half turning in my chair, to see the door opening and Pastor Roberts stepping through. The room brightened for an instant, light from the room beyond racing down the aisle but stopping short of the casket. He turned to shut it behind him with a solid click, a final sound, the punctuation to his question. He clasped his hands in front of him, staring at me, waiting.

"I've said my goodbyes."

"Have you?"

He was moving before I could react, at my side in a few swift strides and reaching for me, pulling me up and dragging me forward. I stumbled, and he righted me, kept me on my feet, and only stopped when were beside the casket, staring down into Vivian's face. My hip touched the polished wood, real and solid, and so much closer than I'd planned to be. The pastor's grip on my arm pinched, fingers digging into soft flesh, so near to me that I could smell the spicy cologne he wore, something dark and woodsy and at odds with the room full of roses.

"You should apologize."

"What?" I tried to pull away, but his grip tightened.

"You should apologize." He repeated, staring at Vivian, granite and steel in his voice. "She did everything for you. Everything after your father died. And this is how you repay her?

"Running away, abandoning her, and now you can't even honor her final wishes. She'd be horrified. Your father would be disappointed. You are an ungrateful and selfish child."

I listened in stunned silence, the tremble I'd been

fighting to control taking over, anger and shame heating me from the inside. It was all true. I'd abandoned her, turned my back on blood, and run as far away as possible, all the way across the country, until I'd been stopped by a rocky coastline, the sea a barrier I couldn't cross.

"You have no idea what you're talking about," I whispered.

"I'm sorry, I didn't mean to interrupt." A woman's voice broke across us, the door open behind her, other curious faces looking in. "I believe the viewing hours have started?"

I didn't know her, but there was something familiar about her. In her voice and around her eyes, a tilt I almost recognized. She watched us curiously, eyes coming to rest on the pastor's hard fingers digging into my upper arm. His grip relaxed under her gaze, dropping away like an iron shackle, and I placed my hand over the spot and took a step back.

"Not at all," he said with a smile. Everything about him changed with the words; he was now a pleasant man who had come to mourn a member of his flock, offering comfort to the only child of the deceased. "I'm Pastor Roberts. It's so good of you to come to pay your respects. I know it would have meant the world to Vivian."

The woman glanced between us, raising an eyebrow at me in question. I gave her a tight smile and stepped back, leaving them together as I went to sit in the very back of the room. The corner was dimmer here, and I could remain in the shadows until I could comfortably leave. I wanted to go right now, walk out without a backward glance, but the idea of them gossiping even more than they were already got under my skin. In a lot of ways, I'd reverted in coming back here, slipped into the habits of my childhood thoughtlessly, becoming again the little girl full of doubt and fear.

I watched the woman as she looked down at Vivian, face full of an emotion I couldn't name. Not sadness or any kindness, but something hard.

"She's at peace now," Pastor Roberts said.

"I'm sure she is," the woman replied, a sourness beneath her words.

His brows drew together. "I'm sorry, but you look very familiar, but I don't believe we've met before. Are you related to Mrs. Taylor? May I ask your name?"

"No."

The woman gave Vivian one last look and turned her back on the pastor, striding up the aisle toward the open door without looking back. I watched her go, curiosity getting the better of me, wondering how this stranger might have known Vivian. She was the first person who appeared to dislike her.

The pastor watched her go as well, thoughtful, eyes narrowed. I turned away before he could turn his gaze on me, studying my hands folded carefully in my lap. Others began to file in now, clustering around the casket, telling each other how wonderful Vivian had been. The pastor greeted each person, shaking hands and squeezing shoulders gently, comforting gestures so at odds with the way he'd touched me.

I let him take on the role of family. If I'd cared more, I would have been the one up there, thanking each person for their condolences. But I couldn't stand to hear it anymore, the same thing said a hundred different ways over and over. A few people sat in the chairs, sitting together in small groups, talking softly about the dead woman in the room. I caught snippets of conversation here and there.

The woman they spoke about was unrecognizable to

me. Who they thought she was versus the reality shocked me. And what would they think about her if they knew the truth? But no, they wouldn't accept it. Their minds were set when it came to me.

"Are you Emma Taylor?"

I looked up at the question, meeting the eyes of a thin young man, brown hair going long, and gold-rimmed glasses perched on his nose. He smiled at me and held out a hand, waiting for me to take it.

"Yes."

"It's a pleasure to meet you. I'm Andrew Barns."

"Andrew?"

The church ladies had mentioned him, a part-time helper, someone to look in on Vivian. I took his hand, his grip strong and the smile he gave me unwavering.

"Mind if I sit?" He gestured at the chair beside me.

"No, not at all." I looked around the room. A few people had noticed he'd taken a seat beside me, but most were too busy sharing stories about the recently departed, bonding over the lovely woman they were all sure she'd been. "A few members of the church told me you were a home health aide? You helped look after Vivian at the end?"

He nodded, glancing at me and then around the room, rubbing his palms down his khakis, smoothing the fabric down. For a moment his glasses reflected the over-lit casket and flowers, an invisible watcher. *What do you see?*

"Yes, I was. I'm so sorry for your loss."

"Thank you," I said, closing my mouth tightly over the protest he didn't need to hear. "Were you close?"

"Not exactly."

My eyebrows rose at the edge in his voice. No, he hadn't been an admirer. The second person here today who hadn't bought into her bullshit. It was a surprise, a refreshing bright point in the murky shadows of this room. It was full now. I wasn't sure when it had happened. I'd been so focused on memory, sifting through my past, searching for the buried pieces. Andrew was a welcome distraction.

"You're one of the few then," I said. "Everyone seemed to be close to her."

Andrew glanced around the room before leaning toward me, glasses flashing, one hand balling into a fist against this thigh.

"I don't think she was who she said she was." His whisper brushed past me, traveling over the raised hairs on my arm, lingering in my ear. "She tried to make me believe she was something else. A different kind of person. Do you know what I'm talking about?"

I nodded, focusing on the casket and the people coming and going. Pastor Roberts was speaking softly to an older woman—gray hair, blue blouse, matching purse. She turned to me, pale eyes full of anger, and I hastily looked away. I could feel their eyes, harsh intention, watching as the young man beside me whispered.

"I would come by the house and things would be moved, small things, things she would ask me for help with when I was there. I didn't notice right away, but then it was so obvious once I did."

"What do you mean?"

I couldn't wrap my head around what he was trying to tell me. It was there, something important under the urgency in his voice, wrapped up in his inability to lay it out as clearly as possible.

"When the hospital initially set up the services, I was told she was paraplegic and diagnosed with stage four breast cancer. She wasn't treating it, there was just pain management, and all I really had to do was stop by the house and help with small things. The nurses would handle the meds. I saw them a handful of times, but they never stayed long. I don't think they realized it."

"Realized what?"

"She wasn't paralyzed."

My heart froze.

"What?" I choked on the word, struggling to breathe as my chest tightened. Not paralyzed. Not dependent. Not a victim. Her pale face and smiling eyes, the pleasure there as Pastor Roberts's hand connected with my cheek. "Are you sure?"

He nodded, head continuing to move, eyes lit with manic energy. He was coming clean, passing on a weight he could no longer carry. I recognized it, understanding how badly he needed to be free of the secret. I'd felt like that before.

"I wasn't one hundred percent sure until the last visit. I'd asked one of the visiting nurses if she'd noticed anything odd. I only had suspicions about Vivian at that point. Nothing solid. And the nurse said she'd seen nothing out of the usual. I didn't know how to tell her what I'd seen, how to explain it. And I was afraid they'd think I was crazy. They would have told me it was just the old house. Your mom had them all wrapped around her finger. She'd had me wrapped around her finger."

Your mom.

"What happened?" I turned to him, placing a hand on his arm, hoping to steady us both. His leg bounced, eyes searching my face, intent and considering my question. I squeezed his arm slightly. "Tell me what happened."

He began to speak, words coming carefully, each maneuvered into place after several seconds of deliberation. He kept his voice low, and I leaned toward him, desperate to catch every last breath.

"I came Mondays, Wednesdays, and Fridays. Every week. I did for months. I offered to come by on the weekends, but Vivian set the schedule. It took weeks to pick up on the little things, but then I started to pay attention, to notice. She was so...distracting." He paused, closing his eyes, swallowing. "She liked attention, you know? So things were good as long as I fawned over her. But the expression I'd catch on her face sometimes when she didn't realize I was watching her. There wasn't anything warm in her expression."

Across the room a woman laughed. I stopped breathing. Had it been Vivian? No. She was dead. She was right there, dead in a casket, pumped full of embalming fluid and smelling like a dead thing. Vivian was dead.

Am I?

I shook my head, trying to understand. "You said she wasn't paralyzed. But I grew up in that house, with her. She was in a car accident when I was a child. My dad died."

"She wasn't." He gripped my hand, fingers digging into my flesh, his face pale. "I came on a Sunday. I wasn't scheduled, but I'd called, and no one answered. I had a last-minute appointment to deal with on Monday, and I wasn't going to make it. When I got there, I knocked, but no one answered, so I let myself in with the key she'd given me.

"Usually, I'd find her in the sitting room or maybe the dining room, with paperwork or her diary. She was always writing. She said she wrote letters to all her old friends from college. But I couldn't find her. She wasn't anywhere. I called out for her, thinking maybe she was in the restroom or her bedroom, but no one answered."

He shivered, closing his eyes, and let out a breath.

"I finally checked her room. I knocked before opening the door, worried maybe she'd fallen and hurt herself. Anything could have happened. And she was on so much pain medication for the cancer. She wasn't in her room."

I squeezed my hands together, knuckles white, my pulse racing. I nodded for him to go on, to put words to the horror creeping up on me—goose flesh rose all over me, hair standing on end.

"The wheelchair was beside the dressing table."

I could see her room, empty but expectant, knowing at any moment the woman of the house would come breezing in on a cloud of perfume. She'd moved so gracefully when I was small. So light on her feet. I'd watched her dance once at one of the house parties—a swirl of floral summer cotton, hair fanning out around her face as she twirled, lovely hand to her throat as she laughed, ruby flashing. Why would she have given that up? Her freedom. Her independence. Her ability to move through the world without hindrance or pain.

But she'd found another kind of freedom after the accident. The town had curled around her like a dying blossom, there in every way possible, fawning and petting the beautiful broken woman. She was only happy if everyone was watching her.

"What happened then?" I asked softly.

"It was so quiet in the house, but it didn't feel empty. I was going down the hall, toward the front door, and I thought I heard someone walking around upstairs." His voice trailed off into a whisper and he added, "Vivian."

"Did you check?"

He shook his head. "I kept going. It didn't feel right. There was something off. All the hair on my body stood up, and my heart was racing. I had to get out of the house. If I stayed, if I even turned around, something bad was going to happen.

"I went through the foyer and hurried for the front door. But then I heard something right behind me. At the top of the stairs. Like someone had come to stand there as quietly as possible. I didn't stop. I kept going. I didn't even shut the door behind me. I got in my car and never even looked in the rearview mirror."

He expelled a heavy breath, a flush creeping across his cheeks, the threat of tears in his voice. The experience had scared him badly. I knew exactly how he felt.

"I was going to call my boss on Monday and let him know I couldn't go back, but he called me first. Vivian had called and told him she was going to have the nurses come in more often and she wouldn't need me. She told him to thank me for everything and to let me know how much she appreciated my thoughtfulness and discretion."

"You never said anything?"

"I thought about it. I really did. But this whole place loved her, and who was I going to tell? And what would I say? Something weird happened in her house? They'd laugh and say all old houses are haunted or I let my imagination get the better of me." He let go of my arm, pulling back, leaning into the padded chair. "I saw her a few weeks ago. She was sitting in that classic Mercedes on my street, and when I passed her, I thought I'd seen a ghost." He laughed, brittle and tired, reaching up to touch his cheek. "I was so relieved when they told me she'd passed."

"Car? The attorney said she sold."

"Maybe she rented one. Maybe it wasn't her." He shrugged. "But it looked like her."

I leaned toward him, needing to keep this between us,

afraid of anyone in the room overhearing it. "But why are you here? Now?"

"She talked about you," he paused, squeezing his eyes shut as if his head ached. "It wasn't kind. I thought, maybe if you came, I could tell you. If it were me, with this kind of history, I'd want to know."

I nodded, keeping my voice low, the pull of Vivian so strong that it brought her past back to this place—another blossom pulling in tight. "Thank you for telling me."

"You're welcome." He stood, smoothing out his button-up shirt, running a hand over his short hair. "I'm glad I did. I feel better for letting you know."

He might have felt better, but I didn't.

Voices rose and fell in muted conversation around me. The town brought together to mourn an influential figure. But what had she done? The church ladies talked about house parties and volunteering at the church—garage and bake sales, fundraising projects, and organizational skills to rival a five-star general.

It was hard to imagine her doing those things—lowering herself to those simple projects. But maybe she had been those things all along and I'd been too focused on my inner world, the one she shaped by the hour, to see what happened beyond my narrow borders. Still, over-hearing how they spoke of her, the contributions to the community, the mark she'd left on these people, it was hard to reconcile that with the woman I knew.

They chattered like grackles, high-pitched like sparrows, squabbling like blue jays—these busybodies and townsfolk, their gazes hard and suspicious as they passed me over, passed me by. Beady eyes and sharp beaks. I looked down at my hands folded carefully in my lap—

fingers not too tight, not too loose. Calm. Collected. Ladylike.

Emma. Emma. Emma.

Again and again, I heard my name. But it wasn't directed at me; no one was trying to get my attention. It was all about me, to each other, hands covering mouths, backs slightly turned. I couldn't stand it anymore. I stood, ready to leave, unable to bear the pressure of Pastor Roberts any longer.

The room grew quiet, and then all conversation stopped. I glanced to the door, hand in my purse, searching for my keys, and Jake walked in—coming through the doors as if the world was ending and he was there to watch it burn. He wore what he normally did, jeans and a T-shirt, dark hair slightly mussed, as if he'd driven with the windows down on the way here. So casual, glittering blue eyes, face hard and closed off as he scanned the room.

Me. He was looking for *me.*

Our gazes locked, and his face softened, guard slipping, vulnerable to a breathless moment strung between us on a delicate thread. *Let me in.* I smiled, a sharp sting as my lip stretched, the spot tender, and it was only for him—relief and welcome, pleasure at simply seeing his face again. He began to work his way toward me, ignoring the others in the room, the atmosphere dropping, a storm building momentum.

My heart picked up, beating quickly, excitement filling me as I realized his absence had affected me. Even with the strange woman and meeting Andrew, I'd been so alone. Now I wasn't. He smelled like rain and green things, the fresh scent clinging to him and enveloping me as he came to stand beside me.

"You came," I said.

"I said I would." He nodded, turning slightly to keep Vivian at his back. "It started raining, and it took me a little bit more time to get here. Should I have worn a suit?"

"What?" I shook my head. "No. Not at all."

I glanced around the room. The men were wearing nice things, not suits or Sunday best, but more than T-shirts. The women mostly wore dresses or dressy blouses with cardigans. Jake was underdressed, but I didn't care. The only thing that mattered was that he'd shown up for me.

"Ignore them," I said. "Their opinions don't matter."

Sadie appeared at my elbow, latching on to me, grip tight, demanding my attention. Her eyes were locked on Jake, distaste evident, and she didn't bother to whisper.

"Emma, your momma might have had a soft spot for him, but honey, you need to cut him loose. There's no reason in the world for a nice girl like yourself to be associating with a murderer."

"Ma'am, respectfully," Jake held out a hand, his voice even. "You don't know what you're talking about."

"Yes, I do." She puffed up like a chicken—ruffled feathers and small angry eyes. "I know a killer when I see one."

I stared at her, mouth open slightly with shock. A glance around the room told me she was going voice to what they were thinking, what so many of them wanted to say. For whatever reason, they hadn't. Out of respect for the dead? Some kind of honor when it came to Vivian's daughter, no matter how ungrateful she was? But Sadie hadn't hesitated to give her opinion.

Your momma might have had a soft spot for him.

My mind spun, the room darkening at the edges. Anger arrived and passed over me, becoming something else. True fury, screaming rage. It came from the way she spoke about these people like she knew them—Vivian and Jake. As if she might understand better than me how they fit in my life.

I'd wondered how Jake knew Vivian. There was something there, more than just two people living in the same town. All those clippings told me that, the collection of his criminal history, the sad story of his life.

What had she known?

The thought that Vivian could invade even this part of my life, this thing with Jake that wasn't really a thing, made it all worse. This room full of nosey people, the pastor watching with his sanctimonious sneer. And beside me, tall and silent, Jake. He didn't say a word in response. No denial. No asking for quiet. Nothing.

"Emma, honey, come on now. You come on with me. Irene and the ladies are having dinner after this. We'd love for you to join us. Nothing fancy, just some fried catfish. We've got some wonderful stories about Vivian to share. I'm sure you've got a few of your own."

Sadie tried to coax me closer, keeping her voice gentle, her grip on my arm tight. Other voices joined her, no one I recognized, entreating softly, their sharp edges concealed in kind words. I shook my head, stepping away, but she refused to release me.

"Jake White is a murderer. Plain and simple." Irene joined Sadie, pale eyes accusing, arms crossed over her skinny chest. Her gaze went from my face to his, her tone hardening. "I know you killed Alice, Jake. The whole town does. They'll figure out another way to bring charges against you. And when they do, I'll be right there in court. They'll kill you dead, Jake White. I'll be there to see it."

Her words revolted me, my stomach churning with acid, the urge to cry overtaking me. Not with sadness, but anger. I'd had enough. I peeled Sadie's fingers from my arm, stepping out of reach when she moved to reclaim her hold. I turned to Jake, to offer support or comfort, but he had his back to the room, poised to leave.

Sadie and Irene continued, loudly proclaiming his assumed guilt, poised to leave. Others began to whisper, avid hungry gazes taking it all in, reveling in the deliciousness of the scene. Vivian in her nest of red satin wearing her favorite red dress, the pastor overseeing it all, and the town murderer come to destroy their peace, their mourning.

And it had been her daughter, me, who had brought him here.

"Stop it," I said, looking from one woman to the other, then around the room. "What's wrong with you?"

"We're looking out for you," Irene hissed. "Just like your momma would have if she were here."

I pointed to the casket. "She is here. Right there. And I really don't think she cares as much as you think she does."

Silence spread, expanding outward, moving through the room—bomb or bloom, unfurling, continuing, exploding. I covered my mouth. As shocked as they were by what I'd said. Pastor Roberts began to make his way toward us, excusing himself through the crowd.

When had it gotten so large? When had all these people arrived?

"Emma." Jake's voice cut across the silence, his face set, giving nothing away. "Do you want a ride?"

"No," Sadie hissed. "She isn't leaving here with you."

His eyes didn't leave my face. I couldn't read him.

"I brought my car," I stammered, not understanding what he was offering exactly. I held my keys up, a show-and-tell example that I could share with the whole class. "I don't need a ride."

"Emma, would you come with me please?" Pastor

Roberts reached me, frown lines creasing his serious face, his hands behind his back as if to keep them to himself.

I stepped back, toward the door, toward Jake. With horror, I realized Jake was gone. Between holding up my keys and the pastor saying my name, he'd gone. Gone. Vanished. Abandoning me to my chosen fate.

"Where's Jake?" I looked around wildly. "Where did he go?"

"Emma dear, this is for the best. He doesn't belong around decent people." Sadie reached for me, grasping claw like fingers curling toward me.

Shaking my head, I stepped back, out of reach. I moved quickly, out of Vivian's room, down the hall, and through the reception area; a group of people turned to watch me, their voices faltering. Sadie and the others were behind me, calling for me, begging me to come back.

"Jake?"

Faces turned to me, curious and surprised, startled, unsettled, but none of them Jake. Through the glass doors, I caught a glimpse of the parking lot and a familiar truck backing out of a spot near the front, coming slowly around to leave the parking lot.

I pushed through the glass doors, running, the group of church ladies calling out my name, following me through the doors and out into the light rain. If there were any kind of justice in the world, their carefully blown-out hair and overly done up faces would melt.

What if he didn't see me? What if this was it and we never spoke again? I waved, trying to get Jake's attention. He hadn't seen me; he didn't know. The brake lights vanished, and the truck moved, easing forward. Panic, pure and overwhelming, grabbed me and shook me.

"Jake!" I hollered, flat out running now, splashing through puddles.

The women continued to call, voices high, pitched to reach me, grasping.

"Jake! Wait!"

I don't know if he heard me or finally saw me. Maybe he had a feeling. But the brake lights flashed on, and he leaned across the seat to push the passenger side door open. I didn't hesitate, I hurried toward it, taking it for what it was—a lifeline.

"Emma Taylor, don't you dare!"

Reaching the truck, I glanced back, several women in the parking lot, Pastor Roberts standing at the open door. Mr. Laurent was there too. Half the town seemed to be. I slid into the cab of the truck, warm air blowing on my feet as I pulled the door shut and snapped my seatbelt on.

"Go," I said, eyes glued to the rearview mirror, watching as the funeral home receded.

Rain beat down against the windshield, the wipers squeaking with each pass across the glass, sheets of it running down the windows. The dull hammering of the water filled my ears, matching my thumping heart. I turned to Jake, relieved, and suddenly incredibly irritated. He glanced at me, eyes sweeping my face, taking in my wet hair and damp clothes.

"What kind of asshole just leaves a girl stranded like that?"

CHAPTER FIFTEEN

SATURDAY

The truck came to a stop, quick and abrupt, and ready to take off again as soon as I was out. Beyond the windshield, Magnolia House rose high into a night with no stars or moon. Low clouds rolled across the sky, promising more rain and leaving us expectant— watchful and waiting. I'd left the light in the foyer on—a warm yellow light from the chandelier, swaying gently, sending tiny rainbows shivering across the wallpaper.

But it wasn't on now.

"You getting out?" he asked.

I shot him a look, irritated that he was so ready to get rid of me. "In a hurry?"

He just stared, and I couldn't tell what he was thinking, the color of his blue eyes deeper in the dark, his handsome face shadowed and unreadable. I wanted to touch him, place my hand against his cheek, and feel him there beside me. There was something unearthly about him, ghost-like, in the glow of the dashboard lights.

Stay.

I looked away, back to the house, touching the sore spot

on my lip. What I wanted didn't matter, and if I said something right now, it would probably be dumb. So I didn't say anything at all.

The house seemed to be waiting for someone to come along and wake it up.

I didn't want to go inside. Not alone.

Jake unbuckled and leaned toward me, the scent of his cologne—fresh and bright—filling the space between us. My heart skipped as he reached for me. He was going to kiss me, and I knew if he did it wouldn't stop there. I wouldn't want it to.

But he reached past me, pulling the door handle and giving it a shove. It swung open, letting in the muggy night and the chirp of crickets. The dome light washed over us, showing me that he hadn't planned to kiss me at all. He just wanted me out of his truck.

I blinked as he settled back in his seat, and a wave of embarrassment flooded me, drowning everything else out —fear of the house, a flash of hope. I fumbled my purse onto my shoulder and got out, slamming the door shut.

Moving toward the house blindly, I listened to the truck slowly ease away. Fine. Once again, I'd been the only one who'd felt something. It didn't matter that I wanted him if he didn't want me. We kept dancing up to this line; I could feel him there with me, and then he'd pull back, retreat.

The house was red, reflecting the taillights, throwing back strange shadows and altering the darkness around me. I took a step toward it and stopped, shivering, suddenly cold in the heat. The white siding glowed eerily, the place pale red and aware. Watching me.

More than anything I wished the light hadn't burned out. I wished this was any other house, any other place. I'd wait until he was gone, until the house no longer reminded me of blood. Then I would go up the steps and inside, I would never let on that for a moment, here, bathed in crimson light, I thought the place was alive. The light switch would work, and I would retreat to the quiet of my dad's study until dawn.

And I would pretend that everything beyond that locked study door was as it should be.

But the lights didn't fade, didn't retreat into the night. I took another step toward the house, back stiff, wondering why he hadn't gone. He'd been in a hurry and such a jerk not even ten seconds ago. Then the engine turned off, and the lights went out. It startled me, blind in the sudden darkness as I turned toward Jake getting out of the truck.

"Come on," he said, stalking toward me.

"What're you doing?" I asked, taking a step back.

"Walking you home and trying not to be an asshole about it." He gestured at the house, raising his eyebrows.

I snorted. "Well, you're not doing a very good job."

"I thought I'd give it another shot." He glanced down at me and almost smiled.

I couldn't help the laugh then; it was loud in the night, surprising us both but I didn't care.

"You need more practice."

"Maybe I'll practice with you."

His smile widened, and my heart thumped. I didn't even notice the steps as he led me up them, aware of how close he was. We lingered for a moment under the blue ceiling of the verandah, paused in the darkness, on the edge of something I couldn't put a name to.

"Keys?" he asked.

I fumbled with them, trying to figure out which one opened the front door. There were only four, but I ended up going through each of them before finding the one that fit.

The lock clicked, and the grandfather clock struck the hour as the door swung open. The shut-in smell of dust and old things whispered out, rushing past us to run free in the night.

"What happened to the lights?"

"I don't know," I said, hesitating to step inside.

Vivian was here somewhere, still here, and she wasn't ready to let go.

The floorboards creaked as I entered—old wood, built to expand and contract with the weather, to bend and not break. Crossing the hall, hand out for the light switch, I sensed my awareness of the dark house around me grew. It crouched in the rooms beyond the arches, the morning room and parlor, unseen eyes heating two solid points in my back. I turned to the morning room, a black hole exerting force and pulling me in.

And in it?

Nothing.

Nothing but my fear of the dark and the threat that this house would eat me whole.

Turning the light on was imperative—lifesaving. I needed it bright and yellow and warm enough to fill up the house, to blur the edges of my body with my surroundings. I felt along the wall, the switch farther away than I'd remembered, and flipped it.

No light.

I flipped it again, heart slamming in my throat, the quiet house closing in. The hair on my arms stood up, a shiver racing across me, leaving me cold.

It was time to leave.

I turned, ready to run, ready to leave Magnolia House forever. It didn't want me here, and I didn't want to be here.

It would suit me just fine to walk away now and let the attorney handle it all.

But Jake was closer than I'd expected, and I turned, crashing into him. I yelped and pushed, forgetting for an instant that I hadn't been alone after all and that someone alive and breathing was with me. He made a soothing noise and wrapped his arms around me. He held me without speaking, keeping me close with one arm around my waist and the other around my shoulders. I trembled, the house crouched at my back, but Jake was solid and real.

"Anything in this house ever work?" he asked after a minute.

"Sometimes."

"Does it do this a lot?"

"The wiring has never been any good. And the breakers get flipped all the time. Or the bulbs burn out suddenly. Something usually happens like that."

"Where're the breakers?"

"Pantry in the kitchen."

I felt him move, digging in his pocket, and he pulled out his cell phone. I didn't bother with mine—it would be dead, as it always was. But his lit up, blinding and harsh, illuminating his face, casting shadows. Then the light vanished—dead and gone—leaving me blinking and seeing stars in the abrupt darkness.

"Stupid phone," he muttered.

"It's okay," I said. "That happens a lot around here too."

He unwrapped me, one hand finding mine in the dark, engulfing mine, and I clung to him. We moved down the hall toward the kitchen together. Somewhere deep inside the house, a clock began to tick, so faint it was almost inaudible. Not the big grandfather clock in the foyer, this was one I'd missed in my original inspection of the house. It put my teeth on edge, lurking at the edge of hearing, counting down each moment so slowly.

Reaching the kitchen Jake tried the switch on the wall, but it was out as well.

"Do you have a flashlight? Candles?"

"There are matches by the stove, and there should be candles in the drawer by the fridge. Or maybe in one of the lower cabinets. I know I saw some, but I don't remember where exactly."

He let go of my hand, and I missed him immediately, the space he'd been horribly now empty. He moved toward the fridge, passing the window above the sink. He became a dark shape moving past the gray rectangle, a ghost in my kitchen. Suppressing a shiver, I crossed to the stove. It was an old gas beast, one you had to light yourself and hope it didn't explode.

The matchbox rattled when I touched it, a tangible sound of relief and comfort—the promise of light. It was one of those large cardboard, industrial packages, rough places the color of red bricks on either side of the packaging to pull the match head across, to strike it on.

"Found the matches," I said, shaking the box, rattling the contents like a castanet.

Jake grunted a response, moving around the kitchen, opening drawers and cabinets—rattling silverware—still searching for candles. My hands shook as I opened the box, the tremor new to me, the fear of the dark surprising.

I'd never been afraid before. I'd lived in this house without electricity, roaming the confines of my room and the upper floors, familiar with each warped spot in the floors, how many steps it took from my room to the stairs. Not once living in my own apartment, in an alien city, had I been afraid. But this place made me itch for floodlights and nightlights, kerosene lanterns, and bright white LEDs.

Magnolia House was under my skin, clawing into muscle, intent on reaching my bones.

I fumbled with the box, and the contents spilled, rattling out, tiny slivers of wood scattering across the kitchen floor and sliding beyond my reach. With a groan, I knelt, sweeping my hands across the linoleum and dragging a handful back.

I struck one against the box, and sparks flashed, small and faint, a teasing hint of fire. I tried again. Light, this time, small but bright and hot, grew, alive in the darkness. As my hand shook. the flame devoured the sliver of wood hungrily, already nearing my fingers. Shadows jumped and shivered as the flame flickered, and I held it higher, illuminating Jake a few feet away.

Jake watched me in the light, kneeling on the floor in the pile of matches, his eyes a reflection of fire. There was no expression on his face. I didn't recognize him, didn't know him. A new fear touched me, fresh and sharp, a warning from one person after another.

You should stay away from him.

The match burned down—flame licking my licking fingers. I yelped and dropped it, the light vanishing and leaving a hole in my vision. I fumbled for another match, striking it against the box again and again. It failed to catch, and I dropped it, groping for another.

Jake moved, coming toward me, his heavy boots creaking. He knelt beside me, one hand coming up to mine as I struck the match, flame catching. He helped to shield the fire, and our eyes met in the small circle of light.

This man I thought I knew. Someone I understood. He was the stranger who had driven me home only to return with a sack full of junk food. This was a man who had stopped someone from hurting me. This was someone who had come into this dark house with me to make sure it was safe—to bring me light.

I wanted to kiss him. The thought surprised me. Right now, at this moment, I wanted his mouth on mine more than I wanted anything else.

Kiss me.

His gaze dropped to my mouth. I sucked in a breath, lips parted, and heart pounding. The match burned down, singeing my fingers.

"Shit!"

I dropped it, blind again, but this time I wasn't alone.

Jake caught my hand and pulled me toward him, pressing my fingers to his lips, brushing a soft kiss against burned skin. I shuddered, a small noise of pleasure and surprise escaping me. His mouth moved, kissing the palm of my hand, then the delicate inside of my wrist. I reached out with my other hand, cupping his face—coarse stubble and warm skin. I was on fire, lit like a match, wanting his mouth on me.

A crash, the shattering of broken glass, broke the moment. The light in the hall snapped on, yellow and harsh, stretching into the kitchen, falling on my face. Jake remained in shadow.

I hesitated, my hand on his face, waiting for him to kiss me again. I wanted him badly. I wanted him to want me as badly as I wanted him. But we were frozen, locked in the moment, and as much as I wanted to push us forward, I hesitated. I couldn't. I wanted him to do it, for him to make the choice. Because God help me, I'd already made mine.

I pulled my hand away—heart sinking. He didn't stop me.

"What was that?"

"The light came back."

We spoke at the same time. He stood, half turned toward the hall and the direction of the noise. Light fell across his features, and once again he was impassive, as if he'd never touched me in the dark. I opened my mouth to say something, anything, to distract myself from what I was thinking.

"Let's check the fuse box," he said.

I stood up, brushing my hands together, smoothing away the lingering sensation of his kisses. I pointed to the pantry door. "It's in there, on the wall to the right. There isn't a light in there though."

He nodded and crouched down to pick up a candle. It was one of Vivian's long white tapers, the kind she'd put in all the candelabras—burning on mantles and in front of mirrors, the flames doubled and tripled, the light growing.

"Here."

I held out the box of matches, weightless yet heavy—containing disappointment and confusion, the promise of illumination. He studied my face, eyes roving over my features, searching. When he didn't move to take the box, I bent and picked up a match, striking it in a swift motion that sent the flame dancing. He took it, our fingers touching briefly, and he lit the candle.

For a moment, he remained where he was, kneeling in front of me, face lifted to mine. Candlelight slid over him, over us both, as we watched each other. In another part of the house, something crashed to the floor—mirror, porcelain figure, crystal dish. The light in the hall went out.

The candle flame jumped as he stood, moving to the pantry with me following right behind. I opened the door for him, holding my breath as he walked past me and took the light with him.

"How old is the wiring?" he asked, opening the box, and exposing the snarled contents.

"I don't know. Really old. The house was built in the 1800s, and electricity was added downstairs sometime in the 1930s with a little bit of updating around the '60s."

"What about the upstairs?"

"No electricity. Grandparents decided it was too expensive to do the whole house. But it really wasn't too bad living up there without it." I stopped, biting the inside of my cheek.

"Your bedroom was upstairs?" he asked, an edge to his voice.

I nodded.

"And your mom didn't have the second floor updated?"

I raised one shoulder in a shrug, perfect indifference, practiced and remembered in this place. A flicker of something dark flashed in his eyes, too quick for me to understand. Anger? Disgust? Was it for the girl I'd been or the woman I was now? Did it really matter? No, in this place they were the same. I was the same.

He turned back to the box—a confusion of fuses, switches, wires, and paper labels covered in spidery cursive. After resetting them all several times, and a few curses, the lights in the kitchen snapped on. It was a shock, an explosion of light, going from the half-light of the candle to this full-blown electric glow.

"You really need to have an electrician fix this mess. It's going to catch fire any minute and burn the whole place down."

"Are you an electrician?" I asked.

He narrowed his eyes at me. "No."

"Are you going to pay for one?"

"No."

"Then don't worry about it."

I turned away, retreating to the kitchen, returning to the matches on the floor. He didn't say anything, but I heard the metal box shut and then the pantry door. I collected the matches slowly, a few at a time, placing them carefully back in the box. When I finished, I turned to see him leaning against the counter, watching me, with his arms crossed.

"What?" I asked.

He straightened. "Want me to check the rest of the house? Figure out what that crash was?"

"Why?"

"Because you looked afraid to come inside earlier."

I hesitated, dreading the moment I'd be alone.

All old houses made noises. They settled and groaned, creaked in high winds, expanded with rain. Some houses held on to scents—wearing baking bread or floor polish like good perfume, reflecting different sunrises, recalling past sunsets. A house *remembered*.

Was it only the memory Vivian's wheelchair I heard each night, rolling back and forth—that familiar faint squeak, the heavy sigh, the scent of jasmine and magnolia blossoms lingering? I told myself that's all it could be. But this was Vivian's house, and deep down I knew it would be whatever she wanted it to be. And she always refused to be forgotten.

Jake watched me, seeing all of it pass across my face. I'd always been so good at hiding my thoughts. I'd had to for years. But with Jake somehow, I'd become transparent, emotions visible and on display.

"No, it's okay." I shook my head. "Thanks for the ride and fixing the lights."

Without a word, he walked past me.

He was going. A sigh escaped me, partly relief but more disappointment. He'd leave, drive away, and I would wave until the red taillights faded before retreating to the study. Vivian would roam the halls, and I wouldn't be able to think of anything other than his lips on my fingertips in the dark.

It seemed like a story, a piece of fiction inserted into my life. *Main character has romantic moment in old house.* It was the kind of thing that didn't happen in real life—not in my life.

But here in the kitchen, with the scent of burned matches between us, he'd pressed the tenderest of kisses to the inside of my wrist. My stomach clenched with the memory, skin tingling with sensation.

Jake stopped at the first door outside the kitchen, another pantry of sorts, a place to store and organize cleaning supplies. He looked inside thoroughly, moving a mop to see the back corner, before firmly shutting the door. He moved to the next door. The room was empty now, but it had been a sewing room at some point. My dad's study was beyond that.

"What are you doing?"

"Checking the house."

"For what?"

"Ax murders. Monsters. Giant spiders. Whatever it is that you're afraid of."

I moved into the hall, heading for my dad's study, wanting to block the door. I didn't want him to see that I was sleeping on the sofa in there. In this whole house, with all of these rooms, even if only downstairs had electricity, it seemed odd. He'd think I was being strange. He'd take one look in there and know I was hiding.

"I'm not afraid," I said. "Thanks again for fixing the lights. I really appreciate it, but you don't have to stay. You must have a lot going on tonight. I've already taken up a bunch of your time."

I put my back to the study door, hand on the knob. I met Jake's blue gaze and ignored the question on his face. He leaned in, crowding me, reaching for my hand on the knob. His hand was warm on mine. He was so close, so near to me that I had to catch my breath. He was studying me thoughtfully.

"What are you afraid of, Emma?" he asked softly.

My name in his mouth, the tone low and soothing, made me shiver. I shook my head and tried not to stammer. "I'm not afraid."

He was so close I felt his chest move when he took a deep breath; I could almost convince myself I heard his heart beating. But no, that would be mine—fast as a rabbit ready to flee. *Catch me.* A trace of his cologne reached me, fresh and citrusy, and there was stubble coming in along his jaw. He took half a step forward, our bodies touching, and warmth bloomed low in my belly, heat rushing through me.

"Shouldn't you be?"

"No." I lifted my chin. "Why should I be?"

"Because you're alone with a murderer."

I'd read the newspaper articles, and the residents of Back of Beyond continued to gossip. It didn't matter that he'd been acquitted. He'd been the boyfriend. He'd been in and out of trouble: checkered past, spotty history. The papers wrote about him as if he'd been a hardened criminal at the age of eighteen—breaking and entering and assault on public record. But no one could say what had happened exactly, what the context was, how it all connected.

"I'm sure you've heard all the details by now."

"So?"

He chuckled—the sound so warm I had to stop a smile from spreading across my face in response. He considered me, looking at me as if he wasn't sure who I was after all. Like, somehow, I'd changed his mind. He'd been so sure that I was just some spoiled woman coming back to wrap up the details at the big house—the place that cast a long shadow over this tiny backwater town. He'd been less than thrilled to be thrown into my path time and again, somehow both of us in the wrong place at the wrong time.

But this was the first time he'd looked at me like that.

"I'm not afraid of you," I whispered.

"Oh yeah?" He leaned into me, whispering in my ear. "Why not?"

"Because you're checking under the bed for monsters."

He laughed, a real laugh, and for a moment he dropped his head to mine, pressing his cheek against my hair. I sucked in a breath, pulling him into my lungs. Then he was twisting my hand on the knob and easing me against the door until it opened.

I took in the room, going over it as it must appear to him, seeing it with a fresh set of eyes. Bookshelves lined the walls, floor to ceiling, and were packed with hardcover and paperback in all sizes. The old oak desk was worn with constant use and age. A green desk lamp, which was on, and a brown leather chair. Stacks of paperwork covered the surface. File folders and cardboard boxes, pages clipped and stapled and bound together with tan rubber bands.

It looked like a very unorganized person had been inter-rupted mid-sort. And it was true. I didn't know what to do with half of it and wasn't sure what I might need to keep. There were piles to shred, and another to take to the attorney.

The only window in the room faced the back garden and the woods beyond. Sheer white curtains covered it now, but beyond those, I knew the night was ready to be let back in—ready for all the lights in Magnolia House to go out.

To the right of the door was the chesterfield leather sofa. Older than the desk and twice as worn, cracks spread across one arm, and a few buttons missing along the back. My blanket and pillow were wadded up to one side, a laptop, a phone charger, and another stack of papers at the other. There were more papers scattered across the floor. My suitcase was open at the end of the sofa, clothes everywhere, and even I was unable to tell what was clean or dirty. A pair of pink underwear sat right on top of the mess, and all around the room were empty coke cans.

I darted forward, snatching up the underwear and knocking a can over. It rolled across the floor with a tinny sound. I saw it the way he must be seeing it. A complete wreck being lived in by a slob. And it was very obviously lived in. He probably thought I was crazy, living in this room, sleeping on this sofa in a house full of beds. I waited for him to say something, to ask questions, to look at me with a trace of distaste. But he didn't. He glanced around, took it all in, and turned back to the hall.

"Wait," I said, going after him. "Where are you going?"

He kept moving, heading for the next door. "I've got more rooms to check. We still haven't found whatever broke. Or caused it to break."

"You're really going to check every room?"

He nodded.

"The whole house?"

"The whole house."

I checked my watch, the one I'd been forced to wear since my cell phone kept dying. A morbid thought crossed my mind, invasive and predatory: Who would stop it if I died? I shook myself, shoved the image down.

"It's almost one in the morning. It's crazy to check the whole house. Aren't you tired? Don't you want to sleep?"

"Are you tired?" he asked, pausing with a hand on the next door down the hall.

I tried to remember what the room was. Another empty space that could have been anything. Most of these rooms had been empty all my life, my childhood echoing in this half-abandoned space.

"I'm very tired," I admitted. I was exhausted. The fear had receded enough to let the exhaustion of the day sink in. My body felt heavy, like it wasn't really mine, and I was trying very hard to resist the urge to go back to the sofa and lay down. It had been such a long day. And even though I was still afraid of the house, of what was lingering here with me, sleep was beckoning, insistent. It was unavoidable and wasn't going to take no for an answer.

He pulled out his phone and checked the time. The bright blue light lit up his face; jaw covered in a shadow of stubble; lips pressed in a thin line.

"You're right," he said, slipping the phone back in his pocket. "I didn't realize how late it was."

"It's okay," I said.

"You should get some sleep."

"Yeah." I nodded, glancing back at the study. "I need it. I'll walk you to the door and make sure it's locked. Wouldn't want to waste all your effort and let a monster in after you've gone to all this trouble to check."

He laughed, a real laugh of pleasure that startled me. I hadn't heard him sound so genuine, so relaxed. I smiled, pleasure rippling through me that I'd been able to do it. He followed me out to the foyer.

I stopped abruptly when we reached it. One of the mirrors had fallen from the wall and shattered, reflective pieces scattered across the hardwood—catching our movement, showing us a fragmented reality. I groaned. The mess would have to wait for daylight. I couldn't face cleaning it up now.

"We should sweep that up." He sounded a little surprised.

"No," I said, stepping around it. "I'll clean it up in the morning. And get those bulbs replaced too."

Overhead several of the bulbs in the chandelier had gone out. It happened every time, replaced and new, suddenly dead. I should probably have an electrician come out like Jake had suggested. I was almost done wrapping up all of Vivian's affairs. I should leave the electrician to whoever owned the house next. But the thought of coming back to a dark house again, even after I'd left all the lights on, was enough to make me reconsider.

I reached the door and turned to him with a smile, ready to say goodnight. But he closed it, turning the lock. The sound of the bolt shooting home echoed in the entryway, the finality of it shooting up my spine with excitement.

"What are you doing?"

"You're right, it's late. I'd lost track of the time. I'm exhausted, and the last thing I need is to fall asleep at the wheel or get pulled over for swerving on the road. Morning isn't that far away. Would you mind?"

I opened my mouth but had no clue what to say.

"You should get some sleep too. The dark circles under your eyes make you look half dead."

I touched my cheek, forehead wrinkling. "That bad?"

"Terrible," he confirmed.

Gently he took my arm, steering me carefully around the broken mirror and back to the study. My heart pounded, filling my ears, leaving me deaf to anything else. His hand on my arm was so warm, and I wondered if his hands would be just as warm on other parts of my body. Fear and desire mixed strangely, a coiling knot reworked constantly, the tension in my body both at once.

He shut the door firmly behind us once we reached the study, and I crossed to the sofa, hand to my arm where he'd been touching me. I perched there, watching him, trepidation joining the tension.

"Mind if I take my boots off?"

I shook my head. "Not at all."

He kicked them off easily, steel-toed boots that reminded me of cowboy boots without the cowboy. He set them neatly beside the door, gray T-shirt taut across his broad shoulders, smooth against the muscles of his back. Then I realized he was watching me. He raised an eyebrow, the hint of a smile playing around his mouth.

"Can I offer you something?" I stammered. "Coke? Tea?"

Maybe you'd like to have me?

"Nah, thanks for the offer. I might read for a bit if you don't mind the light being on."

"No, it's okay. I sleep with the light on anyway." I sounded five years old, and I cringed as the words left my mouth. "I mean, I don't usually sleep with the light on. I'm not a child. I just sleep with the light on here." I trailed off, voice dying into nothing. Trying to explain it had only made it worse.

But didn't say anything, simply nodded and moved to the shelves farthest from me. Scanning them slowly, he tilted his head to read the book spines, reaching out to touch one or two. I waited for half a second or more, surprised he was here, in this room with me. If he'd wanted to kiss me, he would have. But he hadn't. Was he really afraid of falling asleep behind the wheel? Or afraid he'd be pulled over by a police officer that believed he'd killed Alice.

Fear.

I wasn't afraid of him. Back of Beyond might've believed he was a murderer, but I'd read all the newspaper articles. There had been no physical evidence. He'd been acquitted.

The trepidation I felt, the knot in my stomach, had nothing to do with fear.

I wasn't afraid he'd hurt me or that he was who they all claimed him to be.

What I felt was desire.

The sheet I'd been using had slipped to the floor when I'd gotten up this morning, and I took my time fixing it now. I took my time arranging the blanket and pillow, fluffing and straightening until I couldn't put it off any longer. Exhaustion weighed heavily on me, pulling at my shoulders, and urging me to sleep. Slipping my shoes off, I kicked them to the side, and curled on the sofa, still wearing my jeans and T-shirt.

Jake had found a book and settled with his back up against the door. He seemed at ease, as if he slept in strange rooms on a regular basis. I wondered if he did.

"Jake," I whispered.

He looked up and met my eyes.

"There's another pillow under the clothes there by the suitcase, if you want it."

He put the book down, a paperback history of the

Roman Empire, and leaned toward the mess of my suitcase. Pushing clothes aside, he pulled the pillow free, the pillowcase deep teal with sprigs of white flowers, from my bed at home, and tucked it behind him, settling back.

I watched him read, turning pages, the crisp sound of paper against paper filling the study. The house was so quiet—eerily quiet. But I was grateful. I would gladly accept silence. Adjusting the pillow beneath my head, I stretched out, yawning.

"Why are you here?" I asked, unable to keep the curiosity contained any longer.

"I told you." He glanced up and then back to the book and turned a page. His voice was soft, so soft in the small room. "I'm tired. I don't trust myself to drive."

"I don't believe you."

"You don't have to."

I sat up, propped up on an elbow, glaring at him now. "Why are you here Jake? Here, right now, sitting on the hardwood floor of this house? Isn't your butt sore already?"

He stared at me with his fathomless, unknowable blue eyes.

"What do you want me to say?"

"You kissed my hand in the kitchen." My voice was small—small as kisses in a darkened room, soft lips to fingertips, the nearness of another beating heart. What had changed between that moment and when the light in the hall had snapped on, revealing him to me? I didn't know. I didn't understand any of it.

"You're right." His eyes dropped back to the book, and another page turned. "You looked afraid to be alone in the house, and for whatever reason, I decided to stay. Though right now I'm wondering why I did."

"You're here because I really am a child afraid of the

dark. Because you pity me." I flopped back to the pillow, closing my eyes, cheeks burning. I'd been wondering if he'd kiss me, wanting him to, and that had been the furthest thought from his mind. I didn't want his pity. It was the last thing I wanted. Or anyone else's pity. It was just more proof that I needed to get out of this place as quickly as possible. I could go back to being Emma Taylor and not Vivian Taylor's daughter.

"Maybe a little." After a moment he asked, "Do you want me to leave?"

I rolled onto my side, my back to him, pulling my knees up. Did I want to be alone in the house?

"No," I whispered. The evening had been hard, full of terrible things, and I'd made it worse. I always made things worse. "Jake?"

"Mmm?"

"I'm sorry I called you an asshole."

"Don't worry about it," he replied, voice smooth, and so very calm. "I've been called worse."

"Just because you have, it doesn't make what I said right. Or okay. I'm sorry."

Another page turned as he read on, unbothered. Vivian had said so many things to me, words flung with savage force, hard as the crystal ashtray she'd thrown at me once that had blackened my eye. The bruise had faded, the words remained.

"Thank you, Emma. Goodnight."

His voice was soft, tender, and I almost turned to face him. But tears had gathered in my eyes, and I didn't want him to see me cry. I lay there, listening to the house, to him. I tried to clear my mind, to push all of the things that were waiting for me to deal with them away—focus on my own breathing. *In and out, out and in.*

I was relieved he'd stayed, and he'd accepted my apology. I hadn't wanted to spend the night alone. Not in Magnolia House, buried beneath the weight of the past, the heaviness that lay across my shoulders as soon as I walked through the door. At least for tonight, the weight was less suffocating.

"Goodnight, Jake," I mumbled before finally giving in and falling asleep.

CHAPTER SIXTEEN

SATURDAY

I woke with a start, going from dead asleep to completely awake—heart pounding, throat tight. Looking around wildly, breath shallow, I took in the study—my mess, blanket half on the floor, light on. I checked my watch. Three in the morning.

The witching hour.

Jake was at the door, back to me, hand on the doorknob, frozen in the act of opening the door. I opened my mouth to speak, to warn him, plead with him to lock the door and step away, when I heard it.

Vivian was rolling down the hall.

It was such a quiet sound, almost not there, but to me, it was a brass marching band blasting raucous music in my face. My ears ached with the sound. It was at the other end of the house, but it was getting closer.

"Don't open it," I hissed, sitting up, voice high in panic.

The rest of the blanket slipped to the floor, sending a stack of paperwork sliding sideways in a muted rustle of pages. Jake turned to me, face pale, and put a finger to his lips. I nodded, pulling my knees up to my chest and wrapping my arms around them.

Old houses remember things. They collect and hold the lives of their occupants, carrying on even when those people have moved on—passed on. So many people had lived in this house. I'd grown up with their ghosts and Vivian's superstitions. I'd heard the faint laughter and smelled blackberry pie when the oven was cold, caught glimpses out of the corner of my eye, and walked into an empty room knowing someone else had just left. There'd been the faint trace of perfume, the sudden absence in the air. Magnolia House had never been truly empty.

But this was Vivian.

Vivian, the monster of my childhood.

Vivian, the woman who haunted my dreams.

No one can hurt you like a mother can.

Jake moved his hand from the knob to the lock beneath it. He turned it slowly, so quietly it barely made a sound, and took a step back. I could see how tense he was, stiff, with his shoulders back. I could feel it too, jaw clenched as I waited, teeth aching as I watched the door. We held our breath, listening to the rolling glide of the wheelchair on polished floorboards. The sound neared, still quiet, almost muted, as if there were no weight to it at all. No reality. But it was real. It *felt* real.

Go away.

I concentrated on the thought, repeating it with every cell in my body, the way I'd done when Vivian would call me to come downstairs as a kid, praying she'd forget about me.

Go away. Go away. Go away.

The sound stopped on the other side of the door. I strained to hear anything, the smallest movement or sound. I leaned forward, nauseous with expectation and fear. Nothing happened. The silence of the old house, never exactly quiet, crept in. Beyond the window, the wind picked up, rustling the rose bushes against the siding—thorns scratching old paint. Inside there were the small noises of the house moving with the wind.

We were frozen in place.

I had to breathe, unable to keep the tension going and needing to let go. I let it out, relieved that the other sound had stopped, her sound. She was gone. If she had ever been there at all.

The knob began to turn, creaking, moving so slowly I might have missed it except for the noise. I slapped a hand over my mouth, smothering the desire to scream. Tears gathered in my eyes, rolling down my cheeks. I was transfixed. If I concentrated on it and stared with unblinking eyes, the lock would hold. But if I looked away the door would open, swing inward on silent hinges, and whatever was on the other side would come in.

It was my own personal magic, a superstition ingrained since childhood.

Don't blink.

The brass knob turned, moving in the other direction now, slowly, so slowly back and forth. I bit into the palm of my hand, not hard, putting firm pressure on myself, forcing my nerves to focus there.

Jasmine filled the air, not the star jasmine the house wore—a living sweet green scent. This was the unforgettable scent of expensive perfume bottled in Paris, purchased at a specialty shop in New Orleans, and handdelivered every six months.

Vivian's perfume.

Jake stepped back.

The lock held.

The knob slowly moved back into place, whatever was on the other side letting go.

He turned to me, shaken but holding it together, maybe refusing to believe what he'd heard. Refusing to accept what had just happened. A part of me—the Oregon, tiny apartment, career in the English department part—was in denial as well. But the other part, the girl who'd been raised with ghosts, who had known superstitions were there for a reason, wasn't denying anything.

Still, even as her perfume lingered in the room, I didn't want to accept that Vivian was here. This wasn't the first night I'd heard something in the house. But this was the first time the scent of jasmine had come to me, the first time it had tried the door. *She.* I'd worked so hard to escape her all my life, but even now I couldn't get away. I couldn't break the ties that bound us together.

I held my hand out for Jake, and he came to me, sitting beside me on the sofa and pulling me to him without a word. He tucked me against him, my head on his chest, as he wrapped his arms around me, resting his head against my hair. A muscle in his jaw jumped, and I waited for him to say something, anything. He remained quiet. Maybe he was still listening like I was.

He stroked my hair, running a soothing hand over me again and again—for himself or me, I couldn't be sure. Calm lay between us, but it was delicate, something I wanted to disturb. Now wasn't the time for questions. Those would come later, and I'd have to consider what answers to give. I wasn't sure where to start. Or how far back to go.

We sat like that until the dark rectangle of the window began to lighten, the faintest of gray coming through the curtains. Daylight, dim, barely there, but growing stronger with each breath I took, had arrived. I relaxed, exhausted, and stretched so thin I might shatter into a thousand pieces.

The night was over.

I fell asleep with Jake's arms around me, the light beyond the window getting stronger.

SUNDAY

You can't go back and change the beginning, but, you can start where you are and change the ending.

- C.S. Lewis

CHAPTER SEVENTEEN

SUNDAY

Birds sang somewhere nearby—sparrows or redwing blackbirds, sweet voices raised to greet the sun. I kept my eyes closed, listening to the notes rise and fall so close to the window that they must have been in the bushes beneath it. I was still curled in Jake's lap, but his arm was no longer around me like it had been in the night. He breathed steadily, possibly still asleep.

I lay there, listening, peace filling me. The night was a distant place—disconnected, a strange reality. I wondered what time it was and what would happen when Jake woke up. What had changed in the night? Had it changed us? Not that there was an *us* to change. But things had been building, tension vibrating, and there was *something* here between Jake and me.

Last night he'd kissed my hand in the dark.

I opened my eyes finally, unable to put it off any longer. Sunshine filtered through the lace curtains, brighter than the lamp alight on the desk, and it changed everything— the cool morning light of an overcast day. The room was different in this light, the space so unlike the one I'd fallen asleep in.

"Good morning," Jake said.

His voice startled me, and I sat up, smoothing a hand over my hair and rubbing sleep from my eyes. He was watching me, and I gave him a small smile, wondering at his expression, the softness there. He reached out, bridging the distance between us, and traced the line of my eyebrow, his eyes moving over my face. My breath caught with surprise, heart pounding, my body tingling with the connection.

I cleared my throat, looking down at my hands—short nails, cuticles rough—curling them together, hiding the flaw. I looked up, meeting his eyes, and forced myself to speak. "Did you sleep?"

He shrugged. "A little."

I didn't know what to say about the night. How could I bring it up now, when the world was so fresh and, even in the overcast light of morning, so bright? He'd seemed as afraid of what lay beyond the door as I had been. But it was hard to believe in it all when the sun shone, and the birds sang, and his touch was so distracting. I smiled again, for lack of anything better to do.

"I like you a little too much Emma Taylor."

He brushed a lock of my hair back gently, tracing the line of my cheekbone, and touching the healing spot on my lip. I held my breath, pinned with excitement and longing, wondering why there was a line of worry between his brows.

"Too much for what, Jake White?" I asked.

He chuckled and said with a smile. "My own good."

I studied his face, searching his clear blue gaze as his

smile faded. A hole opened inside of me, and doubt flowed out even as it sucked at the little bit of confidence I'd had.

"You'll be gone in a few days," he said, voice matter-of-fact and direct, reading the falter in my expression.

There was more beneath his words, hovering in the room around us, clinging to us both. What he didn't say, I already knew. What was the point of starting anything when I'd leave and never come back? I'd been very clear about my desire to put this place behind me as soon as possible. I couldn't fault him for not wanting a short-lived romantic situation that would be over so soon. I squashed the disappointment, refusing to acknowledge that it didn't change how I felt when he was in the room.

I nodded and stood, stifling another yawn. "How do you feel about coffee? You want some?"

"You got creamer?"

"Sure do."

"Then I want coffee," he said, standing with me, stretching his hands above his head. The hem of his T-shirt rose, exposing a flash of tan stomach. "Not gonna lie, it feels good to change positions. I didn't want to wake you up, but my legs were starting to fall asleep."

I laughed. "You could have woken me up. I wouldn't have minded."

He shook his head, taking a step toward me, closing the distance as if he hadn't just pointed out that I'd be gone in a few days. He ran the back of his hand down my arm. "You looked peaceful. I figured you needed as much sleep as you can get."

My breath caught in my chest—voice stolen by the casual caress.

"If you show me where that coffee is, I'll make it," he

said, easing past me as if hadn't stopped my heart with a soft touch.

———

Bees flew lazily from flower to flower in the overgrown beds of the kitchen garden—basil running to seed, leggy parsley, and mint. Wildflowers had crept in to join the mix—bright yellow coneflower swaying, pale purple chicory, and vervain. I loved the riot of it all, the madness of the forest and bayou creeping up on this place from the back, as if it might overtake the house by surprise.

The morning was warm around us—as it always was, as it always would be. Despite that, I enjoyed the heat from the coffee mug in my hands, cradling the warmth, holding on to it and resisting the urge to touch Jake. He sat so close, I could lean to my right and touch his arm, rest my head against his shoulder.

We'd moved around each other in the kitchen, comfortably quiet, passing through the first hour of the morning as if we'd done it all before. As if our future held more mornings like these. We'd settled on the back steps, beside the wheelchair ramp, unable to escape the reminder of whose house I occupied at the moment.

From here the wreckage of the carriage house to the left was clearly visible. I hadn't been out back in the daylight much and it was out of sight as you came down the drive. A ruin of splintered timbers and blackened wood, a base of scorched bricks, all overrun with wisteria and wildflowers, blackberry brambles beginning to take hold to host bees and butterflies.

"It burned down right after you left," Jake said, sipping his coffee, considering the tumbled remains. "Not sure what happened exactly though. The insurance company ruled it as an accident. One of those acts of God."

"How do you know?" I asked, the question sharper than intended—cutting with suspicion and uncertainty. Time and again he'd hinted at a connection to Vivian, known things only someone who'd spent time with her could know. And still, I wasn't sure how they could have come to know each other, how Vivian would know this outsider of a man.

"You don't remember me, do you?"

I shook my head, wondering where I could have seen him before. I searched my past, the memories of my childhood, the last few brutal years here when my life had been so focused on surviving. I'd made myself small, shrinking and pulling in, terrified of being noticed because it would detract from Vivian.

"I worked every job I could in the summers and during the school year. Once I graduated, I worked all the time. I delivered papers, mowed lawns, and picked up hours at Josh's shop. The guy I did landscaping for had the contract for Magnolia House. I think I saw you all of about ten times before you left."

"Here?" I pointed to the dirt, the soil I'd grown up on. "You saw me here. At this house?"

Jake smiled, enjoying my surprise. "Yeah, here. You were awful quiet. I don't think I ever heard you speak, and I swear I had no idea what color your eyes were until I picked you up off the side of the road the other day. You never looked up. You were always staring at your feet."

I nodded, staring at my coffee mug now, scouring my memory for a glimpse of young Jake White. He would have been a year ahead of me in school and preparing for graduation when I'd escaped. I must have seen him somewhere in town or school, passed by him without realizing that he'd almost kiss me in the dark. And he'd seen me here, a younger version of myself, the girl I'd abandoned.

"Vivian kept me on after the trial. Josh too. It was hard to find work afterward, hard to go anywhere. I worked as much as I could and kept my head down. But that was after you left, all of that. I don't know when you left home exactly though. Vivian told everyone you'd gone to live with a distant relative. At the time, I thought 'good for her, getting out of this place,' and honestly, I was jealous."

"You continued working for her? You were here at the end?"

He nodded, not meeting my eyes, keeping something inside himself, hiding it. "I didn't come out every week. She wasn't really keeping the gardens up. She just wanted the yard right around the house mowed. You want me to clean it up? Keep mowing?"

"No, I'm not going to worry about it." I shook my head, watching the way morning light fell across the garden, sifting through the oak trees at the edge of the property. "I don't remember you at all. I remember we had a gardener and sometimes he had a helper."

Jake nodded. "That would have been me."

I searched my memory—sounds of a riding lawnmower filling my ears, the snap of pruning shears, men laughing together. The gardener, Marcus or Mark, had been older, gray at the temples, and weatherworn. He always wore a wide-brimmed hat kept in place by a strap under his chin and a blue bandanna double knotted around his neck. Sometimes he'd had a teenager with him, someone a little older than me, tall with shaggy dark hair, someone on the verge of really coming into themselves, growing into long legs and big hands. Jake White. I'd never realized it.

"Why did you keep coming out here?"

I couldn't imagine anyone wanting to come to this place, over and over, of their own free will. Had he experienced anything like Andrew Barns had? If they were to sit down together to compare stories, would they align somewhere along the way? The devil would be in the details—could he confirm or deny the truth of her physical condition?

"It was hard there for a while. Vivian was good to me," he said.

The words didn't sound right. The way he said them, the emotion behind them, was like something coiled and ready to strike—an alligator made of secrets lurking beneath the surface he presented.

"Was she?" I asked, tone hard and unforgiving.

How anyone could find comfort with Vivian, that she would be kind to anyone without a motive, was alien to me. He looked up, meeting my eyes, and for the first time, I saw him. So clearly. The hurt and anger, the pain of it all, the loneliness.

"You have no idea what it was like after the trial."

No. He was right. I didn't. And he would never be able to understand what it had been like to have her as a mother. I didn't try to fill the silence. Nothing I could say would be right. Our wounds were too raw, even all these years later.

"Services aren't until later, right?" he asked.

"Not until six. I wish it were sooner so I could just get it all out of the way."

"What will you do until then?"

I lifted a shoulder in a half-hearted shrug. "I've got the house to sort through. There's not as much here as I was worried there might be, but it's enough to keep me busy."

"You hired Laura Kennedy for the estate sale?"

"Yeah," I shot him a look. "How did you know?"

"Would you believe it if I told you I work for them too?"

I laughed. "You truly are a jack of all trades."

"A Jake of all trades."

He smiled, eyes laughing, and I wanted to kiss him so badly I itched with it—skin vibrating with his nearness, the potential thick like honey. That expression on his face, lit up and happy, in the moment with me here in the sunshine. He was a handsome man, and the silent moodiness he wore most of the time was compelling, but when he smiled, he was someone else. Jake was irresistible.

"Yes," I laughed.

"If you want help moving things around or getting ready for the sale, I wouldn't mind coming out."

I sucked in a breath, caught off guard. His words from the study flew through me, *You're leaving in a few days*. How easy would it be for us then? To be around each other more, lingering over coffee together like this, sharing our pasts so easily. At what point would it go from being casual to something I wouldn't be able to forget?

"Yeah, maybe after the services." I tried to keep my tone casual, the hope tempered with the reality of our situation. "You'll be at the services?"

I wasn't sure he would be, not after yesterday, but I needed him more than ever. It was unfair to him, to step in and be a lightning rod in this situation, taking so much of the focus from me. But I wasn't sure I'd be able to walk into the church alone later.

He nodded. "You want that ride into town? Pick up your car?"

"Sure," I said, swallowing the last of my coffee. "You ready now?"

"If you are."

I nodded. "I'll grab my things."

———

I couldn't stop the groan when I saw the Town Car parked on the driver's side of the rental in the parking lot of the funeral home. Sadie and Irene were in the front, mouths pressed flat, and there was another pair of ladies in the back. I didn't know their names, but I recognized them from the viewing the day before. The group watched the truck pull in like a pack of wild hogs—dangerous and ready to take what they could get out of the situation.

"You think they waited out here all night?" Jake asked as he pulled in on the other side of the rental and parked.

"Sipping coffee and sharing gruesome predictions?" I suggested.

"Yeah," he said, smiling at me. "Like a gossip stakeout."

"They must be thrilled to have so much to talk about for the next fifty years," I said with a laugh.

"I think they'll make it last much longer than that."

Sadie and Irene were arguing—both red in the face with their hands in the air. One of the women from the back seat leaned forward to join their conversation.

"What do you think they're fighting about?"

"I'll give you two guesses," he said.

"Well, wish me luck out there. Thanks for the ride," I said, pulling the rental key from my purse.

He nodded; blue eyes focused on mine. "Any time."

I smiled and pushed the truck door open, sliding out and turning to wave at him. But he'd gotten out of the truck too, the driver's side door slamming shut as he came around the back. The Town Car doors opened, and Sadie stepped out, staring at us over the roof of the sedan, while Irene and the ladies in the back rolled theirs down so the others could hear everything without missing a word.

"What're you doing?" I whispered to Jake.

"Walking you to your car."

"Is this you still working on your manners?" I asked, glancing at the women. "You didn't get it out of your system last night?"

"Emma Taylor!" Sadie waved a finger at me, vibrating with anger, her voice shrill in the morning, rivaling the grackles lingering in the parking lot. "You keep getting into cars with that man, and one of these days you won't be getting out of it."

"Sure enough," Irene said with a nod, arms crossed. "You'll end up just like Alice."

"Thanks for coming out for Vivian last night," I said, addressing them directly but without making eye contact. I kept moving, keys out, Jake silent at my side. "I'm sure I'll see you later too. I know it would make her happy that her friends had all attended."

They both began to talk at the same time, their voices mingling, canceling each other out. I ignored them, slipping between the Town Car and the rental, avoiding the curious gazes of the ladies in the back and Irene's glower. They continued talking, voices rising now. Nothing changed. Nothing was new. Their message remained the same despite my disinterest in it. The only thing I could do was hope eventually they'd give up and I'd have some peace.

"Well," I said, raising my voice and pressing the unlock button on the fob until it beeped several times. "It's been nice seeing y'all!"

Jake came up beside me, leaning around me to open the car door, looking up at the sky as he did. "The services aren't until this evening, right? You've got the whole day to kill."

Kill the day.

It caught in my ear, my head, twirling slowly in place. I jingled the keys, a jarring musical note, breaking up the silent question. *Do you want me to spend it with you?* I almost asked. I knew what I wanted my answer to be. But what did he want?

"You ready for some help out there at the big house, Emma? Irene can follow you straight there. We got plenty of time today."

Sadie, hands on hips, glared at me—carefully blown-out curls quivering, chest heaving with emotion. I almost pointed out that she'd catch more flies with honey than vinegar, but I don't think it would have sweetened her expression at all. Jake squinted at me, mouth twitching with the hint of a smile.

"You want Irene and Sadie following you home?" he asked softly.

"No," I said, shaking my head firmly.

"Well then," he said, leaning into me, "I've got an idea."

"Wha—"

He pressed a quick kiss to my half-open mouth, catching me off guard, catching the church ladies off guard. They gasped, horrified and disgusted, voices high with shock. My ears buzzed, and I couldn't make sense of their words, only the tone. I didn't care what they were saying anyway.

"You know," he said, loud enough that they could hear the invitation, "if you ever feel like fishing, I've got an extra pole you could use."

He took a step back, hands in pockets, smiling as he headed for his truck.

"I hate fishing," I said, shading my eyes, and watching him go.

"You don't have to fish."

The smile he gave me warmed me right down to my toes.

"Emma Taylor, don't you dare!" Sadie yelled. "That man is going to hell! And if you're not careful you'll be going with him!"

CHAPTER EIGHTEEN

SUNDAY

I went without a second thought. I had to go. I refused to examine it too closely, to pull back the layers of desire to what might be lurking beneath it. It was enough right now to know that I wanted to be near him, in his orbit. Rolling down the gravel track that led to his cabin, I set it all aside, not buried or forgotten, but saved for later, for another day.

In all of this—coming home and discovering I'd remained in Vivian's shadow, the things happening in the house, and with my ears still ringing with the harsh voices of the church ladies—I needed someone. And Jake was who I wanted. Despite the warnings, the insistent gossip, my own internal voice warning me to keep a little of myself back, to keep this man at arm's length, I couldn't.

Every chance I got, I ran toward Jake.

We were strangers pulled and pushed together, our pasts tangled, unraveling, and we were still waiting to see if they connected to our futures. His and mine. I was beginning to think they were. But he would have to be the one to decide in the end.

Parking behind his truck, I sucked in a calming breath and checked my reflection in the visor mirror. With my face scrubbed clean and bare of makeup, I looked younger, a little raw—a woman dealing with an unexpected death, a haunted house, nosey small-town gossips, and in desperate need of a decade of uninterrupted sleep. My brown shoulder-length hair needed smoothing, the humidity forever lingering in the almost curls, the frizz unescapable. I pushed it behind my ears, pressing my lips together with resignation that this was it and it wasn't going to get any better, and got out of the car.

Jake came out onto the porch to greet me. He must have seen me pull up and been waiting, giving me a moment with the mirror. I felt like an idiot now, knowing he must have watched me taking a personal inventory. His eyebrows went up in silent question.

"Don't look so surprised to see me," I said. "I'm here to take you up on your generous fishing offer."

He smiled. "I thought you said you didn't fish?"

"I don't," I agreed. "But that won't stop me from tagging along."

He nodded, looking away from me to boat dock, a flicker of an unreadable expression crossing his features. My stomach twisted with the way his brows came together briefly in consideration, the weighing of options, deciding my fate. His eyes came back to me, softer and more open.

"Come on then," he said, motioning for me to follow him to the dock. "Let's get while the getting's good."

I smiled. My dad had used that phrase a lot. Something he'd picked up from someone else as a kid. I hadn't heard it once in Oregon. Hearing it now, in the hot sunshine with this man, made me fiercely miss the things from my childhood that had been good. I wanted those good things again. I wanted the memories of my dad, the sayings that lurked within me waiting to be rediscovered.

Following Jake, we passed beneath the overhanging trees that grew around the house, moving from shade to sunshine—dappled light, harsh before being relieved by shadow. I watched his back, thin cotton moving over muscle, and swallowed, warm tension building in my stomach, excitement and anticipation bubbling through me.

I want you to want me.

The song lyric wove through my brain, striking like a gong, vibrating. I hesitated, wondering if being here was fair to him. I was leaving, and when I was gone I'd leave this whole disaster behind. But he'd still be here, living in it, trying to survive this small town. Wanting him was selfish. Especially when he'd said he liked me too much. And yet he'd invited me here.

"Having second thoughts?"

I looked up, meeting his blue eyes, and shook my head. He smiled, like he knew what I'd been thinking, like maybe he'd been thinking it too. Hot sunshine soaked into my shoulders and top of my head, heating split ends and eyelashes—butterflies filled me, fluttering in my blood, in my head.

The dock creaked beneath me as I stepped onto it, the weatherworn wood baked hard in the heat and throwing it back at me. I shaded my eyes and looked around, over the water, glittering reflections and feathery dancing shadows beneath cypress trees. I glanced back to the house sitting deep in the shade.

"Aren't you going to lock the door?" I asked.

"Why?" He shrugged, stepping into the swaying boat and tugging at the rope tied to the dock. It slithered free, a hushing sound on the edge of hearing, a gentle slapping of water on the sides of the craft as it drifted, ready to pull away.

"What if someone breaks in?"

"I've got nothing to take."

"But—"

"Emma," he said, bitterness coloring his words as he gave me a look. "You really think someone would break into my house?"

Murderer. Killer.

"No," I said, dropping my gaze. "I guess not."

He held out a hand, a silent offer to help me into the boat, patiently waiting. I took it, the roughness of his fingers wrapping around mine, strength in his grip as he steadied me, sent my heart pounding. The boat dipped, wallowing as it took on my weight, and he steered me to one of two narrow benches. The craft was narrow and flat-bottomed, with an engine at one end and a blunt nose at the other. There were fishing rods, a tackle box, and an ice chest tucked between the benches, with a net tucked along the side.

"You were already on your way out?" I asked, realizing how close I'd been to missing him.

"I wasn't sure you'd take me up on the invitation." He shot me a look, eyes flashing to my face and away. "But you got here just in time. Another couple of minutes and the place would have been empty."

"Glad I caught you then."

He didn't respond as the engine sputtered to life, too loud for a moment for conversation. I wanted him to say he was glad too. But as the engine evened out, we didn't speak as he navigated, maneuvering the boat away from the dock, out into the wider waterways. I leaned into the breeze, the wind pushing my hair away from my face, tugging at my T-shirt. I exhaled and my shoulders relaxed, some of the stress of the day falling away.

"It's nice, isn't it?" Jake said, voice raised above the noise.

"What?" I turned to him, unsure of what he'd said.

He waved at the water with his free hand. "It's nice. Being out on the water. Away from it all. Nothing can get you out here. Not even the ghosts."

I nodded, hoping he was right.

We stopped in a spot that looked like all the others we'd passed—cypress and water lilies all around, a little cove of sorts tucked out of the main waterway. I studied the flowers as he set up his fishing gear, transfixed by dragon-flies and water bugs. I leaned against the side of the boat, enjoying the blankness of my mind. I clutched it tight, invisible fingers digging in.

Overhead clouds drifted lazily across the sun—casting us in shade and then releasing us to intense inspection. The water, so still, reflected the world back to us, the sky mirrored and seemingly another place, a different world. In that one, did a mother love a daughter? Had the father of the family survived? If the daughter had stayed in this town, would she have known Jake?

Jake.

His name was desire and curiosity, butterflies and fire in my blood. I glanced at him, startled to find his eyes on me, watching me the way I'd watched the water, his own wondering visible in his expression. This was the first time

I'd been able to read him, to understand completely before he looked away.

"Why look at me like that and then look away?" I asked softly, turning my attention back to the water, a flush creeping across my face. It was too much, too much familiarity. I was asking for something that wasn't mine—his honesty, his emotion.

"Aren't you leaving in a few days?"

His voice was as soft as mine had been—the constant edge dulled. The air was different between us out here on the water, away from town, away from the people who thought we were something other than we were. They were wrong about me. They had to be wrong about him too.

"I have to. I can't stay in this place."

He made a noise of agreement, understanding without needing an explanation. Why hadn't he left? A dead town, the residents wrapped up in their harsh pocket of religion, the way the woods filled up at night with strange noises and distant lights. It was all so isolated, a forgotten corner of the world, the only way in or out a decaying old bridge across a creek that flooded at the drop of a hat. Someday the bridge would collapse, and they might never repair it. Then Back of Beyond would truly be forgotten. And he'd still be here, living and working under their harsh judgment.

"Then why does it matter how I look at you?"

I opened my mouth, caught between being honest and preserving what little bit of pride I had left. I didn't want to tell him how I thought of him at night, how he crossed my mind during the day, and I found myself looking for him around every corner I turned.

"I guess it doesn't," I laughed.

"You shouldn't let what people think get under your skin," he said.

"You're one to talk." I snorted, skimming my fingers over the water, searching for fish. The water was a clear brown here, and the first few feet were visible. I didn't know what lay at the bottom, what plants might cling to the mud down there and what creatures swam through it all. He was like this place, only the surface visible, the light unable to penetrate farther down.

"I'm serious. You're leaving in a few days, and this place will be behind you. Don't waste your time worrying about these people. You aren't going to change their minds about Vivian."

I sighed. "Is it so wrong to want it though? She had them all fooled."

"You're going to have to make peace with the fact they don't care. Even if you could present them with some kind of solid evidence, they wouldn't care. These people make up their minds, and nothing will change things for them but death."

I nodded, considering his words, genuinely trying to take them in and settle them down in my mind. He was right. Of course, he was. I wasn't going to change anyone's opinion here, and I needed to let it go and move on. Soon, so soon, I'd be gone, and they could go back to gossiping about the family that had lived in Magnolia House.

"Unless you have found something in the house?"

It was barely a question, the words soft, his tone lifting the last word up slowly, as if he expected the whole thing to be dashed from his fingers. I turned to him, shading my eyes, and studying his features.

"Like what?"

He shrugged, squinting out over the water, mouth set in

a hard line; a muscle in his jaw jumped. His hand on the tiller tightened, knuckles going white. I waited, needing to know what he meant, curious about what he might know, how it all connected to that house and that woman.

"I don't know."

"A letter of confession maybe? Or a lockbox with a gun?"

Or a newspaper clipping inside a diary. A few words scrawled in her looping cursive: *They found her.*

"Maybe. I don't know. Guilty could look like all kinds of things with her."

"Yeah, maybe." I agreed, mind racing.

What did he suspect her of? What did I? I wasn't sure yet, not one hundred percent. There were things I was finding in the house, uncovering in the wake of her death, that made it all the more obvious that she was nothing like the person people had believed her to be. Vivian had photos of them, Alice and Jake, a very in love young couple—high school sweethearts.

I'd believed Vivian was capable of anything, absolutely anything. Why was I hesitating when it came to this? But she'd been in a wheelchair since the accident, bound to the house by invisible chains, limited in a way that would make it impossible to come and go without being noticed. And Alice's murder had happened well after Vivian had been told she'd never walk again, after the crying and wailing that had come with that diagnosis, the anger that followed.

So much anger.

What would she have thought of beautiful Alice with her hold on Jake?

I studied him, dark hair and blue eyes, probably one of the most handsome men I'd ever met. He moved through the world with a kind of confidence I envied. It hadn't been easy in any way, and yet he came through it all. And when he smiled, a dimple flashed and lit me up inside like a bonfire.

I put an arm over my face, blocking out the sun, wondering how sunburned I'd be later. Jake took his baseball hat off and dropped it on my head, the band too big, the front of it falling over my eyes.

"Thanks," I said, adjusting it, grateful for the shade.

"Sure," he chuckled, the sound between us so natural. "Don't mention it."

We passed a few hours in the sun, birds calling to each other, insects buzzing, we headed back. The hours had flown—a strange mix of emotional tension and longing, each shared glance eons long while the time raced by. But we had a funeral to attend. A woman to lay to rest. A past to bury.

I wasn't sure who wanted to skip it more, me or Jake.

———

When we reached the dock, Jake tied the boat up and offered me a hand up. I stood, swaying with the motion, skin prickling with his nearness. I'd wanted to ask him about the kiss in the parking lot. Several times I'd thought I would; there had been an opening in the conversion, a gap where a kiss would have fit perfectly.

But I'd run out of time. If I didn't ask now, would I ever?

"Did you kiss me back there because you wanted to? Or because you wanted to irritate and rile up the locals?"

I stood in his shadow, the boat rocking beneath us, his blue eyes on my face. I wanted to lean forward, fall into him, and find out if he would catch me. I bit my lip, looking away, unable to take the pressure of his stare. He reached out, cupping my cheek, smoothing a thumb over my lip. I closed my eyes, leaning into his touch, sucking in a breath that filled my lungs, dizzy with his heat.

The boat moved, swaying as he lowered his face to mine, his breath mixing with my own. The sun hot on my skin, cool compared to his touch, cotton warming, head buzzing with anticipation. I waited, eyes closed, wanting his lips on mine, wanting to open beneath him like a flower. No, not a flower, nothing as delicate, I wanted to swallow him like a storm, pull him in and hold on for as long as he would let me.

"Open your eyes," he whispered, the words rushing through me.

I did, lashes fluttering, blood pounding. He was so close, the baseball cap pushed back a little, shading my face. We stood in our own pocket of shadow, the shade between our bodies, the both of us burning hotter than the sun.

"What?" I said, voice low, the word almost not there.

He leaned in, our eyes locked, and he pressed a soft kiss against my mouth. It was so tender, tentative, and he watched me waiting to see if I would pull away. I didn't. I reached for him, wrapping my arms around his neck, pressing my body to his, and closing my eyes as the kiss deepened. His hands moved over my body, firm and pressing me to him, holding on tight.

I broke away, shading my eyes, studying his face.

"Why do you think I kissed you?" he asked, voice low and rough.

"Because I'm leaving in a few days and you've got nothing else to lose."

"I've never had anything to lose, Emma." The corner of his mouth hitched up, dimple flashing.

"Not even your heart?"

The words were out of my mouth without passing through my brain—thudding through me, shocking my system. I held my breath, terror filling me, instant regret at sticking my foot so far in my mouth I was surprised I could even close it now. He studied me, his hand coming up to cup my face, gentle—as if I might crumble and he was trying to hold me together.

"You should go get ready for the funeral," he said. "You're running out of time."

He was right. We were both running out of time.

I nodded, letting him help me out of the boat and firmly onto the solid dock. It felt like coming back to reality, to a place I wasn't ready to be, back within reach of Magnolia House. I made my way to the car, fumbling the keys out of my pocket, feeling his gaze on me. But when I turned to wave, he was concentrating on unloading the boat, focused on anything but me.

CHAPTER NINETEEN

SUNDAY

I sat in the car, the engine groaning with heat stress, the air conditioner fighting to keep me cool. Beads of sweat rolled down between my shoulder blades, my bra too tight around my ribs, as cicadas droned on and the sound buzzed in my teeth. I clenched my jaw around the vibration, holding in the overwhelming anxiousness rising in my chest.

When I couldn't put it off any longer, I got out of the car, stepping out into the glare of the lowering sun, laid bare for inspection for all those still making their way to the church. Smoothing the simple black dress down, wriggling my toes in the black flats, I pulled in a steadying breath.

What was the worst that could happen? It wasn't as if there could be a repeat of last night. People respected the church. They'd all be on their best behavior. I touched my lip. I'd managed to forget about the split, so focused on remembered kisses and desperate for more, and it was healing—already better.

Crossing from the parking lot to the sidewalk leading up to the church, I searched for a familiar face. Strangers met my gaze, some flat and emotionless, others with that sneer I'd come to expect. The First Baptist Lunch Committee, that gaggle of gossiping women, nodded to me, not committing to a greeting or pausing to shake my hand or offer a hug. They watched me, eyes moving over my dress and shoes, the purse hanging from my shoulder, my hair still slightly damp from the shower. Their dissatisfaction was evident.

A shiver of sharks.

I'd read about that when I was a kid in one of my dad's books—*Animal Behaviors and the Natural World*. A group of sharks was called a shiver. It described these ladies perfectly—cold and watchful, waiting for first blood as I approached the open church doors.

Subdued piano music filled the air, coming from inside the building, the gentle hymn played with reverence. I recognized it from my childhood but couldn't put a name to it. One of those songs we'd stood to sing, red leather songbook in hand, Vivian's voice rising over the congregation.

The music passed through me, over me, continuing out into the parking lot and street, joining the Southern summer and cicadas droning on into the evening sun. The scent of roses followed the music, spilling through the doors—deeply floral, green, and sweet.

They would be crimson. A shade similar to the color of lipstick she favored.

I never wanted to smell another rose as long as I lived.

Pastor Roberts did not come out to greet me, left in me in the sun, searching for the little bit of comfort I'd managed to uncover in this place. I hesitated, several feet from the threshold.

Fight or flight.

Run or stay.

The music stopped, cicadas startled silent in its absence. Thunderous silence overtaking it all—heavy as guilt. A gnawing sensation filled me, a terrible moment hurtling toward me and unavoidable, inescapable.

Jake hadn't come. He'd said he would but what did that mean? I was more a stranger than anything else, a woman shoved into his life because someone else had died. That was our only connection. I wanted to believe a kiss had changed us, that the dark interior of Magnolia House had bound us together. But we were still strangers.

I hated to face the crowded church alone.

And I wouldn't.

I wasn't going to sit in the first row with the congregation at my back and Pastor Roberts on the dais looking down on me. I refused to sit for his judgment. I wasn't staying. I would be gone in a few days. I would never see any of these people again. Still, the urge to fall into line, to do the thing that was expected, to participate in this farce despite my feelings, was strong. To fit in, conform, and maybe be accepted, was an instinct that was very hard to ignore.

I put a hand to my stomach, pressing against the flip-flopping sensation, and took a deep breath. The first step toward my car was the hardest. There was whispering behind me now, voices swelling like the sea, rising as they waited for me to enter so the services could start. But another step took me in the opposite direction. Then another. My formal black flats clicked against the sun-washed sidewalk, flecks of reflective mica winking up at me as I went.

Behind me, the pastor called out, my name like pelting ice, cold and hard enough to knock the ninety-degree heat aside.

Don't let him see you flinch, baby.

Dad's voice. A phrase he'd never spoken but all him just the same.

"Where are you running off to?"

A different voice stopped me, not the lingering memory of my dad, but a solid and present voice I trusted. The parking lot was in sight, the rental car baking in the sun, my keys flashing silver in my hand. But I'd been waiting for this voice.

"I thought you weren't coming," I said, stopping in the middle of the sidewalk.

Jake was crossing the lawn from where he'd parked in the street to the right of the parking lot. He wore a dark-gray suit, crisp white shirt, and tie tucked into a matching vest, with shoes shined to a glossy finish. With the grease-stained T-shirt gone and his hair slicked back, he almost looked like a different person. Maybe a version of himself he didn't like to be for anyone else.

But he'd come here for me.

"I'm sorry I'm late," he said, closing the distance between us. "I couldn't find my tie."

"You only have one?" I asked with a smile.

"Why would you need more than one?" He returned the smile, a dimple flashing before he looked past me to the church. "They waiting on you?"

I nodded.

"Well then, let's see if the whole place bursts into flames when I step inside. There are several people in there that have sworn up and down it would. I'd like to see if they're right."

He held out his arm, waiting for me to take it, intense eyes on my face. I glanced at the church. I could still leave. I could run. But I could face them all with Jake beside me. I put my arm through his and he pulled me close, my hip brushing against his as we turned back to the church. The fabric of his coat was smooth, the feel of him warm and solid beneath my fingertips. We found a rhythm, our shoes an echo of each other, soft clicking as we walked with purpose toward the open doors.

"What if they're right?"

"Then we're near the exit."

"And the others?" I laughed and looked up into his face, studying the hard lines, the sharp cheekbones, the way his mouth twitched with some dark pleasure.

"Maybe the doors will lock as we close them."

I squeezed his arm. "You can't say that. That's a terrible thing to say."

"Is it?" He looked down at me, the smile gone, consideration in his eyes. "If you don't want me to, I won't."

I nodded, stomach tightening as we neared the doors, tension pulling my shoulders taut. No turning back. No running. We'd face it together. Two outcasts. Two of the most hated people in Back of Beyond. Maybe the church would catch on fire, our voices incendiary, our presence blasphemy. But I would take him, a suspected murderer, over everyone in that building, any day of the week.

We went up the steps, moving in unison, an army of two facing certain death, headed into a battle we could never win. Then we were over the threshold and into the air conditioning, the interior dim after the intense sunshine, the church pews full of faces turning to watch our arrival.

———

I never thought I would walk down the center aisle of a packed church. People dreamed of wearing white and being surrounded by friends and family. The moment when the room stands to watch you pass, the murmurs of pleasure at seeing you, tears collecting in eyes, hands pressed to damp cheeks. Roses would scent the air, weddings and funerals had that in common, the beginning and the end of all things.

We arrived in black, happy mourners to a funeral where the congregation wept. With a scuffle of shoes on hardwood, a few people stood—a man with a plaid shirt stretched tight over his gut, a woman in a blue floral print dress, a couple toward the front in starched Sunday best. The room was silent, each person holding their breath, a layer of shock laid over us like a summer quilt.

At the head of the aisle, Pastor Roberts waited, face blank, eyes burning with furious fire. I continued forward, fighting the heat of his anger, pushing forward even as everything in my body told me to run.

We stopped at the first pew, the whole row empty, reserved for the family of Vivian Taylor.

Jake guided me to a seat, waiting to sit until I had. The pew was hard beneath me, bare wood with no padding, a box of tissues tucked against the arm. Beneath the seat were bibles and hymn books, little white tithe envelopes and short pencils. Overhead several fans spun with the barest hint of a sound, contending with the air conditioner and the rustle of people moving behind us like a flock of murderous pigeons.

I hadn't allowed myself to look beyond the pastor until that moment, to see Vivian in all her splendor at the head of the church. The last time we'd been here together had been one of the worst moments in my life. I resisted the urge to touch my cheek as Jake sat beside me, his knee brushing mine, a gentle pressure to remind me was here and on my side.

Someone cleared their throat, the sound overly loud in the respectful quiet, and spoke. "He shouldn't be here, Pastor Roberts."

"He needs to leave!"

"Get him out now!"

Other protests erupted as people agreed, voices mixing and melding to become one. I clasped my hands together, pressing tight, knuckles going white as a frenzy of anger built. Jake reached over, taking one of my hands in his, smoothing a thumb against my palm in soothing gesture. His warmth grounded me and kept the anger in the room from closing in and choking me.

"Even sinners are welcome in church," Pastor Roberts said, raising his hands in a pacifying gesture. "I understand your concerns, but we are here to remember Vivian Taylor. We shouldn't let anything take away from that."

There were a few grumbles as people sat, fabric rustling and muttered disagreement slowly dying away. Pastor Roberts turned to us, focusing on our clasped hands, a flicker of unpleasant emotion in his eyes. I looked away, straight ahead, and tried to ignore the squirming unease churning inside. After a long pause, he began to speak in the smooth way I remembered from childhood. I tuned the words out, taking in the rhythm they made, not listening to the message.

The spot between my shoulder blades itched, the back of my head burning, as most of the focus in the room remained on us. Despite the pastor's words, there were barely audible grumbles of disgust mixing with his voice.

Jake kept my hand in his, knee pressed to mine, as the funeral continued. Vivian would have been furious that so much attention had been taken from her. The scene I'd created would have earned incredible viciousness behind closed doors. Instead, Pastor Roberts directed all his anger and frustration at us throughout the ceremony.

Several people spoke, the eulogy read by a woman from the church who claimed to know Vivian so well. They spoke of kindness and soft gentleness, the rock she'd been for the community, and her involvement in the church and other charitable organizations through the years. They would never be the same without her. She had left a hole in the fabric of their lives.

Vivian would be missed.

I didn't recognize the woman they spoke about. She was a wholly different creature than the person who had birthed me, raised me, terrorized me. As each mourner stepped away from the podium, they glared at us, hard faces and eyes, trying to shame Jake into leaving. Or make sure I was aware of how spectacularly I had failed as a daughter.

How many of them had been here the day I'd pushed Vivian out of the wheelchair? If they hadn't been present, they would know the story. Something like that would have spread like a cold, passed on contact and within sneezing distance. I swept it aside, working to clear my mind, needing to make it through this moment. After this, beyond this act in the tragedy that was Magnolia House and Back of Beyond, would be the cremation. The final stop in Vivian's journey.

When music began to play, I knew it was over. Mourners stood, moving toward the casket to say their final goodbyes.

"Are you ready? Do you want to say goodbye?" Jake whispered in my ear, leaning into me, shoulder brushing mine.

I shook my head, squeezing his hand before I stood. The

scent of jasmine perfume hit me, that artificial sweet floral note overwhelming the fresh roses for an instant. I looked around, wondering who might be wearing the brand Vivian favored. But no one stood near us, no one could have gone past and left scent memory trailing in their wake.

"Emma Taylor," Pastor Roberts's voice rang out, the room quieting. "You will say goodbye to your mother."

I paused, shocked at his tone—thundering command and rebuke.

"No," Jake said. "She doesn't need to do that here, in front of the whole church. She's done enough to pacify all of you."

Murmurs, faces pinched around sour thoughts, others watching with curious malice as the town murderer defended the town outcast and villainous daughter.

"For once in her life she needs to do the right thing."

The words were a growl, a threat.

"I've said my goodbyes." I met Pastor Roberts's eyes, facing the forceful distaste. "It's time for you to say yours."

Jake gave my hand a reassuring squeeze as we walked down the aisle and pushed through the closed front door. An older woman I didn't recognize rushed after us, stopping me on the front steps with a firm hand on my arm, nothing gentle in her voice. More condemnation from the congregation, more anger at how I'd handled things. Everything about her, stance and glare, threatened passive aggression because she was too afraid or weak to be direct.

"I'll be placing flowers on your family mausoleum when I visit. My Walter is only a few rows away, and Vivian deserves to be remembered. With you living so far away, I know it will be a comfort to you knowing she will be. I want you to know that we'll all be doing the right thing."

I shook my head, taking a step back.

"She won't be there." Pastor Roberts cut through the conversation, speaking from the doorway of the church, a faint smile on his face.

"What do you mean?" the woman asked.

"Emma has made the choice to ignore her mother's final wishes. Vivian is being cremated this very evening." His words fed the growing anger, the building resentment. "And Emma has refused to tell me what will happen with her ashes."

The woman put a hand to her mouth, eyes wide. "Pastor, no. That can't be. That's horrible."

Others were gathering on the church steps now, silent and intent. I opened my mouth, the urge to defend myself so strong, so necessary.

"Don't. It doesn't do any good. You've done what you think is right. It's time to let it go," Jake whispered, taking my arm and turning me gently away. He glanced over his shoulder, back to the crowd watching us.

"You are the most ungrateful child I've ever met, Emma Taylor." She sneered my name, pouring nastiness into each syllable, as her voice followed us, climbing higher, going shrill. "I hope you know what kind of man you're spending time with, Emma Taylor."

"Ignore her," Jake said, squeezing my hand again.

I nodded, swallowing, my mouth dry, knees trembling. I wanted to yell at them, point hard fingers at them, let loose all of my fear and grief on them. But I was on the verge of tears, and that was the last thing I wanted to give them.

"Emma! Emma Taylor, you stop right there."

I stopped, back straight, stomach dropping, and turned to face Pastor Roberts.

"This is the last time I'm going to ask you to do the right thing. You have a chance. It won't make up for everything, but Vivian meant a lot to us, and we would like to see her final wishes honored."

I had reached my breaking point with this man.

"Do the right thing? Are you joking?"

"I'm very serious. You've shown you don't have her best interests at heart. You shouldn't be handling her final arrangements."

He took a step toward me, mouth open to continue, but stopped when Jake took a step between us.

"You think you knew Vivian?" I spoke through clenched teeth. "You didn't. None of you did. Vivian was a monster. You can't tell me that none of you saw how she treated me after my dad died."

"I don't know what you're talking about." A flicker of emotion passed over his face, the self-righteous expression wavering.

"Stop." I held up a hand. "Isn't lying a sin, Pastor Roberts? Of all people, I would have thought you'd be the least likely to lie. It doesn't suit you. I can see it on your face. If you didn't know for sure, you had a suspicion."

"You were difficult after your dad passed. Your mother and I spoke about you many times. Even after you abandoned her. She did the best she could and provided for you. You had shelter and food, didn't you? And the only thing I saw was a spoiled, ungrateful child who assaulted her mother."

Don't let the bastards grind you down, baby.

Dad. Always dad with the constant encouragement and belief I could make it through all this and out the other side even as I doubted it.

I laughed, the sound bursting from my chest, reverberating through the parking lot. It filled my ears, my head, and for a moment it sounded as if it were Vivian laughing.

"You're a willfully ignorant old man in a dying town. I don't have to explain anything to you or justify myself. Not anymore."

Turning away, fumbling my keys out of my purse, I crossed to the rental car. Jake was right behind me, following closely. Pastor Roberts was rooted to the sidewalk, staring after us.

"I was wondering how long it would take you to say something," Jake said.

I unlocked the car and opened the door before I met his eyes. "Too long."

"Better late than never," he said with a shrug.

"Maybe so," I said, with a tight smile. "Thank you for coming. For being here. I know it's uncomfortable. All of these people," I waved at the church, "are terrible."

"Yep," he said, keeping his eyes on me, searching my face. "But you won't have to deal with them anymore."

"Not after the estate sale, no. And that will be over soon enough."

He nodded. "So, what now?"

I blew out a sigh. "Vivian will be cremated. They're going to take her to the crematorium right away. It's over in Fairview. I'll be there waiting for her."

His brows came together. "Is that a usual thing? Will they let you?"

I need to know," I said, lowering my voice. "I need to see it all end."

"I get that." Jake glanced around the parking lot and then up at the sky. "I have to get out of this suit, it's driving me crazy, but would you like company afterward?"

"At Magnolia House?"

He nodded.

I bit my lip, looking down at my shoes, wondering where all that might lead if I accepted his offer.

"Yes."

A simple answer. A single word. But it altered our reality, changed the air between us, and stopped the cicada song for an instant.

"I'll change and then meet you. That okay?"

"Yeah, sounds good."

I half turned away, back to the open doors of the church, the world coming to a focus around a casket hidden from view. I needed to be at the crematorium tonight. I had to make sure. I had to be certain she was really gone, that her place in the world had been taken from her, and she would never ever get it back.

Jake touched my shoulder and pulled me toward him. He slid a hand up the back of my neck, bringing our faces together. My heart stopped. He was going to kiss me, here, in this church parking lot, in front of all these people. I leaned forward, into him, face tilted up and not knowing what I wanted. Kiss me here? Now? He smiled, maybe he saw it all on my face, but he rested his forehead against mine, and closed his eyes. When he spoke, his voice was low and soft, a well of emotion behind the words.

"I'm proud of you, Emma Taylor."

Fireworks shot through me, bringing light to all the dark forgotten places of my soul. *I'm proud of you.* It had been so long since I'd heard those words. Not since my dad. And they meant more to me than I could express. Tears gathered on my lashes, and I released the breath I'd been holding, letting the ball of stress drop.

"Ms. Taylor, I would like one last word."

Pastor Roberts approached, eyes hard, mouth a thin line in his pale face. In the sun he seemed to have aged more, beyond the shadows of his church, out in the light of day where he could no longer hide. He was just a man after all. Not the bogeyman of my childhood. Not someone I owed anything to. No more explanations. No more justifications.

"I don't have anything else to say to you," I said, half turning away.

His hand closed like a vice around my wrist. "But I have something to say to you."

I looked down at his hand, the pressure of his grip growing, anger feeding it. Too many men had put their hands on me here, too many people had made assumptions about me or jumped to conclusions. Jake took a step forward, the anger that lingered below the surface beginning to bubble.

"Remove your hand," he said, voice low and soft, deadly like a coiled snake.

Pastor Roberts sneered at him, lip curling around his words. "You don't belong here. You should leave before someone decides to escort you off the premises."

There was a crowd gathered on the church steps, a handful of men coming down the walk with intent expressions. There would be a fight, it didn't matter if Jake or one of the other men threw the first punch, there would be no winners walking away.

"Stop," I said, forcing calm into my voice, steel into my spine. "Let go right now. I have nothing else to say to you and I refuse to listen to any more of your opinions."

"Opinions?" he laughed, shaking my arm, refusing to let go. "Facts. Even now, after all these years and all her prayers, you're still the ungrateful brat. You're cruel for the sake of cruelty, an unnatural child, a hateful child."

"I'm done listening to you," I said, jerking my arm away and stepping back.

He followed me, hand out and reaching for me still, sputtering about duty and loyalty. Jake stopped him, stepping between us with his hands up. I clicked the unlock button on the rental until it beeped, lights flashing. I wasn't going to hurry, I wouldn't run. I'd been so close before, but I wouldn't now. The pastor had bullied me, determined to get his way—Vivian's way—and I wasn't going to let him see my fear.

Jake reached the car just as I did, reaching in front of me to open the driver's side door. I slid in, and he moved to block me from view of the church, hiding me from anyone who might be watching. I swiped at my cheeks, relieved to find them dry, even as the urge to cry with anger and frustration filled me. I'd always been an angry crier, and right now I would've given anything not to have an audience. I shoved the key into the ignition and twisted it, holding my breath until the engine caught and the car started.

"Be safe," Jake said.

I nodded, pulling the seatbelt on and releasing a deep breath. Looking up into Jake's face I smiled, small and a little damp, on the verge of spilling real tears. But I was grateful for his kindness, the gentleness he'd shown me, and the strength it took to show up in a place you knew you weren't wanted. He shut the door, stepping back from the car, patting the hood as I put it into drive.

"I'll see you at Magnolia House."

CHAPTER TWENTY

SUNDAY

How quickly does a casket burn? How fast would it be consumed, the body within licked by flame, blackened, broken down until only the bones were left? I'd looked it up. I had to know. The answer varied, two to four hours, with a cool-down period and then processing. A total of seven to ten days to get the ashes back.

Mr. Fontenot came highly recommended by Mr. Laurent—they looked so alike they could have been brothers—and he promised I would have Vivian's remains within the week. I told him it didn't matter as long as I got to be there when she was rolled into the oven. He had looked at me oddly, maybe realizing for the first time that there had been something more to my story, our story. The story of Poor Vivian. Beautiful Vivian. The story of an ungrateful daughter and the long-suffering mother confined to a wheelchair.

Vivian had been an incredible actress.

A beautiful casket. Expensive. Vivian had spared no expense.

If it had been my choice, it would have been simple pine and inexpensive. I wouldn't have wasted money on her. But she'd taken that choice away from me. And really, I was thankful. I hated to feel that here, with her at the end. I'd spent so much time turning my past into armor—using the pain. But here I was laid bare, raw after the scene with the pastor, the distasteful stares of strangers. Assumptions. All of them so sure they knew the circumstances and the extent of my cruelty.

There was a small room where family could stand, watch the casket slide out of view, a curtain drawing closed as the bundle made its way to the fire. But everything else happened out of sight. Mr. Fontenot took me to a back room. Employees only. The public wasn't allowed back here; it was off-limits, forbidden.

I watched as the casket was rolled in, fire burning hotly: hungry and bright.

Take her. Keep her. But release me.

I prayed this would be enough. That witnessing this would be the point where everything broke—my past and present, severed, torn asunder. I stayed for almost an hour. I couldn't pull myself away. Mr. Fontenot faded into the background, leaving me to my pain, a brief moment of grief. After all, all of it, she had been my mother.

But this was the last time I would think of her that way. A heaviness settled over me, shoulders weighed down, feet sore and ready to take me from this place, propel me to a plane that would take me home.

"Thank you," I said, turning away, and glancing around for the exit.

"This way," Mr. Fontenot said, coming forward, eyes down, face blank.

He showed me to a steel door with a push bar, heavy and solid, and opened it silently into the world. The afternoon had become night, and I stumbled out as the door clicked shut behind me. The industrial light above the door was hazy with flying insects—June bugs searching for love, moths drawn to artificial flame.

"Want a ride home?"

I looked up at the words, startled, taken off guard. I'd expected loneliness. I thought I would carry the flames through the night, hold them close to me, keep them to ward off the creak of floorboards and half-seen images from the corner of my eye. I thought I would be alone tonight.

"Jake."

He was leaning against his truck, a figure in the dark, beyond the halo of light. I couldn't see his face, would never recognize the figure was his if I hadn't recognized the voice. That voice. I longed for it, for words whispered in my ear, breath brushing my skin, lips so close to mine.

"I thought you were meeting me at the house."

"I thought you might not want to be alone when you came out."

I hesitated, the building at my back, the reality of it all beneath the star-filled sky, and the whoosh of gas igniting buzzing in my ears. "You're right."

"Let me take you home."

I nodded. There was a promise in his words, his voice. Something we had danced around: thrown glances, hands brushing, the nearness of each other like hot sunshine. The kiss on the boat overshadowed it all, his mouth on mine.

"What happens now?" He tilted his chin at the building, what it held, what it promised.

"I'll have her ashes back in about a week. I can pick them up, or they'll mail them."

"What will you do with her?"

"Don't know yet."

He pushed off the truck, coming toward me, stepping into the industrial orange that bathed the back of the building—face soft, eyes tender.

"I'm sorry, Emma."

Simple words. Words that came easily to people, said in passing, without any real thought or emotion behind them. But not from him. He meant it, offered it with his whole heart. I held my breath as he reached out, cupping my cheek. I leaned into him, holding his hand to my face, stealing a little bit of his warmth.

"Come on," he said. "Let's get you home."

He took my hand, guiding me to the truck, and opened the door; a hand on my elbow to help me inside, the door shutting softly as I clicked the seatbelt in place. He got in too, the engine turning over, headlights picking out the pine trees around the parking lot. My car, forlorn in the night, and abandoned. But I'd come back for it. Eventually, I'd have to.

We didn't speak as he drove, and I was grateful for the silence. Neither of us needed small talk as we passed through town. I watched houses go by, lighted windows, the one red light in the town square unnaturally vibrant. Then we were beyond it, past the brightly lit gas station, passing the *Hell Is Real* sign.

Hell is other people.

Jean Paul Sartre had written that. I'd seen the play once, *No Exit*, and the line had been burned into my soul. Later, much later, I'd come across a collection of plays in a used bookstore in Portland and that one had been in it. A dog-eared and yellowing copy, with a green fabric cover, gold embossing. I missed my books—longed for beautiful words and worlds to fall into.

Take me anywhere with you.

———

The house waited, picked out in the truck headlights, darkness wide and all-encompassing beyond the circle of warmth. I kept coming back to this place in the dark, unable to escape the nighttime hours. This is how I would remember it when I left, in disconnected dreams and flash-backs, crouched in the bayou and watching the world go by.

Jake turned the engine off and came round to open my door, waiting as I slid out, feet hitting gravel with a crunch. I made a noise, half a *thank you*, but couldn't bring myself to say it louder. I'd made it back and was exhausted, hit suddenly with the conversations I'd had and the weight of my inadequate defenses. Jake walked beside me without speaking, up the stairs, hesitating on the verandah as I pulled the key from my purse. I pushed it into the lock but didn't turn the handle.

"Are you staying?"

It was more than that. It was an invitation, a silent plea. *Stay with me.* Stay because I might go crazy in the night. I would go mad with fear and never be the same. This woman, this self I had built and come to accept, would be ruined. *Stay and keep me safe.*

"If you want me to."

I nodded, not trusting my voice, and pushed the door open. Vivian's house greeted us.

You're back. I knew you would be.

And it was her voice. Not gone as I had hoped it would be in my head. Not silent. Inescapable. Relentless.

I can't stop you from coming in, but I'll be happy when you're gone.

The house and Vivian, two voices, one thought.

"Still sleeping in the study?"

He moved into the foyer to flip on light switches. Relief flooded me when they came on.

"I wouldn't sleep anywhere else."

"I don't blame you."

He walked beside me down the hall, hand entwined with mine, facing this with me—memories and terror, a long night filled with expectation. The lamp in the study was on, and the room was full of muted greenish-gold light. I was glad I'd remembered to do that before I'd left. *I'll leave the light on for you.*

My wrinkled sheet and pillow were a smushed lump on the sofa, the sloth shirt I'd been sleeping in tossed over the back. It was simultaneously the most comfortable and uncomfortable-looking place to sleep.

I yawned, exhausted, the desire to sleep hitting me all at once—the Sandman overtaking me, determined to put me out. Grabbing an oversized T-shirt from my suitcase, I kicked off my shoes one at a time. I slipped it on and fumbled with my funeral clothes beneath it—awkward and self-conscious as I worked my bra off without taking the dressy shirt off. His eyes were on me, touching me, but I didn't look up. I moved to the sofa and curled onto half of it, a ball of woman and sheet, molding the cool pillow into a more comfortable position, and closed my eyes.

I heard the zipper on his jeans slide down, the thump of shoes being kicked off—rustling fabric, the scent of soap.

"Stretch out some," he said, a hand on my shoulder.

Then the weight of him beside me, coming to hold me in the narrow space. I moved to rest my head on his shoulder, sliding a leg over his, yawning as I settled in.

He smoothed down the fabric of my T-shirt. The motion was soothing, nothing was offered but comfort. And that was what I needed most. Out there on the verandah, I'd thought it was something else. A physical release. A blank, mindless moment of passion. But not here in the study, surrounded by my father's books, not waiting for the sound of a wheelchair moving down the hall. He gave me exactly what I needed.

"Don't let me go," I mumbled.

"No," he said. "I'm not letting you go."

He spoke so softly I thought I dreamed it.

MONDAY

I know you're tired but come,
this is the way.

- Rumi

CHAPTER TWENTY-ONE

MONDAY

I was free.

Vivian was gone.

The night had passed, and nothing had moved through Magnolia House.

I made an extra strong pot of coffee as the sun rose, the two of us moving through the kitchen in that familiar way I'd enjoyed so much from the other morning. We sat in the dining room, the polished surface of the table reflecting the room—our blurred figures caught and held, the windows rectangles of light stretching across polished maple. I traced the rim of my mug, the contents trembling slightly.

We ate white bread with butter and jelly, a single piece folded in half, rolled around the strawberry jam. It reminded me of all the dinners I'd had at this table, forced to sit motionless, to eat exactly what Vivian permitted. There had been plenty of nights I'd gone to bed hungry, I'd cooked enough dinner for two and yet been left starving when she insisted I should watch my weight.

Not anymore.

I savored each bite, here with Jake, drinking coffee and

eating without plates, drops of jam on the polished surface of the table. A weight had been lifted. I smiled as jam dripped from my sandwich, the mix of slightly bitter coffee and sweetness on my tongue was perfect.

"You want some help cleaning up the house today?" Jake asked, leaning back in the chair, sunlight from the window warming his features. "Laura said she'd be here today, right?"

"Yeah, sometime this morning." I nodded, sipping coffee. "Wouldn't Josh miss you though?"

"Nah, it's good. My hours are pretty flexible," he said, turning his mug in a circle on the table. "And I let him know Laura would be setting up a sale today and tomorrow."

"Thanks for sticking around," I said, smiling.

"Anytime," he said, saluting me with his coffee mug.

It was easy. So easy, to sit, drink coffee, and eat bread and butter with this man. So few things in my life had been easy. Nothing had ever felt like this. I smiled, feeling it stretch out in my soul—like a car in a puddle of sunshine—and I wanted to laugh.

"What?" Jake asked, half smiling as he watched me.

"Nothing." I shook my head, shoving the last bite into my mouth, brushing crumbs from my face. I chewed quickly, swallowing before continuing. "This is nice, you know?"

Jake looked down at the table, moving his mug, his own jelly sandwich eaten. I waited for him to agree, to echo my heart, to have his smile match mine. Knocking resounded through the house—tap, tap, tap—the polite arrival of someone ready to be greeted.

"That should be Laura," I said, pushing out of my chair, propelling myself toward the front door and away from the strange silence that had overtaken the dining room.

———

Room by room—furniture, porcelain figurines, paintings, dishes, linens, books—the contents were catalogued and sorted. Laura moved through it all at a pace I could barely keep up with. I'd assumed it would take hours. But she sorted the house out with a clipboard and pencil, going down a checklist and scribbling notes in the margins.

Jake lingered at the edges of our conversation, unobtrusive, and seemingly uninterested. I'm not sure at what point he retreated to the study with another cup of coffee. At one point we'd passed the open door, and he'd been at the desk sorting through a stack of books.

"Well, there isn't much, and it shouldn't take long. Owen, Colton, and Jake will all be helping to set up the sale tomorrow." Laura said, flipping through her notes. "What about your mother's room?"

The question brought me up short. Of course, I needed to deal with that room. Her room. Of all the places in the house, she lingered there the most. I could feel her there in a way I couldn't explain. But I knew. Even now I didn't want to go in there.

"Is there anything you want to add to the sale in there?"

"I'm not sure," I said, glancing over my shoulder, half expecting Vivian to be there. No one was there. The house was empty aside from myself, Jake, and Laura.

I thought I told you to stay out of my room, Emma.

Was that a memory or something else? Her voice cut through my thoughts so clearly, as if she had been standing beside me after all.

"Would you like me to take a look?" Laura prompted.

I nodded. "Let's go take a look."

I led the way—through the foyer and down the hall to

the last door on the right. The window showed an over-cast sky, clouds low and heavy, and a fly buzzed against the glass, tapping as it tried to escape. I wanted to free it, let it loose, but the window hadn't been opened in as long as I could remember. Never once in my life. I didn't even know if it could open. And it didn't matter. No matter how many flies I tried to shoo from the house or little carcasses I cleaned up, there were always more at this window.

I tensed for the searing frost of the doorknob, a physical manifestation of anger from someone dead and gone. I didn't know how I would explain that to Laura. *Oh you know, old houses.* If I shrugged and smiled, would she accept the non-answer? Maybe. But the knob was room tempera-ture and turned easily in my hand, the door swinging open on hinges that might have been freshly oiled if I didn't know any better.

"After you," I said, stepping aside so she could enter the room first.

"There's a lot of good stuff in here." Laura looked around, hands on hips, running a practiced eye over the room. "I'm sure all of it would sell. The dressing table espe-cially. I've got several people who have asked me to keep an eye open for pieces just like that."

I looked at the little table with the velvet stool before it, the trifold mirror reflecting the room. Vivian stood behind me, the woman I remembered from before the accident, tall in shiny black heels, with perfectly styled dark curls. The hair on the back of my neck and arms rose as cold engulfed me, rolling waves hitting me in the gut, and nausea followed. I clutched my stomach and shifted so I was no longer seeing the room reflected in the glass.

"Are you okay, Emma?" Laura asked.

I nodded; vision blurry. "I don't think I want to put anything here in the sale."

"Are you sure? I'm positive I could sell it all." Her brows came together as she studied my face, searching for the reason I'd changed my mind about selling it all as soon as possible.

"Yes," I nodded, swallowing.

"All right then," she said, not sounding sure about my decision at all. "If you change your mind, let me know."

"I will. Absolutely. Thank you for taking a look."

I hurried to the door, putting my hand on the knob and waiting for her to follow. She did so reluctantly, taking one more look around the room, calculating profit margins and desirability. I smiled tightly as she passed me, unable to meet her eyes, knowing there would be more questions I couldn't answer. As I pulled the door shut, I looked at the mirror; I couldn't help myself, couldn't stop as my eyes were dragged to the spot I had seen Vivian moments before.

But the room was empty.

———

"We should go ahead with the sale tomorrow. The hurricane might miss us, but I'd rather do it now than wait and see."

"That sounds perfect," I agreed.

"You got somewhere safe to go if it makes landfall?" Laura asked.

"No, I'll be here. I guess it's safe enough."

"You let me know if you want to ride it out with us. We'd be more than happy to have you. Or Jake might be willing to share a roof with you for a while."

She smiled, an expression that held a knowing secret, as

she glanced to where he stood going through a stack of old hardback books. A flush crept up my cheeks, ears burning. Was it that obvious then? Or had she heard the town gossip? It might have been both. I was an open book, and every page had Jake's name on it.

"I like the idea of getting the sale over as soon as possible," I said, clearing my throat. "Maybe I'll be on my way to Oregon before the storm hits."

She gave me a considering look, as if she might not believe I was in such a hurry to be gone after all, but nodded. "Earlier is best. What doesn't sell, we'll give you a flat rate for and move it to our shop. Though, lord knows, you should have plenty of business. Everyone for ten square miles wants a look at this place."

"Really? I thought the house would have been full of Vivian's admirers at the end. Everyone here to support her and poking around, you know?"

"Not that I know of. I just know what I've overheard at the shop, and it seemed that most people believe that Magnolia House is full of one-of-a-kind treasures that Vivian watched over like a dragon. Hordes of antiques and all that."

I made a noise, part surprise and curiosity.

"At least it means you'll have a packed house. Fingers crossed it all sells and Jake won't be forced to move too many things on his own."

"Yeah," I said.

"Well, I'll get out of your hair. Tomorrow we'll be here around six in the morning to start the setup, and the sale should start around eight. Don't worry too much about moving things, but if you feel up to it, put the smaller stuff, knickknacks and dishes on the counters and tables. The things upstairs could be moved down. But like I said, don't worry about it too much. I'll have several helpers in the morning, and we move pretty fast."

"Thank you for everything," I said, extending my hand. "You've made this all so easy. I can't thank you enough."

"It's been my pleasure, Emma." Laura shook my hand, smiling and already moving toward the front door. "If I'm being honest, I'm one of those people who always wanted a look inside this place."

"Is it what you expected?" I smiled, glancing up at the blank space on the wall where Vivian's portrait had hung.

"It hasn't disappointed." She hesitated, mouth open, ready to say more, but she shook her head.

"What?" I asked.

"It feels a little full to me. Cold in places." She shrugged. "You know what I'm talking about?"

I shook my head.

"Good thing you're not superstitious," Laura said, a smile flashing across her face. "We'll see you first thing in the morning."

We went and picked up the rental in Fairview before starting on the house. I made a joke about returning it if Jake was going to drive me around the whole time and to my surprise, he shot me a toe-curling smile. I was only half joking though. It spent more time parked in inconvenient locations than not.

Returning to the house we began upstairs. Little by little moving things down—boxes full of linens, books that had somehow missed being put with the others, random collections of brass candlesticks, and delicate porcelain figurines. I started piles in the foyer, odds and ends appearing one by one.

Laura had said they would sort it all and price it, arrange it on tables and set it out to catch a buyer's eye. But I wanted to see it all first, a kind of morbid curiosity, like turning over a rock knowing a million tiny pale crawling things will come scurrying out but needing to see it anyway.

We didn't talk as we worked, passing each other, depositing items to return to wherever we'd uncovered them. Coming together and parting, again and again, a dance of organizing and removal. A hundred times I'd opened my mouth to say something, but nothing came out. I wanted to thank him for the help, for the gentleness he'd shown me last night, for the kiss in hot sunshine, for the way he'd cupped my face in the dark.

I couldn't manage to get the words out. And then we were too busy.

The attics were empty now. Not that there had been much up there in the first place. I'd taped shut the boxes of newspaper clippings and written *TRASH* in big black marker across the tops. I didn't need to read through them again, and I didn't want Jake to see them. After that I'd moved to the second floor, my floor, and had begun to go through the rooms that still had things in them.

Most had been empty, or nearly so. Only the room to the left of the stairs, at the opposite end from my childhood room, had much of anything. This room had boxes stacked neatly, a single row, floor to ceiling, of clothes. Each was carefully labeled with the year and contents. Not all of them seemed to belong to Vivian. A few with my father's name were here and there. I thought for sure, somewhere, I would find my name scrawled on something, anything.

But I hadn't found it yet.

I could hear Jake downstairs, boots on wood, the creak of a door, the sharp click of it latching. Dust filled my nose and coated the back of my throat, sticking and making it hard to breathe. Sweat beaded on my brow and rolled between my shoulder blades. It was so hot upstairs, away from the ceiling fans and the effort the ancient air conditioner made. The windows had been painted shut years ago and would never open now.

I pulled down a random box; Vivian's initials and the date, August 1992, and the word *blazers* were written on the top. I picked at the packing tape, pulling up an edge and peeling it away with a flourish.

The inside of the box was carefully lined with white tissue paper, each item of clothing wrapped in its own crinkling package. I lifted the first layer, exposing a red linen jacket with gold buttons embossed with anchors. Jasmine filled the room, her perfume fresh and heavy as if she'd slipped silently in behind me and at any moment I would feel her hand rest on my shoulder.

The feeling was so intense, so vivid, I fought the urge to turn around.

The hair rose on my arms and the back of my neck. I sucked in a breath, trying to calm my pounding heart, concentrating on the gold buttons, the way light caught on the surface and slipped along the curves—anchors and sailors' knots. I waited until the sense of watchfulness passed, lifting and leaving me alone in the room again.

The jacket was heavy, pockets weighted down and lumpy. I patted them down, feeling the objects through the cloth. In the left pocket, it felt like a small bottle. I shook the jacket out, leaves of rumpled half-transparent tissue paper drifting away.

A small bottle fell out, similar to others I'd seen on her dressing table—cylindrical and heavy cut crystal, a brass spray top. At some point it had come from that fancy shop in New Orleans too. I sniffed it carefully, a small amount of clear liquid sloshing, but it didn't smell of anything. I expected an old perfume smell—that slightly rancid scent of jasmine gone bad, the alcohol smell that sometimes came through. But this smelled of nothing.

I patted the other pocket. Stiff paper, not the wispy tissue used for packing; this felt like a sheet of paper folded up. Flipping the jacket over I dug into the pocket and pulled out a white envelope.

It was blank and sealed—nothing to give away the contents. I felt the envelope, trying to decide if it was empty. No, there was something in there. It felt like a piece of paper folded over, thick but not too thick. I turned it over in my hands, rubbing a thumb over the sealed flap.

"You ready for a break yet?"

I jumped, dropping the jacket and bottle as I turned. It rolled away, making a half-moon across the floor, coming to rest against the box I'd pulled the jacket from. Jake stood in the door, leaning into it, watching me with unreadable eyes. I nodded, aware that his gaze had shifted to the pile of red fabric on the floor.

"What did you find?"

"Nothing," I said, too quickly, with too much guilt.

The word was automatic, leftover from too many confrontations with Vivian. I didn't know why I'd said it, standing there like a fool, hands empty and flushed cheeks.

"You want lunch?"

"Yeah, that sounds good."

I stepped over the jacket on the floor, leaving the box open, knowing it would be there when I returned. A thread of worry wove through me, an invisible tie to the jacket and the envelope I'd left on the floor.

———

Lunch was turkey sandwiches on white bread, and we ate potato chips straight from the bag—greasy fingers brushing as we both reached in at once, messy but wonderful because he sat beside me. We were on the back porch again, watching the swaying green trees and listening to the music of the bayou. The sky was overcast, threatening rain, and promising storms. The hurricane was coming. It was in the air, the breeze bringing it—salty seas and saw grass from along the coast, that sharp fresh scent that only came with heavy rain.

"You think it'll hit us?" I asked.

"I don't doubt it."

"You got some kind of intuition? The ability to see the future?" I was half joking, half serious.

"Nothing so mystical. My knee aches with it. The change in air pressure."

"I can't feel it."

"You got any old football injuries?"

I laughed. "No."

"Might be why then."

His smile. I wanted more of it the more I saw it. I wanted more and more of him all the time. But the moment at the dining table lurked beneath each word, each thought. He'd paused, there had been an expression I couldn't understand, and then Laura had knocked. If she hadn't, what would he have said?

I sipped my coke, enjoying the cold fizz, wishing last night had been the end of it all. I was so sure it had been, but what I'd felt in Vivian's room hadn't been my imagination. What did it take to unhaunt your life? What other ties did I need to break?

"You know you don't have to do everything tonight?" Jake asked.

He'd been watching me. I hadn't noticed before, but he'd caught the way my brows had come together when Vivian had crossed my mind. I smoothed my face out, smiling, and forcing myself to believe, even for an instant, that all was right with the world.

"Yeah, I know. But I'd rather stay busy. And this feels like the home stretch." I held my arms up, reaching for the sky. "I'm almost home."

"You're so close," he agreed, tone more reserved than before.

The moment stretched between us, silence and a thousand questions.

"You sure you don't mind helping?" I asked, wanting to break it, needing conversation to keep the doubt away.

"Not at all. I'm happy to, boss." He grinned at me. "What would you like me to work on next?"

"How do you feel about kitchens?"

Jake laughed. "I think you're about to tell me I really like them."

"It's because you do!" I laughed, enjoying the expression on his face. "In fact, you love them even more when all the dishes and glassware are on the counters."

"See," Jake held up a finger, mouth twitching with a suppressed smile. "I always knew there was something off about my kitchen. Now I know! Just empty all the cabinets."

"Yep!" I laughed and held out my hand. "And if you empty all mine, I'll buy you dinner."

"How could I ever refuse?"

My heart was in my throat, his smile everything. Expectation for his touch roared through me, and it took everything I had not to throw myself into his arms and press my lips to his perfect mouth. He took my hand, his warm and callused around mine, and we shook to seal the deal.

———

The paper tore easily, a jagged wound appearing as I forced it open, exposing the contents—a yellowing piece of lined paper, torn roughly from a notebook, the edge ragged. I opened it slowly, breath caught, skin prickling with goose bumps. The hair on the back of my neck rose as I saw the writing, going cold all over as I read the name signed at the bottom.

> Viv –
> You said if I ever had any problems you'd help me out. You got time tomorrow afternoon?
> Alice

Who the hell would ever call Vivian, Viv? My mouth hung open at the thought. Vivian, the formal and demanding Southern belle would never have condescended to having her name shortened like that. Vivian would never have answered to anything other than her full name laced with a heavy dose of respect and flattery.

But someone had gotten away with giving her a nickname.

Alice.

Jake's Alice.

I traced the words. It was the penmanship of a young woman—big bubbly letters, the way she dotted the I in her name. I could imagine how she would have written her and Jake's initials in a heart with an arrow through it.

And she'd given Vivian this note.

How had Vivian known her? And Jake? I couldn't understand how the three of them could have been connected. He'd worked to keep the gardens up, he'd been here all the time, coming and going. Had Alice come with him once? Had Vivian invited her inside for some iced tea and a chat?

The hair on my arms rose, the back of my neck going cold, as I stared at the note. Magnolia House creaked, floorboards shifting, a light rain pattering across the roof. I glanced at the window, half expecting the hurricane to have made early landfall with my luck lately. But it was a passing cloud just spitting rain, as my dad would have said.

I put the note back in the envelope, concentrating on the motion, focused on the movement as my mind raced. If Jake didn't already know they were connected, he had every right to.

Problems.

There was only one boy in this situation. And the whole town believed without a doubt that he'd murdered Alice because she was going to leave him. Had she talked to Vivian about this before she'd died? Had Jake lost his temper after all?

I'd never considered who might have killed Alice if Jake was innocent. I'd never doubted him, not really. He was rough around the edges, didn't suffer fools, and hadn't hesitated to handle the situation with Jonah.

He didn't handle the situation the right way.

Officer Hatcomb didn't have any doubts about Jake.

I was leaving in a few days. I would never come back. What did it matter if I found this letter and I never spoke to Jake again? What did I think was going to happen anyway when I returned to Oregon?

There wasn't even anything here to propose going long-distance over.

A few kisses and sharing a sofa for a couple of nights didn't mean there was a relationship.

Even though a small part of me really wanted to find out just exactly what was going on between us. It wasn't nothing. But was it anything?

I tore through the remaining contents of the box the blazer had come from. More of Vivian's things—very obviously Vivian. Expensive fabrics in classic cuts, the kinds of clothes that cost so much money they didn't have to shout about it—subdued, elegant. But at the bottom of the box, between two layers of tissue, were a set of clothes I couldn't imagine Vivian wearing.

A simple pale-blue tank top and jean shorts with a ragged hem.

I'd never seen Vivian in jeans. Not once in my whole life.

I wrapped the clothes, perfume bottle, and letter in the blazer with the anchor buttons and set them aside to take downstairs. Then I emptied the rest of the boxes, each and every one. I checked every pocket, patting down the satin-lined blazers, linen pants with sharp creases still holding strong, the silk blouses with embroidered collars. There was nothing else. Each item of clothing had been dry-cleaned and soon the floor around me was covered in white tissue paper.

There was nothing else to find. Not a dime left in a shoe, not a bobby pin or receipt.

The note and bottle had been left intentionally.

Vivian had left them for me.

CHAPTER TWENTY-TWO

MONDAY

Jake was in the kitchen, sorting through all the things taken out of the cabinets. I was counting it as a kind of progress. Maybe not the good kind since it had only been to transfer what was inside to the outside, but on the other hand, at least the cabinets were empty now. I was arranging stacks of antique porcelain dishes on the dining room table—soup plates, chargers, bread plates, and finger bowls.

All of it completely beautiful and useless.

The blazer was a crimson roll of fabric on the mahogany buffet table to my left. I'd moved it several times now—from the chair beside me to the table, table to shelf, shelf to buffet. I'd opened my mouth a dozen times to ask Jake about Alice and Vivian but chickened out each time. What if I was stirring up bad blood? I didn't want to demand he tell me about Alice and force him to share what must have been incredibly painful memories. I bit my lip, mind going around again, weighing pros and cons.

A crash echoed out from the kitchen, a tinkling sound of

tiny things sliding across the linoleum, rushing into corners. Silence rolled in behind it, filling up the expanded space, the house holding its breath.

"Hey! Everything okay?" I called.

No response.

I left the teacups I'd been sorting—Blue Willow and Ming Dragon Red—and made my way to the kitchen. Calling out again to see if he was okay. Outside, the wind picked up, pushing at the siding, sending jasmine vines tapping against the windows. The change in the weather altered the mood of the house, leaving us in cool, dim shadows.

"Hey, Jake, you okay?" I asked, coming into the kitchen and looking around.

Jake stood in the middle of the room, head down, fist clenched around something. The box of keys I'd pulled out from the lower cabinet where the candles had been lay scattered at his feet. Silver and brass keys of varying styles and sizes fanned outwards from him, reaching into the corners of the room, some even as far as where I stood.

And Jake was holding one, staring down at it, turning it over and over in his hands, the light catching the worn metal.

"What happened?" I asked, stepping into the room and sliding on several keys.

He opened his fist, extending each finger slowly, to reveal a key—light caught on the worn metal. Without looking up he began to speak, voice whisper soft.

"I'm not sure how old I was when I saw her the first time. We were kids, you know? This place is so small, and all the other little towns pooled their kids into one school. You were there, you know."

"What're you talking about?" I swallowed, the tension in the room reaching me, settling in my gut.

"She was smiling, teeth crooked and so tan from being outside all summer. She was basically sunburned. She'd come to live with her daddy after something happened with her mom. She'd been sick or something, and she couldn't take care of Alice anymore."

I sucked in a breath.

Alice.

"When we were seventeen or so I asked her out. She'd laughed right in my face, bent over and stomped a foot. Made a huge scene. And I knew it was a no. I turned bright red, and I swear I would have given anything to have had the earth open up and swallow me whole. Everyone was watching, I'd done it right after school had let out Friday afternoon. I'd been working up to it all week."

Jake looked at me then, a quick glance, but I wasn't sure he saw me. There was so much memory reflected in his eyes, the past clouding his vision. And then he chuckled, a soft sound, a moment of surprised delight—something small and wonderful turning into something big and beautiful.

"And you know what she finally said? 'Jake White, what the hell took you so long?' She kissed me right there, in front of God and everybody. I thought my heart might explode."

He paused and held the key up to the light. I could see a jagged star cut into the grip. The key from the envelope the attorney had given me. The key Vivian had left for me that fit no lock in this house.

"Sometimes you look back on old relationships and you can see why they ended, hindsight being twenty-twenty and the benefit of old age. I don't know about you, but I never considered high school my best years. But Alice? We were good together. The kind of high school sweethearts who get married at eighteen, have two kids in a nice house, growing old together kind. The long-term kind. The forever kind."

My heart twisted. For him, for myself, for all the wanting I'd felt these last few days. Below that was a thread of jealousy. Jealous of a poor murdered girl that he'd loved so much. A woman he still loved. I hated myself for it, ashamed and going red with his words washing over me.

"I turned eighteen that fall but she was a few months younger. We were talking after-high school plans. I was going to join the Army, get out of this place and make some decent money. She was going with me. There wasn't money for rings, but I promised her that the minute that first paycheck hit my hands, we'd be ring shopping.

"I was taking metal shop that last semester, and she'd given me a copy of her house key. I never would have used it. I'd never even thought about it. I wasn't going to disrespect her daddy. I liked him. I really did. And I thought he'd liked me too. And what I wanted from her wasn't something we needed to be sneaking around about. I wanted her heart, her future. I'd already given her mine."

He stopped, chest rising and falling, breathing audible, like he'd run ten miles. Tears shivered on my eyelashes, threatening to fall, but I couldn't move. I needed to hear all of this as badly as he needed to say it right now. I needed to know.

"But she'd given me a key anyway, with a smile and a kiss. One afternoon I decided to try and cut a heart in it. I thought it would be easy, but I messed it up right away and turned it into a star. Not a great star. But it looked better than the deformed heart I'd tried to cut. I traded keys with her that afternoon, taking her old key and watching as she slid the new one with the star on her keychain."

Jake let out a shuddering breath, and I wiped at my eyes.

"Her smile. You should have seen it. Nothing else like it."

He stopped talking, breathing heavily. The air in the room was thick, almost gone, warped with his words and the distress rolling off him in waves. I opened my mouth but couldn't speak. I didn't know what to say.

"You know, they never found it. They found her keys, the car key and locker key and bike-lock key and mailbox key. But not the house key. And I'd been so helpful, marked it so clearly for them. They looked all over. And I looked all over. But no one ever found it."

The key glittered as he tossed it up into the air and caught it, closing his fingers tight around the metal.

"That hurt a little. More than I'd like to admit maybe. Even now. I couldn't afford a ring, and she swore she didn't want one. I wasn't able to give her anything tangible. I was working my ass off mowing lawns on the weekends and working under the table for Josh. Every last penny went into savings for the two of us. I had nothing to give. Not until that stupid star. A stupid shape cut into a house key. Like any of it mattered."

I took a step forward, reaching out to him. "It mattered. It does matter."

He looked up then, focusing on me, seeing me for the first time. There was so much anger in his gaze, boiling over and bubbling, and it forced me back.

"They never found it, Emma. Do you understand that? Everyone looked, the sheriff thought it was suspicious that her house key was missing. He thought I'd taken it. Her dad swore up and down his daughter would never have given me a key to their house. He looked at me like he didn't know me, like I hadn't eaten dinner with them five days a week for the last year. I was a stranger suddenly."

His knuckles went white as he tightened his fist.

"A jealous boyfriend. She'd been accepted to several colleges. Had her pick of schools, even out-of-state places. No one believed she'd be moving out of this place with me. Some poor as dirt, dead end loser with grease under his nails."

I'd seen the newspaper clippings telling his story. This story of high school sweethearts turned sour. The jealous boyfriend who couldn't let go. The girl on her way up and out, a young woman who was going to *be* someone. And he'd taken all of that from her. They all believed it. They all *knew*. Even the kids he'd gone to school with, all grown up now and one or two wearing a uniform. They were all certain, right down to their bones, about Jake White.

My heart quickened, growing cold as I listened. There was so much anger in him, simmering for years beneath the standoffish calm he cultivated. A person was capable of anything. No one knew what they would do until they were in that situation. Before the incident in the parking lot, I would have said he was innocent—quiet and reserved, something sad and broken in his past, but not something he broke himself.

"Why is this in Vivian's house, Emma? Why is it in a junk box with a hundred other keys? Why the hell would this key be here?" His eyes narrowed as his voice rose, a flush creeping up his neck.

I shook my head. I wanted to know as badly as he did. But I couldn't think under his glare of accusation. This was more emotion than I'd seen from him. He'd been an asshole, and he'd been laid back, and everything in between. I'd even made him laugh. But through it all, there had been this sense of stillness, of cultivated calm. But not now. Now it was gone, burned away, leaving smoking coals and ash.

A tiny part of me, buried deep inside my chest, was asking, *Did you kill her? Did Vivian help cover it up?*

"Why is her key in this house?" he repeated, low and soft now, anger turned to fury.

"I don't know," I whispered, shaking my head. "It was in an envelope the attorney gave me. Vivian left it for me. I put it in that box when I got home."

He looked at me like I was crazy. Like I was stupid. Like I was lying.

"Do you know they almost convicted me of her murder? The whole town thinks I did it. Her dad moved away a few years after, and you know, I'd been grateful at the time because it flat-out hurt to look at him. And my dumb ass stayed here, took all their bullshit. I'd wanted to get out with her. But if she wasn't with me, it wasn't worth leaving. Fucking stupid."

Tucking the key in his back pocket, he took a step toward me. I couldn't help it, I wished I hadn't, but I took a step back—moving away, retreating. The desire to flee hit me, the urge to run, fight or flight kicking in. I'd never been a fighter, but I'd long ago perfected the art of running away.

"They've gotten under your skin and into your head, and now you're wondering if it's all true. I know you're a little afraid of me. I can see it. But you've also been easing closer, a little bit at a time. I think you like me more than you should. And you think I'm dangerous, and whether you admit it to yourself or not, that's part of what you like about me. You want a little bit of danger."

He came closer, and I retreated until I hit the door frame. He'd put the emotional wall back up, smoothing out his features, a calm lie. My heart pounded, and I could feel his heat, the heaviness in the air between us.

"Did you kill her?" I asked, pulling in a ragged breath.

I'd never asked him, tried to push the thought away when it popped up. But I had to know, I had to hear it from him. My chest was tight, the world coming down to him, ears full of his ragged breathing.

Jake leaned into me, the distance between us vanishing, as he put his lips to my ear, one hand on my hip. I turned into him, unable to deny the thrill that shot through me, the warmth of his body that I craved. He smelled like worn leather and sunshine, the way the world heated up underneath a pale sky and bright sun. There was the scent of soap beneath that, and the lingering freshness of mint.

His lips brushed my ear, my breath catching, my hands coming up but not touching him. I couldn't bring myself to touch him. I didn't know if I'd push him away or pull him close, if I would apologize some more or tilt my face to his, hoping he'd kiss me.

I would kiss him back.

Would I be kissing a killer?

"Do you think I killed her?" He paused, waiting for me to respond, carrying on when I didn't. "Her name was Alice. She was smart and funny and beautiful. When she came into a room, it lit up. She brought the light in with her. She'd turn everyone's head. She made them all laugh and smile. We all loved her. I loved her."

I shook my head, not understanding where he was driving us, moving us both toward a point of no return. Whatever was coming, some dark secret he knew, it would change us, it would break apart this moment. I wanted that; I feared it.

He brushed one hand up my arm, tracing the line of my shoulder, moving to cup the back of my head. Everywhere he touched me felt white hot. His hand on my hip, on my neck, his mouth brushing my ear. He pushed closer, hips and thighs brushing mine, curving my body to fit his until there was nothing left.

"That's what you want to know, isn't it? You want me to tell you all about her, you want to know all the things your mother knew. You're just like her, did you know that? You're just like your goddamned mother."

I shoved him then, twisting away. But he held me, pressing me into the wall, pinning me in place.

"Stop," he growled, tightening his grip. "You want to know how I killed her? You want to know how they found her body, without a mark on her, naked and white in the swamp? I dumped her there, out there for the alligators and bugs and vultures because I didn't give a shit about her. Do you want all the gory details?"

I began to tremble, fear and desire tangling together, a strange mix of have and have not. He buried his face in my hair, against my skin, like a lover, his heat something I craved. I shook my head, trying to deny it, to squash the questions and slow-burning desire. I wanted it all. I wanted to know everything.

"Ask me," he said, voice dropping. "Ask me anything you want."

I hesitated, frozen, everything inside pure chaos. I sucked in a breath, expanding my lungs as much as I could with him so close, my breasts flat against his chest. And I couldn't stop myself from finally touching him, letting my hands come to rest on his sides, gently, barely making contact. Another breath, so big I thought my lungs might burst, and then I let it go.

"You don't have to tell me anything." I held on to the rest of it, the words rolling around in my mouth, waiting to be said. I had to say them, I needed them out, between us. "I don't care if you killed her. It doesn't change how I feel about you."

He froze, not breathing, not moving, a statue made of anger and shock. The moment drew out, expectation thrumming, my skin tingling. He let out a breath, and with it, I thought he would tell me everything.

It would all come out.

All of it.

I knew it wouldn't make a difference. I *didn't* care. I'd been avoiding it, circling the emotion, thought and desire, pushing them away when they came too close. He could tell me anything, right here in this room, and I'd accept it.

"You're as bad as they are. Believing the lies even as the truth stares you right in the face. You're the daughter of a monster. Why should I expect any better?" He sneered, the expression part hurt and part disgust.

"I don't—" I stammered, shocked at his words, the venom in them.

"At least I don't look like the killer."

He stepped away, taking his heat with him, leaving me exposed and cold. He turned and walked away, floorboards creaking beneath his heavy boots, moving down the hall and toward the front door before I could stop him. I stayed where I was, staring at nothing, listening to the front door crash open and then slam shut. The engine of the truck rolled over, roaring into life, loud in the silence he'd left behind.

I listened as he drove away, still leaning against the wall

until there was nothing left to hear. I was alone in the house again, with only my thoughts and insecurities, a thousand questions and no answers. His last few words circled in my head, leaving me uncomfortable and with a sense of rising dread.

At least I don't look like the killer.

TUESDAY

Some of us think holding on makes us strong;
but sometimes it is letting go.

-Hermann Hesse

CHAPTER TWENTY-THREE
TUESDAY

I became aware of a woman staring at me. She passed amongst the tables set up on the lawn and the yard equipment pulled from the shed. The house was open too; there were already people moving around inside, voices lowered as they gossiped about me, pausing at the foot of the stairs to consider moving past the sign that said, *closed to visitors.*

I sat in the far corner of the verandah, watching people come and go. A few stopped to say hello and tell me how sorry they were about Vivian. Over and over, the words came, hovering like flies, *I'm so sorry for your loss, I'm sorry about your momma.* I hated hearing it.

But all of these people meant the contents of the house sold quickly—bone china, knickknacks, champagne glasses with paper-thin rims, leaded crystal candy bowls, fine linen table clothes and embroidered bedsheets. Vivian had filled the downstairs with beautiful things and these people were here to carry them away. Even the larger pieces of furniture were selling.

It was a relief. I'd been worried no one would come, but

I should have known better. Back of Beyond and the surrounding areas would never turn down the opportunity to get a look inside Magnolia House.

But the woman who watched me didn't pick anything up or check price tags. She wasn't here for the contents of the house. She was here for something else.

I watched her out of the corner of my eye, not wanting to meet her gaze directly, uncomfortable with the sense of impending confrontation. It would be in defense of Vivian. Everyone here felt the need to remind me how I'd failed as a daughter and human being.

She was older, with short smooth gray hair and blue eyes. A large diamond sparkled on her left hand, nails manicured and buffed to a shine. Her clothes were modest but expensive looking, the purse clamped to her side buttery-soft leather. There was something about her face, the set of her mouth, her cheekbones, that tugged at a memory. I didn't know where I'd seen her before, but I was sure I had.

I knew she would come to me. She was just working up the courage to climb the steps. It was coming, the words, the determination to say them to me. So I waited. I waited and watched her as she watched me, until finally she gave up and approached.

"Are you Emma?" the woman asked.

"Yes, I'm Emma Taylor." I nodded, a knot tightening in my stomach, skin prickling with her question. I dreaded her words, whatever accusation she would make. "Can I help you?"

"You look like your mother." Her high-class Southern drawl held a hint of disgust. Then she sighed, resigned. "But you look like your dad too."

My head jerked up with that, surprised. No one ever said I looked like him.

"Yes, you do a little. There's more Vivian in you than I would like to see, but some things can't be helped. I'm Denise Taylor Shepard. Brian's little sister."

My mouth fell open. I had an aunt? I'd never met any of my extended family. I'd never known they even existed. The portraits in the house were of long-dead ancestors, but I had no way of confirming they were actual relations. My parents had never spoken about family, as if they'd come out of the blue from nowhere and nothing. And after the car accident, there had only been the two of us.

"Vivian never told me I had any other family."

"Well, I'm not surprised." One perfect brow on the woman's face rose, her expression conveying perfectly what she thought about Vivian. "We wouldn't have told anyone about her either. The feeling was mutual. But your dad? He didn't tell you about us?"

Us. Plural. I had more family out there. Maybe I had more aunts and uncles, cousins, and grandparents.

Vivian had once told me her family was all gone—dead and buried, a cold look in her eye. My dad had never said a word about his. And I had never asked, never pressed him for more information. But I had been a child. Any questions I had came later, when I was older, and then there was only Vivian to explain away the absence of others in our life.

You have no other family. There is only us, Emma.

The woman, Denise, my aunt, studied my face thoughtfully before holding out a hand. I took it, her grip steady as she said, "It is lovely to finally meet you, Emma. Like I said, I'm Denise Taylor Shepard. And I came to see if Vivian was really dead."

I sucked in a breath, skin tingling, toes curling in my sneakers.

"Does it shock you?" she asked. "I'm sorry if it does, but I had to know."

I shook my head. "It doesn't shock me."

The thing that had been coming toward me, inescapable, had arrived. It was in this woman's tone of voice. It was in the way she had to know if Vivian was dead. She'd needed to know like I had.

"You needed to see if she was dead too," I said.

I repeated it stupidly, like a child. But the words had shocked me; they'd hit so close to my own heart, my own reason for coming. A corner of her mouth lifted, a smirk of pleasure in something that should have been painful, triumph and hard joy in her eyes.

"Yes, I needed to see she was dead. Is that why you've come home?"

I nodded, looking out over the lawn and the tables, people milling around and throwing glances my way. They were always so curious, all of the people who'd been born here, who would die in this place believing in something so intensely it blinded them to the truth.

"So you've figured it all out? Vivian and the whole sordid mess?"

"Mess?" I searched her face, wondering how much was going to change with this conversation. A lot. It filled the air between us, electric as a thunderstorm, as inescapable as the impending hurricane.

"Well, if you haven't heard the story, I can tell you what I know. I don't know everything though. Your dad kept a lot of things from us."

"Why would he do that?"

But I didn't have to ask. Vivian. It was always Vivian.

"We didn't approve of the woman he'd decided to marry. He cut us off, all of us. But now I'm not sure if it wasn't Vivian doing the cutting." Her tone was hard and sharp, chips of stone tumbling down a mountain, gaining momentum.

I stood, gesturing to the front door. "Would you like to come inside? There's still furniture in the living room. Can I get you something to drink? Tea or water?"

"No, nothing to drink thank you. I won't be here long."

At least I remembered the duties of a good Southern hostess. My mind spun with the idea of who my dad had been before Vivian as I moved toward the front door and she followed. My skin prickled under her attention, the questions she sought answers to in her own mind. Was I like my dad enough for her to share what she knew? Or would she see too much Vivian in my face? Would she keep back an important detail?

Her eyes touched every inch of the entryway, the formal living room we crossed into, the arch on the opposite side with the more informal parlor. She looked at it all as if it were from a memory, a place forgotten and now rediscovered. Her mouth pinched tight around whatever was waiting to come out, words in her throat, at the tip of her tongue. I gestured to the small grouping of furniture, and she moved toward the chair opposite the sofa.

"Have you been here before?" I asked, sitting with my hands in my lap, fighting the urge to pick at my cuticles.

A bitter laugh came out, her eyes sweeping across the crown molding along the top of the wall, the intricate details, the chandelier, and the medallion above our heads. The crystals shivered beneath her gaze, tinkling ever so slightly in a room with no airflow or breeze.

"I used to spend summers here a long time ago. The whole family did. But after Brian inherited the house and married Vivian, we were no longer welcome. I haven't been here since before they were married."

My mouth made an O, but no sound came out.

I understood better than anyone that blood didn't make you family. This woman was my aunt, a relative I'd never even known I had, but that didn't mean she was family. I didn't know how much information I could press her for, or if too many questions would stop the flow of information I was hoping for. I cleared my throat.

"I had no idea this was my dad's house. Vivian made it sound as if it had always belonged to her, been passed down on her side of the family." I stood, hand over my mouth as the news sunk in, and turned to look toward the lawn covered with the contents of the house. "I'll stop the sale. I'll buy everything back."

"No, Emma. It's okay," she gestured for me to sit down, her voice soothing. "Brian packed up everything with senti-mental value and had it shipped to us a long time ago. I think he felt guilty eventually, for cutting us off. Maybe, given enough time, we would have reconciled at some point."

"I'm so sorry," I said.

"No need to apologize, you've done nothing wrong. Do you mind if I ask what your plans are for the house?" She kept her face and voice smooth, giving nothing away.

"I don't have any plans for it," I said, lifting one shoul-der. "I'd considered selling it. I don't plan to live here."

"If you do decide to sell, would you mind getting in touch with me first?"

"Of course."

I nodded, part of me still wanting to chase away all the

buyers on the front lawn. She'd said the sentimental things had been passed on to her already but what if there was something he'd missed? What if there was something tucked away and undiscovered in the house? But I already knew I'd be calling her sometime in the near future about this place. I could feel how badly she wanted it.

"We basically grew up here. It feels like a hundred years ago." She smiled tightly and crossed her legs, gaze moving over the room thoughtfully. "And after our grandparents passed, it went to Brian."

Brian. She said it like she missed him, his name familiar in her mouth, in her mind. She spoke his name as if he weren't dead and, at any moment, we'd hear the study door open and he'd come strolling out, hands in the pockets of the sweater he always wore, glasses reflecting back the room, our faces caught side by side. He would come and sit with her, take her hand in his and pat it, and smile as if no time had passed.

Hey, Denise, what's taken you so long?

My breath caught. I wished he would. I wanted that to be the truth, he'd be alive and well, he'd hug me and tell me it was all okay. He'd help me survive this. But the only thing that would be coming out of the house would be Vivian. Vivian and the shushing, hushing, whispering sound of the wheelchair moving over the floorboards.

Denise perched on the edge of the chair with her purse in her lap, hands folded neatly over it, as if at any moment she would jump up and walk out. I could almost hear the tap, tap, tap of sharp-heeled, expensive shoes as she hurried away, knowledge dropped like a bomb and exploding in my head. I didn't want the few delicate memories I had of my dad ripped apart. They were a few of the only things I had that didn't belong to Vivian.

"So he didn't tell you about his family. And I'm guessing she didn't tell you about hers?"

I nodded.

"Shall I start at the beginning then?"

"Yes," I whispered, voice hoarse, throat closing around the word.

"It's heartbreaking to know he didn't share anything with you, even the smallest thing." She studied my face. "I always hoped we'd meet you one day."

I licked my lips, mouth drying out, heart frantic in my chest. Her words lit a fire in my gut, heat touching my cheeks, flaming through me. Anger at Vivian, even some anger with my dad.

All of my life, I'd moved through the world alone—a spectator, an observer of all things living. Even when I was free of her, beyond this place, I'd been unable to connect with people. I was missing that piece, the thing most people seemed to have, a grappling hook, a way to connect to other ships passing in the night.

"You knew about me?"

"Eventually. We found out he'd had a little girl, you, right before your first birthday. I reached out, hopeful, wanting to bridge the gap. But he wouldn't even tell me your name. He had no interest in reconnecting. None at all."

I swallowed, wondering why he'd been so firm, not understanding the desire to cut family off when they'd done nothing but love you the best they could. He must have had his reasons, solid and concrete, rock-hard reasons. But I couldn't even begin to understand them now.

"She didn't invite us to the funeral. Didn't even give us the option of being there. 'You're not welcome, and you'll never meet Emma.'" Her voice changed for a moment, becoming a snotty shadow of Vivian's. "That's how we found out your name."

I hadn't been to his funeral either. Vivian hadn't thought it necessary that I attend. I dreamed about it though, how I thought it might have been, a simple casket sliding into the tomb, white stone and green moss, the sky overcast, the stark darkness wrapping Vivian, the blackness of her soul worn openly on her skin—silk and sheer layers of chiffon, the way her shoulders sagged as Pastor Roberts pushed her in the new wheelchair. But I hadn't been there; I couldn't say how it had gone.

All I knew for sure was that Vivian had gone directly from the hospital to the graveside.

Later, much later, I'd gone to sit on the shallow steps of the family tomb—lonely, sad, and small. I'd pressed my hand to his name, wishing I could push through stone, wanting to know if he was really in there. Part of me had believed he hadn't really died. He'd come home any day now. He wasn't really gone. I needed to see him to know, but Vivian had taken that away from me, the chance to say goodbye. It had been hard to leave the grave knowing I was returning to a house where my remaining parent didn't love me.

Denise cleared her throat. "It's been a little strange knowing you were out there, carrying a name I'd grown up with, related to us but not knowing us. We eventually heard you'd left town, but no one seemed to know where you'd gone."

"I'm sorry we didn't get the chance to meet sooner." I gave her a soft smile, meaning it with everything I had.

She returned the smile, a kinder one than before, face softening. "It would have been nice. I think you'll like your cousins. You'll like the whole family when you meet them."

Her voice trailed off as she studied my expression. I couldn't tell for sure what she saw. A mix of emotions flashed through like photographs, one after another, a quick succession—curiosity, doubt, worry, happiness.

"If you'd like to meet us," she amended. "I know we should have reached out sooner. We should have made an effort to find you. But…"

I held up a hand, wanting to reassure her, understanding why her voice trailed off into uncertainty. "I'm nothing like Vivian. I would love to know my family."

She nodded, pleased. "Wonderful. I'll give you all my contact info, and after you've finished with things here, you can come for a visit."

"That would be lovely," I said, excitement fluttering in my veins, a new anxiety building.

How many of these relatives would see Vivian in my face? How many would be willing to accept me? While Denise seemed ready, I knew how Vivian affected people. Too many people saw a shadow of her in me—an inferior copy of her beauty—and if they distrusted her, they might distrust me as well.

We sat in silence for a few more moments. There was something else, below the reaching out and bringing the past forward, connecting me to them. She had something else to say.

"Was there something else?" I prompted.

"Has anyone from town talked to you about her?"

I shrugged, uncomfortable with the question. "Things with Vivian were complicated."

"Has there been negative talk?"

"No." A bitter laugh escaped, sharp and slicing through the air. "Everyone loved her."

Denise nodded, hands gripping her purse more tightly,

knuckles whitening. "She was very charming when she wanted to be. The woman could put anyone under her spell."

"Even you?"

"For a time." She looked down at her hands, perfectly manicured nails, the diamond ring. "But if she couldn't get what she wanted from you, things turned sour very quickly."

"Yes," I agreed. "All relationships with Vivian were transactional."

"I don't think Brian ever believed the allegations. And of course, nothing was ever made public. I think that was because her family wanted to keep it quiet and save face. Nothing to tarnish their good family name."

"What allegations?"

Denise released a sigh, heavy with knowledge and weary of the world. "There were whispers about her grandmother in an extended care facility. Dementia had been an issue for several years, and there was a large sum of money to be released upon her death. From what I understand, Vivian wasn't the only one waiting. One day the grandmother was fine, and the next, gone. Of course, old folks can go like that. But Vivian had been present at her passing, and a few pieces of jewelry had disappeared."

"How do you know?"

"Brian shared a few things before the marriage. He was defending her, trying to show us how unfairly her family had treated her. Building sympathy. The wedding was coming up, and our parents kept wondering when we'd meet her family. It never happened."

"They didn't show up at the wedding?"

"No." She shook her head, bitterness touching her and

passing, a shadow over carefully made-up features. "None of her family attended. There were a handful of friends from college, but no one close. She didn't have a maid of honor or bridesmaids. She convinced Brian they didn't need them. It was a very strange sort of wedding for our family. Not at all the grand affair my parents had dreamed about for their eldest son."

"What about her college friends? Did you talk to them?"

"Of course. I was curious and beginning to be suspicious. What kind of woman from a well-off and respected family doesn't have anyone show up for her at church? Maybe that sort of thing is done more now—elopements and spontaneous weddings in Las Vegas." A genteel sneer colored her voice. "But not here. And especially not then."

"Did her friends have anything to say about her missing family?"

"Well," Denise began, letting the pause draw out, leaving it hanging in the air between us. "There were three girls. Two didn't know her well at all. They had a class in common, but that was all. They hadn't even been given written invitations. Apparently, she'd casually mentioned she was getting married, and they'd jokingly asked to come."

"I didn't realize she was in college when they got married."

"She didn't go back after she became a Taylor."

"Do you know what degree she was working toward?"

"No, we never spoke more than a few words to each other." She shook her head and shrugged. "Anytime I asked any kind of question, she changed the subject. She was good at that. One moment I'd be intent on getting an answer, and the next she'd steered the conversation away and into something much more casual. Weather. Food. The local flower competitions. Afterward, I always felt a bit of a fool, letting myself get distracted, caught off guard by how charmingly she'd asked my opinion on something."

"I know that feeling," I said.

"Yes, I suspect you do." Sympathy slid across her face, there and gone before it could become pity. "The last friend, the third girl who came, didn't stay long. As a matter of fact, she left right after I spoke to her."

The hair on the back of my neck stood up, cold touching me, lingering between my shoulder blades. "Why?"

"Vivian saw us talking. I was asking questions, being nosy and trying to get some kind of answer. The girl was rather candid, but she turned white as a ghost when she caught Vivian's eye across the room. I don't think I've ever seen so much hate in a stare before. Nothing even half as vicious in a snake." She stopped, met my eyes across the sitting room, and put everything she had into her next words. "But maybe in a killer."

"What did the girl tell you?" I whispered.

I could feel pieces of the puzzle dropping into place.

"People seemed to be drawn to her no matter what—pulled in by her charm and kept by fear. This girl was afraid of her. They had been in the same sorority together."

"Had been? I thought she was still in school?"

Denise nodded slowly. "Exactly. But this girl said Vivian had been asked to leave. It had been kept quiet, her family had gotten involved, but a girl from their sorority had gone missing. One of the girls on Vivian's floor. No one knew what happened exactly, but the police asked a lot of questions. How well had Vivian known the girl, had they been friends, who spent time with her? I don't know if they ever found her, the girl at the wedding implied they didn't. But

Vivian was never formally investigated, and soon her involvement was pushed aside by other things."

"But why was her sorority sister there if they weren't in the sorority together anymore? If she was afraid of Vivian why even be there at all?"

"Maybe she had something on this girl. Maybe they had some kind of understanding. I can't begin to guess what it might have been."

"Do you remember her name? Could I find her? Ask?"

"No. I should have written her information down. It was stupid of me not to; I know it now and I knew it then. But I was so focused on Brian and Vivian. Then when he cut us off, I put some of these pieces together. Even now, I have nothing concrete. I have second-hand information and a reputation for being bitter about my brother's wife."

I studied my hands, folded carefully in my lap, nails trimmed short, a scrape on my middle finger. Details. I needed to remember each thing, each morsel of information. My mind was racing. I knew what it meant, to have these things coalesce in this place, but I didn't know what to do about it. Or if there was anything I should do.

Jake flashed through my mind, standing in the kitchen, angrier than I'd ever seen him. Jake holding the key to his girlfriend's house. Jake looking like his world collapsed for a second time.

Where did he fit in all of this?

"So." I cleared my throat, looking up at her, focusing. "You think she killed her grandmother? This girl from school? But how? I don't understand. How could she have not been a suspect? Someone must have looked twice at her, figured out her involvement. I can't believe that no one put it together. None of this makes sense."

The questions poured out of me, a million more waiting

to be spoken aloud. I was overwhelmed with them, stuttering and speechless all at once. I wanted answers—needed them—but this woman seemed unable to give them or maybe just unwilling to share them in this moment.

"I don't know," Denise whispered, desperation coloring her voice. "But I think she killed Brian too."

Andrew in the funeral home, his knee bouncing, fear coloring his voice even then—*I don't think she was paralyzed.*

I sat back, closing my eyes, tears collecting on my lashes.

"I can't prove anything," she said, voice cutting across the darkness in my head, offering kindness and sympathy. "But I'm being honest with you—my blood, my niece. I came to make sure she was dead because I have good reasons to double-check."

"This is a lot," I said, squeezing my eyes tight, white stars burning and bursting.

"I know I must sound crazy to you—"

"No," I sat up, opening my eyes and focusing on her. "No. You don't sound crazy."

"Sometime, when you're ready, I hope you'll come see us." She studied my face, considering me. "It's a lot. I understand that you've come home to put all these things to rest and ended up with more questions. But I would like to hear your stories too. I'd like to know what Brian was like as a father."

I wiped at the tears on my face.

"Here," she said, digging in her purse, searching for something, and made a noise of triumph when she found it. "This is my information."

I took the folded piece of paper she offered, opening it and seeing the address and number, a place in Mobile,

Alabama, that would probably be expensive and well-kept. The handwriting was lovely, feathery cursive with loops and flourishes. *Denise Taylor Shepard.*

My father's sister, family I'd never known I had.

I didn't know how to feel about it yet.

"When you're ready," Denise said.

"Thank you. I'll call. There's so much I want to know about my dad."

"Oh!" Denise went back to her purse, digging farther. "I'm so glad you said that, I almost forgot. This is for you too."

She passed over a black and white photo of a boy. He wore a suit, the kind you'd wear to Easter service at the Baptist Church. Black shoes shined. Hair smoothed and carefully brushed to the side. He was squinting into the sun, face scrunched, little hands shoved into the pockets of his trousers. I couldn't tell how old he was; I was terrible at guessing the ages of children.

He looked like me.

"Brian was eight there. Your father, he hated wearing a suit, but our daddy insisted."

I touched the photograph, his small, slightly blurry face.

"Thank you," I whispered.

I followed her out onto the porch, surprised to find the sale still going on. The world had shifted while we'd been inside, and a hundred years seemed to have passed. But coming out into the daylight, I realized hardly any time had passed at all. Our conversation had been quick and to the point, and I'd learned more than I'd ever hoped to.

How quiet would the house be tonight?

How alone would I be?

Denise waved as she got into the shiny red Mercedes she'd arrived in.

An aunt. A family. People out there who wanted to meet me, know me.

I wasn't alone anymore.

CHAPTER TWENTY-FOUR

TUESDAY

The conversation circled through me. Denise's revelations added to the internal list I'd been compiling. Vivian, mysterious and compelling, charming and beautiful—lover and killer. I sat in my father's study, flipping through folders in his desk, copies of electric bills and invoices for exterminators. I listened for the creak of wooden floors, for the familiar roll of wheels, the way the old house groaned with the weight of her passage even now.

I stood abruptly and went to the kitchen for the flashlight. I needed to see it suddenly—the last place we'd been together. Maybe I was compelled. Driven. Obligated by memory or fate, pushed forward by Vivian's ghost. Her voice wove through my time here, so alive, even now. Her words piercing and venomous, her memory cutting through the quiet of the house. But when I grabbed the flashlight and opened the door, nothing was said, nothing coming up from the past, from Vivian or my dad. So maybe it was me, only my own mind compelling me out into the dark.

The flashlight flickered and danced, winking on and off as I stood on the porch, warm light flooding the overgrown lawn before dropping me into singing darkness—insects and frogs, a wind touching leaves and swaying branches. The always sounds of the night, the constant sounds you could count on when you opened the front door.

The flashlight didn't work in the house. It wouldn't even turn on. It didn't matter how many batteries I changed or if I screwed and unscrewed the little bulb. The house didn't want it. I was relieved when it finally caught again at the bottom of the steps, the light steadying out as I moved farther away from the facade strangled by honey-suckle vines—pale yellow-white flowers bobbed in the breeze, leafy tendrils reaching out. An oil lamp flickered in the entryway, ensuring I'd return to light, however dim.

I waded into the tall grass, an expedition of one toward a remembered destination, the path between the house and the jetty unrecognizable, disappeared over the years I'd been gone. After my dad had passed, she'd stopped main-taining it, and I'd only set foot on it that last time, the last night we'd lived beneath the same roof.

That night had changed everything. I'd reached a fork in the road and hesitated. That hesitation had almost cost my life. I bit the inside of my cheek, chest tightening, heart constricting into a tight fist. Why? Why did I want to relive this? Why did I need to see this place beneath a moonless sky, the sound of slow-moving water growing, subtle and persistent?

Come on down, see my dark rolling water, and meet these gold-green eyes.

The bayou called, murmuring sweet nothings as I approached, the grass damp from the passing rain showers that afternoon, my socks and shoes soaking it up. I slapped a biting insect on my arm and the back of my neck, regretting the lack of bug spray or long sleeves. I'd be eaten alive before I made it back to the house.

Eaten alive.

It wasn't just the insects that would eat me alive.

All those years ago, right before I left, deciding I had to get out or I'd never make it, I'd walked this path with her. The wheelchair had been a nightmare to push through the rutted earth, half mud and vanishing gravel, the wheels sticking and bumping over the uneven ground. She endured it silently, her face a perfect mask, while anger bubbled in the air between us. But she'd wanted me to take her out here, to the place I'd shared with my father, fishing excursions executed here, stolen moments in which I felt loved. She wanted to take those things away from me, strip me down to nothing. I could feel her anticipation.

I'd pushed her out of the chair that morning in the church, dumped her onto hardwood floors, her body smacking the ground, her face going white. The glittering triumph in her gaze as the pastor's hand connected with my cheek, the gasps and raised voices from the congregation. But it had been silent since we'd arrived home, my skin icy hot, stomach upset and threatening to expel the little bit of food I'd eaten.

We'd each gone to our rooms. I'd crept up the stairs and shut the door, laying down on top of the quilt and pulling my knees up to my chest, hugging myself as my mind raced. It wasn't done. It would never be done. And nothing would ever change.

It was only going to get worse.

I shivered with the memory. How bleakness had settled

over me, stone by stone, heavy and crushing, my future an unfolding blossom of horrible darkness. Then her voice had come to me, traveled up the halls, raised high and harsh. I'd stopped breathing, listening, hoping I'd been mistaken, but her voice had come again, louder the second time.

Emma, come here.

I'd gone, leaving my shoes tucked beneath my bed, bare feet on the floors, curling my toes into the carpet on the stairs. She waited for me at the bottom, watching my movements with unfathomable eyes.

Predator's eyes.

Take me to the jetty.

Her voice was flat and dead calm, lips curved, hinting at some inner pleasure. I'd half turned to go get my shoes, but she'd stopped me, insisting we didn't have time and I'd be fine without them. The gravel had bruised and cut my feet, the soles sore for at least a week afterward. The memory of that night overshadowed so much of what happened in the years following.

I stopped halfway to the jetty now, the flashlight picking out the cypress growing at the edge of the water, a group of cattails swaying, the earth beneath me damp and willing to swallow me whole if I let it. If I wanted it to.

Let me eat you, whispered the bayou.

The water and sky, the earth, the whole place, waiting for me to succumb and join her. But maybe it wasn't, maybe it was watching to see if I could make it out again, if I could leave this place with my soul intact. Not fighting to keep me but fighting to help me go.

No matter what had happened that night, there were still memories of my dad here, and those outweighed what happened in the end.

Almost.

Memory trailing like a banner, snapping in the wind of emotion, I pushed through the last few yards to the edge of the water and the decaying wooden jetty crouched low over it. The bayou was high, the structure on the verge of being submerged, and my weight might be enough to sink it.

I slapped another mosquito on my arm, the bite sharp, the spot swelling. I'd be covered in bumps by the time I went back.

If you make it back inside.

Her voice or mine? I wasn't sure anymore. In my mind they had begun to blur, swirling together like blood in water, mixing ever so slowly, until there was no discernible difference between the two. I swung the flashlight around, over the surface of the water, skimming waterlilies and other plants, a small frog jumping from a rotting log with a plop, rings rippling out. The jetty didn't look like it would hold my weight, as if it had been waiting all these years for my return so it could sink into the black water with me on it.

Do it.

I stepped onto it, the wood shivering, bobbing, rolling beneath my feet. It was long and skinny, stretching out into the swamp, with room for boats to be tied up on each side. The far end dipped beneath the surface, vanishing in the dark, the path forward sinking even as my feet touched the rotting planks.

We'd fished from the end, taken a small boat out, and my dad had told jokes and shared stories about fishing when he was younger. There had never been any mention of his father or possible siblings; in my mind he'd been a child fishing alone, creating music with his voice and a tapping foot against a muddy riverbank.

But the last time I'd stood here, it had been much different.

How much did I want to remember? How much could I forget?

She'd begun speaking softly to me, voice so low that I didn't catch it at first, weaving a calming story, the tone barely masking the malice. My feet throbbed and tears gathered in the corners of my eyes as she went on. Even now, remembering the girl I'd been, hearing again those words, made me cry.

I never wanted you.

You were a mistake.

Your father was a fool.

You ruined my life.

You shouldn't be alive.

No one wants you here.

Everyone hates you.

No one would ever believe you.

You're a liar.

You're an abuser.

You should be dead.

You don't want to be here.

You aren't happy here.

You should walk off the end of the dock.

"Walk into the water."

My own voice startled me, her final words escaping my lungs, passing over my tongue. I snapped my teeth shut, clenching my jaw, keeping the rest of it in, the physical memory so strong I had to fight to keep upright.

There had been a moon that night, full and high in the sky, the water silvered beneath it. As a child, there in the dark with Vivian, I'd wondered what it would take to skim the surface, walk on water like Christ, walk away from this place and the monster wearing a beautiful face.

Would it have been so bad? To slip beneath the surface and escape the shame of the church, the hatred of the people in town, and finally cool my burning cheek? At that moment, with her voice weaving a vision of release, I'd thought it might be the right thing to do.

I squeezed my left wrist, the bones hard beneath fragile skin, knowing that if she'd been here, she would do her best to break them again, grip me so tight, do everything in her power to make me believe the world would be a better place if I disappeared into the bayou.

It would only be drowning if I were lucky, lungs full of water, gasping and bubbling down. It would have been more likely to be alligators. I'd seen them doing death rolls on nature programs, been warned all through school to be careful around water, and had alligator safety drilled into me from a young age.

They could move quickly, climb trees, and were patient.

I swung the flashlight over the water again, searching now for that telltale reflection, watchful eyes in the night. Several dozen pairs of eyes I hadn't noticed before caught the beam, one lazily moving through the water toward the jetty. Large eyes, the dark shape of the snout the size of a skateboard, the body propelled forward with smooth flicks from the powerful tail. I stood frozen, locked in memory, Vivian's hand on my wrist as an alligator approached.

Reality or memory? Now or then?

Beneath me, the jetty bobbed gently with the current, swaying with the motion of the water, the end sinking farther down, easing into it as if it were cold and wasn't ready to get wet all at once, timid. A swish of movement in the water caught my attention, and I swung the flashlight up, illuminating more curious alligators swimming in my direction.

There was no high ground here. In the past, when the water hadn't been so high and the jetty newer, it had risen above the water, the bank higher, offering more safety. But now there was no bank, water lapping up into the grass, crawling toward the house. I glanced behind me, the electric lights off again, but the oil lamp I'd left burning in the hall cast a faint glow. It was so far away in the dark, beyond my reach, and right now the safest place to be.

Something bumped the jetty, the wood beneath me shifting, and I had to adjust my weight to keep my footing. The eyes were closer, alligators drifting toward me, slow but intent. The jetty moved again, the end already in the water groaning as it sunk farther, as something large forced it down.

Baby, I don't know what you're waitin' on, but it's time to go. Now.

My dad. Out here where we'd been happy, away from the house, away from her. He was here too, in this place. A sigh of relief escaped me, a wind so fierce I shook with it, tears slipping down my cheeks. This was what I needed—to know he was still in this place, that she hadn't been able to ruin it.

A dark shape emerged from the water at the end of the jetty. Slow steps carried it forward, the whole thing sinking as it took on the weight of the alligator. My heart stopped, my hand slipping from my wrist, Vivian's hold on me gone, vanished at the sight of the giant reptile coming toward me.

It was hard to tell in the beam of my flashlight, with most of the body still in the water, but it had to be at least six feet. I'd seen plenty of gators growing up, but this was the biggest one I'd ever seen. It opened its mouth, the pink-white interior bright in the light, and hissed.

I dropped the flashlight, the yellow glow spinning, hitting the water with a splash. In the last few seconds of light, I saw the giant gator take another step forward, others in the water sliding closer. Beneath me the wood sank, my feet getting wet, the water creeping up my jeans. Dark water swirled, eddying around me, the light gone.

I wasn't going to waste time looking for the flashlight. I knew if I bent to search for it, something would've grabbed me. I took a step back onto the soggy ground, relieved to leave the decaying jetty behind, water sloshing as the reptile moved with me. Heart racing, a gut-churning panic gripping me, and I moved as quickly as possible.

"You gotta keep movin'."

I repeated it aloud, my own voice driving me forward, through the muddy edges where land met water, and into the tall grass. Behind me the hissing came, following, coming for me. At any moment the jaws would close on me, a sharp pain hitting as teeth sank through flesh. But maybe I wouldn't feel it, maybe shock would kick in, and I would never know I was being eaten alive.

Sobbing, stumbling forward, I kept going for the house until the golden glow of the lamp reached out to caress me. Pushing through the last of the tall grass, I ran up the steps, wheezing, a sharp pain in my side. I turned at the top, knowing I would see the alligator behind me, so sure it would follow me up the stairs.

But the patch of gravel at the bottom of the steps was empty. A ragged path wove through the tall grass where I'd pushed free, and beyond that was nothing but darkness. I let go a shaky breath, wiping at the tears on my cheeks, tasting salt.

Behind me, deep within the house, music played. I hadn't heard the song in years, but I recognized it. Vivian's favorite song. Elvis Presley's voice caressed the air, moving toward me, over me, and asking a question I had no answer for.

Are you lonesome tonight?

CHAPTER TWENTY-FIVE

TUESDAY

I hesitated on the verandah, hand on the doorknob, weight on the tips of my toes and ready to run. Music came from somewhere inside the house, something I labeled internally as vintage country—that twangy sound caught in my ear, twitching the muscles in my legs.

It wasn't what I would have chosen, not even what I would have expected from Vivian most of the time, but I'd seen my parents dancing in the kitchen once when I'd been barely old enough to walk, holding on to the doorframe as my dad twirled her across the linoleum.

I touched my cheek, shocked at the memory, the way it had come forward out of the music—another ghost. I hadn't had a single memory of them happy together, where he'd seemed a willing partner in it their marriage. But this memory, recalled at the source, had to be true. They'd been laughing, eyes for only each other, and happy. Even so little, I knew happiness when I saw it.

It was the same song. Maybe even the same time of day. And the music was coming from the back of the house, possibly the kitchen.

Go on, then.

His voice or hers in my head? Or for once maybe, my own? I wasn't sure. I pushed the door open, easing inside, one careful step at a time. I could hear nothing else, only my own breathing and the music, the soft shuffle of my feet on the floor. Behind me, out in the dark I'd run from, even the night noises had faded.

The song began to repeat, caught in a loop. I shivered. It seemed more intentional even than the music playing on its own. The message within it, lyrics and melody strung together, one of melancholy sadness.

Hers or mine?

No, it would be his. The dance was his memory, a flash of happiness in an otherwise bleak place. Most of my memories were of Vivian berating him, yelling, throwing expensive things across the room—slamming doors and breaking glass echoing through the house. Our lives, shattering over and over, coalescing around Vivian, crashing apart in a rage or freezing solid with her vicious cold.

I hesitated in the hall, straining my ears. The music was fainter here, farther away than it had been when I'd passed through the front door. I groaned, unable to keep it in. It was coming from upstairs. I would need a light to find it, silence it. I would never be able to sleep with the song playing through the night.

Or leave. I could leave. I could run out the door and see where the wind might push me. I'd done so much of that already. Running, running. A rabbit searching for a good place to hide, an easily startled bird bursting from cover again and again. I had told myself that I would stand my ground, that I'd had enough, but I kept going back on it. Still the child beneath the adult varnish, the scared and timid girl.

I wasn't going to leave tonight. I half expected an alligator to be waiting between me and the car. It would be better to get a candle and turn the music off.

Grabbing a candle and a small box of matches from the kitchen, I moved to the foot of the stairs, looking up into the second-story darkness, the music a physical force waiting to be breached. The candle shook in my hand, flame jumping as I lit it, and fumbled the matchbox into my pocket.

One careful step at a time, I went up.

I followed the music, moving more slowly now, dreading what I might discover. I wanted to know, needed to stop it, and lure the quiet of the house back out of the corners. *But.* Nothing else beyond that word, *but.* I didn't want to put a name to what could happen after the discovery.

Shadows leapt and jumped away from the light, shifting toward me and away, a tide commanded by a capricious moon. I fought to keep the candle still, biting the inside of my cheek, the hair on the back of my neck standing on end.

The hall could hold anything, anyone.

The music came from the room where the boxes of clothes had been. But I'd watched Laura and her helpers move each one downstairs, the contents haphazardly replaced only to be put out in bins and on hangers for the sale.

Except for the red blazer. It was in the study, tucked into an out-of-the-way corner.

The door was shut, music coming through from the other side. I was nauseous, stomach cramping with fear. But I forced myself forward, reaching out with a trembling hand to turn the knob.

The door swung inward, smooth and silent, the candle-light flowing in, pausing only a few feet in. My ears ached with music; it was so loud, a physical force now that the door was open. A single step would take me over the threshold, into the room I couldn't see, but my feet were frozen.

The candle went out.

Light vanished, gone, absent.

I blinked, seeing nothing, ears buzzing hot. The music filled me, repeating, Elvis making promises if only his lover would return. I couldn't move. Everything, every single fiber in my entire being urged me to run. *RUN.* But I couldn't. I stood, facing the pitch-black room, tears streaming down my face.

A floorboard creaked, taking weight, groaning as something moved in the room.

The sound released me. I screamed, the sound ripping up from the bottom of my lungs, throwing myself back toward the stairs. I screamed as I went down them, falling the last few steps, landing heavily on my hands and knees.

I prayed. I begged.

Please, God. Please. God. Please.

Scrambling up, throwing myself toward the hall, I ran for the study. I slammed into the door, shoving it open and swinging inside, shoving it closed with both hands. Snot dripped from my nose, and I hiccuped sobs as I worked the only magic I knew—I turned the lock.

The bolt slid home, the almost inaudible *click* as it locked in place.

The music stopped—sharp, notes cut in half, a sudden void.

Magnolia House was silent.

WEDNESDAY

It's like freedom out there, can you see it?

- Seeker

CHAPTER TWENTY-SIX

WEDNESDAY

I tasted cold mornings and overcast skies as I crossed the threshold into Vivian's room, passing from that part of the house to this—this life to the next. It was a weight tugging on my soul, a heaviness I desperately wanted to release—double knotted and coated in memory, the kind of sickly sweet that clings to your hands and leaves a bitter taste on the tongue.

Silence greeted me.

Had I been expecting her to comment on my entrance? I shook it off, not wanting the added weight of expectation. Hazy daylight filtered between the curtains, the room as it always had been, a space I'd been afraid to intrude on. Even now, I wanted an excuse not to be there.

Come on, hurricane. What are you waiting for?

You baby. My dad's voice, distant here in the house, vanishing by degrees. *It's waiting for you.*

I was here for a reason. I was looking for something. I didn't know what, but I'd know it when I saw it. I'd tried to make short forays into this space, her space, carving pockets of time from my day—carefully set aside and defined by a ticking clock. But I never lingered; I never stayed.

But now I needed something. Answers. I needed them badly, and this was the only place left to look. It was time to clean it all out and shut it down. Done and dusted. I would walk out of this place, brush it from my hands, the bottoms of my feet. And finally, finally, I would be done with her.

The room was as it always was. Despite nights filled with the sounds of her moving through the house, the hush of wheels and the soft click of locks. Even after the music last night, this room remained the same.

I'd half expected to find her sitting at the dressing table.

I shook myself, moving to the dresser, tugging open the top drawer to peek inside. I don't know what I'd expected. Nothing. Anything. But a jewelry box was not it. She would have set the beautifully etched glass box out, placed just right to catch the light, and admired it daily. Leaving it tucked away in a drawer felt wrong to me.

That sense of strangeness lingered as I lifted it out, big enough that I had to use both hands. I ran a finger over the initials on the top, *VST*. Vivian Scarlett Taylor. I'd never seen the box before, which wasn't much of a surprise. The house had been full of things that had been off-limits. I sat on the floor, legs crossed, placing the box in front of me.

Two breaths, one in and one out, before opening the lid and looking inside. Music tinkled out, high and sharp, little tines hitting metal stubs, a wheel turning beneath a clear piece of glass. I didn't recognize the song. Had she wound it one last time? Knowing I would be the one to find it? The last person to hear the song?

I shivered, the constant watchfulness of the house drawing closer, the other rooms listening in. *This is it,* they seemed to whisper, half-forgotten voices caught between creaking beams and papered walls.

But there wasn't much to see. Half the box was the music piece, the other half a smallish square. I picked through the costume jewelry, gaudy pieces that were so unlike Vivian—rhinestones and plastic, cheap metal, a broken necklace. Beneath those, wedged into the bottom of the box was a polaroid. It was facedown, puckered back to me, and if I'd only glanced inside the box and not gone through it, I would have missed the photo.

I pried it free and turned it over.

A man and a woman.

No.

Two young adults, teenagers really. There was that soft look in the girl's face, rounded, without the lines time would gift her, no sharp edges. The boy was tall and dark, tank top showing off a summer tan and muscles, teeth white and straight, his smile intense and focused on the girl.

She was pretty, sandy haired and slim, wearing a blue tank top and cut-off jeans shorts. She barely came up to his shoulder, fitted to him as if made for that exact spot at his side. His arm was around her, pulling her close, and she was laughing up at him, the two caught in a moment before the smiles vanished into a kiss.

They stared at each other, ignoring whoever had taken the photo, uncaring about the world beyond their bubble.

Jake.

A gut punch. A lightning bolt of certainty. Jake and Alice. The lovers. The couple that could have made it out of this town, could have been something if he hadn't been crazy. If he hadn't been jealous. If he hadn't been a hundred things, a thousand speculations.

He killed her, you know.

Alice.

I studied her, the tilt of her head, hair was pulled back in a messy ponytail, a hair tie on one wrist. I must have seen them around, this shining couple, but they were a year ahead of me, and I'd been living in Vivian's shadow. I tried to pull her up from memory, recall a moving image of her in my mind, but I couldn't. I only had a few of Jake, glimpses caught through the window as he mowed the lawn or trimmed roses. But I'd been curled in on myself, concentrating on surviving, and hadn't looked much beyond the tips of my fingers.

I flipped the photo back and forth, checking that there weren't any names or dates written on it. Not that I needed names. I set it aside, sifting through the contents of the jewelry box more carefully, turning over each piece, inspecting and cataloging before setting it aside.

I didn't recognize any of it. The pieces didn't make sense to me. Tucked in a box she would have loved, but out of sight; jewelry she wouldn't have worn, even if it meant life or death. Not hidden exactly, but away from any casual glance.

Twisted with a necklace was a thin black hair tie. I stopped, breath catching sharply against my breastbone, fingers tingling. It burned, hot in my hand like a lump of coal plucked from a fire. I couldn't let go. There were hundreds of millions of black hair ties, as common as anything, wrapped around girl's wrists, forgotten at the bottom of bags, left in the car or on a dresser.

Vivian had never used them.

There was no way it was the same as the one on Alice in the photo. The world didn't work like that, these thin threads coming together here in my hands, tingling and hot and making it hard for me to breathe. A black hair tie looked like any other, interchangeable, anonymous. A few thin strands of blonde hair were knotted around the band —as if it had been yanked out in a hurry, the wearer rushing, a situation that couldn't wait and had to be met with hair down.

I dropped it. It fell on top of the little pile of glittering trash.

The room was cold again—like the constant chill of the walk-in freezer of the first restaurant I'd waitressed at. It was fine when you first ducked in, searching for whatever the cook had sent you to find, but the longer you stood there searching, the colder it got. The longer I sat in this room, the colder it got.

Gotta get the job done, baby.

Dad's voice. His words floating up from memory, the cheerful lilt spiraling in my ear. Get the job done. I kept repeating it to myself, it was a constant loop in my brain, but these things stopped me every time. Small things, odd things, about Vivian.

Vivian the killer.

But what did a woman I'd never met before know about the woman who raised me?

What did I know about her?

Why had Vivian kept broken and cheap things in a beautiful box that played a lovely little tune each time it was opened?

A treasure chest.

I left it on the floor, going back to the dresser and opening the next drawer, and on down until I'd emptied them all. Clothes lay in neat piles on the floor—satin nightdresses edged in lace, expensive red underwear without tags, shirts with French labels. Even her socks felt expensive, fine smooth cotton in several colors—white, black, and navy blue.

There were cashmere sweaters with sachets of her jasmine perfume between them, recalling her in my memory, bringing her into the room in a physical way that made me look over my shoulder and check the mirrors.

I moved to the wardrobe—huge, too big to fit through the door, it would have to be taken apart to get it out of the room. Throwing the doors open, I stood back, looking at the rows of expensive dresses, the shelves with more folded sweaters. There were shoes at the bottom, lined up in careful rows, polished and beautiful—satin and patent leather.

Beneath a pair of loafers—a delicate fawn color, reminding me of the deer in the woods—was a gray metal lockbox. Industrial. Alien. Ominous. And right here, right out in the open. I could have been in here at any point and found it. I could have known sooner.

Whatever was in this box, it was what I'd been looking for.

And without even opening, it I knew what I would find.

Grabbing it, I turned and hurried out of the room, leaving the door open behind me. I wanted to be somewhere else when I opened it. I needed to be somewhere safe. I crossed the threshold into the study and released the breath I'd been holding—passing from danger to safety, holding my breath as a kind of charm.

My cell phone was on, the screen bright, blinding. I'd left it plugged in and sitting on my dad's desk—hopeful it would charge but keeping my expectation realistic. The screen had been dark for days, and it refused to hold a charge even when it was plugged in. But the screen glowed blue now, unnaturally bright and jarring in this dim space —blinding me with promise.

I set the box down, metallic click against hard wood, and grabbed the phone. I'd saved Jake's number when Josh gave it to me along with his address. But I'd never tried it. I hadn't seen Jake with a cell phone, and I'd wondered if he was one of the few people holding out against the modern age, refusing to be at the beck and call of others through a phone. But it was late now, so late it was early. He'd be home, wouldn't he?

One bar showed in the corner—small and alone, weak and barely there, but it would have to be enough.

Quickly, before the phone died again and the connection to the world beyond these walls vanished, I pulled up Jake's name and hit the call button. My hand shook, heart pounding, breathless and jittery as I watched it connect. The line began to ring. It was a tinny sound, as if coming from a distance, old wires struggling to make the connection instead of digital towers and radio waves working to make it happen.

"Hello?"

His voice came from miles away, so many, and he was fainter than the ringing line had been. I began to speak rapidly, wanting to make sure he'd hear at least my apology if nothing else.

"Jake, I was so wrong. I'm sorry. Even after everything, I should've known Vivian was responsible. I was so focused on putting the past behind me, trying to forget her, to pretend so much of it had never happened. And then for an awful moment, I wondered if you two had been connected in other ways."

"Emma—"

"Wait, please. I lied to myself for so long. I wanted to

believe the accident that killed my dad was just that, an accident. Even after everything she'd done, after the emotional torture, I refused to believe she'd kill him. But Jake, I never once believed you killed Alice. Never. It's true, I let this place get under my skin, and I shouldn't have. I'm sorry."

I was panting, heart racing, wanting with everything I had for him to believe me with. Hoping my words would be enough. I owed him so much more than an apology, I'd doubted him, even after everything I'd discovered. I'd been so determined to ignore that Vivian had been—more of a monster than I ever thought possible. But I couldn't ignore it any longer. And I'd let it hurt the one person in Back of Beyond who'd shown me any kind of kindness.

"I don't know if it's enough," I said, voice dropping, finally slowing. "I found some things in the house. In Vivian's room. I found a letter and a photo." I paused, wondering if he'd believe me. "I found things. In the house, among Vivian's belongings. They have to do with you and Alice. I think Vivian killed Alice."

Silence on the line, heavy, weighted with grief. Then he spoke and his words twisted in my gut.

"I've thought—known—it was her for years. I needed to be positive. I gave up years ago on anyone else understanding. But I needed to find out for myself. That's why I kept going to Magnolia House. There were so many times I thought she'd let the truth slip. But I'd realize later that she'd shared just enough to keep me coming back. She never said anything solid, nothing I could take to the police. No one would have believed me anyway."

"But they will now."

"It doesn't matter. The key is proof enough for me. It might not be for anyone else. But it is for me. I was angry in the kitchen. When you backed away from me like I was some kind of killer, after everything…I wanted to hurt you for believing their lies."

"Jake," I whispered, "I'm so sorry."

I waited, but he didn't respond. I bit my lip, wondering what else I could say.

"I'm going to take it to the police. To Officer Hatcomb. They'll know. Jake, I'm sorry I doubted you, even for a second. I'm sorry I didn't want to believe it was her."

No response. I held my breath, waiting, hoping he would understand. Hoping this would be enough. Maybe it would never be anything other than parting on good terms. I could hope for more, but I didn't deserve more.

"Hello?" I asked, heart thudding, cold filling my chest. "Jake?"

When he didn't answer, I looked at my phone. It was dead. Completely. No bars, no charge. The screen was black. When had it died? Had he heard my apology? I didn't know. I could only hope. And I wasn't sure I had any of that left at this point.

THURSDAY

We're all just walking each other home.

- Ram Dass

CHAPTER TWENTY-SEVEN

THURSDAY

The lockbox was heavy, something more than paperwork weighing it down. In all the keys I'd found in the house, there hadn't been anything this small, nothing to fit a tiny lock keeping the box closed. I'd set it aside, intending to come back.

I hadn't until now.

Magnolia House was almost empty—furniture sold, dishes boxed up and taken away. There was the lingering feeling of the people who had come—curious about this house and the woman who had lived here. But they'd moved on, taken bits and pieces with them, full of stories of Vivian's daughter presiding over the sale.

This box was the last piece, the last of the unknown, another thing I would uncover and leave behind. I refused to take any piece of Vivian with me—refused to give her shelter in my life, in a corner in my apartment. I would break this open, satisfy my own curiosity, and burn the contents if I wanted to.

I checked the box of keys again, in case I might have missed a tiny set. I checked the other drawers and then braved her room, the heavy watchfulness of it, but it wasn't there.

No keys then. It would have to be opened another way. The screen door gave a metallic screech as I pushed through it. It slammed behind me, and I couldn't help but feel I'd been kicked out of the house. I was a visitor in a ghost's house.

A visitor pawing through the possessions of someone still very much present.

But I'd reached the endpoint. I'd finally had enough. This box was the last of it, the end of it, and tomorrow I would be gone. My mind was suddenly made up. There was nothing in this town for me, never had been. She'd given me nothing but the desire to live as far away from her and this place as possible.

In the small work shed, full of cobwebs and rusting tools, a dead riding lawn mower and shelves full of paint cans, I found a shovel. It wasn't as rusted as everything else, newer, cleaner. What had she wanted it for? It was another question that would go unanswered. I wasn't going to stick around and search for one. There was a good chance I would never discover the answer anyway.

I carried the shovel and box back to the kitchen garden, setting the box squarely on the brick path; on an exhale I brought the shovel up and down on the silver-colored lock. It didn't budge, and I brought the shovel up again, raised higher this time. A final act of rebellion, of destruction, of deceit, the final time I'd make any effort to know anything at all about Vivian.

Metal met metal with a crash and the box jumped with the contact.

It opened.

I knelt on the bricks, jeans soaking up moisture, gravel

digging into my knees. I lifted the lid back to expose the contents—a perfume bottle similar to the one in the jacket, another envelope, and a lock of blond hair in a plastic bag.

Shaking, I reached for the letter, biting the inside of my cheek, as I turned it over to read the name written on the front.

Jake.

Jake in Vivian's beautiful cursive.

There was no sheet of ripped out paper, no yellowing pages. The piece of paper inside was white and thick, expensive and elegant, it would last and last, and live on. Just as Vivian had intended it to.

> *Jake,*
>
> *You will never know how much you tortured me. Someday, I hope you understand what I have done for you. The gift I have given you. Someday, you will understand the extent to which people go for love. Alice was such a child and incapable of being the woman you needed in life. You are better off without her, sweet boy.*
>
> *Vivian*

I stared at the note—beautiful penmanship, the V of her name large and taking up half the page. It was hard to tell when she'd written it. The paper didn't feel old, it wasn't brittle or torn, the ink wasn't faded. She could have written it a few months ago. She could have written it the day she died. That felt right to me, a confession made from her death bed, a final grasping reach to control people even after she was gone.

My hands were shaking. I could feel my rapid pulse, the tightness in my chest as I breathed—concentrating on the sensation of air filling my lungs.

It was time to go. Get while the getting was good. If I remained to linger over these mysteries, she would eat me alive. That was why she'd left the diary for me—left these bits and pieces of her life waiting. She'd meant to trap me in Magnolia House. Keep me here after I'd tried so hard to get away.

And it had almost worked.

I'd gotten wrapped up in it all, in her, and I'd ignored that little voice in the back of my mind screaming for the self-preservation instinct to kick in. I'd finally had enough. I was done with the whole place—the town, the people, the whole damn state. I wanted the roll of Pacific waves in my head, the deep green smells of moss and trees. I wanted my own room. I wanted my own bed.

Most of all, I was done with this house.

I threw the door to her room open, shoving it so hard it crashed against the wall and popped back, vibrating on the hinges. The space beyond was dim and quiet, rainy daylight filtering through half-closed velvet curtains and windows covered in jasmine.

Hurricane Angie was here—a fitting name for a destructive force of nature bearing down on this out-of-the-way place—the edges of the storm throwing down sheets of rain, water pooling in the low spots, ditches and creeks filling, the hollows in the yard out front becoming tiny ponds. The bayou would be rising, creeping nearer, reaching for this untouchable house. But Magnolia House wasn't untouchable. Not anymore.

My cell service had been nonexistent in town, but anytime I'd neared the interstate, all the storm warnings and waiting messages would pop up. One right after the other, hurricane and flood warnings in capital letters filling the screen. Then I'd pass out of service, I would delete them one by one, forgetting they'd been there. But I couldn't ignore the approaching storm anymore. It was here, and Magnolia House was right in the path.

I crossed to the windows and pulled the curtains wide, swirling fabric out and away, the heavy velvet sending dust rolling across the floor. The windowpanes were wavy, that old glass original to the house, bending and reflecting light strangely. Rain pelted against the house, the earth taking each hit, the trees swaying with the wind, caught and forced into unnatural motion.

This storm would take the house.

It was so loud I could feel it in my bones, at the back of my throat and eyes, a building pressure, the worst of it yet to come. An inevitable roll of it all coming down on us, on me. And finally, after all this time, hitting Magnolia House.

For generations, my family had preserved this place. Protected the house and the legacy. But it died with me. Maybe the house itself hadn't been at fault, maybe it had been a passive bystander, an observer. And if so, then maybe it would understand this about it exactly. This was about Vivian. This was about scorching the earth and salting it; this was a cleansing that had been a long time coming.

I turned back to the room, the glittering sparking madness Vivian had surrounded herself with. I hadn't put any of it out in the estate sale. Maybe I should have. I could have let it strangers pick through it all, take pieces of her away, bring those shards of herself into their homes. But it had felt wrong. It wasn't something I'd want to invite into my own house. I couldn't let it happen to other people.

Crossing to the dresser, I swept all of the figures and bowls into my arms. The crystal bowl with the rose petals dropped, shattering on the floor, shards of light sliding across the room. I stared at it, the broken beauty of it, the destruction.

It clicked inside of me, two pieces coming together, meeting and locking as if it had always been. Maybe this was where I'd been going all along, how it had to be.

Yes.

Running down the hall, my arms full, I smiled grimly; cheeks stretched tight, dark laughter bubbling but not breaking the surface. I hadn't had a plan, not really, not when I'd opened her door and looked in. But I needed some kind of closure here, something that could be a line in the sand, a before and after point in my life.

Now I knew what that meant.

I fumbled the kitchen door open and pushed through the screen door, passing from the cool quiet of the house into a warm steady rain. I paused, gasping in humidity. Inside the house it had seemed to rage, throwing tree branches across the sky, heavy-fisted rain hitting the siding.

But here on the verandah, out in the open, it felt calmer. It was still windy, still raining, but it wasn't as violent. Large drops, scattered, hit me, soaking my clothes, eyelashes and hair collecting water, the wind howling around me. It was gathering, a roar building, and it was coming for me. But it wasn't here yet.

In the middle of the kitchen garden, where the brick paths intersected and formed a circle, I dumped the armful I'd taken there, crystal breaking and silver bouncing, the tinkling crash of it all filling my head.

I ran back inside, the slam of the screen door following me down the hall, a silent cry and question.

What do you think you are doing?

Without pausing, I went straight for the vanity in her room, taking the engraved powder box and bud vase, the black and white beauty shot of a young Vivian Taylor. She'd been so lovely, truly a woman that turned every head and stopped men in their tracks. But even in the photo, there was an edge to her smile, a slice of cruelty, and lack of warmth. Or maybe I saw it because I'd known her, because I'd survived her.

I brought those outside as well—glass shattering when it hit red brick, the powder box exploding, the finely milled face powder spilling out, going up in the air. The rain beat it down quickly, washing it into cracks.

I went back again and again, rain soaking my clothes, plastering my hair to my skull, my cheeks. It must have been cold, but I didn't feel it. I was warm on the inside, all of the frustration and fear of so many years building into something hotter than flame. If I was ever cold again, I'd think about this moment.

An armful of dresses from her closet came next—pale and soft, flowing fabric in floral and geometric patterns. One or two solid colors, reds and blues, those deep, rich tones that made me think of cut stones and precious gems. I tossed those into the pile and went back to the kitchen for matches.

At the kitchen window, I paused, staring out without really seeing anything. The matches wouldn't be enough in this weather. It would never burn. I went to the butler's pantry and took down one of the oil lamps. It didn't have a wick, and there hadn't been any in the whole house. I couldn't understand why Vivian would keep them if she had no way to use them. But now I was glad.

It took a little effort to remove the bit of metal from the glass, where the wick would have gone and the oil was added. Finally, I had it free, and I carried it carefully outside, covered in gooseflesh and stomach flip-flopping. I poured the oil over the fabric, silk and cotton, sheer chiffon and sturdy satin, and the scent reminded me of bonfires.

I knelt, opening the box of matches carefully, rain hitting my shoulders, a quick patter before the wind whipped it away. The first match I struck was blown out, a flash of light there and gone. I curved around the second match, body and hands becoming a cave, and tried again. A little orange flame shivered into life, clinging desperately to the thin stick.

I tossed it at the pile and held my breath, waiting for it to be blown out, expecting it to vanish. But it landed in a damp spot of kerosene and bloomed. My breath caught in my chest, hitching and lungs tight, excitement filling me, the thrill of triumph surging beneath my skin. I lit another match and added it, the fire low and beaten by rain, but it was there and growing, fed by kerosene, and driven by wind, my little orange flame shivered and survived.

I added more clothes, the contents of her dresser, underwear and bras, and a thick camel-colored coat I found in the back of the closet. There was a handkerchief in one pocket, white with a tiny, embroidered magnolia bloom in one corner. I stuffed it back in the pocket and added both to the fire.

I had to add more oil. I smothered the fire with my next armload, the flames disappearing under all of it. But I got it lit again, adding more oil, smiling as it caught flickering hold again.

The curtains came down with a lot of hard pulling, the velvet finally tearing away from the rod. They were so big I could only carry one out at a time. I added these more carefully, making sure I didn't drown the fire this time, adding more oil, and building a nest out of all of it. I added each one, one at a time, carefully, lovingly.

It was growing, my bonfire of destruction, of memory, a place to get rid of all those things, come to terms with them, accept them, leave them here and go on without them. I wasn't going to carry this anymore, this weight, the constant, needling insecurity and fear. It was staying here.

I emptied her closet and dresser, taking the drawer from the bedside table out and adding it to the pile. Fire licked along the varnished surface, and I poured oil there, savoring the stab of pleasure as it bit into the wood despite the rain. I yanked down the canopy, the whole thing splitting from the ceiling and falling free, the gold fleur-de-lis almost hitting me. That went into the fire too.

I pulled the deep blue quilt from the bed, exposing pale-pink satin sheets. I threw the pillows into the corner, knocking over the bedside lamp with a crash. It didn't break, and I realized I was glad it hadn't, not in here, in the house. I'd found my line then, the one I wouldn't cross. Wholesale destruction outside, minimal damage inside, and I wouldn't be sad when it all got blown away in a few hours.

Knowing the hurricane was coming, the pressure of it—an ax over my head waiting to fall—was something of a relief. I wasn't leaving Back of Beyond with my tail between my legs because even in death Vivian had gotten the better of me. This was something else. I was leaving on my own terms. I'd come to lay her to rest, quiet my past, and untangle the places where our lives were still connected. She'd left a knot for me to unravel—a twisted mess of a life.

My mother, the monster.

And a greater monster than I ever could have dreamed. All the cruelties of my childhood, the coldness and privation, it was nothing compared to the experiences of others. I'd been lucky. I was lonely and sad and things had been hard, but she hadn't physically or sexually abused me, she hadn't denied me food or clothing or shelter. She'd terrorized me and urged me to sink into the swamp. But she hadn't killed me. She'd only scared me.

I refused to let her scare me now.

CHAPTER TWENTY-EIGHT

THURSDAY

The lockbox rattled in the passenger seat. The contents vibrated to a frequency I could almost understand, the words it contained, the confession of a crime held tight inside. I wasn't sure if it would do any good after all this time. If anyone would care. They'd made up their minds about Jake a long time ago. It might get shoved into a closet, left to gather dust, and forgotten about. It might end up in the trash. It might never be opened at all.

But what they did with it didn't matter. I needed to do it, for myself, for the sake of my own soul and the ability to sleep at night. And Jake. I needed to do it for Jake. He said it didn't matter anymore that they hated him, didn't trust him, believed the worst about him. Maybe it truly didn't hurt, not the way it would hurt me, but he deserved to have the truth about Vivian out there.

A door being shut, slammed and shattered with the force, the final nail in the coffin, the last note of a song. Part of me wondered if this was what she'd wanted all along. For Magnolia House to give me her secrets, for one final shocking act to light up the world. She'd taken such pleasure in deceiving people, twisting them, forcing their minds into complicated patterns that fit around her like a puzzle. Maybe this was the last piece of the puzzle.

I didn't know. I didn't really understand it. Maybe she'd thought I'd keep this all to myself, let it grow and fester in my soul, until it slowly consumed me. But she couldn't have known that Jake and I would cross paths. Jake had changed everything.

At the police station I stopped, heart racing, watching the plate-glass front window for movement. The place was empty, lights on and no one home. Had they evacuated because of the storm? Were they all at home and prepared to ride it out? But maybe someone had stayed, maybe Officer Hatcomb would come out from the back when I knocked.

I ducked out of the car, clutching the lockbox, hurrying to the front door of the building. The awning blocked most of the rain, but the wind kept blowing it this way and that, random drops pattering across the glass and then the sidewalk, hitting me and moving on. The office behind the plate glass glowed, neat desks and closed office doors beyond, chairs for visitors lined up and waiting. It was a place out of a feel-good movie, a place that never had to arrest people, and the biggest crime the little town faced was who dug up the flowers in a neighbor's yard.

I knew better. I'd witnessed what happened behind closed doors and felt gravel beneath me in the dark.

I tried the handle anyway, but it was locked. Putting my hand to the glass, I peered inside, searching for any sign someone might be there, lingering after hours. No. It was empty.

I could come back. I could wait in the car for the morning. But that would mean waiting out the storm and whatever might come after it. If the bridge washed out, I'd be stuck. I shivered at the thought. Being in this place one moment longer than I had to made my skin crawl. I set the box on the ground in front of the door. My hand shook as I wrote a note, cold and emotion getting under my skin. I addressed it all to Officer Hatcomb, with a short explanation and my contact information if he decided to follow up.

There was a drop box beside the door, similar to ones I'd seen in post offices, and I shoved the lockbox through. It rattled, dropping with a crash, and was gone from sight. I waited, watching the room beyond the glass, wondering if the noise would have conjured someone. But the space remained abandoned, and my hands were empty. There wasn't any reason to linger.

Pulling away from the curb, I glanced behind me one last time: the little police department, the gutters in the town square filling with water, the trees swaying with the storm. It vanished from sight quickly, lost in the turn of the wheel, behind me before I could take a breath.

"Goodbye," I whispered.

To no one, to the town, to the place I'd grown up.

Goodbye.

———

Rain pummeled the car, obscuring the view beyond the windshield and hammering to be let inside. *Where are you going?* it asked, it needed to know. My heart wanted to know too, my soul wondering what I would do when I arrived, how much of myself would I be willing to lay out.

All of me. Some of me. None of me.

I drove slowly, pausing as I reached water on the roads,

the bayou rising, curious about asphalt and road signs. Would the alligators come too? The fish? Would wading birds pick their way carefully through flooded front yards as alligators waited in the flowerbeds? I wouldn't be here to find out.

When I came to his mailbox, I stopped, windshield wipers battling the rain, a frantic pace my heart followed.

Here.

Stay or go. Return with a thousand unanswered questions, haunted, not by a dead woman who could no longer hurt me, but by the regret of never asking Jake how he felt about me. Never asking Jake to choose me.

I wanted him. I wanted him more than I had ever wanted anything. It could be a force of destruction for good, a pivotal point in my life where I would look back and know, deep in my bones, that it had been a crossroads. But I didn't need the luxury of hindsight. I knew now, right now sitting in the car beside his mailbox, that this was it. Beyond lay a future I couldn't predict, I couldn't know. But if I kept driving, if I never stopped, I knew what my days would be filled with, how my routine would settle and keep going.

Sometimes you gotta take a chance, baby. You don't know until you leap.

I cut the wheel to the right, bumping along the gravel road turning to mud, splashing through puddles, and hoping against hope that I'd be able to make it out again. The headlights only reached so far, the rain heavy and getting heavier. It felt like miles of driving, slow inching minutes to reach a destination that filled me with crackling nerves and anticipation so fierce it left me breathless.

The lights of the cabin were visible before the headlights hit it—warm yellow, a beacon in the night. Parking near his truck, I hesitated, a moment of self-doubt touching me, lingering. I had to steel myself for the act of knocking on the door, meeting his direct gaze. Those blue eyes, full of everything I wanted. Even the pain. Even the hurt. I would take it all.

I ran through the rain, soaked in only a few steps, gasping as I stopped on the porch. My heart pounded, painful in my chest, stomach full of moths and butterflies. It was a chance. Bigger than any I'd ever taken. A gamble of epic proportions. Life or death, fate versus a random universe, the chance that a shared trauma might be part of what could keep us together, close enough to let other things build, for something like love to curl between us like new honeysuckle vines.

I knocked, knuckles on wood solid and real, the gesture more confident than I felt. I bit the inside of my cheek and wrapped my arms around myself, watching the windows for the first hint, the first glimpse of Jake, wanting more than anything for him to open the door and accept what I offered.

Take me.

When I saw him through the glass, my stomach dropped and my mouth went dry. He wore jeans and a gray T-shirt; he held a kitchen sponge in one hand, a dishtowel over a shoulder. He paused when he saw me, brows drawing together. I swallowed, suddenly unsure what I would say, doubting my voice. For a moment I thought he wouldn't answer the door, he'd let me stand out here in the rain until I got tired of waiting.

But with a shake of his head, he reached for the door, music escaping as he opened it.

"Emma." His voice was a gut punch, full of suspicion and touched with disbelief. "What're you doing here?"

"I'm sorry," I blurted out, louder than I'd meant to and not what I thought I'd have said first. But it was the most important thing. I repeated it, watching the expression in his eyes change, going soft.

"I don't know when the phone cut out, I don't know if you heard everything. I'm sorry I let this stupid place get under my skin. I'm sorry I let Vivian mess with my head. I knew better. I did. And you deserve better Jake."

I held my hands out, trying to shape the words, bend them into a better shape, a more attractive sound—imbue them with everything roiling inside of me. "I'm sorry."

He watched me, glancing behind me to the car still running, the headlights cutting into the night. He spoke finally, the words sinking into me like stones, weighing me down.

"There are some things sorry doesn't fix."

"I know," I nodded, taking a step forward. "I know. And you're right. But I'm sorry, I am, and I had to tell you. I needed to talk to you. And I'm not sure it would be enough for me either."

His face was blank, the sponge dripping water on the floor beside him, the song changing in the background. I kept talking, rushing forward, approaching a precipice. Fall or fly, sink or swim.

"I took a lockbox to the police station—for Officer Hatcomb. It was Vivian's. There was a letter. And a photo of you. I tried to tell you on the phone."

He nodded. "I caught part of that."

"It's proof. I should have brought it, I should have let you see it." I held up my hands, feeling stupid now with the realization. Of all the people in the world who deserved this validation, it was Jake. "I guess I hoped I'm sorry would be enough. For you, from me, it would be." My voice trailed off as I studied his face, searching for any sign that my words were reaching the place I'd hoped to touch. His heart. His soul. "Come home with me, Jake. Not to that house, not here. Come to Oregon."

"You don't know me."

"I do. I know enough. And who the hell really knows anyone, anyway when they take a chance and decide to live together?"

He gave me a half smile, dimple flashing. "Plenty of people."

"Okay, yeah, maybe. But some don't."

"Is that what you're asking me? To live with you in Oregon?"

"I'm asking you to take a chance." I sucked in a deep breath, and released it with my words, letting it all pour out of me. "I think outside of this place we could be different people. I think I could change your future."

He didn't say anything, and tears were beginning to sting behind my eyes.

Come on, come on, I wished, I hoped, I pleaded.

"And you've changed mine."

He shook his head. "I don't know, Emma. It's a lot to ask."

"I know."

"I just don't—"

No. It was a no. A crushing, final, no. I couldn't stay. I couldn't hear anything else. He'd be nice; he'd say something he thought might help me feel better about it all. Something that would eclipse whatever the pain might have been if he'd been cruel in his refusal.

"It's okay," I said, holding up a hand, stepping back. "I get it. You don't have to say anything else. I'm so sorry. I'm so sorry about all of it."

I turned away, hunching my shoulders against the rain as I went down the steps, hurrying for the car. I got in, shivering, heart aching, and pressed a fist to my breastbone, trying to ease the pain, my whole body hurting as I scrubbed tears from my cheeks—soaked to the bone with water and sorrow. The car was cold, rain drumming on the roof, heavy drops that promised floods and retribution—ready to run me out of town and wash me away.

The hurricane would wash it all away, and we'd all start fresh after the flood.

This was it. I'd done what I could. I'd shown him the poor shriveled thing that was my heart—doubts and suspicions, the desire to be loved and the potential I thought I had, I hoped I had, to give it all back.

Give me a chance, take a chance.

But he'd turned me away. And really, after everything, I couldn't blame him. I would have done the same. I probably would have done it a lot sooner.

The engine screeched when I turned the key in the ignition, reminding me it was already running, demanding I pay attention. I swallowed, blinking back tears, focusing on what lay beyond the windshield. This was the last time. I'd never be back. I stared, memorizing the tilted lines of the old cabin, the cypress trees and swamp water, the jetty, and remembering kisses exchanged in sunlight.

Never again.

Foot on the break I shifted the car into reverse, glancing over my shoulder, easing off the pedal. I would drive out of the swamp, over the bridge, and out of the Back of Beyond, Louisiana. Soon the invasive humidity would be forgotten, the Southern hint in my voice smoothed out, and I'd go on knowing Vivian was truly gone, no longer out there in the world waiting for me. Dead and buried.

I had an apartment full of plants waiting for me, the sound of the ocean beyond my window, and cool nights filled with sharp stars overhead. The place I'd wanted to be this whole time, longed for, and dreamed about.

Home.

The lights in the cabin went off. I paused, a tingle racing up my spine.

Jake came charging out of the house carrying a black duffle bag, running through the rain toward the car. My heart hammered in my chest echoing the downpour, ears ringing as he splashed through the rain. I fumbled with the locks, mouth open in shock as he opened the door and got in, tossing the bag into the backseat. The rain came in with him, wind and heat and the scent of hurricanes. He slammed the door closed, shutting out the curious rain, leaving it to fall against the windows, fighting to get a look inside—curious about this strange pair in the car.

I stared, full of expectation and joy coiled so tight it hurt to breathe.

"Let's see what happens in Oregon," he said. "You ready to go?"

I nodded, unable to speak. Jake reached for me, pulling me into a kiss that lit me up, set me on fire like a million matches striking at once. The kiss was fierce, mouth open, hands in my hair as I gripped the front of his shirt. I leaned into him, the rain drumming on the roof of the car, swamp rising all around us, the hurricane threatening to blow us both away.

I didn't care.

The future waited, and I would take nothing into it from this place.

Nothing but Jake.

ABOUT THE AUTHOR

Kathryn Trattner has loved fairy tales, folk stories, and mythology all of her life. Her hand-down favorites have always been East of the Sun, West of the Moon and the story of Persephone and Hades. When not writing or reading she's traveling as much as possible and taking thousands of photos that probably won't get edited later. She lives in Oklahoma with her wonderful partner, two very busy children, one of the friendliest dogs ever, and the ghost of an extremely grumpy cat who never liked anyone at all.

If you enjoyed *Magnolia House* please consider leaving a review and signing up for my newsletter. You'll get information on new releases and sneak peeks!

sign up for Kathryn Trattner's Newsletter

www.kathryntrattner.com

 facebook.com/kathryntrattner

 twitter.com/k_trattner

 instagram.com/k.trattner.author

 bookbub.com/authors/kathryn-trattner

ALSO BY KATHRYN TRATTNER

Deep Water and Other Stories

Mistress of Death

The Scent of Leaves

Magic and Myth: Short Stories

The Glass Palace

Magnolia House

<u>The Blood and Rubies Series</u>

The Dead Saint

The Living Saint

Steel and Starlight